P9-CWE-793

Last to Die

ALSO BY JAMES GRIPPANDO

Beyond Suspicion

A King's Ransom

Under Cover of Darkness

Found Money

The Abduction

The Informant

The Pardon

LAST TO DIE

A NOVEL

JAMES GRIPPANDO

HarperCollins*Publishers*

This is a work of fiction. The characters, incidents, and dialogues are products of the author's imagination and are not to be construed as real. Any resemblance to actual persons, living or dead, is entirely coincidental.

LAST TO DIE. Copyright © 2003 by James Grippando. All rights reserved. Printed in the United States of America. No part of this book may be used or reproduced in any manner whatsoever without written permission except in the case of brief quotations embodied in critical articles and reviews. For information, address HarperCollins Publishers Inc., 10 East 53rd Street, New York, NY 10022.

HarperCollins books may be purchased for educational, business, or sales promotional use. For information, please write: Special Markets Department, HarperCollins Publishers Inc., 10 East 53rd Street, New York, NY 10022.

FIRST EDITION

Printed on acid-free paper

Library of Congress Cataloging-in-Publication Data

Grippando, James.
  Last to die / James Grippando.—1st ed.
    p. cm.
  ISBN 0-06-000555-6 (alk. paper)
  1. Miami (Fla.)—Fiction. I. Title.
PS3557.R534 L3 2003
813'.54—dc21   2002038741

03 04 05 06 07 ❖ / RRD 10 9 8 7 6 5 4 3 2 1

For Tiffany.

It just keeps getting better.

Acknowledgments

Carolyn Marino and Richard Pine were as usual a tremendous help in shaping this story, but my gratitude goes way beyond that. Whenever aspiring writers ask my advice, I tell them that rule number one is "Keep it fun." I'm not sure how you do that without the best editor and agent in the business, but thankfully that's something I don't have to worry about.

As always, I am indebted to my readers/critics-at-large for the comments on early manuscripts, Dr. Gloria M. Grippando (thanks, Mom), Eleanor Rayner, Amy Kovner, and Cece Sanford. Wesley Reid was more helpful than he realizes on traveling in Africa (be careful what you say, it might end up in a book), and on the legal side I am again grateful to probate attorney Clay Craig for his insights into "the Slayer Statute" and other mysterious doings in the world of "Whisper Court." Of course, the mistakes are all mine, including those in *Found Money*. (Okay, Clay, are we square now?)

Many people contributed to my understanding of modern-day child slave trading in Africa, including Sudarsan Raghavan and Sumana Chatterjee; the staff of U.S. Senator Tom Harkin, Chairman, Senate Agricultural Committee; and a long list of other people at Anti-Slavery International, the U.S. Department of Labor, the United Nations, International Labour Organisation, Free the Slaves, and the Child Labor Coalition. Thank you as well to the Chocolate Manufacturers Association of the United States of America, American Cocoa Research Institute, and the World Cocoa Foundation, which provided information on the international chocolate industry and the harvest of cocoa.

Once again, I got a little help on character names, this time from the Roberts family, whose generous contribution at the annual auction in support of St. Thomas Episcopal Parish School in Coral Gables, Florida, earned them a fictional trip to Africa. For an extra five hundred bucks, I would have packed you bug spray. Better luck next year.

Finally, for Tiffany—Thank you, I love you, I could write a book about you. But I promise you, I won't.

Last to Die

Prologue: 1996

At last, the old house was quiet. Sally Fenning sat alone at her kitchen table, three stacks of bills before her—due, overdue, and hopeless.

She didn't know where to start. Tonight's tips had been pathetic, hardly worth the aggravation of being a waitress. "Waitress" actually dignified what she did, slogging pitchers of beer and platters of spicy chicken wings to drunk tourists who grabbed an eyeful of T&A with every move she made. In her flimsy nylon jogging shorts and skintight tank top with the plunging neckline, she sometimes felt as though she might as well be dancing naked on tables. At least the pay wouldn't suck.

She pitched the telephone cancellation notice into the trash. They always sent two before actually cutting off service.

Things hadn't always been this bad. She and her husband once owned a little Italian restaurant in Miami Shores, found success, expanded, and promptly fell on their faces. Don't mess with a good thing, was her take on expansion. But Mike was hell-bent on growth, dead-certain that they'd be selling franchises in five years. They used personal credit cards to finance the build-out, suckered by those low introductory rates that lasted six months, followed by a rate so high that your calculator overheats when you compute what you're paying over the life of the loan. The paint on the walls was barely dry when a no-name tropical storm slammed into their shopping strip and sent their red-and-white-checkered tablecloths floating into the parking lot. No flood insurance. The restaurant never reopened. Three years later her husband was working two jobs and she was a Hooters Girl, hardly a dent made in the principal balance on their restaurant debt.

Some people said she had no pride. But she had *too much* pride—too much to just throw in the towel and file for bankruptcy.

"Mommeeeeee," came the little voice from the bedroom at the end of the hall. Their four-year-old daughter was not a great sleeper, and calling out for Mommy at midnight was becoming routine.

She looked up from her check ledger but didn't move from her chair. "Katherine, go to sleep, please."

"But I want a story."

She hesitated. It was late, but working till eleven o'clock, five nights a week, didn't allow her the luxury of putting her child to bed. That was Mike's job, before he headed out for the eight-to-midnight shift as a security guard, or his mother's, who was good enough to come over every night and watch television while Katherine slept, filling the gap between the time Mike left for his second job and Sally came home from hers. The thought of reading to her daughter made Sally's heart melt. She rose from the table and went to the bedroom. "All right. One story."

"Yeah!"

"But then you have to go to sleep. Promise?"

"Promise."

She slid into the bed beside Katherine, her back against the headboard. Her daughter nuzzled close to her. "What story do you want?"

"This one," the little girl said as she took the book from the nightstand.

"*Where the Wild Things Are*," said Sally, reading the title. She knew it well, the story of a little boy whose imagination transforms his bedroom into a scary place where he must confront an island filled with monsters and become their ruler. Sally remembered how her own mother used to read the same story to her when she was going through her nightmare stage as a little girl. Twenty years later, the message was the same: Fear is all in your head.

"Are you still having nightmares, sweetheart?"

She returned to the kitchen, but she didn't have the stomach to go back to those stacks of bills. The rent was due, and Lord only knew where that was going to come from. Renting a house instead of an apartment was an extravagance in their financial straits, even if it was a dumpy old two-bedroom/one-bath that any builder would have considered a tear-down. But Sally had grown up in an apartment, no yard, no privacy, no chimney for Santa to climb down on Christmas Eve. Katherine deserved better, even if it meant forcing the landlord to throw them out on the street.

She opened the refrigerator and poured herself a glass of orange juice.

"Mommy, I want something to drink."

Sally turned, but Katherine wasn't there. She was still in bed. *That girl has ESP.* "Go to sleep, baby."

"But, Mommy, please. I didn't see you all day."

That got to her, tapping straight into a working mother's guilt. One last time, she went to her daughter and sat on the edge of the bed. The light from the hallway was just enough to reveal the fear in her eyes.

"Are you still scared?"

Katherine nodded.

Sally felt her forehead. It was clammy with sweat but not from fever. She was just overheated from lying in bed with the covers pulled over her head. "Why are you so afraid?"

"The monster."

"If I lie down with you for a little while, will you go to sleep?"

"I want to sleep in your room. Just till Daddy comes home."

"Honey, you're a big girl now. This is your room."

"But the monster."

"There is no monster."

"You sure?"

"I'm positive."

"You look, please?"

She sighed, exasperated. "Yes, I'll look." She got down and checked under the bed. "Nothing under here."

"Mmmm hmmm."

"Why?"

"Scared."

"What are you scared of?"

"Monster."

"There are no monsters."

"Yes, over there," she said, pointing toward the drapes that covered the sliding glass door.

"No, honey. There are no monsters out there."

"Uh-huh, for real."

"Come on. Let's read the story."

Sally felt her daughter's face press against her heart as she read aloud. She gave each monster its own voice, not too scary, so as not to frighten Katherine. She was asleep before the little boy named Max made it back from the faraway island to the safety of his own room. Sally quietly slid out of bed, kissed Katherine on the forehead, and tiptoed out of the room.

Back to the bills. Greenleaf Financing. That was a beauty. Two thousand dollars' worth of computer equipment and restaurant software that they'd leased over a five-year period for total payments of twenty-eight thousand dollars. What a deal.

"Mommy." It was another call from the bedroom.

"What is it, honey?"

"Scared. There's monsters."

She pushed away from the kitchen table and went to the bedroom, but she stopped short in the doorway, refusing to let herself be manipulated into coming inside. "There's no such thing as monsters."

"But, Mommy—"

"It's time to go to sleep."

"Can you leave the light on?"

"I'll leave the hall light on."

"Thank you, Mommy. You the best."

It was hard to be firm with someone who told you you're the best and truly believed it. She smiled and said, "Good night. I love you."

"I love you, too."

"No, no. Over there." She was pointing toward the drapes again, the ones that covered the sliding glass door.

Sally hesitated. Even in the dim lighting she could make out the playful pink images of birds, rabbits, and other nursery-rhyme animals that danced across the balloon draperies. Hardly the stuff of a monster's cloak, but her heart still fluttered. The fear in her daughter's eyes seemed so genuine.

"There's no monster."

"Go check, Mommy. Please."

She looked harder this time. Strange, but she found herself wondering if the rabbit was in the same place it had been a minute ago, or if it had moved. It seemed that it was no longer lined up with the little yellow duck on the other panel. She thought her eyes were playing tricks, until she saw it again.

That rabbit moved. Ever so slightly, it had *definitely* moved.

The air conditioner clicked off, and the knot in her belly loosened as the draperies settled back into place. The cool draft from the air conditioner had evidently caught the pleats, causing the subtle shift. No monsters.

"Will you, Mommy?"

"Will I what?"

"Look for the monster."

"Okay. I'll check."

She didn't move.

"Mommy, go."

She suddenly felt foolish. She had actually considered switching on the lamp, then chided herself for even thinking about doing something that might convey her own irrational fear to her daughter. All this talk of monsters was actually getting to her, making her feel alone, making her realize how defenseless they really were, how vulnerable they might be, separated from the outside world and everyone in it by a flimsy lock and a mere pane of glass.

Stop it. She started across the room, one step at a time. It seemed to be taking forever. She was taking half steps, she realized, another sign of fear.

This is crazy.

Finally, she made it. She glanced back toward the bed and saw Katherine peering out from beneath the blanket, all but her eyes and the top of her head hidden. Sally's pulse quickened as she reached out and gently pinched the fabric's edge between her thumb and index finger, getting no closer to the sliding glass door than was absolutely necessary. Katherine ducked beneath the covers. Sally drew a deep breath. In a slow, tentative motion she pulled back the panel.

Nothing.

"See," said Sally. "I told you. No monsters."

Katherine was still hiding beneath the covers. In a muffled voice she said, "The other end. Check the other end, too."

Sally hesitated. She wasn't sure if it was instinct or paranoia that was telling her not to go there, but she couldn't let Katherine see her silly fears. She took a half step, then another, moving closer to the draperies' edge—the far edge where that bunny had moved.

"Careful, Mommy."

"There's nothing to worry about, sweetheart." She didn't like the sound of her own voice. It was as if she were trying to convince herself.

Her gaze drifted across the draperies, a happy portrait of dancing ducks and singing birds. Finally, her eyes locked on the bunny, and she waited. She wasn't sure what she was looking for, exactly, just movement of any kind. But she knew that if you stared at anything long enough it would seem to move, the way stars seem to swirl in the night sky if you lie on your back and stare up long enough. Still, she couldn't tear her eyes away. The bunny was motionless, and then it happened. Maybe it was an illusion, like swirling stars, but the bunny's chest seemed to swell and then shrink. It was as if it were breathing.

As if something behind it had just taken a breath.

"Is it okay, Mommy?"

On impulse, she grabbed the cord and pulled. The drapes flew open, and she froze. She was staring at her own faint reflection in the sliding glass door. Behind her, in the bed, Katherine's head emerged from beneath the covers.

Sally gave her own fears a moment to subside, then tried to play it cool. "See. I told you there were no mon—"

The closet door burst open, and from the corner of her eye Sally saw a blur in the darkness coming toward her. She heard her own scream and then her daughter's cry. "Mommy!"

The blur hit her full speed and broadside, smashing her against the wall. She turned and let her fist fly with all her might, but it was all too quick, and he was far too strong. A blow to her belly took her breath away. Her head snapped back as the attacker grabbed her by the hair. She clawed at his face with her nails, but it was covered with a nylon stocking. Her body twisted, her daughter screamed, and Sally's eyes widened as she saw the shiny blade glisten in the stream of light from the hallway. It was coming toward her, as if in slow motion, but she felt powerless to stop it. She twisted once more, a futile effort to escape.

Her blouse came up, and she watched the blade disappear as the man's fist met her flesh.

She screamed and fell to the floor, gasping for air, trying to stop the hot, wet river of pain that was flowing from the hole below her ribs.

Blood. So much blood.

"Mommy, Mommy!"

Katherine's cries gave her strength, and somehow she sprang into action and grabbed her attacker by the ankles. It was like tackling a mule, and his kick stopped her cold. She tried to rise again, but the room was swirling.

"Don't hurt . . . my daughter," she said, but she could barely get the words out.

He kicked her once more, harder this time. She felt her teeth crack, and the salty taste of blood filled her mouth. She struggled to lift her head, but it dropped to the floor.

"Mommy, the monster! The monster!"

Her daughter's screams faded, and Sally's world went black.

PART ONE

Five Years Later

One

────

The rainstorm was blinding, and Sally was way behind schedule. She hadn't intended to be late, fashionably or otherwise.
She just wasn't good with directions, and this wasn't exactly her neck
of the woods.

Sheets of water pelted the windshield, sounding like marbles
bouncing off glass. She adjusted the wipers, but they were already
working at full speed. She couldn't remember rain like this in years,
not since she and her first husband lost their restaurant to that no-
name tropical storm.

Orange taillights flashed ahead. A stream of cars was inching
down the highway at the speed of cooling lava. She slowed to somewhere below the school-zone limit, then checked her watch. Eleven
twenty-five.

Damn. He'd just have to wait. She'd get there, eventually.

Their meeting had been arranged by telephone. They'd spoken
only once, and his instructions were simple enough. Thursday, 11 P.M.
Don't be late. She didn't dare reschedule, not even in this weather.
This was her man. She was sure of it.

Just ahead, a neon sign blinked erratically, as if shaken by the
storm. It was like trying to read an eye chart at the bottom of a lake,
and she could only make out part of it: S-P-something-something-K-
Y-apostrophe-S.

"Sparky's," she read aloud. This was the place. She steered off the
highway and pulled into the flooded parking lot. Under all this water,

she could only guess as to the exact location of the parking spot. She killed the engine and checked her face in the rearview mirror. Lightning flashed—a close one. It lit up the inside of her car and unleashed a crack of thunder that sent shivers down her spine. It frightened her, then triggered a bemused smile. How ironic would that have been? After all this planning, to get hit by lightning.

She took a deep breath and exhaled. *No turning back now. Just go for it.*

She jumped down from the car and started her mad dash across the parking lot in the pouring rain. Almost immediately a blast of wind snatched her umbrella from her hand and pitched it somewhere into the next county. Wearing no coat, she covered her head with her hands and just kept running, splashing with each footfall. In a matter of seconds she reached the door, soaked to her undergarments, her wet jeans and white blouse pasted to her body.

A muscle-bound guy wearing a Gold's Gym T-shirt was standing at the entrance, and he opened the door for her. "Wet T-shirt contest's not till tomorrow, lady."

"You wish," she said, then headed straight to the restroom to see if she could dry off. She looked in the mirror and gasped. Her nipples were staring back at her, right through her bra and wet blouse.

Good God!

She punched the hand dryer, hoping for hot air. Nothing. She tried again, and again, but to no avail. She reached for a paper towel, but the dispenser was empty. Toilet paper would have to do. She went to the stall, found a loose roll atop the tank, and proceeded to dab furiously from head to foot. It was single-ply paper, not terribly absorbent. She went through the entire roll. She exited the stall, took another look at her reflection in the mirror, and gasped even louder this time. Her entire body was covered with shredded remnants of cheap toilet paper.

You look like a milkweed.

She started laughing, not sure why. She laughed so hard it almost hurt. Then, with her hands braced on the edge of the sink, she leaned forward and hung her head. She could feel her emotional energy drifting up to that ever-present knot of tension at the base of her skull. Her shoulders started to heave, and the laughter turned to tears. She fought it off and quickly regained her composure.

"You are a total wreck," she said to her reflection.

She brushed off as much of the toilet paper as she could, fixed her makeup, and said the hell with it. Nothing was going to stop this meeting from happening. She took a deep breath for courage and exited into the bar.

The crowd surprised her, not so much its makeup, which was about what she'd expected, but more the simple fact that there was such a big crowd on a nasty night like this. A group of truckers was playing black-jack by the jukebox. Leather-clad bikers and their bleached-blond girl-friends had a monopoly on the pool table, as if waiting out the storm. T-shirts, jeans, and flannel shirts seemed to be the dress code for a seat at the bar. These folks were hard-core, and this was clearly a place that depended on its regulars.

"Can I help you, miss?" the bartender asked.

"Not just yet, thanks. I'm looking for someone."

"Yeah? Who?"

Sally hesitated, not exactly sure how to answer that. "Just, uh, sort of a blind date."

"That must be Jimmy," said one of the men at the bar.

The others laughed. Sally smiled awkwardly, the inside joke com-pletely lost on her. The bartender explained, "Jimmy's the umpire in our softball league. They don't come any blinder."

"Ah, I get it," she said. They laughed again at this Jimmy's expense. Sally broke away and continued across the bar before their interest could return to the lost girl in the wet clothes. Her gaze fixed on the third booth from the back, near the broken air-hockey table. A black guy with penetrating eyes and no smile was staring back at her. He was wearing a dark blue shirt with black pants, which made Sally smile to herself. Never before had she laid eyes on him, but his look and those clothes were exactly what he'd described over the tele-phone. It was him.

She walked toward the booth and said, "I'm Sally."

"I know."

"How'd you—" she started to ask, then stopped. There wasn't a woman in the joint who looked like her.

"Have a seat," he said.

She slid into the booth and sat across from him. "Sorry I'm late. Raining like crazy."

He reached across the table and plucked a shred of toilet paper from her sleeve. "What's it raining now, fake snow?"

"That's toilet paper."

He raised an eyebrow.

"Long story," she said. "It was all over me. Five minutes ago I looked like a milkweed."

"With breasts."

She folded her arms across her chest. "Yes, well. Some things can't be helped."

"You want something to drink?"

"No, thank you."

He swirled the ice cubes around in his half-empty glass. Rum and Coke, she guessed, since that was the special of the night. The Coke looked completely flat, about what she expected from Sparky's.

"I watched you drive up," he said. "Nice car."

"If you like cars."

"I do. From the looks of things, you do, too."

"Not really. My husband did."

"You mean your second husband or your first?"

She shifted uncomfortably. They hadn't discussed her marital status on the telephone. "My second."

"The French one?"

"What did you do, check up on me?"

"I check on all my clients."

"I'm not your client yet."

"You will be. Rarely do the ones who look like you come this far and back down."

"How do you mean, look like me?"

"Young. Rich. Gorgeous. Pissed off."

"You call this gorgeous?"

"I'm assuming this isn't your best look."

"Fair assumption."

"What about the pissed-off part. That fair, too?"

"I'm not really pissed off."

"Then what are you?"

"I don't see how my feelings are at all relevant. The only thing that matters is whether you want to do business, Mr.—whatever your name is."

"You can call me Tatum."

"That your name?"

"Nickname."

"Like Tatum O'Neal?"

He grimaced, sucking down his drink. "No, not like fucking Tatum O'Neal. Tatum like Jack Tatum."

"Who's Jack Tatum?"

"Meanest football player that ever lived. Defensive back, Oakland Raiders. He's the guy who popped Darryl Stingley and turned him quadriplegic. They used to call him Assassin. Hell, he liked to call himself Assassin."

"Is that what you call yourself, too? Assassin?"

He leaned into the table, his expression turning very serious. "Isn't that why you're here?"

She was about to answer, but the bartender was suddenly standing beside their booth. He glared at Sally and said, "What you meetin' with this guy for?"

"Excuse me?" she said.

"This piece of dirt sittin' on the other side of the table. What you meetin' with him for?"

She looked at Tatum, then back at the bartender. "That's really none of your business."

"This is my bar. It's definitely my business."

Tatum spoke up. "Theo, just put a cork in it, will you?"

"I want you out of here."

"Ain't finished my drink yet."

"You got five minutes," said Theo. "Then be gone." He turned and walked back to his place behind the bar.

"What's with him?" asked Sally.

"Tightass. Guy finds some lawyer to get him off death row, thinks he's better 'n everyone else."

"You don't think he knows what we're here talking about, do you?"

"Hell no. He probably thinks I'm pimping you."

Her rain-soaked blouse suddenly felt even more clingy. "I guess I brought that on myself."

"Never mind him. Let's cut the crap and get down to it."

"I didn't bring any money."

"Naturally. I didn't give you a price yet."

"How much is it going to be?"

"Depends."

"On what?"

"How complicated the job is."

"What do you need to know?"

"For starters, what exactly do you want? Two broken ribs? A concussion? Stitches? Mess with his face, don't mess with his face? I can put the guy in the hospital for a month, if you want."

"I want more than that."

"More?"

She looked one way, then the other, as if to make sure they were alone. "I want this person dead."

Tatum didn't answer.

She said, "How much for that?"

He burrowed his tongue into his cheek, thinking, as if sizing her up all over again. "That depends, too."

"On what?"

"Well, who's your target?"

She lowered her eyes, then looked straight at him. "You're not going to believe it."

"Try me."

She almost chuckled, then shook it off. "I'm way serious. You are *really* not going to believe it."

Two

Her day had finally arrived.

Sally felt a rush of adrenaline as she sat at her kitchen table enjoying her morning coffee. No cream, two packs of artificial sweetener. A toasted plain bagel with no butter or cream cheese, just a side of raspberry preserves that went untouched. A small glass of juice, fresh-squeezed from the pink grapefruit that her gardener had handpicked from the tree in her backyard. It was her usual weekday breakfast, and today was to be no different from any other.

Except that today, she knew, would change everything.

"More coffee, ma'am?" asked Dinah, her live-in domestic.

"No, thank you." She laid her newspaper aside and headed upstairs to the bedroom. The house had two large master suites on the second story. Hers was on the east side, facing the bay, decorated in an airy, British Colonial style that was reminiscent of the Caribbean islands. His was on the west, a much darker room with wood-beamed ceilings and an African motif. Sally didn't like all the dead animals on the walls, so they used his room only when he wasn't abroad, which was about every other month for their entire eighteen months of marriage. The arrangement had lasted just long enough for her to reach the first financial milestone of an elaborate prenuptial agreement. Eighteen months equaled eighteen million dollars, plus the house—big money for Sally, chump change for Jean Luc Trudeau. Lucky for her, she'd had the foresight to take the eighteen million not in cash but in stock in her husband's company, which promptly went public and— *kaboom!*—she was suddenly worth forty-six million dollars. She could have earned another quarter-million for each additional month, and there were certainly worse men to be married to than Jean Luc. He was rich, successful, reasonably handsome, and plenty generous to his third and much younger wife. But Sally wasn't happy. People said she was never happy. She didn't apologize for that. She had her reasons.

Sally stepped into her dressing room, draped her robe over the back of a chair, and pulled on a pair of sheer panty hose. Naked from the waist up, she stood in silence before the three-way mirror. Slowly, she raised both arms, her twenty-nine-year-old body seeming to defy the pull of gravity as she turned. In the full-length panel she saw it, still visible after all this time. A two-inch pink scar at the base of the rib cage. She felt it with the tips of her fingers, lightly at first, then touching more firmly, and finally pressing until it hurt, as if she were trying to stop the bleeding all over again. Years later, and it was still there. Cosmetic surgery could have hidden it, but that would only have destroyed her most important daily reminder that she had in fact survived the attack. Sadly, her first marriage had not survived.

Tragically, neither had her daughter.

"Anything to iron today, Miss Sally?"

Instinctively, she covered her breasts at the sound of a voice, but she was alone in the dressing room. Dinah was waiting on the other side of the closed door.

"I don't think so," she answered, pulling on her robe.

As the sound of Dinah's footsteps faded away, Sally opened the door and walked to the bathroom to fix her hair and makeup. She returned to the dressing room to select an outfit, which took longer than usual, as she wanted it to be just right. She settled on a basic blue Chanel suit with a peach blouse and new Ferragamo shoes, finishing the look with a strand of pearls with matching earrings. Her platinum and diamond wedding band—two rows of stones for a total of four karats—felt like overkill, as always, but she wore it anyway. She thought she'd put it away for good with the divorce, but today it served a purpose.

Sally stepped back and took one last look in the mirror—a good, long look. For the first time in ages, she allowed herself a trace of a genuine smile.

This is your day, girl.

She grabbed her purse and headed downstairs, leaving through the front doors to the porte cochere, where her Mercedes convertible was parked and waiting with the top down. Her hair was secure in a French twist, but she nevertheless donned the Princess Grace look, a white scarf and dark sunglasses. She climbed behind the wheel, started the engine, and followed the brick driveway to the iron gate. It opened automatically, and she exited to the street.

She drove at a leisurely pace through her neighborhood, the warm south Florida sun on her face. It was a glorious day, even by Miami standards. Seventy degrees, relatively low humidity, a cloudless blue sky. Growing up as a girl, she'd always wanted to live in the Venetian Isles. They sat side by side in the bay, like four giant stepping-stones between the mainland and the larger island of Miami Beach proper. Homes on the waterfront were a boater's dream, many with drop-dead views of cruise ships in port and the colorful skyline of downtown Miami beyond. Technically speaking, it was her dream come true to have a nine-thousand-square-foot house in the midst of this urban paradise.

Be careful what you wish for.

Sally stopped to pay the toll, then continued across the Venetian Causeway. A couple of old Cuban men were fishing on the Miami side of the bridge, right beneath the sign that read ABSOLUTELY NO FISHING.

She was just north of downtown Miami, not exactly the safest part of town, but it was an area in transition. In the not-too-distant past, she would have driven miles out of her way to avoid cutting through here.

She crossed Biscayne Boulevard, made a couple of quick turns, and stopped at the traffic light. The entrance ramp to the interstate was just ahead, the lone escape route to about a dozen east-west lanes perched directly above her. She could hear the expressway traffic, the steady drone of countless cars and noisy trucks echoing all around her.

She usually timed her approach so that she could breeze through with no red lights, especially at night, but that wasn't always possible. Like clockwork, the homeless guys emerged from their cardboard homes beneath the on-ramp. Armed with tattered rags and plastic squirt bottles filled with dirty water, they seemed determined to clean the world's windshields. There were two of them. One came toward her, and the other went to the SUV in front of her.

The SUV burned rubber and ran the red light, leaving Sally alone at the intersection, just her and the window washers. It was mid-morning, but in the dark shadows it seemed like dusk. Interstate 395 and the ramps that fed into it crisscrossed overhead like concrete ribbons. Sally's window washer took a different strategy than the guy with the SUV, approaching not from the side but from the front of the vehicle. She couldn't have run the red light without running over him.

"No thanks," she shouted.

He kept coming, smiling, taking aim with his squirt bottle. The other washer returned to his home beneath the ramp, apparently having conceded the Mercedes to his competition.

"I said, 'No thanks.'"

He walked all the way up to the front of her car, standing close enough to snap off her hood ornament. Suddenly, the darkness seemed to break. They were surrounded by scattered beams of sunshine, as if the clouds had shifted just enough to allow patches of daylight to break through the crevices in the maze-like expressway overhead. The longest, brightest ray seemed to fix on her big diamond ring. It was sparkling like fireworks. On any other day, she might have discreetly slid her hand from atop the steering wheel and dropped it in her lap. But not today.

The man was still staring at her through the windshield. Then, slowly, he raised his arm and took aim, straight at her face. She waited for the stream of greasy water to hit the glass, but it didn't come. A moment later, she realized that he wasn't holding a squirt bottle.

She froze, her eyes fixed on the black hole at the end of the polished metal barrel. It lasted only a split second, but it was as if she were suddenly floating outside her own body, watching the scene unfold. In her mind's eye, she could see the flash of powder from the barrel, see the windshield shatter, see her head snapping back, her body slumping forward, and the spray of blood on the leather seats. She could even hear the horn blasting as her face hit the steering wheel and came to rest there. And for the second time in the same day, she saw herself smiling a genuine smile.

With the lonely crack of a revolver that echoed off concrete, her living nightmare was finally over.

Three

The sun was setting as Jack Swyteck pulled into his driveway. He lived on Key Biscayne, an island practically in the shadows of downtown Miami, but a world apart. Across the bay, beyond the sprawling metropolis and somewhere over the distant Everglades, fluffy bands of pink, orange, and magenta were slowly dissolving into the darkness of night. It wasn't until all color had vanished from the sky that it suddenly dawned on him what day it was. Exactly one year to the day that he and Cindy began the separation that ended their five-year marriage in divorce.

Happy Anniversary, he told himself.

Jack was a trial lawyer who specialized in criminal defense work, though he was open to just about anything if it interested him. By the same token, he turned away cases that he didn't find interesting, the upshot being that he liked what he did but didn't make a ton of money doing it. Profit had never been his goal. He had spent his first four years out of law school at the Freedom Institute, a ragtag group of idealists who defended death row inmates. At the time, Jack's father, Harry Swyteck, was Florida's law-and-order governor and staunchly pro–death penalty. Jack's job didn't sit well with him, but that was sort of the idea. Four years of tweaking his old man proved to be plenty, and in case anyone had written him off as a bleeding heart liberal, he completely shifted gears and made a name for himself as a fair but aggressive federal prosecutor. He left the U.S. attorney's office on good terms, but almost two years later he was still trying to find his stride in private practice. To be sure, everything from a messy divorce to a dead client in his bathtub had served as "distractions" along the way, and he was determined to give his own firm a fair shot before changing professional course again.

"Hey, Theo!" he called out across the lawn.

Theo didn't seem to hear him. He was busily scrubbing down his twenty-four-foot sport fisherman, which at the moment was suspended by davits and hanging over the water. The one saving grace of Jack's austere rental house was the fact that it was on the water with its own dock. This was his third rental since the divorce, part of his whirlwind quest to find the perfect digs for a divorced man with no kids, no addictions, and surprisingly little interest in dating. His latest experiment was a "Mackle home," a simple three-bedroom, one bathroom, cinder-block structure with a small screened-in porch and, of course, no central air conditioning. In the early 1950s, the Mackle brothers built scores of these basic beach homes, mostly for WWII veterans and their young families. Back then, Key Biscayne was little more than a mosquito swamp, so Mackle homes were about the cheapest housing around, with a typical closing price of twelve thousand dollars. Today, the lot alone went for about twelve grand *per foot* of linear waterfront. It seemed that about every third or fourth day a developer would drop by, aching to enter Jack's living room with a bulldozer and blueprints. His was the last of the waterfront Mackles still standing.

"Yo, Theo!"

Still no response. Working on a boat with the music blasting was enough to put Theo in another world. Since Jack didn't own a boat, he let Theo dock his behind the house. It was perfect for Theo, who ran his bar at night, fished and slept all day on the boat. He was one of those rare friends who never seemed to age, which wasn't to say that he didn't *look* older from one year to the next. He just refused to grow up, which made him fun to have around. Sometimes.

Theo was hosing down the deck as Jack approached. "Catch anything?" asked Jack.

Theo kept cleaning and said, "Not a damn thing."

"It's like they say: That's why they call it fishin', not —"

Theo turned the hose on him, giving his suit a good splash.

"Catchin'," said Jack. He was dripping wet but pretended that it hadn't happened, wiping the water from his face.

"You know, Swyteck, sometimes you are just so full of —"

"Wisdom?"

"Yeah. That's exactly what I was gonna say. Wisdom."

"I guess it takes a real genius to taunt an ex-con who's holding a garden hose," said Jack as he brushed the water from his pinstripes.

Theo climbed out of the boat, smiled, and gave Jack a bear hug so big that his feet left the ground. Theo had the height of an NBA all-star, the brawn of a football linebacker.

Jack took a step back, surprised. "What's that for?"

"Happy Anniversary, buddy."

Jack wasn't sure how Theo knew, but he figured he must have mentioned something to him about the one-year milestone. "I wouldn't exactly call it a *happy* anniversary."

"Aw, come on. You gonna hold a grudge because I splashed you with a little water?"

"Exactly what anniversary are you talking about?" asked Jack.

"What anniversary are *you* talking about?"

"It was a year ago today that Cindy and I separated."

"Cindy? Who the hell gives a rat's ass about her? I was talking about *us*."

"Us?"

"Yes. Ten years ago this week. You and me met for the first time. Remember?"

Jack thought for a second. "Not really."

"Now you're hurtin' my feelings. I remember everything about it. It was a Friday morning. Guard comes and gets me from my cell, tells me I have a meetin' with my new court-appointed lawyer from the Freedom Institute. Of course, I'm sittin' on death row without a damn thing to do, except lay there and ask myself, 'Theo, would you like the mustard sauce or drawn butter with your last meal of stone crabs and fried sweet potatoes?' So I'm bouncin' off the walls at the thought of a new lawyer. So I go down, and there you are, sittin' on the other side of the glass."

"What did you think when you saw me?"

"Honestly?"

"Honestly."

"Typical white Ivy League graduate with a save-the-black-man guilt complex."

"Gee. And all this time I thought I'd made a lousy first impression."

Theo narrowed his eyes, as if quizzing him. "Remember the first thing I said to you?"

"Probably something along the lines of 'Got any money, dude?'"

"No, smart ass. I looked you right in the eye and said, 'Jack, there's something you need to know right up front: I am an innocent man.'"

"I do remember that."

"And do you remember what you said?"

"No."

"You said, 'Mr. Knight'—you called me Mr. Knight back then— 'there's something *you* need to know right up-front: I think you're a big, fat, fucking liar.'"

"Did I really say that?"

"Oh, yeah. Exact quote."

"Wow. You must have thought I was an asshole."

"I still think you're an asshole."

"Thanks."

Theo smiled, then grabbed him by the shoulders and planted a big kiss on his cheek. "Happy Anniversary. Asshole."

Jack smiled. Theo and his kisses. A last-minute release from death row for a crime you truly didn't commit could make you want to hug everyone for the rest of your life. Or it could have the opposite effect. It all depended on the man.

Theo said, "Grab that cooler, will ya'?"

Jack took it by the handles, and Theo gathered up the fishing poles with the other gear. Empty bottles rattled inside the cooler as the men crossed the lawn to the driveway. Theo popped the trunk.

Jack put the cooler inside, then helped Theo break down the poles and mount them on the roof rack.

"Anything else?" asked Jack.

"Yeah, actually. I need a favor. Big one."

"What?"

"Did you happen to see that story in the local section a few days ago? That rich woman who got shot in the head while waiting on the red light to get on the expressway?"

"I might have skimmed it. I've been in trial too long. Not seeing much news."

Theo opened the car door, pulled something from the console, and handed it to Jack. It was a newspaper clipping. "Read this."

There were only a few paragraphs with a photo of the victim. Jack read quickly. "Sad."

"Is that all you can say?"

"It's sad. What more can I say?"

"You could look at her picture and say, damn, she's the most beautiful woman I've ever seen in my life."

"Okay, she's beautiful. Does that mean I should be sadder?"

"Yes, Mr. Politically Correct, it *does* make it sadder. That's what everyone wants to be. Young, rich, beautiful. And now she's dead. Doesn't get any sadder than that."

"Theo, where are you headed with this?"

"Did you read how much she was worth?"

"Yeah. Something like . . . whatever it said."

He took back the clipping and pointed to the figure. "Forty-six million."

Jack read it again. "That's a lotta dough."

"Damn straight. Now, this is not a trick question, but I want you to try and guess when was the last time a bona fide babe worth forty-six million dollars came walking into my bar."

"You saw her in Sparky's?"

"About two and a half weeks ago."

"What was she doing there?"

"Talking to a contract killer."

"A what?"

"You heard me."

"You mean she was meeting with someone who kills people for money?"

"I don't mean someone who shoots contracts for a living."

Jack scratched his head, thinking. "You sure it was her?"

"You think I'm gonna forget a face like that?" he said, showing the photo once more.

Jack saw his point. "So, she talks to a contract killer, and two weeks later, she's the one who turns up dead."

"That's right," said Theo.

"What do you make of that?"

"Smells bad."

"I'll give you that," said Jack. "But what do you want me to do?"

"First off, there's a letter I want to ask you about. It's from the dead woman's lawyer."

"Written to you?"

"No. To the contract killer she was talking to in my bar."

"You have the letter?"

"No. I seen it."

"How?"

"Never mind that. Let's just say I'm acting as a go-between here."

"What exactly are you going between?"

Theo grabbed a pack of Kools from his dashboard, then lit one. "You and . . . you know."

"The contract killer? No way."

"Hear me out. The whole letter is two sentences long. It simply tells him to be in the law offices of Vivien Grasso Monday for an important meeting about the death of Sally Fenning."

"So, you want me to advise a contract killer whether he should go to this meeting or not?"

"No. I want you to go with him."

Jack coughed, as if choking with disbelief. "What makes you think I'd be even remotely interested in that?"

"Because I asked."

"Why are you asking?"

Theo took a drag from his cigarette, blowing smoke as he spoke. "Because I think this boy's in a mess of trouble."

"Is he a friend of yours?"

"Not in the least."

"Then give me one good reason why I should walk into another lawyer's office representing a contract killer."

"First of all, except for me and maybe a few badasses between here and Las Vegas, no one knows he's a contract killer."

"Give me another good reason."

"Because you're my buddy."

"Hmmmm."

"Because I've been playing payback ever since you got me off death row, and I ain't never asked you for nothin' in return."

"Okay. We're getting there. But lay another one on me."

Theo lowered his eyes, as if reluctant to answer. Finally, he looked at Jack and said in a quiet, serious tone, "Because he's my brother."

Jack, too, turned serious.

"So, you'll meet with him?" asked Theo.

Jack didn't answer right away, but there was never any doubt what his answer would be. "Sure," he said. "For you, I'll meet with him."

Four

He looked a lot like Theo, was Jack's first impression. Theo in his badass mode.

Jack met Theo's brother "Tatum" in the sunny courtyard outside the downtown public library. He was dressed semi-casual, a sport jacket with no tie, as if Theo had told him to try to look respectable. The jacket looked a little tight in the shoulders, a common problem for muscular men who bought off the rack. It was the lunch hour, and plenty of people were seated at the tables around them in the shade of broad white umbrellas. Some were reading, some were talking and sharing lunch with friends, a few were shooing away pesky pigeons. Tables were far enough apart to keep anyone from overhearing their conversation. It wasn't the normal setting for an attorney-client meeting, but a hit man wasn't exactly a normal client. Jack wasn't worried, but he'd nonetheless followed his instincts and set up the meeting not in the solitude of his law office but in a public place with lots of potential witnesses. Just in case.

"Good to see you again, Mack."

"It's Jack," he said as they shook hands.

"Sorry."

Just what the world needs, thought Jack. *A hit man who doesn't know Jack from Mack.*

They sat on opposite sides of the table. Jack had arrived early and had already finished his chicken salad on pita. There was no table service, and Jack offered to wait while Tatum went through the line, but he declined, seemingly eager to get started.

"How long's it been?" asked Tatum. "Ten years?"

"Eight. Since Theo's release from prison."

"I assume Theo's filled you in as to my goings-on since then."

"Probably more than you would have liked."

"And you're okay with it?"

"Let me put it this way. I'm here because Theo asked me for a favor."

"But you're my lawyer, right? Everything we say is, you know—"

"Privileged, yes."

"You gonna eat that pickle?" he said, pointing to Jack's plate.

"Help yourself."

Tatum grabbed it, bit off the tip, wagged the rest of it like an extra finger as he spoke. "Now, Theo did tell you that I'm not in the con-tract line of work anymore, didn't he?"

"He said as far as he knew, you hadn't done a job in three years."

"That's the truth," he said, pronouncing it like *troot*. "That makes you feel better about this, right?"

"Look, my typical client is not a nun. I've even defended people who'd killed for money, just like you. I'm not judging you. I'm doing a friend a favor."

"Theo says you're good."

"Good enough to get an innocent man off death row."

"That's not as easy as it sounds. Especially when everyone thought he was guilty."

"Everyone except his lawyer."

"And his brother," said Tatum.

"And his brother," said Jack, acknowledging it. "You were there, standing right with him."

"I was the *only* one who stood by him."

"Maybe this is his way of saying thank you. You got thirty minutes."

Tatum popped the rest of his pickle into his mouth. "Where should we start?"

"Let's start with Sally Fenning. How did you two hook up?"

"You gonna finish those chips?" he said, poking at Jack's plate.

"Go for 'em."

He spoke with a mouthful of Ruffles. "She called me."

"Out of the blue?"

"Yeah. Totally."

"She had to get your number somehow. What did she do, look in the Yellow Pages under 'Problem Solvers'?"

"I got no idea how she found me."

"Stop the bullshit, or your free thirty minutes are over."

He was looking for a napkin to wipe his greasy fingers, then just licked them, one by one. "Friend of a friend hooked us up."

"Which friend?"

Tatum leaned back, crossed one leg over the other. Jack felt a digression coming on.

Tatum said, "I don't know how much you know about this woman, but she had some problems in her past."

"You mean she was in trouble with the law?"

"No, not like that. Emotional problems. She was attacked, or something, I don't know exactly. But she hired a bodyguard every now and then, when she was feeling scared, for whatever the reason. Anyway, her bodyguard knew me."

"He called you?"

"No, we was playing pool together one night."

"What did he say?"

"Said, 'I got a client who wants to get in touch with you. Can I give her your number?' I said sure."

"What did you think it was all about?"

"Probably she needed me to beat the shit out of somebody."

"I thought you said you were out of the contract business."

"I don't do hits anymore. Puttin' people in the hospital, that's another story."

"You're okay with serious bodily injury, but you draw the line at murder. Is that it?"

"Somethin' like that. To be honest, it's more about the money."

"I'm not sure I follow you."

"It's a tough business in Miami. These days, you got Colombians, Russians, Jamaicans, Arabs, Israelis, Cubans, Italians, Nicaraguans—everybody and his brother willing to do a job for a measly five hundred bucks. How's a guy supposed to make a living?"

"Join the union?"

"You think this is a joke? This is business, pal, and it's like everything else these days. You specialize. In my case, I turned myself into the guy who knows how to inflict just the right amount of pain, someone who can get results without killing the goose that lays the golden egg. That's a real skill. And it pays real money."

"So, you're a shakedown specialist."

"No. I'm in the art business."

"The art of what? Face rearrangement?"

He leaned forward, elbows on the table. "The art of persuasion."

His glare tightened, as if he were trying to give Jack some sense of just how persuasive he could be. Jack didn't flinch. "So, Sally Fenning wanted to make use of your persuasive powers?"

He settled back in his chair, taking some of the edge off. "That was my first impression."

"And you went to meet her?"

"Right. I told her to meet me at Sparky's."

"Why there?"

"I always meet in a public place. Keeps the unexpected from happening."

"But why Theo's bar?"

"He's my brother. He hates what I do for a living, sometimes he even threatens to throw my ass out. But if I go to Theo's, I can be sure of one thing: Ain't no nosy bartender gonna be listening in on my conversation. Theo don't want to hear none of it. Can't be so sure of my privacy if I go to some other bar."

"Okay. You got to Theo's bar. Then what?"

"She wanted to hire me."

"To do what?"

"Like I says before. I thought she wanted me to work some guy over."

"But that wasn't it?"

"No. She wanted someone dead."

"Who?"

He chuckled to himself. "This is where it gets . . . strange."

"How do you mean?"

"She wanted me to shoot her."

Jack hesitated. He'd heard plenty of strange stories in his career, but this one was up there. "Would you call that an unusual request?"

"Not unheard of. But yeah, like I said, strange."

"Why would a person hire someone else to kill them? Why not just go home and stick your head in the oven?"

"You kiddin' me? People always got their reasons. Buddy of mine did a guy once who lost big bucks in the stock market. Millions. Couldn't go on, but he didn't want his wife and kids to think he was a coward. So he hires a hit man to make his death look like a drive-by shooting. Worked like a charm. You should have read the obituary," he said with a chuckle. "All about how much poor, departed John loved life."

"Is that what Sally was concerned about? What other people would think?"

"I don't know."

"Did you shoot her?"

He looked away, laughing.

Jack stuck with it and asked again, "Did you shoot her?"

Tatum's smile faded. "No."

"Why not?"

"Because I told you: I don't do that anymore."

"Did you tell her that?"

"Told her lots of things. Mostly I told her she was being stupid. She's a knockout, obviously loaded with money. I says, this is crazy. Get help, lady. This ain't like changing your hair color or even gettin' your tits done. You can't go back. Know what I mean?"

"Is that how you left it, then? She asked you to shoot her, you said no?"

"That was it."

"Did she ask for the names of any of your friends who might do the job?"

"No. But I don't just give out names like that." He seemed to catch himself, then added, "Because I don't have friends like that anymore."

"Tell me about the letter you got from Sally's lawyer."

"Not much to tell. Just says she would like me to be in her office for an important meeting relating to the death of Sally Fenning."

"Can I see it?"

"Sure. Got it right here." He pulled it from his inside jacket pocket, then handed it to Jack, who gave it a quick study.

"Clarence Knight your real name?"

"Yeah. Not sure how she got it."

"I take it you didn't give Sally your real name."

"No. Just Tatum, nickname."

"Like Tatum O'Neal, huh?"

"Fucking-A, no, not like Tatum O'Neal. What in the hell planet do you white people live on? Jack Tatum, the meanest, baddest football player—"

"Yeah, whatever," said Jack. "So, somehow Sally got your real name and passed it on to her lawyer."

"Like I said, her bodyguard hooked us up together, so he could have given Sally my real name. Which is more proof that I didn't kill this woman. You think my buddy would give her my name or that I'd give her my actual nickname if I was going to commit murder? I'd be doing aliases, big time."

"In a normal hit, yeah. But maybe you don't have to be so careful about throwing your name around when the person doing the hiring is going to be dead after the hit."

Tatum flashed a peculiar smile and said, "You a pretty sharp guy, Swyteck."

"Vivien Grasso," said Jack, reading the lawyer's name from the letterhead.

"You know her?" asked Tatum.

"Indirectly. She was a big supporter of my father when he ran for governor. Probate is her specialty. So I assume this letter has something to do with the administration of Sally's estate."

"What's that got to do with me?"

"Did you ask her?"

"I was hoping you would. As my attorney."

Jack laid the letter on the table. "I promised Theo I'd meet with you. I didn't say I'd take it any farther than that."

"I can pay you."

"It's not the money."

"Then what, you don't like me?"

"This isn't a date. I don't have to like you."

"Or maybe you think you're Perry Mason and only represent innocent people. Well, let me tell you something: If someone's trying to pin this woman's murder on me, I *am* innocent. So what do you say, Perry? You my lawyer?"

"It's not that easy. I'm pretty busy right now."

"This has to be a lot juicier than whatever else you got on your plate."

"You'd be surprised."

"Right. Take a look at this picture," he said as he handed Jack the same newspaper clipping that Theo had shown him.

Jack took it but said nothing. Tatum said, "Here's a gorgeous, twenty-nine-year-old woman. She's just finagled forty-six million dollars from some rich, old fool she was married to for a year and a half. First thing she does is go around looking to hire someone who'll blow her brains out. Don't it make you wonder what's the deal here?"

Jack stared into Sally's eyes, looking for signs of trouble. Her photo stared right back.

"Don't it, Jack?"

"It has a certain pull."

"Tell me this much: Would you meet with this probate lawyer, if you was me?"

"Not without a lawyer of my own."

"Then come with me. Worst that can happen, you make three bills an hour."

"If it was all about money, I'd be working for the mob."

Tatum leaned into the table, as if on the level. "Let me lay it on the line here. Yeah, I popped a few guys. That's all in the past. Trust me, the world don't miss the scum I did away with. I never killed no one like this woman here, this Sally Fenning."

Jack gave him a hard look.

"Come on," said Tatum, groaning. "I think someone's trying to fuck me here. Sure, I did some bad shit in my life. But this time, damn it, I'm innocent. For a real-life criminal defense lawyer like you, that's about as good as it gets, ain't it?"

Jack nearly smiled. The guy had a point. "Just about."

"So you with me?"

"I'll think about it."

Jack offered the letter back, but Tatum held up his hands, refusing. "Keep it. You might need it."

Jack folded the letter and tucked it into his pocket. "*Might*," he said.

Five

On Friday night Jack went back to high school. The Cavaliers of Coral Gables Senior High were battling Miami Lakes on the gridiron, and he thought it would be fun to take his Little Brother to cheer on his alma mater. Jack was part of the local Big Brothers Big Sisters of America program, and he liked nothing better than to take Nate places that his mother didn't take him—like football games and more football games. It seemed like a nice thing to do for a single mother trying to raise a boy on her own, which was why he'd volunteered in the first place. Nate turned out to be a great kid, which was why Jack loved doing it.

Tonight, however, Jack had an agenda of his own.

As usual, there was a good crowd on hand. Jack and Nate flowed with the stream of excited fans through the turnstyle at the main entrance gate. The marching band was on the field, putting their collective heart into the familiar school fight song. The grandstands were filling up quickly, as a lighted scoreboard at the far end of the field blinked down to fourteen minutes and counting till kickoff. A long line of football players suddenly rushed past him and Nate. Their pregame warm-up was over, and they were hooting and hollering all the way back to the locker room for last-minute game prep.

It had been almost twenty years since Jack played varsity ball, and for a moment he could hardly believe that he'd ever actually looked that young in his gray and crimson uniform.

"Did they wear helmets back when you played?" asked Nate. He was eight years old and sometimes had a way of making Jack feel like eighty.

"Not always," said Jack. "Which explains an awful lot."

"Like what?"

"Nothing," he said, pulling Nate along as they walked toward the stands.

"Why do you always say that?"

"Say what?"

"Whenever I ask what you mean, you always say 'nothing.'"

"I don't always do that."

"Uh-huh. My mom says you do it, too."

"Oh, she does, does she?"

"She says you're afraid to let people know what's really inside your head."

"She really said that?"

"Does that sound like something I would make up?"

Jack smiled, though it troubled him to think that Nate's mother saw him as someone who erected emotional barriers. Funny, but his ex-wife used to say the same thing. "Don't want people inside my head, huh? What exactly is that supposed to mean, anyway?"

"Nothing," Nate said smugly.

"Wise guy."

It was the sixth game of the season, no losses so far, and Jack could feel the excitement around the stadium. They'd arrived too late to get prime seats, but Jack wasn't in a hurry to sit anyway. He waited behind the bleachers at the fifty-yard-line entrance, watching the fans pass by. This section was where players' parents usually sat, and the Cavaliers' quarterback was Justin Grasso. His mother, Vivien Grasso, never missed a game.

Jack had intended to call Vivien before the weekend but was caught up in an arbitration proceeding in Orlando. Her letter to Tatum Knight had scheduled the mystery meeting for Monday afternoon. Jack figured he'd accidentally-on-purpose bump into Vivien at the game, find out what it was all about, and then decide whether it sounded interesting enough to offset the hassle of dealing with a loose cannon like Tatum as a client. Jack wasn't overly picky, but it had been one of those weeks where it seemed that if it weren't for clients, judges, and other lawyers, the practice of law wouldn't be such a bad way to make a living.

"Let's go," said Nate.

"Just a minute," said Jack. Vivien was headed toward them, and Jack had a bead on her in the crowd. He hadn't seen her since his father's farewell party as governor, but she looked the same—lean and athletic, little to no makeup, as if she'd gone for a twenty-mile run, jumped in the shower, and rushed over to see her son rip the visiting team to pieces. No one wondered where the star player for Gables High got his abilities.

"Jack Swyteck," she said with a smile. "How's your old man?"

"Doing great. I think he's fishing in North Carolina this month."

"Slacker. We need to get him out of retirement and run for Senate. Unless maybe his son is interested in politics."

"My interest is limited to voting. Even then, it's pretty much limited to voting for immediate family members."

She laughed. Jack was about to introduce her to Nate, but the boy was already engrossed in deep conversation about Harry Potter with Vivien's ten-year-old son. It was the diversion Jack needed.

"Funny I ran into you," said Jack, lying. "I was meaning to call you."

"What about?"

"Friend of a friend situation. A guy named Clarence Knight."

She seemed to be searching her mind, then it registered. "Oh, yeah. One of the Sally Fenning heirs."

"*Heirs?*" said Jack.

"I sent him a letter inviting him to the reading of the will. You're coming with him?"

"I don't know yet."

"A will contest isn't your cup of tea, huh?"

"There's a contest?"

"I shouldn't have said that. Could be, I suppose. But no one's said anything. Yet."

"Are you telling me I should or shouldn't get involved in this?"

"Forget what I said," she said, smiling. "Just a lawyer's cynicism. Anytime there's this much money at stake, you expect the heirs to fight."

"You're sure Tatum Knight is an heir?"

Nate spoke up, as close as he ever came to whining. "Come on, Jack, let's go. We're going to miss the kickoff."

"Just a minute, buddy."

Vivien said, "The boy's right. We are going to miss kickoff. Call me in my office Monday morning. We'll talk. And say hi to your daddy for me," she said as she walked away.

"I will. Good luck tonight."

"Go Cavaliers!"

Jack watched Vivien and her young son disappear into the crowd. The steady stream of spectators continued past him to their seats. Nate tugged at his arm.

"Hello up there!" said Nate. "Can we go watch the game now?"

Tatum Knight, an heir? Jack couldn't get the thought out of his head.

Nate asked, "What's that goofy look on your face for?"

"What goofy look?"

"You look like you just stepped in bat vomit."

"I think maybe I just did."

"Gross! Really?"

"No, I didn't mean really."

"Then what did you mean?"

"Nothing."

"Nothing, nothing, nothing. You did it *again!*" said Nate.

Jack smiled. "So I did. Come on, let's go watch football." He put his arm around Nate and led him toward the bleachers.

Six

Kelsey was getting to know Sally Fenning.

Kelsey Craven worked for Jack Swyteck. Her latest assignment was to pull together information on the two tragedies that punctuated Sally's life, her own senseless shooting at an intersection and the murder of her daughter five years earlier. She wasn't an investigator, so she'd gathered things that were publicly available, mostly from the Internet, such as newspaper articles and even an old Web site relating to Sally's search for her daughter's killer.

It wasn't a full-time job, but a few hours a week was all she could give Jack. In addition to being Nate's mother, Kelsey was a third-year law student at the University of Miami. Law was her second career, something she'd decided to do after divorcing the man who'd convinced her that a ballet dancer was too stupid to get into law school. She'd danced professionally for two years before a knee injury ended her career, then she'd gotten married and had Nate. From the day he'd walked it was clear that Nate would never be a dancer, but she followed her dream anyway and opened her own studio, sharing her passion with children, mostly little girls. She still taught dance but no longer owned the studio, having sold the business to pay for law school. She made a little extra money as a law clerk, doing legal research and writing for Jack Swyteck, P.A. Sometimes he sent her on fact-finding missions, like the one on Sally Fenning. This wasn't the most intellectually challenging assignment, but it had turned out to be one of the more interesting ones.

Without a doubt, it was the only one that had ever made her cry.

The doorbell rang. Kelsey put her notes and newspaper clippings aside, then rose from the table and went to the front door. Through the peephole she saw Jack with Nate's head on his shoulder, the boy sound asleep. She opened the door and let him inside.

"Straight back to the bedroom," she whispered.

Jack carried Nate down the hall, Kelsey right behind them. She hurried ahead to the bedroom, adjusted the dimmer switch so that there was just enough light to see, and pulled back the covers. Jack laid the boy on the bed, then spoke in a whisper.

"Sorry I kept him out so late."

"No problem. It's not a school night. I'm sure he had a great time."

"A total blast."

"Thanks for taking him."

"You're welcome."

Their eyes met and held. It was suddenly awkward, as if neither one knew exactly how to say good night when it was just the two of them in the bedroom, no crazy Nate buzzing all around them. Jack said, "Guess I better get going."

"Can you stay a minute?"

"I—uh, yeah. I guess."

"I found some interesting stuff on Sally Fenning. We could have some coffee and go over it."

"Sounds good."

"I'll be just a minute."

Jack turned and headed for the kitchen. Kelsey tried to get Nate into his pajamas without waking him, but it was a losing battle. No matter how gently you tried to pull a T-shirt off a sleeping child, it always seemed to want to take his head with it.

"Mommy, stop."

"Let me help you."

"No, no. I'm a big boy. I can do it myself."

"All right. You do it."

"I need privacy."

He was cranky, obviously overtired. She handed him the pajamas. "Take these in the bathroom with you. And so long as you're awake, be sure to brush your teeth."

He grumbled and marched off to the bathroom. Kelsey smiled to herself, though she was slightly saddened at the thought of her little boy all grown up and too embarrassed to get dressed in front of his mother. He was back in thirty seconds, wearing his pajama top backward.

"Good night, Mom," said Nate, crawling into bed.

"Where's my hug and kiss?"

He came to her and squeezed tightly.

"Oh, you're so strong." She broke the embrace and asked, "Teeth all brushed?"

"Yes."

"Let me see."

His mouth tightened, as if amazed by the way his mother always knew. He lowered his eyes and asked, "Have you ever thought about . . . you and Jack."

She lifted his chin and looked him straight in the eye. "Me and Jack, what?"

"You know. Do you think he's handsome?"

"Yes. Jack is very good-looking."

"He's nice, right?"

"Extremely."

"Do you like him?"

"Yes," she said cautiously, seeing where his little mind was headed. "But there will never be anything romantic between us."

"Why not?"

"Because . . ." She wasn't sure how to answer. It was a question she'd asked herself more than just a few times: Why *not* Jack? "Because he's even worse than you are at trying to change the subject."

"I'm not changing the—"

"Let me see those teeth."

His lips parted slowly. The Oreo cookies were a dead giveaway. Kelsey pointed him back toward the bathroom. "March. And don't forget the ones in back."

He was groaning as he scurried down the hallway. He was a good kid who listened well, definitely the sole bright spot from her short-lived marriage. Her ex-husband was a smart and charming college professor who taught comparative studies. Unfortunately, the thing he liked to compare most was married sex to sex on the side.

Nate was practically sleepwalking when he returned from the bathroom. She put him to bed, and he was in dreamland before she left the room.

Jack was alone in the kitchen, enjoying the collage of photographs on the side-by-side refrigerator-freezer doors. It was a veritable time-line of Nate's life, from birth to third grade, pacifiers to baseball mitts. Some were of Nate alone, but most were of Nate and his mom. They had the same big, hazel eyes, the same smile. Nate was looking more and more like his mother as he grew older, which was a good thing. All ballerinas seemed to have a handsome air about them when up onstage, and Kelsey was one of the truly beautiful ones who didn't seem to dissolve into skin and bones when you got close.

"Did you see the latest one of you and Nate?"

Jack started at the sound of her voice. Kelsey entered the room, then pointed to a snapshot near the refrigerator door handle. It was Nate, Jack, and a life-size Tigger.

"Wow. I made the fridge," said Jack.

"No higher place of honor in this house."

"Like getting a star on Hollywood Boulevard."

"Well, let's not get crazy. It's only Scotch tape and magnets. Today Jack Swyteck, tomorrow Derek Jeter. Know what I mean?"

Jack smiled and said, "He is eight."

"Yes, he is," she said, sounding almost as if it overwhelmed her. She crossed the room to the coffeemaker. "Want some decaf? I made it just before you got here."

"Yes, thanks."

Jack took a seat. She poured two cups at the counter and then brought them to the table. She sat opposite him, next to her laptop computer.

Jack stirred a teaspoon of sugar into his coffee and said, "I ran into Vivien Grasso tonight. The lawyer handling Sally's estate."

"And?"

"She wrote that letter to Tatum because he's named in Sally's will."

She coughed on her coffee. Jack had told her all about Tatum, as his discussions with her were protected by the attorney-client privilege, even though Kelsey was still only a law clerk. Kelsey said, "Wait a minute. You're saying she hired a guy to kill her, and then she named him in her will?"

"That's what I'm told."

"Doesn't that strike you as bizarre?"

"Yes. Assuming that Tatum is telling me the truth."

"Well, let's assume that he is for the moment. Why would Sally name him as a beneficiary?"

"Could be his fee for having agreed to kill her," said Jack. "But that's a really goofy way to do it."

"Could be a setup," said Kelsey.

"How do you mean?"

"He isn't really a beneficiary. Vivien Grasso is just saying that he is. Maybe she thinks Tatum killed Sally and she simply wants to get him in a room where she can grill him."

"I didn't get that impression from Vivien."

"Or how about this? Maybe Vivien thinks that someone else in the room—one of the other beneficiaries—hired Tatum to kill Sally. It could be that the lawyer just wants to test the reaction of each of the beneficiaries when Tatum walks into the room."

"I like the way your mind works, but I think it's working overtime right now."

She opened the cookie jar and passed it his way. The Oreos were all gone but the crumbs, Nate's favorite. Jack was stuck with shortbread.

Kelsey closed up the jar and asked, "So, what do you think's going on?"

"I'm pretty content to just go to the meeting and find out."

"Aren't you worried about representing a scumbag hit man?"

"No. But I am worried about representing someone who lies to me."

"So you'll represent a murderer but not a liar?"

"I didn't say that."

"So you won't represent murderers or liars?"

"There's only one kind of person whom I will categorically refuse to represent. I may or may not represent a murderer. I may or may not represent a liar. But I absolutely, positively will not agree to represent anyone who lies *to me.*"

"You sound like someone who's been burned."

"You could say that."

"Personally or professionally?" She seemed to reconsider the question, then said, "Sorry. That's none of my business."

"It's fine. The answer is both."

"Do you think Tatum Knight is lying to you?"

"That's what I'm wrestling with."

"For what it's worth, I hope you do get involved in this."

"Why?"

"I don't even know this woman, so it seems almost silly to say I care. But on some level, I feel drawn into it. Her whole life's a tragedy, really."

He glanced at her computer and said, "Sounds like you found a few things on Sally Fenning."

"You told me she was attacked a few years ago. But there's more to it than that."

"That's all Tatum told me."

"He left out the most important part." She flipped through her notes, then took a moment to bring him up to speed on the original attack, the death of her daughter. Jack listened in silence, wondering why Tatum hadn't shared these details. Assuming he knew.

"That's horrible," said Jack.

"Yes. It is."

"But it might help explain some things," said Jack. "Maybe she couldn't cope with the murder of her only child. She marries some rich older man, thinking maybe money would make her happy. But it only makes her more miserable. So she finally hires someone to kill her."

"Which means that perhaps Tatum is telling you the truth. She did ask him to kill her."

"Or maybe he's only telling me a half truth. Maybe she asked him to kill her. And he didn't say no."

"Possible," said Kelsey. "Except that I don't totally buy it."

"Why not?" said Jack. "If something happened to Nate, God forbid, don't you think it would at least cross your mind that life isn't worth living?"

"Not under Sally's circumstances."

"How do you mean?"

"If something horrible like that happened to my child, I wouldn't rest till the day they nailed the guy who did it."

"You mean they never caught the guy who killed Sally's daughter?"

"Never even an arrest. This afternoon I called to see if I could pull the file out of police archives, but I got nowhere. It hasn't been archived. It's still technically an open investigation."

"Interesting," said Jack, the wheels turning in his head. "This woman suffers the worst tragedy imaginable. Her four-year-old daughter is murdered viciously in her own home. Five years go by, she's just gotten her hands on forty-six million dollars, compliments of her second husband, and that's when she decides that life isn't worth living."

"Assuming Tatum is to be believed."

"That's the big assumption," said Jack.

"So what are you going to do?"

"The meeting with Vivien Grasso is Monday. That doesn't leave me a lot of time, so I guess I'll do the only thing I can."

"Dump the case, move on?"

"No way." He took one last hit of coffee, then looked her in the eye and said, "I'm going to find out if Tatum Knight is believable."

Seven

First thing Saturday morning, Theo Knight drove to Mo's Gym on Miami Beach.

The Beach had a long boxing tradition, dating back even before a young and overconfident Cassius Clay trained and fought there to snatch the world heavyweight title away from the most feared champion of his era, Sonny Liston. Mo's was a no-frills facility that catered strictly to amateurs. Not the kind of amateurs who flocked to self-defense classes after the September 11 terrorist attacks. These were serious tough guys, amateurs only in the sense that they had no license to box and didn't at all aspire to be the next Muhammad Ali. They just loved to go at it, man to man, and Mo's was good training for the more important fighting they did outside the ring. Anyone who walked into Mo's had better know the ropes, so to speak, and he had better not freak at the sight of his own blood.

Theo found a chair near the center ring, where his brother, Tatum, was beating the holy hell out of someone who obviously had no idea who the Knight brothers were.

Theo and Tatum had fought plenty, no ring, no gloves, no glory. Toughing it out with gangs wasn't exactly the life Theo would have chosen for himself, but the illegitimate sons of a drug addict didn't have many choices. Their aunt did her best to raise Theo and his older brother, but with five of her own, it wasn't easy. Tatum was always in trouble, and Theo inherited a bad-boy reputation and a slew of enemies without even trying. Not that Theo was a saint. By the time he'd dropped out of high school, he'd done his share of car thefts, small-time stuff. Compared to Tatum, he was the good brother—until the night he'd decided to help himself to a little cash in a convenience store and walked into a living nightmare. It was the kind of trouble people expected of Tatum, not Theo. Over the years, he'd managed to push that night into a corner of his brain that he never visited. But as he sat there watching his brother pulverize his opponent, he found his mind slipping back in time, the memories spurred on by the smells and sights of Mo's, the fighting all around him, the gang graffiti on the walls, the walk and talk of dead-end kids.

Four o'clock in the morning, and the city sidewalks were still hot. It was mid-July in Miami, and for three consecutive days there had been no afternoon rain to cool things down. Fifteen-year-old Theo sat in the passenger seat of a low-riding Chevy, the windows rolled down, the music blasting from rear speakers that filled half of the trunk. He wore his Nike cap backward, the price tag still dangling from the bill. Sweat pasted his black, baggy Miami Heat jersey to his back. A Mercedes-Benz hood ornament hung from a thick gold chain around his neck. It was the required uniform of the Grove Lords, a gang of badass teenage punks from Coconut Grove led by chief thief Lionel Brown.

The car stopped at the red light on Flagler Street, a main east-west drag that ran from downtown Miami to the Everglades. They were just beyond the Little Havana neighborhood, outside the Miami city limits, in a rundown commercial area that catered to shoppers in search of used tires, stolen jewelry, or a good porn flick. On weekends it was always congested, but in the wee hours of Wednesday morning traffic was light.

"Chug it," said Lionel from the driver's seat.

Theo took the half-pint of rum, exhaled, and sucked it down. It burned the back of his throat, then his senses numbed and he felt the rush. He got every last drop.

"My man," said Lionel.

Theo suddenly felt dizzy. "Where we going?"

"Shelby's."

"What's that?"

"What's *that*?" Lionel was smiling for no apparent reason. "That be your ticket, my man." Lionel took a right turn off Flagler. The Chevy sped down a side street, then came to a quick halt at the dark end of an alley.

"Seriously, what is it?" said Theo.

"A convenience store."

"What you want me to buy?"

"You ain't buyin' nothin'. Walk up that alley, turn left at the sidewalk. Shelby's is open twenty-four hours. You goes in, grab the cash, get the hell out. I'll wait here."

"How I gonna just grab the money? What if he gots a gun?"

Lionel chuckled and shook his head. "Theo, man, don't be such a pussy."

"I ain't no pussy."

"You gettin' the easy ticket, okay. It ain't usually this easy to become a Grove Lord, but your brother, Tatum, well, he got pull. You understand what I'm sayin'?"

"No. What the hell's so easy about robbin' a convenience store with no gun?"

"You don't need no gun."

"What you want me to do, walk in and say please?"

"Ain't no one to say please to."

"Say what?"

Lionel checked his big sports watch. "It four twenty-five now. Shelby's got one clerk from three-thirty to five-thirty. Every morning at four-thirty, that one clerk has to go out back in the alley and set up for deliveries."

"He don't lock the front door?"

"Sometime he do. Sometime he forget." Lionel handed him a small crowbar and said, "Take this. In case he don't forget."

Theo stared at the crowbar in his hand.

Lionel said, "You want to be a Grove Lord, or don't you?"

"Shit, yeah."

"You got five minutes to prove it. Then I'm gone, wit or wit'out you."

Their eyes locked, then Theo yanked the door handle and jumped out. He was no long-distance runner, but a hundred yards straight down an alley was quick work for him. The passageway was narrow and dark with just a lone street lamp at the front opening. He took it at full speed, zigzagging around a row of Dumpsters and leaping over a pile of garbage. At the sidewalk he slowed to a casual stroll, and turned left toward Shelby's. The crowbar was tucked in his belt, hidden by his long, black jersey.

Shelby's faced a parking lot, which it shared with a Laundromat that had closed hours earlier. To Theo's relief, the lot was empty. He kept walking, briskly but not so fast as to draw attention to himself. Neon signs glowed in the plate-glass storefront. The trash can at the front door was overflowing, and little white plastic shopping bags dotted the sidewalk like a field of dandelions. It was only a few meters, but it seemed to take forever to reach the door. He glanced inside. No sign of the clerk anywhere. Had to be out back, just as Lionel had promised. The crowbar seemed heavier in his pocket as he reached for the door and pulled the handle. The latch clicked, and the door opened. Theo was almost giddy at the thought: the clerk had forgotten to lock it.

Dumbshit.

Theo walked inside, past the eight-foot-high display of canned soda, past the snack rack, past seven hundred different kinds of gum and mints. He stepped carefully but quickly, making not a sound in his sneakers. He reached the checkout counter and stopped. The cash register was right in front of him. He listened, straining to hear anything that might tell him where the clerk had gone, but he heard only the hum of the refrigerated units behind him.

Theo checked his watch. Two minutes had passed. He had three minutes to grab the cash and meet Lionel in back. His pulse quickened. He could feel himself sweating, and for a moment he couldn't move, paralyzed by the voices in his head, his aunt telling him to high-tail it out of there, his older brother, Tatum, yelling, *Pussy, pussy, pussy!* Without another moment's thought, he leaped over the counter, yanked the crowbar from his pants, and smashed open the cash register. The drawer sprang open, and he reached for the cash. But there was none. It was completely empty.

What the hell?

"Help me."

Theo froze at the sound of the man's voice. It was faint, so faint that he almost wondered if he'd imagined it.

"Please, somebody."

The voice was coming from the back room. Theo's heart was in his throat, his thoughts a total blur. He just went with his instincts, jumped over the counter, and sprinted for the door.

"God, *please,* help me!"

Theo stopped cold, just a few feet from the door. Lionel would be gone in just ninety seconds, but those pathetic pleas for help had snagged him like a fish on a gaffe. The man sounded like he was dying, and Theo had never let anyone die before. He wasn't sure what to do, but if that was the sound of death, he was pretty damn certain he didn't want to be a Grove Lord.

He turned, raced back toward the stockroom, then stopped cold in the doorway.

"Oh, *man!*"

The clerk was lying flat on his stomach, his chest heaving as he struggled for each breath. Stretched across the entire length of the room, from the walk-in freezer to the stockroom exit, was a dark crimson smear. It was exactly the width of his body, marking the path he'd crawled inch by inch on his belly, bleeding profusely.

The man looked up at Theo and reached out with his hand. His face was battered and bloody, his clothes soaked with blood. He didn't look much older than Theo, practically a kid, maybe Tatum's age. "Help me," he said in a voice that faded.

Theo just stood there, frightened and not sure what to do.

The man gasped, and his face hit the floor. Then, with a suddenness that chilled Theo, his chest stopped moving, his lungs no longer fighting for air. Theo looked on in horror, then trembled at the sight of the little crowbar in his hand, the one Lionel had given him— something about it that he hadn't noticed earlier.

There was a smear of dried blood on it.

"Shit, man," he said aloud, and then instinct again took over. He turned and raced for the front door, falling to the floor as he smashed into the snack rack and toppled over the canned soda display. His ankle turned, and he rolled across the floor in agony.

And then he heard it—the sound of approaching sirens.

On impulse, he picked himself up, burst through the front door, and made a mad dash for the alley, fighting through the pain of his twisted ankle, knowing in his heart that his friend Lionel would be long gone when he got there.

"Theo, my man!"

It was Tatum calling out from the ring, cocky as ever, sparring with a young Latino who was about half his weight. It wasn't his style to box pip-squeaks, but it was always Mr. Machismo with the twenty-seven-inch waist who liked to taunt the baddest dude in the gym. It was as if these muscle-bound weeds had something to prove, like those annoying little poodles in the park that took on the rottweilers. Sooner or later, the big dog was gonna bite.

For Theo's benefit, Tatum wound up like a windmill, toying with his opponent.

Theo just smiled. He didn't love everything about his brother, but he had to love him. Jack Swyteck, his court-appointed lawyer, was the one who finally got him off death row for the murder of that store clerk. But through it all, there was only one other person who'd stuck by him all the way. In a lifelong give and take of sibling love and hate, this was the one great unequalizer, the debt he could never repay. At least that was the way Theo saw it.

Theo walked toward his brother's corner and leaned over the ropes from outside the ring. The unmistakable odor of sweat and old leather tingled his nostrils. He could hear the fighters grunt with each jab, feel the intensity of their concentration. Only the intellectual snobs of the world thought that boxing wasn't a mind game.

"Ever wonder why a boxing ring is actually a square?" asked Theo.

Theo could mess with his brother's head better than anyone—distract him with extraneous thoughts, watch him take a beating. Even from across the ring, Theo could see that he'd broken Tatum's rhythm.

"You got your three-ring circus," said Theo, his tone philosophical. "Olympic rings. Onion rings. Smoke rings. Ringworms."

"Shut up!" said Tatum.

The little guy was gaining confidence, moving around Tatum like a gnat on a lightbulb.

Theo snickered. "Diamond rings, toe rings, nipple rings, navel rings, scrotum rings, even ring around the collar. All them is circles."

"I said, shut *uuuuuup!*"

Theo said, "Then there's a boxing ring. I mean, how is it that a ring has corners?"

Tatum took a quick jack to the jaw, which startled him. "That's it," he said as he landed a left hook that sent the gnat flying across the ring. "Get your ass in here, Theo."

"Thought you'd never ask." Theo climbed through the ropes. The wounded Hispanic kid helped him strap on gloves. Then Theo stepped farther into the ring with his usual style, leaving the mouthpiece behind so as not to rob himself of his most effective weapon—verbal taunting.

"International rules?" said Theo.

"Uh-uh. Knight rules."

Theo had always moved better than his older brother, and that was especially the case this morning, as he was completely fresh. And he seemed to be particularly on fire when it came to casting confusion to the enemy. "Hey, Tatum. How many times a day do you think lightning strikes?"

Tatum didn't respond. Theo connected with a left-right combination.

"Take a guess," said Theo, ever-light on his feet.

"Strikes where?" said Tatum, grunting. The mouthpiece made him sound thick.

"The whole world. How many times a day?"

Theo could see him thinking, see his loss of focus on the fight for just a moment of weakness. He led with a hard right this time, landing another combination that jerked Tatum's head back.

"How many?" said Theo.

"I dunno. Fifty?"

"Hah!" he said as he delivered a quick blow to the belly. Tatum's eyes bulged, as if to confirm the landing.

"Guess again," said Theo.

Tatum was clearly hurting; Theo was holding nothing back. Tatum said, "A hundred."

"A hundred times a day?" said Theo, scoffing. "That your guess?"

Tatum took a swing, but Theo quickly stepped aside and popped Tatum with another head shot. Tatum stumbled but didn't go down.

Theo allowed him to get his footing, just to keep things interesting. "Try a hundred times *a second*," said Theo. "That's how many times lightning strikes every day."

They circled one another slowly, sizing things up, looking for an opening. Tatum came at him, but Theo beat him back with a numbing blow to the forehead.

"Here's the tricky part," said Theo, still dancing in the ring. "How many people you think get killed by lightning?"

Tatum didn't answer. He seemed to be struggling just to stay focused.

"About fifty," said Theo, answering his own question. "A *year*."

Tatum staggered. That last blow to the forehead had been a direct hit. Theo said, "Every second of every minute of every day, lightning strikes the earth a hundred times. But only a few people get a good, direct hit all year long. What does that tell you, Tatum?"

"Stand still and I'll tell you." He took another swing. *Whiff.*

"When somebody says the chances of Theo Knight getting off death row, or chances of Tatum Knight staying out of prison, are about as good as getting hit by lightning, what does that tell you?"

He unleashed another combination, then backed away before Tatum could answer.

"What the hell are you jabbering about, Theo?"

"Don't you get it? It's not that lightning don't strike. You just gotta be standing in the right place."

"You're talking shit."

"I'm talking about missed opportunities. There's all kinds of ways to miss opportunities. Ain't that right, Tatum?"

Tatum just grunted.

"You can blow them all by yourself," said Theo as he landed another punch, then pulled away quickly. "Or sometimes you don't have to do anything at all. Opportunities just pass right by you. Because your older brother went ahead and fucked up everything for you."

Theo could feel the old anger rising from within. With a flurry of punches he came straight at Tatum and pinned him on the ropes. He kept swinging, and Tatum could only curl up and defend.

"Enough!" shouted Tatum.

For an instant, it was as if they were no longer in the ring. They were on the street corner outside their aunt's apartment in Liberty City, and Theo was pounding on his brother for having hocked their aunt's wedding ring to buy some dope. Theo abandoned the boxing mode and wrestled his brother to the mat, locking Tatum's head in a two-handed hold that could have busted his neck. Theo spoke directly into his brother's ear in a low, angry whisper, so that no one could overhear. "I vouched for you with Swyteck. I told him you didn't kill that woman."

"I didn't kill her."

"Don't lie to me!"

"I'm not lying, man. I didn't kill her."

"Swyteck was like lightning for me, you understand? You think a guy like me gets off death row without Jack Swyteck? You think a guy like me gets anywheres at all without a friend like Swyteck?"

"I hear you, okay?"

He shoved Tatum's face into the canvas. "He'll help you, too, man. If you let him. But the last thing he needs is another scumbag client who lies to him."

Theo tightened the headlock. His brother grimaced and said, "No lies, I promise."

"I swear, bro. You lie and embarrass my friend—you blow this opportunity I'm giving you— I'll bust you wide open."

"I'm not lying."

"Did Sally Fenning hire you to kill her?"

"She tried."

"Did you kill her?"

"No. I didn't touch the bitch."

Theo kneed him in the belly, then pushed him down to the canvas. "She wasn't a bitch," he said as he walked to the ropes. "She was a mother."

Theo used his teeth to unlace his gloves, then pulled them off and tossed them into the plastic crate in the corner. He swatted the line of hanging punching bags on the way to the locker room, a boxing rhythm that matched his walk. At his locker, he dug out his cell phone and dialed Jack's number, catching his breath as the phone rang five times in his ear.

"Jacko, hey, it's me."

"What's going on?" said Jack.

Theo blotted away a smear of blood on his wrist. He was sure it wasn't his. "You don't have to worry about my brother smokin' you no more."

"What do you mean?"

"Let's just say Tatum passed a lie detector test. He didn't kill Sally Fenning."

"You sure of that?"

"Sure as I can be."

"Did she hire him to kill her?"

"Tried to. He sticks by that, yeah."

Theo took a seat on the bench, waiting for Jack to speak. He sensed that something was still troubling him. "What now?" asked Theo.

"It's the same thing Kelsey and I were talking about last night. Here's a woman who goes through the worst nightmare imaginable, the brutal murder of her own child, but it takes five years, a new marriage, and a mega-million-dollar prenup settlement for her to decide that she can't go on living anymore."

"Maybe it was just something that ate her up over time."

"That, or maybe something else pushed Sally over the edge. Something more horrible than having your child murdered in your own home."

"What could be worse than that?"

"I don't know. But I aim to find out."

Theo smiled thinly and said, "As usual, boss, I aim to help."

Eight

At 1 P.M. Monday Jack was in the law office of Vivien Grasso. His client, Tatum Knight, was at his side.

Vivien had yet to make an appearance. Her secretary had simply escorted Jack and his client back to the main conference room, where three men and a woman were waiting at the long mahogany table. They were the other beneficiaries, Jack presumed, but he was reluctant to jump to any firm conclusions.

Jack introduced himself and his client to the group, which precipitated an exchange of names only. Everyone seemed cautious, if not suspicious, reluctant to divulge anything about themselves.

"Deirdre Meadows," said Jack, repeating the final introduction as if he recognized the name. She looked familiar, too. Plain but potentially attractive, her simple clothing, minimal makeup, and efficient brown curls befitting of a woman who was perpetually on deadline.

Jack asked, "Don't you write for the *Tribune?*"

"I do," she answered.

"What, they got you covering this story from the inside?"

"No. I was invited to this meeting. Just like everyone else."

"Did you know Sally Fenning?"

"Sort of." She looked away, as if catching herself in a lie. "Not really."

"Are you a beneficiary under the will?"

"I guess we'll find out."

Jack checked around the table. "Does this arrangement strike anyone else as odd? I get the sense that everyone knows there's a lot of money at stake, but no one quite knows why they're here."

"I know why *I'm* here," said the guy across the table. Miguel was his name, and he'd introduced himself only by his first name, as if he were under strict orders to be tight-lipped.

"Be quiet," the older man next to him grumbled. He was short and stocky, like a fireplug in a double-breasted suit. His hair was slick and dyed black, his mustache perfectly groomed, his midsection soft and round, as if he spent all day looking in the mirror from the shoulders up. His name was "Gerry"—just Gerry, as he was evidently operating under the same brilliant first-name-only strategy.

"You two together?" asked Jack.

They answered simultaneously: "Sort of," said Miguel; "None of your business," said Gerry.

Jack said, "Let me guess. Gerry, you're Miguel's lawyer."

Gerry didn't answer.

"That's Geraldo Colletti," said the reporter. "The divorce lawyer. I'm sure you've heard of him. Made quite a name for himself in family court by snaking other lawyers. First thing he tells his client to do is spend some money interviewing the five best divorce lawyers in town. That way, the other spouse can't go out and hire them, because Gerry's client has already revealed enough confidences to make it ethically impossible for them to represent the other side."

"That's hogwash," said Gerry.

"I *have* heard of you," said Jack. "I don't do divorce work, but aren't you the same Gerry who got himself into trouble for running an ad that labeled you 'Gerry the Genius.'"

"*Gentleman* Gerry," he said, obviously annoyed. "And the ad didn't get me in trouble. It was just ineffectual. Apparently, no one wants a divorce lawyer who's a gentleman."

"I see. Tell me, Gentleman Gerry. What's your take on this?"

"We'll know soon enough."

Miguel made a face. "Oh, what the hell are we being so coy about? I'm Miguel Rios, Sally's first husband."

Jack did a double take. "What are *you* doing here?"

"I was invited, just like the rest of you."

"I wasn't aware that you and Sally were . . . on good terms."

"I wouldn't say it was good terms. Don't get me wrong. It's not like I was expecting her to leave me a mile-high pile of shit and an extra-large spoon. I just wasn't expecting her to leave me anything. But when you're worth forty-six million bucks, maybe there's enough to go around for everybody. Even your ex. So here I am."

"For the money?" said Jack.

The lawyer jumped in, as if pained by Miguel's words. "That's enough information, Mr. Rios. We came here to sit and listen, remember?"

"Oh, put a sock in it, Gerry. You don't represent me here, so don't be telling me what to do."

"Hold on," said Jack. "Are you saying that Gerry the Genius is attending this meeting in some capacity other than as your lawyer?"

"Excuse me," said the attorney. "That's *Gentleman* Gerry."

Miguel said, "Genius here got the same letter I got. He's named in Sally's will, too."

Jack leaned back, thinking. "Interesting. We've got an estate worth forty-six million dollars, but so far, the only people who appear to be in the running to inherit any portion of it are a newspaper reporter, an ex-husband, the ex-husband's divorce lawyer, and my client." All eyes shifted to the man at the other end of the table. "Who are you, sir?"

"I'm an attorney."

"Another lawyer," said Jack.

"I'm here on behalf of Mason Rudsky."

Rudsky was a name that everyone but Tatum seemed to recognize immediately. Jack said, "Mason Rudsky, the assistant state attorney?"

"That's the one."

Jack said, "The same Mason Rudsky who oversaw the investigation into the murder of Fenning's little girl?"

"Yes."

Miguel glared at him and said, "The same Mason Rudsky who in five freakin' years never brought an indictment against anybody for the murder of my daughter."

There was anger in the father's voice, and it cut through the room like an Arctic blast.

The door opened, and all rose as Vivien Grasso entered the conference room. "Keep your seats," she said as she took her place at the head of the table.

"Thank you for coming. Sorry for the late start, but I wanted to give everyone a chance to get here. I would begin by saying that there was one other invitee, but I have as yet been unable to nail down a current address for him. I'll assume he's a no-show."

"Who is it?" asked Jack.

"Not important for present purposes. You'll see soon enough when the will is filed with the court. He won't lose any of his rights as beneficiary simply because he failed to attend the reading of the will."

"Does that mean everyone here is a beneficiary?" asked Jack.

"Let's have the will speak for itself, shall we?" Vivien opened her leather dossier and removed the last will and testament of Sally Fenning. Jack felt his heart thumping as she began, trying to imagine how the others must have felt. They—or at least one of them—might be just minutes away from the cushy side of a forty-six-million-dollar inheritance.

But why?

"I, Sally Fenning, being of sound mind and body . . ."

Vivien read slowly, and Jack listened to every word. He was a lawyer, after all. Words were his business, and words were all you had when it came to dealing with the wishes of the dead. But he was beginning to think that whoever wrote this will must have been paid by the word. It went on for several pages, dry and repetitive as hell, about as bearable as a Swyteck family reunion without Zanax.

"When do we get to the good stuff?" asked Tatum. Jack glanced at his client. The big guy's eyes were about to glaze over.

"I'm turning to that now," said Vivien as she slid another document from her dossier. "The trust instrument."

"Trust?" said Jack.

"Bear with me," said Vivien. "This *is* a multimillion-dollar estate, after all. It's a little more complicated than leaving Uncle Ralph the rice maker and a pair of old bowling shoes."

"Take your time," said Jack.

Vivien read on for another fifteen minutes. Although the language was just as dry and legalistic as before, she managed to hold the attention of everyone in the room. Especially at the end, when she mentioned each of the beneficiaries by name.

Jack scribbled down five names as she read them. "The sixth?"

"I told you, you'll get the sixth after I've had a chance to meet with him." Vivien returned to the document, reading all the way down to the date and place of execution. When she finished, she laid the papers on the table before her, saying nothing further.

The others looked at her, then at one another, as if not quite sure they'd heard it correctly. Or perhaps they were just stunned into silence.

Finally, Sally's ex spoke up. "Are you saying she actually left us her money?"

"Forty-six million dollars?" said the Genius. He seemed dumbfounded, somewhere between giddy and on the verge of a panic attack, almost speaking to himself. "I can't believe she left it all to us."

Vivien said, "Well, technically, she didn't leave it to all of you. She's leaving it to one of you."

Tatum scratched his head, made a face. "I'm not followin' any of this. Who gets what, and when do we get it?"

Vivien smiled patiently and said, "Mr. Knight, let me put this in terms that everyone here can understand. All of the assets of Ms. Fenning's estate will go into a trust. There are six potential beneficiaries. One by one, your rights extinguish upon your death. Until there's only one of you left. That's when the trust shall be distributed, principal and any accumulated interest. The last person living has all rights of survivorship."

"Speak English," said Tatum.

Vivien looked at him coolly and said, "Last one to die takes all."

The reporter looked up from her notes. "Is that legal?"

"Sure," said Vivien.

Tatum said, "Let me get this straight. If all these other jokers live eighty-nine years, and I live ninety years, I get the money, but I have to wait ninety years before I gets a single penny."

"Exactly. But you get interest."

"That's bullshit."

"Let me give you another for instance," said the Genius. "Let's say that we all walk out of here, and these fine folks get hit by a bus. And I don't. That means I'm a millionaire?"

"No. There is still one other beneficiary who's not here."

"Him too," said the Genius. "Let's say they're all on the same bus, and it rides over a cliff. Hypothetically speaking, of course."

"Then, yes, you've hit the jackpot. You inherit forty-six million dollars as soon as everyone else is dead. The only condition is that you're still alive when everyone else dies."

"Doesn't matter how they die?"

"No. What matters is when they die."

A tense silence filled the room, which was prolonged by an anxious exchange of eye contact among a group of strangers who now, for some reason, seemed forever linked to one another. Finally, Gerry the Genius said, "It's as if she's encouraging us to bump each other off."

More silence.

Vivien looked each of them in the eye, then said, "I'm not suggesting that anyone here is so inclined, but if any of the beneficiaries under this will were to bump off the others in hopes of inheriting the whole pie—well, just forget about it. Your motive would be obvious, so you'd never get away with it."

Miguel chuckled, more philosophical than angry, as if the beauty of his ex-wife's scheme had suddenly come clear. "So the joke's on us. She makes us feel close to the money, but no one can really get it. At least not soon enough for it to be of any use to us in our lifetime. We'll just go on living and hoping we'll be rich some day, but we're all just going to die as poor as we ever were."

Vivien said, "If you're feeling abused, you can always opt out.

Nothing prevents a beneficiary from rejecting his right to an inheritance."

He looked around the room, seeming to be doing some quick computations in his head as to the odds of his outliving everyone else in the room. "No. I'll play her little game. I'd be happy to take her forty-six million."

"And she'd be happy for you to have it," said Vivien. "And I mean that. Sincerely."

"So all we can do is wait?" asked the reporter. "Just go on living our lives and wait for everyone else to die?"

"That's exactly right," said Vivien.

Gerry the Genius flashed his plastic grin. "And, of course, we should all rest a lot easier and live a lot longer knowing that none of us here is a trained killer."

He laughed too hard at his own joke. They all laughed, but it only made the moment all the more uneasy.

"Yeah," said Tatum, catching Jack's eye as he spoke. "Thank goodness for that."

Nine

Things were moving fast. On Tuesday morning, Jack and Tatum were in court already. The plan was to move things even faster.

Jack didn't often find himself in probate court, and it was a bit of an adjustment for him. In some ways it was the most uncivil of places in the entire civil court system, the bloody arena in which sisters fought brothers and sons betrayed mothers, all in pursuit of family fortunes. Yet it was regarded as a strangely courteous environment, at least among members of the bar. Lawyers held the door for each other, said good morning, shook hands, knew each other by their first names. They even seemed to talk softly when addressing the court, as if in respect for the dead. Here, the stakes were as high as in any courtroom, but the style was different. That was why they called it "Whisper Court."

"Good morning," said Judge Parsons from the bench. He was one of the more respected members of the Miami–Dade County judiciary, a wiry African-American with thick, gray eyebrows and a shaved head that glistened like a brand-new bowling ball.

"Good morning, Your Honor." The reply was a mixed chorus of lawyers and clients. Since the meeting at Vivien Grasso's office, the number of relevant players had grown appreciably. Evidently, none of the beneficiaries was willing to play Sally's forty-six-million-dollar game without topflight legal representation. Ex-husband Miguel Rios had hired Parker Aimes, the five-time chairman of the probate section of the Florida Bar and a distant relative of the late Will Rogers. (The joke was that he'd never met a decedent he didn't like.) Reporter Deirdre Meadows was represented by not one, but two lawyers from Miami's biggest firm. Assistant State Attorney Mason Rudsky had already dumped his first lawyer and replaced him with a former law professor who had literally written the book on Florida's law of estates and trusts. With Vivien Grasso as personal representative of Sally's estate, the introductions were starting to sound like a Who's Who of the probate bar, with one notable exception.

"Your Honor, I'm Gerry Colletti . . . appearing on behalf of Gerry Colletti."

There was a light chuckle in the background, which seemed to annoy Gerry. He was apparently the only person in the courtroom who didn't find it goofy that the client was introducing himself as the lawyer.

The judge said, "Mr. Swyteck, it's your motion that's brought us here. Please proceed."

"It's really quite a simple motion, Judge. As you know, Vivien Grasso is the personal representative of Sally Fenning's estate. The law gives her ten days from the date of Ms. Fenning's death to deposit with the clerk of the court a copy of Ms. Fenning's last will and testament. As of today, ten days have come and gone, and the will is not on file."

"But according to Ms. Grasso, she read the entire will to you at her office."

Vivien rose and said, "That's exactly right, Your Honor."

"That's not *exactly* right," said Jack. "She read the entire will to us, *except* for the identity of the sixth beneficiary."

Vivien said, "If I may explain, Your Honor."

"Please do."

"We're talking about a forty-six-million-dollar estate. Look at the interest this case is generating," she said as she turned and pointed to the public seating behind her.

Jack turned and looked with everyone else. The gallery was nearly full, six rows of shoulder-to-shoulder seating.

The judge asked, "Where did the buzz about this case come from all of a sudden?"

Vivien said, "Obviously you didn't see the paper this morning. Nifty little story about the missing heir in a forty-six-million-dollar game of survival. Doesn't take long for word to get out when one of the beneficiaries is a reporter."

Deirdre Meadows sank low in her chair.

Vivien continued. "Now, why do you think the courtroom is nearly full for a Mickey Mouse motion like this one? I'll tell you why. Because every warm body sitting in the observation gallery this morning works for a lawyer. They're chomping at the bit, just waiting for me to divulge the name of that sixth beneficiary, so that they go running after him with a business card."

Jack took another look, panning across a sea of faces that looked guilty as charged.

The judge flashed a thin smile and said, "Funny, but I'm suddenly reminded of something I watched the other night on the Discovery Channel. A helpless deer was surrounded by a pack of hungry coyotes with teeth bared. The pack slowly closed in, jaws snapping, until finally one of them lunged forward and took hold of a hoof. The others piled on. In a matter of seconds the deer was on its back, limbs extended, drawn-and-quartered as the ravenous coyotes pulled mercilessly for a share of the meal. Anyway, I digress. I guess that's my way of saying that one third of forty-six million dollars is a contingency fee worth fighting over."

"You bet it is," said Vivien. "And that's why I don't want to publicize the name of the sixth beneficiary until I've been able to locate him. If I'm forced to reveal the name, I'm afraid that one of these coyotes, as you say, is likely to reach him before I do. Frankly, I think that's an utterly distasteful way for someone to find out they're a beneficiary under a will."

"I agree," said Jack. "That's why I haven't asked the court to order Ms. Grasso to file the will with the court."

"Then what are you requesting?" asked the judge.

"This is a peculiar situation," said Jack. "Ms. Fenning's will is structured so that the surviving beneficiary inherits the entire estate."

"Which is exactly Ms. Grasso's point," said the judge. "Unless the beneficiaries are willing to wait fifty or more years for the money, they'll either have to figure out some way to get the other beneficiaries disqualified or to work out a settlement. That means they'll need a sharp lawyer, and I have little doubt that there will be plenty of them hunting down our mystery beneficiary once his name is revealed."

"That's one side of it, Your Honor. But consider another possibility. Immediately following the reading of the will at Ms. Grasso's office, I believe it was Mr. Colletti who made a joke to the effect that it's a good thing none of the beneficiaries is a trained killer, or maybe they'd all have to start looking over their shoulders. After leaving the office, it occurred to me: How do we know this unidentified sixth beneficiary *isn't* a trained killer?"

"Do you have reason to believe he is dangerous?" asked the judge.

Jack hesitated. He couldn't very well inform the judge that Sally Fenning tried to hire his own client as a hit man, or that the real reason for his motion was to test his theory that beneficiary number six was the hired gun who *hadn't* turned Sally down.

"I don't know anything about him," said Jack. "But for the sake of personal safety and peace of mind, each of the beneficiaries should know the name of the sixth beneficiary. So I ask the court to order Ms. Grasso to divulge the name to us immediately, under seal, for our eyes only. Then once she finds him, she can make the name public."

"Ms. Grasso, what's wrong with that?" asked the judge.

"In theory, nothing," she replied. "But we have to look at reality here. If I were simply turning the name over to Mr. Swyteck, whom I know and trust, I wouldn't be worried. But let's face it. Once the coyotes sitting on *that* side of the rail realize that everyone sitting on *this* side of the rail knows who the sixth beneficiary is, there's no telling how much money they might pay one of us for that information."

Gerry jumped to his feet. "I resent that, Your Honor! Ms. Grasso was looking right at me when she made that implied accusation."

"I was not."

"Oh, what a crock."

"Enough!" said the judge, throwing his hands in the air. "I won't have lawyers sniping at each other in my courtroom."

Heavens to Mergatroid, no, thought Jack. *Not in Whisper Court.*

The lawyers apologized, but the judge had already made up his mind. "Ms. Grasso, I appreciate your concerns, but I can't suspend filing deadlines based upon your abstract fear that some lawyers may act unethically in pursuit of a hefty contingency fee." He peered out over his reading glasses, scanning the public seating area. "That said, let me make myself absolutely clear to the peanut gallery. If anyone oversteps the bounds of ethics and good taste in pursuit of this sixth beneficiary, they'll have me to deal with."

"Does that mean I'm required to file the will with the court?" asked Vivien.

"Yes. By the end of the day. And in the interest of avoiding a mad stampede on the clerk's office, let's do it this way. Please announce the name of the sixth beneficiary."

"Right here, in open court?"

"No time like the present."

"All right. If that's the court's ruling."

"That's my ruling."

"His name is Alan Sirap."

A rumble emerged from the public seating behind Jack, as scores of courthouse spies reached for pen and paper to scribble down the name. Jack glanced at his client, but Tatum shrugged, as if the name meant nothing to him.

"Anything further?" asked the judge.

No one answered.

"Then we're adjourned." With the bang of a gavel, the judge stepped down from the bench and exited swiftly through a side exit to his chambers.

The lawyers and their clients rose and gathered their briefcases. Colletti took the long way around the big mahogany table, and he didn't stop until he was standing within Jack's personal space. He spoke firmly but in a low voice, so no one but Jack could hear. "If you think you got a leg up because you're buddy-buddy with Vivien

Grasso, think again. I'm not in this to lose. Especially to a client like yours."

"I'd take him over your client any day, Gerry."

"We'll see about that."

Jack watched as Colletti walked up the aisle to the main exit in the back of the courtroom, pushing his way through the crowd, as if he were determined to lead the pack of coyotes from the courthouse.

Ten

I t was an hour before sunset and just minutes before tip-off as Jack threw together a tray of beer, chips, and salsa for the Knicks-Heat game on the tube. The stakes were high. If the Heat lost again, Jack would get a flood of calls and e-mails from friends in New York. *Knicks rule, Heat suck, na, na, na-na, na.* But it was one of those magical Miami nights when Jack would fall asleep to the soothing sounds and smells of Biscayne Bay right outside his open bedroom window, while his buddies up North had just one more day to decide which pair of long johns to wear under their Halloween costumes, so who were the real losers anyway?

"I got good news and bad news," said Theo. He was peering through binoculars and standing on Jack's patio beside the portable television he'd wheeled outside for the game. Jack adjusted the rabbit ears, then set up the goodies on the table beneath the umbrella. Nothing like beer, your best friend, and basketball under the stars.

"What now?" asked Jack.

Theo lowered the binoculars. "The good news is, your neighbor likes to prance around the house naked as a jaybird."

"My neighbor is a seventy-eight-year-old man," said Jack, wincing.

"Yeah. That's, uh, kind of the bad news."

Jack chuckled as he grabbed a beer and fell into the chaise. Theo plopped down beside him and put the whole bowl of chips in his lap.

"You gonna leave some for me?" asked Jack.

"Get your own." Theo reached for the remote control, but Jack snatched it away.

"That's where I draw the line, buddy," said Jack.

"I just wanted to see if Sally Fenning's in the news again."

"What makes you think she would be?"

"The name of the sixth beneficiary is out there now. I wouldn't be a bit surprised if the media finds this Alan Sirap before the lawyers do."

"You got a point."

"Course I got a point. I always got a point. I don't open my mouth unless I got a point. Unless I gotta burp." He belched like a foghorn.

"Could you possibly be any more disgusting?"

"Only on a good day." He put the bowl of chips aside and asked, "So, what are you gonna do about Tatum? You gonna represent him?"

"I already do."

"I don't mean this hourly bullshit you're doing as a favor to me. Are you gonna jump in this case for the long haul or not?"

"I don't know yet."

"Come on. Like the judge said, there'll be plenty of legal back-stabbing to go around, with each of these beneficiaries trying to pick off the other ones. And it's high profile, too. When's the last time you had a case that was in the news like this?"

Jack shot him a wicked glare.

Theo coughed, as if suddenly recalling that the *last* high-profile case had nearly gotten Jack, himself, indicted. "Okay, forget the publicity angle. Let's talk dollars and sense. You got pretty beat up in the divorce. The only thing Cindy didn't take was your car and your best friend, and she probably could've had that too. Imagine me wearing a fucking cap and driving Miss Daisy all around Coral Gables in a Mustang convertible."

"It wasn't worth the fight. I just wanted to move on."

"That doesn't change the facts. You got a nice house here, Jack, but you don't own it, and we're sitting outside watching TV not because it's such a beautiful night, but because you don't even have an air conditioner."

"What's your point?"

"One third of forty-six million dollars—*that's* my point."

"You think I should sign on as Tatum's lawyer?"

"If you don't, someone else will. Why shouldn't it be you? All the other beneficiaries are hiring topflight lawyers."

"The other lawyers have the comfort of knowing that their client didn't kill Sally Fenning."

"So do you."

Jack drank his beer, didn't say anything.

Theo said, "I can't give you a hundred percent proof Tatum didn't kill her. But he gave me his word, brother to brother, in the boxing ring, and there's probably no place more sacred to the Knight brothers than the ring. There's no sure thing in life, especially when you're talking about a shot at a one-third contingency fee on a take of forty-six million bucks."

"I know what you're saying."

"I don't think you do. I'm talking about more than just money. It's who you are, and who you're going to be the rest of your pathetic life."

"Let's not get carried away here."

"This is no bullshit. Tatum and I used to have this saying. There's two kinds of people in this world, risk takers and shit takers."

Jack laughed, but Theo was serious.

Theo said, "Tatum might not be your ideal version of a client, but he's giving you the chance to answer a very important question. So think real hard before you spit out an answer: What do you want to be the rest of your life, Jack Swyteck? A risk taker? Or a shit taker?"

They locked eyes, and then Jack looked away, letting his gaze drift toward the water and a distant sailboat running wing-and-wing toward the mainland. "Tell your brother to stop by the office tomorrow. We'll sign a contingency fee agreement."

PART TWO

Eleven

The Harmattan winds were blowing right on schedule.

It was Rene's third autumn in West Africa, and no one had to tell her that the dusty winds had returned in full force. Her dry eyes and stinging nostrils didn't lie. The winds blew from the deserts of the north, starting as early as October, typically lasting through February. With the dust, however, came occasionally cooler temperatures at night, though cooler was indeed a relative concept in a place where a typical daytime high was ninety-five degrees and the weather on the whole was best described as gaspingly hot. In the next five months they'd have just five days with rainfall, but at least there would be no raging rivers of mud to wash livestock, children, or entire hillside villages into the valley. Life in West Africa was a trade-off, and Rene had learned to accept that. For the foreseeable future, she'd live with dust in her hair, dust on her clothes, dust on her toothbrush, and it was just too damn bad if her friends back home just couldn't understand why the snapshots she sent them had such a flat lifelessness about them. Even under the best of circumstances, it was hard to do photographic justice to the endless grasslands of northern Côte d'Ivoire, unless you were a professional, and Rene was anything but that.

Rene was a pediatrician who had volunteered for a three-year stint with Children First, a human rights organization that was fighting against the forced servitude of children in the cocoa fields. The inspiration had struck her in her last year of residency at Boston Children's Hospital. One night in the lounge, while wolfing down her typical dinner of a diet soda and a candy bar, she read an article about the reemergence of slavery. Studies by the United Nations and the State Department confirmed that approximately fifteen thousand children, aged nine to twelve, had been sold into forced labor on cotton, coffee, and cocoa plantations in Côte d'Ivoire. The situation was only predicted to get worse, as prices for cocoa continued to fall, and almost half of the world's cocoa came from the very region that had stooped to child labor to boost profitability. Her candy bar suddenly didn't taste quite as sweet. It just so happened that she was at one of those "Why did I go to med school?" junctures. Was it time to move to Brookline and wipe snot from the noses of kids who came to checkups in the company of their nannies, or did she yearn for something more? Before she had time to reconsider, she was on a plane to Abidjan, her ultimate destination being Korhogo, capital of the Senoufo country, a nine-hour bus ride north.

Côte d'Ivoire had been rocked by a military coup in 1999, and Rene arrived just in time to find it besieged by a host of medical problems—malnutrition, AIDS, infant mortality, even genital mutilation among some migrant tribes. She did it all, but she tried to focus on the mission that had moved her. Officially, the local governments denied that child slavery existed. Soon enough, however, Rene was able to put a face on the crisis, the faces of children who were routed to her clinic for assistance as they struggled to find their way home to the most impoverished of countries that neighbored Côte d'Ivoire. Children who told her of men luring them away from their families in bus stops and busy shopping markets in countries like Mali, Benin, or Burkina Faso. Many traveled by sea, packed in crowded old ships at ports like Cotonou, ironically a thriving center of slave trade in earlier centuries. Others came by land, trucking through the brush and canoeing across rivers until they reached plantations far from civilization, farther still from home. They stopped only when it was time for the men to get out and negotiate with cocoa farmers near Lake Kossou, when two or three or twelve children at a time would march off to meet other children of the same fate. They lived in overcrowded huts without cots, without plumbing or electricity, but with strict rules against talking, because talking led to complaining, and complaining led to revolt. They told Rene of twelve-hour workdays in the fields, sunup to sundown, and the hunger in their bellies from lousy food, mostly burned bananas, maybe a yam if they were lucky. They showed Rene the scars on their legs, arms, and backs, told her of the beatings when they didn't work fast enough. The beatings when they didn't work long enough. The beatings when they tried to escape. Beatings, beatings, and more beatings. All for no pay to the child, just a promise of perhaps a lump sum payment of ten or fifteen dollars to the child's family, a payment that was frequently never made. No one wanted to call it slavery, but one of the first rules Rene had learned in med school was that if it looks like a duck and quacks like a duck . . .

Chickens clucked behind her, startling her.

"*Ysugri, nassara,*" said the man as he passed her on the street. Excuse me, white woman.

Rene stepped aside. The man had a long wooden pole across his shoulders, balanced on either end by live chickens unhappily hanging by their claws. The official language of Côte d'Ivoire was French, but few Africans spoke it, particularly in the north. Based on his tongue and dress, she guessed the man was from Burkina Faso, a desolate, landlocked country to the north that made Côte d'Ivoire glisten like a model of prosperity.

Rene flowed with the stream of cows, mules, and pedestrians to the city market. Some of the streets were paved, but others were just dirt trails that wound through the city like footpaths to centuries past. She knew her way, but it was easy enough for anyone to find it this time of year, as any gathering of this size stirred up a reddish-pink cloud of dust that was visible from across town. There wasn't much to do in Kohorgo, and the afternoon market was a reliable source of entertainment, if you could stand the heat.

Rene stopped at the corner to sip water from her canteen. Two years earlier, she would never have gone out this time of day, but time had made her more durable. Or crazier.

"*Wanwana, wanwana?*" she heard the tourists ask. Travelers did indeed find Kohorgo, mostly on their way to someplace else, almost always in search of its crude and unusual painted *toiles*, a native form of art that found its way into just about every hotel and expat home in the country in the form of wall hangings, bedspreads, napkins, and tablecloths. The question at the afternoon market was always the same: "How much?"

"Good price," she whispered as she passed a couple of hard-bargaining Australians.

"Thanks, mate," said one of them, and then he went on haggling.

Bargaining was a way of life at the market, though Rene had stitched up more than one tourist who'd failed to realize that once you negotiated one of these artists down to a certain level, it was extremely insulting if you ultimately did not buy.

A blast of wind sent the dust swirling, and Rene covered her face with her scarf. This was a particularly noxious blast, carrying with it the stench of sewer. Perhaps some rain had fallen to the north last night, or the authorities had simply decided it was time to unload the overflow.

The wind eased back a notch, and Rene opened her eyes. Dust continued to swirl, and the market was suddenly a haze, as if she were dreaming. The labyrinth of brown walls and buildings made of mud-brick almost seemed to melt into the earth. Shawls and wraps flapped in the dirty breeze. Animals stirred at the more subtle desert odors blown in from the north. And the tourists kept haggling.

In a few moments she was able to focus once again, and her eyes fixed on a young boy standing on the corner, a boy like many others she'd seen. Skinny legs, muddy trousers, plastic sandals. The tattered shirt, eyes filled with fear. Anyone else would have thought he was lost. But Rene knew the look.

This boy was running.

Slowly, she started moving in his direction, careful not to scare him off. She kept watch without making eye contact, wending her way through the crowd, taking a circuitous route to the street corner that the boy seemed to have claimed—he and scores of other children who passed their days begging in the streets.

The onslaught began as she drew closer, child after child with out-stretched hand.

"*S'il vous plaît, mademoiselle. S'il vous plaît.*" If you were white, even the street children knew enough French to say please in the official language.

It was hard to ignore them, but she couldn't help all of them. Only the slaves among them.

Though surrounded by other children, she never lost sight of the boy. Just ten feet away, her suspicions were confirmed. She could see the blisters on his hands and the crisscrossing of scars around the calves and ankles. Boys in the field cut the cocoa pods with machetes. It took one or two good lengthwise whacks to break open the woody shell and scoop out the beans. A good boy could split open five hundred pods an hour, though with fatigue or lack of experience they often slashed themselves. At least this one still had all his fingers and toes.

Finally, after continuous effort, she managed to plant herself beside him.

"*S'il vous plaît, mademoiselle,*" he said with outstretched hand.

His French was remarkably good, so she replied in the same language. "Don't be afraid," she said. "I've come to help you."

He took a half-step back. Clearly he understood.

"I've helped lots of boys like you," she said. "Boys who work in the cocoa fields."

Other beggars tried to force their way between them, but Rene kept working him. "I'm a doctor."

She pulled a photograph of her clinic from her pocket. She'd found it useful in past cases to be able to show the boys something. "It's just around the corner. Come with me. I can help you get home."

He shook his head, as if he'd heard that one before.

She stepped toward him, then stopped, fearing that she was coming on too strong. "Please," she said. "You don't look like the other children, you understand? Come with me. Let me help you before the child brokers find you again."

He looked into her eyes, and she didn't dare look away. Being a woman was such a huge advantage when talking to a boy who'd been lied to by so many men.

He nodded slowly, and she immediately took his hand. It was the coarse and calloused hand of an old man, surely not of the boy he was. She led him back across the market, down a dusty shortcut she knew to her clinic.

"What's your name?"

"Kamun."

"How old are you?"

"I don't know," he said.

"Do you want some water?"

"Yes."

They stopped, and she let him drink from her canteen.

"Thank you."

She smiled and patted his head. "You're welcome."

At the end of the dusty trail was the Children First clinic, which didn't look like much of a clinic. It was one of the older buildings in the neighborhood, thick walls of mud-brick and an adobe-style roof. But it did have a noisy air-conditioning unit sticking out the window, which seemed to delight the boy.

"Cool," he said, smiling.

"Yes. It is. Come inside."

He followed her in, and she closed the door behind him. He seemed nervous again, so she took him by the hand and let him stand directly in front of the A/C and turned it on full-blast. He smiled, even laughed a little as the cold air dried the sweat on his brow.

Through the holes in his shirt she saw scars across his back, and she wondered how long it had been since he'd laughed like this.

"Come in here," she said. She took him into the other room—there were only two—and sat him on the examination table.

"I want to listen to your heart," she said. She placed the stethoscope on his knee and listened.

"I don't hear your heart," she said.

Finally, he laughed. "That's not my heart," he said.

"Oh, I'm sorry." She put it on his elbow.

He laughed again, and she laughed with him. But if he thought this routine was funny, he was probably younger than she'd guessed. She placed her stethoscope on his heart and listened.

"Good strong heart," she said.

"Yes. That's what *Le Gros* said." *Le Gros*—the Big Man.

"Is that who you worked for?"

"Yes."

"How long?"

"Six."

"Months?"

"No. Harvests."

Rene had been around long enough to know that most cocoa farms had a main harvest lasting several months and a mid-crop harvest lasting several more. Six harvests meant that Kamun had been working almost three years straight.

It's not going to be easy to get this boy home.

"What did you do there?"

He didn't answer, which was to be expected. It generally took them a while to warm up.

"May I take your shirt off?"

He shook his head.

"I noticed some marks on your back. I just want to take a look."

He folded his arms, refusing.

"It's okay. We can do that later."

She paused, then prepared herself to ask the one question she always asked. She knew the answer she'd get, talking to a child who'd never known a home with milk and sugar in the cupboard. But she asked anyway, hoping the answer would help her see purpose in her work and strengthen her resolve, hoping that it wouldn't simply dampen her spirits and break her heart.

"Kamun. Have you ever tasted chocolate?"

"Chocolate?"

"Yes, chocolate. Have you ever tasted it?"

He shook his head. "What is . . . chocolate?"

The main door opened, and a man and woman entered. "Post," they said with their usual cheery smiles.

Rene quietly assured Kamun that they were friends. It was Jim and Judy Roberts, nonmedical volunteers who ran the administrative side of Children First's operation. Rene had liked them from day one on the job, a couple of down-to-earth Oklahomans who didn't do charity just to get their mugs in the society pages and who'd found a meaningful way to spend their retirement together. They were back from their daily jaunt to the post office, Jim the former Iowa State football player having led the way. Rene stepped out of the examination room and asked, "The usual?"

"No," said Mr. Roberts. "There's actually something here for you today."

"Really? Put it on the desk. I'm with a patient."

"It's from a lawyer," he said.

That piqued her interest. She crossed the room and took a look. She didn't recognize the name.

"Who's the boy?" asked Mrs. Roberts.

"Sorry?" said Rene, still focused on the envelope.

"The patient. Who is he?"

"His name is Kamun. I'll introduce you in a minute. This looks kind of important. Maybe I should open it."

Mr. Roberts handed her an opener. She quickly sliced the envelope from end to end, then removed the letter. It was one page long. Her eyes shifted from left to right as she read, then her lashes fluttered and her hand began to shake.

Mr. Roberts asked, "Is everything okay, Rene?"

Instinctively, she brought a hand to her mouth. "It's my sister," she said.

"She's okay, I hope."

Rene looked up from the letter and said, "She's dead."

Mrs. Roberts came to her, put her arm around her. "Oh no."

Rene lowered herself onto the edge of the desk, the quickest place to sit down. "She was shot. A robbery or something. They don't know exactly. In Miami."

Mr. Roberts took her hand. "I'm so sorry, honey."

Mrs. Roberts said, "She was such a sweet girl. I mean, it seems like she was just here with us."

"It's been over two years since she left."

"Really? That long? Oh, time flies. But she was still so young. I think I'm going to cry."

"Please, don't," said Rene.

Mr. Roberts glanced at his wife, as if telling her to be strong for Rene. She cleared her throat and quickly toughened her resolve.

"Thank you," said Rene.

Mr. Roberts grimaced and said, "She really was such a nice person."

"Would you like a minute alone?" asked Mrs. Roberts.

"I'll be fine, really. But thank you both. It's kind of you to say such nice things."

Mrs. Roberts said, "We can arrange for some time off, if you would like."

"I don't expect I'll be going anywhere."

"It's no problem, if you want to go home."

"Sally was the only family I had left. Now she's gone. There's nothing to go back to."

The older woman smiled flatly, as if she were trying to understand. "It's up to you, dear. Whatever you want to do."

Rene returned a sad smile, then started back to the examination room. She stopped in the doorway, then turned and looked at both of them. "I don't want you or the organization to be at all worried about me. I'm not going anywhere."

"Like we said, Rene. It's totally up to you."

With a final nod, she tried to convey that this would be the end of the matter. Then she stepped into the examination room and turned her attention back to Kamun.

Twelve

At noon on Thursday, Jack took Sally Fenning's ex-husband to lunch.

He'd spent the morning in court at the Criminal Justice Center, so they met just a few blocks down the Miami River at the Big Fish Restaurant, one of Jack's favorite lunch spots. For all its miles of breathtaking waterfront, Miami offered amazingly few places that actually allowed you to sit by the water and eat seafood. The Big Fish was right on the Miami River, nothing fancy, just a relaxing place to score fresh dolphin, tuna, or shrimp ceviche while soaking up a historic stretch of river where ninety-foot yachts bound for the West Indies shared the right of way with rusted old container ships filled with stolen SUVs destined for South America. It was a landmark of sorts, a piece of old Miami where mariners from houseboats at the west end of the river sidled up alongside bankers and lawyers from the office towers to the east, where the mouth of the five-and-a-half-mile river emptied into Biscayne Bay. Jack was sentimental about the place, too. It was over broiled grouper and french fries that, as a federal prosecutor, he'd talked his first mobster into testifying for the government.

Jack didn't think he'd ever duplicate the sense of symmetry that came from nailing Tony "the Big Tuna" Dilabio at a place called the Big Fish. But he still felt a rush of adrenaline as he shook hands with Sally's ex-husband.

"Thanks for coming," said Jack.

"No problem."

They took a small table by the window, which overlooked an old fishing pier that had been half-submerged in the river for as long as Jack had been coming here. Miguel was wearing a short-sleeved white shirt and blue, form-fitting bicycle pants. He'd joined the City of Miami Police Department near the tail-end of his marriage to Sally, and he was now part of the downtown bicycle brigade, a small team of officers who patrolled the parks and streets by pedal power on twelve-speeds.

Miguel's full name was Miguel Ortiz Rios, a first-generation Cuban-American. Jack's mother had actually been born in Cuba, but he didn't mention it to Miguel. She died just hours after his birth, so his Latin connection was purely genetic, and he came across about as Cuban as Yankee pot roast. He knew from experience that if he told Miguel he was half Cuban, Miguel would start speaking Spanish, Jack would do his best to respond in kind, and Miguel would quickly revert to English, surmising that Jack was a lying sack of shit gringo who was trying to forge an instant rapport by claiming to be Latino.

"I assume you didn't invite me here to turn me on to the conch fritters," said Miguel.

Jack gave a little smile and said, "That's true. Though the conch fritters are pretty good."

"That's what I'm having," he told the waitress. "Just water to drink."

"I'll have the big tuna," said Jack.

"It's all pretty much the same size," she said.

Jack caught his own Freudian slip. "Sorry. I mean just the tuna. Seared, rare. And an iced tea."

The waitress took their menus and left them alone at the table. The lunch crowd was streaming in, and the conversations around them had merged into a single, steady rumble.

Jack said, "Before we start, Mike —"

"It's Miguel. Only Sally called me Mike."

"Sorry. I just wanted to remind you that you do have the right to have your lawyer here."

"Forget it. Parker Aimes gets a big hit if I take home the forty-six million, but I still gotta pay him a reduced hourly fee if we lose. I'm using him as little as possible."

Interesting, thought Jack, that Miami's top probate lawyer didn't like the ex-husband's chances well enough to take a straight contingency fee arrangement. Jack said, "I have a few things I want to ask about you and Sally, but let me start with the big question. What do you think Sally was up to here?"

"Like I said at the meeting. As far as I know, there isn't a single person on that list of beneficiaries who Sally loved. And a few of them, I know for a fact Sally hated them."

"So she decided to leave forty-six million dollars to people she hates?"

"No," said Miguel. "She left her enemies to *fight* over forty-six million dollars that they would probably never get their hands on."

"You consider yourself one of her enemies?"

"That's a little complicated."

"Give it a shot."

"I never thought of Sally as the enemy. Never. Not even in the darkest times."

"But you did hire yourself a pretty tough divorce lawyer."

"I didn't really hire him. Gerry Colletti did it for me as a friend, freebie."

"He still your friend?"

"I don't think of him as one."

"What happened?"

"Nothing, really. I just finally came around to realize Sally was right about him. He is a scumbag."

"You think that's one of the reasons Sally considered you the enemy? You used a scumbag divorce lawyer?"

"I can see where you might say that, but no. Truth is, I wouldn't let Gerry put the screws to her. I'll give you an example. Sally and me had this restaurant. In fact, we bought it from Gerry. It was a disaster, and we had to close it. All that debt went with me. Whatever assets we had went with Sally. The way I saw it, she was never going to recover psychologically if I put her in a financial hole."

"That's pretty fair-minded."

"After what happened to our daughter, the rules are a little different. You try to work things out."

"Is that the way Sally saw it?"

He gave Jack a sad smile, a slow shake of the head. "Unfortunately, no. Sally was a sweet, loving person. But she changed."

"What changed her?"

His smile was gone. "Our daughter was murdered in our house. That can change you, don't you think?"

Jack lowered his eyes, a little embarrassed for having asked. "It's the most terrible thing I can imagine. And I'm sorry that happened to you and Sally."

"Thanks."

A party of six walked by on their way to another table. Jack waited for them to pass, then said, "But even something as horrible as the death of a child doesn't always tear a marriage apart. Sometimes the parents turn to each other for strength."

"You're talking about the ones who don't blame each other for what happened."

The waitress brought their drinks, then left as quickly as she'd come. Jack stirred a packet of sugar into his iced tea and asked, "Is that what happened to you and Sally? The blame game?"

"I don't know what happened to us. We tried. I *really* tried to be there for her. But she just didn't want help. Not from me, anyway."

"Did she blame you for what happened to your daughter?"

"No."

"Did you blame her?"

He paused, as if not sure how to answer. Finally, he said, "She *thought* I did."

"How did she get that impression?"

"I'm not sure, exactly."

"What's your sense?"

Again he paused, seeming to struggle. "Sally had this . . . job. I didn't really like it."

"The Hooters gig?"

He blinked twice, as if ashamed that Jack knew. "Look, I don't want you to get the wrong idea about Sally. She was a terrific mother. It wasn't like she was going out dancing on tables or something. It's just that, we owned that lousy restaurant I was telling you about. We had a terrible flood, no insurance, and we lost everything. We were bad in debt, needed money like you wouldn't believe. We both had to work crappy jobs to get back on our feet. I just wish she could have found something better."

"Did you ask her to quit?"

"We talked about it. But tips are pretty good at a place like Hooters. Tourists get a little drunk, you know how it is. Anyway, four hours a night there was like eight hours someplace else. So it left her some time for Katherine."

"So she kept the job?"

"Yeah. Big mistake."

"How so?"

Miguel tore open a pack of oyster crackers. "She ended up getting stalked by some loser."

"Stalked?"

"That's the sort of thing I was most afraid of. Some of these creeps who go to these bars think all the waitresses want it, that they're easy. You know what I'm saying?"

"What happened? Somebody started calling her on the phone, following her home—what?"

"I don't know all the details. She didn't even tell me about it till after our daughter was killed."

"Why not?"

"She knew I'd make her quit if I thought some guy was hassling her at work. And she also knew I'd break his neck if we found out who he was."

"Did you ever find out who he was?"

"No. Chickenshit son of a bitch. Sally said he just kept taunting her with anonymous calls from pay phones, hang-ups, that sort of thing. Never got a look at him. Maybe the cops could have helped, if she'd reported it, but she said she didn't want to antagonize him. She thought if she ignored him, he'd go away."

"Did he go away?"

"No way." Miguel lowered his eyes and said sadly, "And it was our daughter who paid."

Jack paused in mid-sip, putting down his tea. "Are you saying this stalker killed your daughter?"

"Can't prove it. Especially since Sally never told anyone about him stalking her until after our daughter was killed. If she had reported him, we would have had something to go on. As it was, the guy just vanished after the murder. Cops had no trail to follow."

"So he was never charged?"

"No one was ever charged."

"Did they ever name any suspects?"

"No. But they did give me a polygraph. Schmucks. Can't find the guy who did it, so they go hassle the daddy."

Jack paused, trying to be delicate. "How did that turn out?"

"Exactly the way Sally and me knew it would. They asked me three different ways: Did you kill your daughter, did you stab your daughter, did you harm your daughter in any way? I passed with flying colors."

"You still think it was the stalker who did it?"

"No doubt in my mind. I mean, who else? How many enemies does an innocent little girl have?"

"Do you blame Sally for the fact that he got away with it?"

"No way. I'm a cop. I'm not the kind of guy who blames the victim."

"I'm glad to hear that."

"But somehow Sally got it fixed in her head that I thought it was all her fault. Once that happened, our marriage was over. I'm sure that's why I'm in her little game now. I was probably the first one on her list."

"But you're not the only one on her list."

"No. Obviously not."

"Why are the others on there? Any idea?"

The waitress brought their food. "Here we go," she said, setting their plates before them. "Anything else I can get you?"

"No, thanks," they said in unison.

The waitress left. Miguel was pouring cocktail sauce on his conch fritters. Jack was still waiting for an answer, but with the waitress's interruption, Miguel had apparently lost track of the question. Jack asked again, "Do you know why the others are on Sally's list?"

Miguel had a mouthful of fritters. He shrugged and said, "You'll have to ask them."

Jack nodded, then looked at his plate of food. But he'd suddenly lost interest in eating. "I intend to," he said.

Thirteen

J ack was back in his office by three o'clock. He had a deposition after lunch, and he'd expected it to last the rest of the day, but the opposition had stormed out early when Jack refused to stop asking the witness to explain how he'd completely singed off his eyebrows if, as alleged, it was Jack's client who'd torched his own business.

"Mr. Valentes, I'm going to keep asking this question until you tell me exactly what happened to those eyebrows."

"What eyebrows?"

"That's my point."

"That's it, Swyteck. We're outta here!"

Miami was a living and breathing anthology of the History of Stupid Criminals.

The strong smell of Cuban coffee hit him as soon as he entered the office. Maria had his afternoon jolt of caffeine ready. She'd been his secretary for almost seven years, starting with his second day on the job as a federal prosecutor and following him into private practice. With the dust barely clear from his divorce, it was comforting to know that he was actually capable of a stable, long-term relationship of any sort with the opposite sex. He didn't consider himself picky in the romance department, but after his marriage to Cindy Paige, he did have certain minimum requirements—sanity being chief among them. Of course, his maternal grandmother, *Abuela*, as he called her, would even waive the sanity test if Jack would just bring home a nice Cuban girl. Too bad Maria was married.

"How'd the depo go, Jack?" she asked as she handed him his *taza* of espresso.

"Same old, same old."

She smiled and shook her head, as if all too aware that a quip like that could mean anything from utter boredom to an all-out fistfight.

Jack headed down the hall to his office, past the conference room that doubled as his library. He noticed Kelsey was busy at the table, doing a Westlaw search on the computer. She was wearing running shoes and black spandex exercise leggings that revealed just enough of the former ballerina to confirm that somewhere under that big, baggy aerobics T-shirt was one amazing body.

"Expecting clients today?" he said as he stuck his head into the room.

She checked her attire. "Sorry. I just stopped by on my way to Body and Soul."

He assumed she wasn't talking about some kind of new-wave religion. "Have a good workout."

"Thanks."

He started out the door, then stopped and came back into the room. "Actually, I have a favor to ask of you."

"Sure. What?"

"It's on the Sally Fenning matter. I met with her ex-husband for lunch."

"How'd that go?"

He took a minute to bring her up to speed, telling her all about the stalker that Miguel thought was responsible for the death of their daughter. He also told her how Sally had apparently come to think that he blamed her for the whole tragedy.

"What's your take?" asked Kelsey. "He the kind of guy who blames the victim?"

"He says he's not. And he didn't come across that way."

"A good guy, or just talks a good game?"

"Not sure. I did pull his divorce file, just to see if there might be any insights."

"And?"

"It played out just the way he said. Even though this shark Gerry Colletti was his lawyer, Miguel kept him on a pretty short leash. Sally got all the assets, Miguel took the debt. Not much of a fight there."

"Which makes you wonder: Why is the divorce lawyer on her list of enemies?"

"Exactly," he said. "And that's exactly where you come in."

Kelsey grabbed her pen and paper, as if eager for the assignment. "Okay."

"Put the pen down. This isn't research."

She smiled. "You mean I'm actually going to get to do something outside the library?"

"Maybe. Here's the deal. I can accept the fact that Sally structured her estate in a way that would torture her ex-husband into thinking that he might someday come into big money. I don't have children, but just from my relationship with Nate, I know that if someone blamed me for the brutal murder of my child, there would be no limit to the anger I would feel."

"Ditto."

"But like you said, that doesn't explain the divorce lawyer. In fact, absolutely nothing came out during my talk with Miguel Rios that shed any light on why Sally felt the same anger toward any of the other beneficiaries."

"You think there's something Mr. Rios is not telling you?"

"Something he's not telling me, or something he just doesn't know."

"How do we plug the hole?"

"I talked to Tatum right after lunch. The way he met Sally was through a referral from her bodyguard. Tatum says the bodyguard is willing to talk with me tonight. He moonlights as a bouncer at a club on South Beach and said he'd give me a few minutes on his break. He could be a real window into Sally's head."

"No doubt about it. How can I help?"

"I'd like you to come with me."

"Wow. Real sleuthing. The kind of work any third-year law student would die for."

"I have to confess. I feel a little guilty about asking you."

"Why? Because you need to interview a knuckle-dragging Neanderthal, and you think he's more likely to talk to a good-looking woman than to Jack Swyteck?"

Jack took a half-step back, surprised. "How . . . did you know that?"

"For one, on a certain level you're as much a Neanderthal as he is, which gives us women a distinct advantage in figuring out what you men are really up to."

"I see."

"Plus, Tatum called the office about a half hour ago. We talked. He said it would be a much more productive meeting if I went along and flashed a little cleavage."

"I didn't ask you to flash cleavage," said Jack.

"Do you want me to or not?"

He didn't answer.

"Jack?"

"I'm thinking," he said. "I'm not sure there's a right answer to that question."

"If you're uncomfortable with this, we can forget the whole thing. I won't go."

"No, I want you to go. If nothing else, it will be good practical experience for you."

"If all I wanted was experience, I'd happily put on a pinstripe suit and go as a Jack Swyteck clone. But as a woman, I bring things to the team that you can't. And there's nothing wrong with that."

"There isn't?"

"No," she said, exasperated. "I'm so tired of this politically correct dogma we try to live under. Let's all celebrate diversity, but God forbid that anyone should point out we're all different. Doesn't that drive you crazy?"

"I just don't want you to think you have to do anything that makes you feel compromised."

"For Pete's sake, we're interviewing a man in a South Beach nightclub. I don't feel compromised by dressing the way a woman would dress. You're much too old school, Jack."

"Old school?"

"It's like the old brains versus beauty debate. Why should a woman be put down for using her sexuality?"

"Because it's demeaning?" he suggested.

"Is it? When you think about it, how is showing off your looks any different from showing off how smart you are? You were born with your brain, the same way you were born with your looks. It's ninety-eight percent genetics. You can't take any more personal credit for your IQ than for the size of your pores. If you ask me, the only people who have a legitimate right to claim they're better than anyone else are people who choose to be nice. That's the one defining characteristic about ourselves that we have total control over. But, of course, if you're truly a nice person, you don't go around bragging that you're better than everyone else."

Jack thought for a moment, silent.

"Did you hear anything I just said?" asked Kelsey.

"Yeah. I was just wondering."

"Wondering what?"

"Does this mean you will or won't be flashing cleavage tonight?"

She wadded up a piece of paper and threw it at him. "Neanderthal."

Jack smiled and said, "I'll pick you up at ten."

"Hopefully not by my hair."

"Only if you're dressed in leopard skin," he said, then headed for his office.

Fourteen

Headquarters for Miami's leading newspaper was at the north end of downtown, right on sparkling Biscayne Bay, with daytime vistas of the cruise ships docked at the Port of Miami and the Art Deco skyline of Miami Beach in the distance. Nightfall, however, made mirrors out of the tinted plate-glass windows, and without the breathtaking views, the fifth-floor newsroom of the *Miami Tribune* had a stark, factory-like feel to it. Sandwiched between beige-carpeted floors and suspended fluorescent lighting was a twisted network of shoulder-high dividers that compartmentalized the gaping room into open workstations for a hundred-fifty reporters and staff writers, each with a video display terminal, gray metal desk, and chirping telephone.

Deirdre Meadows stared at her reflection in her monitor, thinking.

Since learning that Sally Fenning had made her one of six beneficiaries in her forty-six-million-dollar estate, Deirdre had been brainstorming, trying to find the best angle for a story. This one had all the elements. Sally was a beautiful young woman with a tragic past, a multimillionaire second husband, and an intriguing flair for creative estate planning that seemed driven by mysterious motives that Deirdre was itching to unravel. Deirdre had finally settled on a three-part investigative piece: Sally and her daughter as victims, Sally's marriage to a millionaire and her violent death, and Sally as a hand from the grave manipulating the lives of six seemingly disconnected heirs, only one of which would ultimately inherit her entire estate. She'd pitched the idea to the managing editor late that afternoon, only to be shot down immediately.

"Sorry, Deirdre. We just don't have room in the budget for another investigative piece."

"But a ton of the research is done already."

"I've heard that one before."

"It's true," she said. "I'm the one who covered the murder of her child five years ago, so part one is basically done already."

"Which is exactly the part of the story that isn't news anymore."

"The rest won't be as much extra work as you think. For some reason, I'm a beneficiary under her will. For my own good, I have to investigate this anyway, so why not do a story about it?"

He made a face. "That's the more fundamental problem. Call me old-fashioned, but frankly, I don't like stories written by reporters who are part of the story."

"I'm really not part of it. I'm incidental. I think the only reason she made a reporter one of her beneficiaries is so that this story would be written."

"And you think that's a reason we *should* do the story?" he asked, incredulous. "Sounds like a creative form of checkbook journalism to me."

It was downhill from there. Deirdre didn't like his answer, but she didn't want to push so hard that she'd spend the next two months covering the likes of chili-eating contests and high school student government elections.

Deirdre laid her fingers on the keyboard. One option was to simply start writing, churn out a few compelling pages, and go over his head. That was risky, but it was impossible to succeed in this business without taking risks. Newsrooms across the country were filled with talented reporters. No one ever won a Pulitzer Prize by cowering in the face of rejection. Especially when the guy doling out rejection slips was an idiot.

She let her fingers start dancing, tapping out words, only to be interrupted by the ring of her telephone.

"Meadows," she answered.

"Want to know who killed Sally Fenning?" said the man on the line. It was a deep, mechanical voice. He was clearly speaking through one of those voice-altering gadgets that were sold at spy stores and electronics shops on just about every other block in downtown Miami.

Deirdre didn't answer right away. The steady drone of a newsroom full of countless other conversations hummed all around her. She plugged her open ear, as if to make sure she'd heard correctly. "What did you say?"

"I think you heard me."

"Who is this?"

"Would I be altering my voice if I was going to tell you who I am?"

"Why are you calling me?"

"Because I have a story that needs to be told. How'd you like to tell it for me?"

Her heart was thumping. She cradled the phone with her shoulder and scrambled for a pen and paper. "I'm listening."

"I was at the on-ramp to I-395 where she was shot. I saw it happen."

"What did you see?"

"Everything."

"Let's start at the beginning. What were you doing there?"

"No, let's start at the *real* beginning. What's in this for me?"

She paused to choose her words. "I'm not sure what you mean."

"Yes, you do."

"Look, I can't pay you for a story."

"As a reporter for the esteemed *Miami Tribune*, that's true. You can't. But simply as a curious heir to Sally Fenning's estate, what's wrong with compensating someone for their time and inconvenience?"

Her grip tightened on the telephone. She wanted this. Bad. "Why should I believe anything you say?"

"Because I can show you the four-karat-diamond wedding band that Sally Fenning was wearing when she was shot—and that she wasn't wearing when the police found her body."

Deirdre felt chills. Instinctively, she looked over her shoulder, a subconscious confirmation that her supervisors wouldn't approve. "We should talk about this."

"You want to see the ring, don't you."

"Yes."

"Then we meet on my turf, not yours."

She hesitated for a moment, then said, "Where?"

He chuckled. "Not so fast. Give me your cell phone number. I'll call you and tell you where to go."

She gave him the number, then asked, "When should I expect your call?"

"I work till midnight. Have your phone on then."

"Midnight, tonight?"

"Yes. Unless you want to put this off. Or maybe you just want to forget the whole thing, and I'll call someone over at the *Sun-Sentinel*."

"No," she said, checking her eagerness. "That's fine. Tonight's fine."

"One last thing."

"What?"

"I don't want an audience. This is just you and me. Got it?"

She swallowed hard, then said, "Got it."

He said good-bye. The line clicked, and her caller was gone.

Fifteen

———

Jack was driving his Mustang, ten minutes away from Kelsey's house, when his cell phone rang. It was Nate.

"You have to speak up, buddy. I can hardly hear you."

"I can't," said Nate. "Mom thinks I'm asleep. I'm under the covers."

"Then maybe you should hang up and go to sleep."

"No, no, wait. I have to ask you something."

Jack stopped at the traffic light. "What?"

"Are you and my mom going out on a date?"

Jack could hear the hopefulness in Nate's voice, the very thing that had kept Jack from even thinking about an attempt at romance with Kelsey. Dating the mom was a huge no-no in the Big Brothers Big Sisters program. If it didn't work out, it was always the kid who suffered.

"No," said Jack. "This isn't a date. This is work."

"Then why did she try on fifteen different dresses?"

Jack recalled the cleavage debate, but he definitely wasn't going to go there. "That's just what women do, Nate. You'll see some day."

Nate tried to pursue the dating issue further, but Jack put a stop to it. "I'll see you this weekend, okay, buddy?"

"Oh, okay," he said, grumbling. They said good night and hung up.

Jack slowed as he approached Kelsey's house, but he was a few minutes early. He waited in the driveway, giving her enough time to try on dress number sixteen, then at precisely 10 P.M. he walked to the front door and knocked. Kelsey answered with a smile.

"Ready?" she said.

"Yup."

She was wearing red, a good color for the South Beach club circuit. Rather than blatant sex appeal with a heaping helping of cleavage, she'd opted for a more tasteful, striking look, and she'd hit a home run. Her hair was up in a twist, and the dress was strapless, which let the beauty of her long neck and sloping shoulders play out. Jack had never really noticed before, but she had great arms, beautifully sculpted. Her walk was clearly that of a dancer, poised and graceful, perfect posture without a hint of stiffness.

"Nice dress," said Jack.

"This? Oh, thanks. Just something I threw on."

Jack smiled to himself, deciding not to tell that Nate had already ratted her out.

It was a fifteen-minute drive over to South Beach and a thirty-minute wait at the valet entrance to Club Vertigo on busy Washington Avenue. By the time they got inside it was after eleven, which was like the early-bird special in this sleep-till-noon, party-till-dawn neighborhood.

It seemed like forever since Jack had done the South Beach club scene, even longer since he'd done it with a woman who turned heads the way Kelsey did. One thing that never changed about South Beach was the utter lack of subtlety in the way people checked each other out. There was nothing casual about it. This was the stuff by which one's clubbing worth was measured. If South Beach were in Silicon Valley, people would be wearing the high-tech equivalent of Web site counters around their necks. Naturally, the ones with the most hits would vault to the head of the line behind the velvet ropes.

"See your bodyguard friend anywhere?" asked Kelsey.

"I'm not even sure what he looks like."

"Just look for the guy with the thickest neck."

Jack chuckled. "He said to give our name to the woman bartender. She'd call him over."

The line was moving slowly, and they were nearing the entrance. Each time the doors opened, Jack was hit with a flash of swirling lights and a blast of music, and he could feel the vibration in his feet. He suddenly had an unnerving thought, one that made him glad this wasn't a date. He was entering a dance club with a professional dancer. Sort of like going to bed with a sex therapist. *No, no, no. Your hips go this way.* Who needed that?

Finally they were at the velvet rope. The goon at the door gave Jack a once-over, then focused on Kelsey. Her proverbial hit counter was overheating.

"You with him?" he asked, as if he couldn't believe it.

Jack was about to give it right back to him, but Kelsey moved closer and locked arms with Jack. She was clearly just playing the game and pushing the goon's buttons, but Jack liked the feeling nonetheless.

"Is that a problem?" she replied flatly.

Attitude ruled in South Beach, and it both amused and intrigued Jack to see that Kelsey had it in her. The goon unhooked the rope, and with a jerk of his head he signaled them to enter.

Club Vertigo was in an old hotel that had been gutted on the inside and completely reconfigured with a tall and narrow four-story atrium. The main bar and dancing were on the ground floor, and if you looked up into the towering atrium from the center of the dance floor, the mystery behind the club's name immediately unraveled. Several large mirrors suspended at different angles made it difficult at times to discern whether you were looking up or down. With even a slight buzz, the pounding music, swirling lights, and throngs of sweaty bodies were enough to give anyone a sense of vertigo. The sensation worked both ways, with hordes of people-watchers looking down on the dance crowd from second-, third-, and fourth-floor balconies.

Jack gave his name to the female bartender at the main bar and told her he wanted to see Javier. She picked up a phone for about a ten-second conversation, then looked at Jack and said, "Second floor, Room B."

Jack and Kelsey meandered through the crowd and took the stairs to the second floor. A muscular guy dressed in tight black clothing and wearing a thick, gold chain around his neck was standing outside Room B. It was one of the champagne suites, a private room away from the commotion where people could have more intimate gatherings. Sort of a sex and drug club within a sex and drug club. The night was young enough that most of the suites were empty.

"You Tatum's friend?" he asked.

Jack shook hands, then introduced Kelsey.

"Nice to meetchya," he said, looking past her. Javier looked Hispanic, but he talked like a New York Italian. It seemed that everyone on South Beach was pretending to be something they weren't.

"Please," he said, inviting them into the suite. Jack and Kelsey entered first. Javier followed and closed the door behind him, shutting out the noise. The sudden solitude was a strange sensation, like submerging into the silence of the deep end. The room itself was nothing spectacular, just a fake-leather couch, an armchair, smoky glass-topped table, and cheesy red velvet wallpaper.

Jack started to explain what he was after, but Javier stopped him. "Tatum already filled me in," he said. "And I can only give you about ten minutes."

"Let's get to it," said Jack. "Kelsey, why don't you start."

Kelsey gave a little smile, as if to thank Jack for keeping his promise to let her take an active role. She scooted to the edge of the couch, leaning forward slightly, trying to make eye contact. Javier seemed to be looking beyond her, just as he had with their handshake, as if something on the wall behind her had caught his attention.

"How long did you work for Sally?" she asked.

"Few months, on and off."

Kelsey paused, as if she'd expected at least a little eye contact with his response. But he still seemed obsessed with something over her or behind her.

"What did you do for her exactly?" asked Kelsey.

"Bodyguard."

"Did she really need a bodyguard?"

"She was a rich lady. And she scared pretty easy. She'd be alone a lot. Her old man—and I do mean *old* man—was from France or some-place. And you heard about what happened to her and her daughter a few years back."

"Yes," said Kelsey, "we know about that."

"So, she'd be alone, sometimes afraid to even go anywhere. She hired me to drive her around. The mall, restaurants, wherever. I'm not saying she needed me. But I made her feel safe."

Kelsey asked, "Didn't she have any girlfriends?"

"I suppose. None that I saw, though. She struck me as a loner. Real pretty lady, but not a very happy person. Know what I mean?"

Javier was talking to Kelsey, but he wasn't looking at her face. His focus had seemed to shift from the wall behind her to the top of her head. Kelsey tried to sit taller and make eye contact, but his gaze rose with her, as if he'd developed some bizarre fixation with the crown of her skull.

"For crying out loud," said Kelsey. "What are you looking at?"

"Huh?"

"Did a bird shit on the top of my head or what?"

"I don't think so."

"Then what is it? You've been staring at the top of my head from the moment I opened my mouth."

"I'm not looking at your mouth," he said.

"I know. You're staring at the top of my head."

"I understand that this is what you think. But what I'm actually doing is *not* looking at your mouth."

"You're losing me."

"I'm a recovering porn addict."

"A what?"

"I was addicted to porn. I can't look at a woman's mouth without having impure thoughts, which is a very distracting thing when you're trying to have an intelligent conversation. So I don't look at her mouth."

"I see." Kelsey glanced at Jack and said, "Why don't you take it from here, boss?"

"Good idea." Jack handed him a list of the beneficiaries under

Sally's will—her ex-husband, the lawyer, the reporter, the prosecutor, Tatum, and the unknown sixth beneficiary, Alan Sirap.

"Did you ever hear Sally mention any of these people?"

"Tatum, of course. After I linked them up together."

"I'll get to that in a minute. What about these other people?"

"I'm sure she said things about Miguel Rios. Mike, she called him. Her ex, right?"

"Right. What did she say about him?"

"I don't remember anything specific."

"How about the other people? She ever say anything about them?"

He read over the list and shook his head, then stopped himself. "This guy. Gerry Colletti. If I'm not mistaken, he was her ex-husband's divorce lawyer."

"That's right."

"Him I remember her talking about."

"What was that about?"

"We was out driving somewhere one night, and we passed this restaurant on the highway. And she says that used to be Alfredo's."

"Alfredo's?"

"Sally and her ex-husband used to own a little Italian restaurant that went broke. Poured everything they had into it."

"Miguel told me about that," said Jack. "In fact he says it was Colletti who sold it to them."

"That's right. I think him and Gerry were friends way back or something."

"Actually, it sounded to me like Miguel isn't too keen on him anymore. But I'm more interested in what Sally told you about Gerry."

"As I recall, she'd had a couple of glasses of wine and was talking to me pretty freely. She just starts saying how she couldn't stand this Gerry from the day she met him."

"Why not?"

"From the way she described him, he was one of these real slippery guys who turn a girl's stomach. She was telling me about how Gerry took her and her sister out to dinner one night to try to talk Sally into letting her husband buy the restaurant from him."

"Sally has a sister?"

"Yeah."

"What's her name?"

"I don't . . . Rene, I think. She lives in like Africa or some place. According to Sally, she's even more gorgeous than she was. But I find that hard to believe."

Jack glanced at Kelsey, as if to say "Remind me to follow up with this Rene."

Javier said, "Anyway, Gerry takes Sally and her sister out to dinner, buys them three bottles of wine. Sally's convinced that this loser is thinking threesome with two hot sisters. All the while, Sally and her sister are doing their best not to puke at the thought. But my point is that Sally has a real vivid memory of this night. She remembers all the details. It's almost creepy."

"How do you mean?"

"I give you an example. She gets to the part of the story where Gerry is telling her what a cash cow this Alfredo's restaurant is. Gerry keeps going on and on, to the point that she figures he had to be keeping two sets of books, because the P and L didn't show any profit at all. Then finally, she does this impersonation of Gerry. For me, it was one of those spooky moments, like when you *know* that a person has relived this moment over and over again in her mind. She did the mannerisms, the tone of voice, the whole thing. The way she tells it, Gerry leaned into the table, looked her in the eye, and curled his index finger to call her closer, like some child molester trying to lure a schoolgirl into his van. Then he got this drunken grin on his face and whispered into her ear, like it was some big secret he was sharing: 'Alfredo's. It's a gold mine, baby.'"

Jack felt a chill. It was almost too convincing, the way Javier had acted out the pedophile analogy.

"What did Gerry mean by a gold mine?" asked Kelsey. "Was he laundering money there?"

"Nah," Javier said, dismissing it. "Gerry was a total bullshitter. But his little song and dance worked. Sally gave her husband the go-ahead to buy the place. From day one it hemorrhaged money. Eventually it wiped them out."

"Is that why she hates Gerry's guts?" asked Jack.

"From what she told me, she saw this Gerry character as the start of all her problems. It was the end of her happy marriage and her life with her little girl. The beginning of nothing but worries about money. Then she started working at Hooters or some place like that, which was when that stalker started hassling her. You know about that, right?"

"Yeah, Miguel told me. He thinks it was the stalker who murdered his daughter."

"Well, there you go. In Sally's mind, all her problems, including that stalker, could be traced back to Gerry selling them that pig-in-a-poke restaurant."

"That's interesting. Like I said, I don't think Gerry is on Miguel's short list of drinking buddies anymore, but he doesn't seem to have the hatred that Sally had."

"If you could ask Sally, she'd say it's because Miguel is stupid. He thinks their restaurant failed because of the flood that ruined all their improvements. He just didn't want to admit that his own friend screwed him from the get-go."

Jack and Kelsey exchanged glances, as if something was still missing. Jack said, "Anything else come to mind, Javier?"

"That's about it."

"Let's talk about Tatum for a minute. Why is he a beneficiary under Sally's will?"

"Pretty obvious, don't you think?"

"You tell me."

"From what I understand, Sally set this up like a game—survival of the fittest."

"In a sense, yes. Last one living takes all."

"There's more to it than that, right?"

"How do you mean?" asked Jack.

"Tatum says there's two ways to get the money. One is to outlive everybody. The other is to be the only one who doesn't— what do you call it—renounce his inheritance?"

"That's right," said Kelsey. "Anyone can pull out, if they choose."

"There you go," said Javier. "You either gotta outlive everybody, or you gotta persuade the others to throw in the towel. In that kind of game, doesn't it make sense to have at least one person in the mix, like Tatum, who isn't squeamish about blood?"

Jack narrowed his eyes and said, "Are you saying that Sally intended to have these people fight over her money. I don't mean legal battles. I mean fighting, literally."

"If her ex-husband and this Gerry are on the list, yeah, absolutely. I think she would have liked nothing better than for those two guys to end up killing each other trying to get her money."

"So she made Tatum a beneficiary to do what? Get the fists flying?"

"All I can tell you is that one night, Sally asks me if I know any tough guys. Real tough guys. I say sure. That's it. I don't ask questions. I hooked her up with Tatum, and that was that."

Jack said, "Next thing you know, she's shot dead, and Tatum's a beneficiary under her will."

"About the size of it." Javier checked his watch and said, "Look, I gotta get back to work. I work for tips, and filling these suites is my big take for the night."

"Of course," said Jack, rising. "We'll clear out."

"Unless you and the lady want to stay. It's very private."

"No, no," said Jack.

"That's quite all right," said Kelsey.

"You sure?" said Javier. "I'm full service here. Whatever you want, I can get. Drinks, breath mints, ecstasy, condoms."

Kelsey popped like a spring from the couch at his mention of condoms, as if propelled by the thought of what she might have been sitting in. Jack had a feeling that her awesome red dress was destined for Goodwill.

"How about a rain check?" said Jack.

They shook hands and said good night. Then Jack and Kelsey followed the stairs down to the main floor and continued out the exit to the sidewalk. It was almost midnight, and Washington Avenue was kicking into high gear, an eclectic mix of gays and straights, tourists and natives. A stretch limo cruised by, music blasting through the open windows. The back end was an outdoor hot tub bubbling over with twenty-something-year-old hard bodies who were laughing loudly and speaking Portuguese.

"I'm real sorry about this," said Jack as they reached the curb.

"Sorry for what?"

"I asked you to come because I thought it would be fun for you. A more exciting side of lawyering. I didn't mean to throw you to a recovering porn addict."

"You didn't throw me. I volunteered. I'm not going to shrivel up and die because some pathetic loser can't look at my face without thinking about . . . well, whatever he was trying not to think about."

"So you're okay?"

"I'm okay. But as for the speech I gave in your office today—about how using your body is no different than using your brain?"

"Yeah?" said Jack.

"After meeting Javier, let's just say my thoughts are evolving on that front."

"Fair enough," he said with a smile. They stood in silence for a moment, a little awkward, as Jack debated the next move. The yellow light from Club Vertigo's neon sign was playing against Kelsey's eyes, drawing flecks of gold from the intriguing pools of hazel. The divorce had left him pretty rusty at dating, but he hadn't completely lost the ability to read the expression on a woman's face or interpret her posture, the little things that said, "What's next on the agenda?" as opposed to "I'm tired and I want to go home." Part of him wanted to take a shot and ask her out for coffee or something, but it just didn't seem right to be hitting on Nate's mom.

"I really have to let the baby-sitter go," she said. "Maybe another time."

"Another time what?"

She smiled wryly. "For the past thirty seconds you've had one eye on me and the other on Starbucks across the street. So . . . maybe some other time."

He fumbled nervously for the valet ticket in his pocket. "Sure," he said, wondering if he was really that obvious or if she was just that perceptive. "Some other time."

Sixteen

At 1 A.M., the warehouse district west of the Palmetto Expressway had all the charm and personality of Leavenworth after lockdown. The buildings all looked alike, simple cinder-block and sheet-metal construction. Outside each establishment, every inch of ground was covered with nondescript stacks of inventory on pallets. Protecting it all was a nine-foot-high chain-link fence with coiled razor wire running across the top like a man-eating Slinky.

A thick layer of clouds made the night moonless, and street lamps were few and far between. The little red Honda bounced and rattled across potholes so deep that the entire vehicle was coated with muddy splash. Street maintenance was a losing battle here, as countless trucks beyond the legal weight limit pounded the pavement from sunup to sundown, six days a week.

Deirdre Meadows was a long way from home, but instinct told her that she was nearing her destination. She stopped at the end of a deserted street to get her bearings, squinting to make out the dimly lit sign ahead.

"JJ's Italian Tile and Marble," she said, reading aloud.

She checked her notes. *That's it.* Finally, after driving around in circles and checking out at least a dozen other places named So and So's Italian Tile and Marble, she'd found it.

She killed the engine and switched off the car lights. The sudden blackness gave her pause. It was darker outside than she'd realized. She flipped on the dome light to check her purse. Pen and paper, of course. Dictaphone. Cell phone, battery fully charged. It was no panacea, but so long as she had her cell phone, Deirdre would go just about anywhere—anywhere for a story, that is.

The phone call had come just before midnight. Deirdre was in her living room, watching Letterman on television, the cordless phone at her side. She had Caller ID, which told her only that it was coming from a pay phone. It rang twice before she answered.

And one last time, she played it over in her mind.

"Hello." :

"You ready?" he asked. Again, it was a deep, mechanical voice that almost sounded underwater.

"You bet," she answered.

"Go to JJ's Italian Tile and Marble on One hundred thirty-second Court, west of the eight-twenty-six. Drive around back and find the gate entrance along the chain-link fence. There's a padlock on it, but I'll leave it open. Come inside and walk about a hundred yards straight toward the loading dock."

"Why there?"

"Because I said so."

"Look, I'm not so keen about meeting a total stranger behind some building in the middle of the night."

"Then don't come."

"You'll still give me the story?"

"Not if you don't come. And by the way, when I say come, I mean alone."

"Why are you doing it this way?"

"Because I want to know."

"Know what?"

"How bad you want the truth about Sally Fenning."

"What makes you think I want it this bad?"

"Because this story has a pretty good payoff. Like forty-six million dollars."

"How is the identity of Sally's killer going to earn me forty-six million dollars?"

"It won't cinch it, but it will bring you one step closer."

"How?"

"Sally's killer can't inherit anything from her estate. That's the law, right?"

Icicles went down her spine. She'd assumed that her caller was no genius, but apparently he was smart enough to know about the Slayer Statute. "That's right," she said. "Murderers are disqualified from inheriting anything from their victim."

"There you have it. One down, five to go."

"Are you telling me that Sally's killer was one of her six named beneficiaries?"

"I'm saying be at JJ's Italian Tile and Marble in ninety minutes or less. End of story. For now."

Deirdre checked the clock on her dashboard. More than an hour had passed since that conversation, but the question still burned in her ear: How bad *did* she want the story?

Almost as much as the money.

Instinctively, she found herself reaching for the door handle. The door opened, and she stepped out of the car. The expressway was out of sight, somewhere beyond the block of windowless buildings, but she could hear the steady drone of traffic to the east. It seemed strange that hundreds of vehicles were racing by every minute, yet she felt so alone, not another car or human being in sight. Before shutting the door, she reached for the dash and flashed her parking lights. She checked over her shoulder and took a long look down the dark street. A set of orange parking lights flashed in response, then returned to darkness. Her boyfriend. It made her feel a little safer knowing he was just a hundred yards and a speed-dial away on her cell phone. She closed the car door, took a deep breath, and walked toward the gate, pea gravel crunching beneath each footfall.

This had better be good, she told herself.

Seventeen

It was last call at John Martin's on Miracle Mile, the closest thing in downtown Coral Gables to an authentic Irish pub. Dark-paneled walls, Harp lager on tap, and classic pub grub like shepherd's pie or bangers and mash were hardly the norm in south Florida, but John Martin's was a nice diversion. The long, mahogany bar carved by local artisans was a beauty, and every now and then, the owner would book an authentic Irish band that was sure to get feet stomping and hands clapping. Even pretty waitresses with red hair and freckles, however, couldn't completely obscure the fact that this was not exactly County Cork, especially at happy hour, when John Martin's was affectionately known as "Juan Martino's," serving largely a Latin business crowd that, even on St. Paddy's Day, would rather have a mint-colored mojito than a pint of green lager. It might sound strange, but to taste it was to love it.

"Another Jameson's and water?" asked the waitress.

Gerry Colletti swirled the ice cubes in his near-empty glass, then decided that he'd had enough. "No, thanks. We're about done here."

He watched her ass move from side to side as she walked away, then turned his gaze toward the work papers on the table. Seated across from him was Bill Hanson, a man with the look and demeanor of an accountant on April 14, just coffee in his cup. Hanson was an actuary trained in the science of expressing the proverbial length of one's lifeline in terms of mathematical probabilities. Once Gerry realized that he had to outlive the other named beneficiaries in order to inherit the entirety of Sally's estate, he hired Hanson to provide a statistical analysis of how he might fare in the test of longevity that Sally's will had created.

Gerry glanced at the charts and graphs one more time, then pushed them aside. "This all looks impressive, but I hate interpreting this stuff. Just explain it to me, will you, please?"

Hanson seemed disappointed, as if charts and graphs were his pride and joy. "You want the long or short version?"

"I want an answer to the question I hired you to analyze. We got six beneficiaries under Sally Fenning's will. The one who lives the longest gets forty-six million dollars. So, let's just apply the normal criteria that insurance companies use to evaluate the risks posed by any applicant for life insurance. Who's going to live the longest?"

"I can't tell you who is going to live the longest. All I can do is rank them according to the actuarial score I gave them."

"And the score means what?"

"The higher the number, the higher the risk for the insurance company. Which, in your context, means the greater the likelihood of experiencing early death."

"That means I want all these other jokers to have big numbers."

"Exactly. Mind you, this is not as reliable as something I would put together in the case of an actual insurance application. Applicants are required to disclose all kinds of information relating to their family background and health. Here, I've used only what I've been able to dig up on these people."

"I understand."

"I've also thrown into the mix a few factors that I couldn't legally consider in an insurance application. Things that, frankly, might get an insurance company sued."

"But I'm not an insurance company, and anyone who's stupid enough to sue me ought to have their head examined. Just give me what you've got."

"Okay." He cleared his throat, checking his notes. "The highest score goes to the prosecutor. High-stress job, smokes like a chimney, looks to be about forty pounds overweight. He's fifty-eight and his father died of a heart attack at age fifty-five."

"Beautiful. He could go at any time."

Hanson shot him a curious look, seemingly uncomfortable.

Gerry asked, "What's wrong with you?"

"I guess I've never done an analysis where my client is actually rooting for the big bony man with the black hood and sickle."

"I'm not rooting. I just want you to tell it like it is."

"I'm glad you said that. Because the second-highest score goes to you."

"Me? I don't even smoke."

"Yes, you do."

"Socially."

"That aside, the biggest thing working against you is something I can take into consideration only because you're a friend of mine and I know your lifestyle. Basically, you're a horny divorce lawyer who hoses half the women who come through his door."

"Say what?"

"Sorry, Gerry. You asked for my honest analysis. As many sexual partners as you've had and will continue to have, I put you at a high risk for HIV."

"But I use condoms."

"No, you don't."

"How do you know?"

"Because I saw those pictures that Lisa Bartow put on the Internet. You remember your old client Lisa, right? You sued her because she wouldn't pay your bill, and so she retaliated by posting those photographs on the Web of you and her doing—"

"Yeah, yeah, yeah, I remember."

"Funny, I never heard anything more about that dispute. I guess it settled, huh?"

Gerry wasn't smiling. "For an accountant, you seem to think you're one funny guy."

"Just dealing with the facts."

"Fine. So you got me in second place."

"Right. Third is the ex-husband."

"That's ridiculous. How is it that both Miguel and me are at a higher risk for early death than that black guy, Tatum Knight."

"Good point. In all fairness, I had trouble assigning any score at all to Mr. Knight. I don't have any real reliable information on him. For example, family medical is real sketchy. His father is unknown."

"What a surprise."

"He was raised by an aunt. His mother was a druggie, and I haven't been able to nail down whether she's alive or dead."

"Don't waste your time pursuing it. For my purposes, I'll just assume he's the kind of guy who could get blown away next week holding up a liquor store."

"You may be right about that."

"So, bottom line is what?" asked Gerry.

"Hard to draw firm conclusions. Like I say, Tatum Knight is somewhat of a wild card. And then there's that sixth beneficiary who didn't show up for the reading of the will. Until you get me a Social Security number, I can't pull any information to rank him."

"Are you telling me I paid you to do a worthless analysis?"

"No. Purely from a statistical point of view, I don't think it matters who the unknown is or what his score is."

"Why do you say that?"

"In all probability, your biggest worry is still going to be the newspaper reporter."

"Low score?"

"Very low. She just had her twenty-ninth birthday last month. A vegetarian. Runs marathons. Doesn't smoke. And she has amazing family history. Her parents are in their seventies and still alive. Both sets of grandparents are also still living. The oldest is ninety-two. If I was going to bet on who was going to win the longevity race, I'd put my money on her."

Gerry raised his glass and winked. "Don't throw your money away, my friend."

"What does that mean?"

"Nothing. Thanks for the help. I'll call you if I need anything else."

Gerry laid a twenty on the table to cover the bar bill. Hanson gathered up his reports, shook hands, and headed for the front exit to Miracle Mile. Gerry's car was in the back parking lot, so he headed out alone for the rear exit, past the men's room and the wood-carved sign with the old Irish drinking toast: "May you be in heaven one hour before the devil knows you're dead." The final stretch of hallway was the John Martin's walk of fame, two walls lined with autographed black-and-white photographs of probably every local celebrity who had ever tasted beer, from Roy Black, famous criminal defense lawyer, to Dave Barry, funniest man alive. It soured Gerry's stomach to see it. Nearly a full year had passed since Gerry had presented the owner with a framed and autographed eight-by-ten of himself.

Still not up there, you son of a bitch.

The smell of garbage greeted him as he opened the door and stepped into the back alley. A gray cat leaped from the Dumpster, then scurried up the iron fire escape.

The autumn night was unpleasantly warm. After midnight, and still it had felt cooler *inside* the smoke-filled pub. Gerry draped his sport coat over his shoulder and walked toward the parking lot. A weak street lamp illuminated the back of the pub and the rear entrances to several other businesses that had closed hours earlier. It was no darker than the dimly lit bar he'd just left, but the lighting was different, more yellow, and it took time for his eyes to adjust. He noticed that the striped wooden arm was up at the lot's north exit. Apparently the parking attendant had abandoned all hope of collecting a toll from the handful of stragglers.

Gerry reached for his keys as he approached his BMW. Counting his, just three cars and a van remained in the entire lot. Naturally, the crummy van was parked right beside his limited edition, paid-extra-for-it, emerald-black paint job. He walked to the front of his car and looked down the driver's side, checking for fresh dings. It looked clean, but it was too dark to be certain. He considered etching a retaliatory scrape into the side of the van with his key, but just as he started down the narrow opening between his car and the van, the passenger door flew open and hit him squarely in the face. Gerry was knocked backward and fell onto the hood of his car. Someone jumped out and grabbed him by the shirt collar.

"Stop!" Gerry screamed.

The attacker whirled him around and landed a fist to Gerry's right eye. A flurry of punches continued, one blow after another. The man wore leather gloves, but that in no way lessened the beating. His fists felt like iron, as if weighted by rolls of quarters. Gerry had no chance, no way to fight him off. A blow to the belly knocked the wind from him, followed by a direct hit to the side of his head that unleashed a sharp ringing in his ear.

"Stop already!"

There was a pause in the frenzy, and Gerry collapsed onto his back, splayed across the hood of his car. He wasn't seeing or thinking clearly, and just as he raised his head and tried to focus, his attacker grabbed him by the hair and slammed the back of his head into the car hood. Dazed, Gerry slid down the side of the car and landed in a heap.

He didn't move, couldn't even raise his head. A door slammed, and an engine rumbled. The van pulled out. Gerry lay with his cheek against the pavement, his battered eye throbbing as he watched the blurry van disappear into the darkness.

Eighteen

The sign on the metal gate read TILE DELIVERIES ONLY, as if to reconfirm that Deirdre was in the right place. The padlock on the latch was open, just as her caller had promised. The hinges squeaked as Deirdre pulled the gate open. She stepped inside the chain-link fence, then paused in the darkness and listened. She heard nothing but the sound of her own breathing. Goose bumps tickled the back of her neck, but it was a warm night, and she knew it was just nerves.

This was risky, to be sure, but she'd taken bigger risks before for less important stories. Like the night she'd spent downtown, sleeping in a cardboard box beneath the expressway as part of her field research for a day-in-the-life piece on a homeless crack addict, which was never published. Or the time she'd crashed a teenage "rave" party and popped ecstasy so that she could write firsthand about the effects of the drug. She'd nearly fried her brain and ended up in the emergency room, all for eight columns of work that the editors cut to three paragraphs. In retrospect, those seemed like foolish risks. But this story was different. Much more than a byline was at stake.

At first, Deirdre had dismissed Sally Fenning's forty-six-million-dollar test of survival. She didn't seriously think she'd ever see the money. But the more she thought about it, the more she realized: Why not her? There were six beneficiaries. One out of every six people die in accidents—drownings, car crashes, airplane disasters, hunting with morons who didn't know their friends from a duck. Just like that, her odds were down to one-in-five. Florida had the death penalty, so if tonight's source could eliminate yet another beneficiary as Sally's murderer, that would reduce her odds to one-in-four. Who wouldn't take that bet? She was young and healthy. She had a better shot than anyone. She'd be rich. Filthy rich.

And with this story, she might be famous to boot.

She drew a deep breath and entered the back lot. Her caller had told her to go to the loading dock. She could see it straight ahead, fairly well lit by two glowing security lamps. Getting there, however, was a walk through a man-made canyon. The long driveway was just barely wide enough for two trucks to pass in opposite directions, and either side was lined with countless pallets of boxed ceramic tiles, some stacked twenty feet or higher.

She took a step forward, then started at the sound of her cell phone ringing. She grabbed it quickly, recognizing the number as her boyfriend's.

"What are you calling for?"

"I just wanted to make sure you're okay," he said.

"I told you I'd call if I got into trouble."

"I know. But it's too dark, too deserted. I don't like the looks of this, baby."

Deirdre hated it when he called her "baby." "Just stick to the plan, okay? Where would Woodward and Bernstein be today if they'd refused to meet Deep Throat in a dark parking garage?"

"This isn't exactly Watergate you're breaking open. Come on. Let's split."

"No, damn it. I'm not going to blow this chance. Now, sit tight until I call you." She switched off the phone and shoved it in her purse. Strangely, the call from her boyfriend made her that much more determined to go through with this. She continued down the dark driveway toward the loading dock, passing one stacked pallet after another. Between each stack were narrow crevices, perfect hiding spots. As she passed each opening, she peered into the long, black tunnel to make sure no one was lurking in the darkness. With endless rows of stacked boxes, it was like staring into the entrance of a labyrinth.

Her phone rang again, giving her heart a jolt. She snatched it from her purse and answered in an angry voice, "What now?"

"Chill, lady."

Deirdre froze. It wasn't her boyfriend. It was the deep, mechanically altered voice of her source. "Where are you?"

"Never mind that."

"What do you mean, never mind? I'm here. Are we meeting, or not?"

"We're not."

"You son of a bitch. You said—"

"I said you could see Sally's ring first."

She reeled in her anger. "Is it here?"

"Just keep walking toward the loading dock."

She was just a hundred feet away. She checked left, then right, searching for her caller in the dark crevices between stacked pallets. But she saw nothing. "Okay," she said, putting one foot in front of the other. "I'm walking."

"Keep going."

"Are you watching me?" she asked.

"Do you feel watched?" he said.

She checked over her shoulder. "A little."

"Good. Maybe that will keep you from running off with the ring."

"What am I supposed to do with it?"

"Look, but don't touch."

"How will I know it's really hers?"

"The band is engraved on the inside. Read it. Then go check it out. You'll see it's the real thing."

Deirdre was fifty feet away as she entered the circle of light surrounding the loading dock. "When do I find out who killed her?"

"As soon as we strike our deal."

"What deal?"

"My piece of your forty-six-million-dollar inheritance."

"What makes you think I'm going to inherit it?"

"Because you're going to live longer than anyone else."

"How do you know that?"

"Because I'm going to make sure of it."

Deirdre stopped. It wasn't something she'd decided to do. Her feet had just stopped moving. "What are you saying?"

"You and me. A team."

"I'm not interested in being on anybody's team."

"That's not the answer I want to hear."

"I don't care. This is getting too weird."

"Don't blow this, Deirdre. You get half, I get half. You get the story to boot."

"What kind of a sick bastard are you?"

"A greedy, sick bastard. Just like you. Except that I lack your ambition."

Her grip on the phone tightened. "Look, I think I know what you're saying, and let me make myself clear. I don't want any part of any plan you might have to hurt any of those other potential beneficiaries."

"Then why did you come here?"

"For the story."

"And the money."

"You said you knew who Sally's killer was."

"And I'm willing to tell you. But not without a deal on the inheritance."

"I'm not interested in making that kind of deal with you. So you can just keep your ring, keep your story, and keep away from me. Understand?"

She waited for a response, and the silence on the line only heightened her sense of being watched. "I know you're still there," she said. "I'm hanging up now. Listen to what I'm saying. I don't ever want to hear from you again. Got it?"

"Yeah," he said. His voice was especially deep, and the voice altering device only seemed to emphasize his anger. "I got it."

The call ended, and Deirdre immediately rang her boyfriend on speed dial. "Johnny, get over here right now."

"You okay?"

"Yeah, just scared. Meet me at my car." She disconnected, wheeled on one foot, and sprinted for the gate. It was a hundred-yard dash in the dark to the exit, and Deirdre was running full out, gobbling up in no time the same stretch of driveway that had taken several minutes to cover earlier in her timid entrance. Arms pumping, legs churning, she was flying by row after row of stacked pallets. She kept her eyes focused on the gate ahead, ignoring the dark crevices between boxes that had frightened her on the way in. She was at top speed when she reached the fence, and she practically slammed into the chain link.

Outside, her boyfriend's car pulled up next to hers. He jumped out and ran to the gate.

Deirdre reached for the latch and yanked on the padlock. It didn't budge.

"Are you okay?" her boyfriend asked from the other side of the fence.

"Yes, yes. Just—I can't get out of here!"

He tried the padlock. "It's locked."

"Damn," she said. "That creep locked me in."

"Can you climb over?"

She looked up at the tangle of razor wire that ran the length of the nine-foot-high fence. "I would say no."

Her boyfriend's expression suddenly went cold. "I would say you'd better."

Deirdre turned and froze. A pair of Doberman Pinschers emerged from the darkness. They were approaching slowly, like lanky cheetahs stalking their prey, growling with teeth bared.

"Don't move," said her boyfriend.

The watchdogs inched closer. Deirdre looked at one, then the other. The bigger one barked and snapped, then pulled away. Deirdre threw herself back against the fence.

"Don't move," her boyfriend said in an urgent whisper.

"I'm scared!"

"And don't look them in the eye, either. They'll think you're challenging them."

"Johnny, do something!"

"I'm calling the cops. Just don't move a muscle."

"I have a can of mace in my purse."

"Leave it. These dogs are trained to go after people who reach for weapons."

The dogs snarled, saliva dripping. Deirdre's voice shook as she said, "They're going to kill me."

"Not if you don't move."

"We have to do something!"

"Just stay put."

The bigger dog barked again, six or seven quick bursts that rattled off like machine-gun fire. Deirdre screamed, which made the dog snap at her. Deirdre reached for her mace, and the other dog went for her leg. She kicked him away, but the big dog sank his teeth into her wrist and pulled her to the ground.

"Deirdre!"

She kicked and punched wildly, trying desperately to cover her head and roll away. Her arm shook violently in the dog's teeth. Then, suddenly, it released her arm, and both dogs froze. Deirdre was shaking, too frightened to make a move. The dogs had stopped snarling, as if they'd completely lost interest in her. They seemed to be listening to someone or something, but Deirdre heard nothing.

As quickly as they'd come upon her, they turned and ran toward the loading dock. Deirdre's thoughts weren't lucid, but it was as if they'd heard a dog whistle.

Still on the ground, Deirdre checked her arm. The dog's teeth had torn through her clothes and into her skin. She gasped at the sight of her own blood.

"Stay quiet," said Johnny, still on the other side of the fence. "Cops are on their way."

She started at the sound of her ringing cell phone. Her purse had flown off somewhere in the attack, but the noise was coming from behind her. She crawled on all fours, grabbed the phone, and answered.

"Are we a team?" he said. It was that mechanical voice again.

Deirdre grimaced, as her arm was throbbing with pain from the dog bite. "What the hell did you just do?"

"A night watchman will do anything for a little extra cash. Even disappear and loan me his dog whistle. Funny how that works, isn't it?"

"I don't think this is funny at all. Let me out of here!"

"Relax. I'm giving you a choice, Deirdre."

"What choice?"

"A very simple choice. You can be a winner, or you can be a loser. It's that simple."

"What the hell are you talking about?"

"We'll talk later, after you've calmed down. In the meantime, you breathe a word about this to anyone—I mean *anyone*—and you're definitely a loser. Big-time loser. You hear?"

She didn't answer.

"Do you *hear*?" he said.

"Yes."

"Good. The key to the lock is taped to the light pole. Now get the hell out of here."

With a chirp of her phone, the call was over. Deirdre rolled onto her side and put pressure on her arm to stop the bleeding, fighting back tears in the darkness.

Nineteen

Probate Judge Leonard Parsons looked mad as hell. Worse, he was looking down from the bench and straight at Jack's client.

The phone call from the judge's chambers had come at 9 A.M. A battered Gerry Colletti had filed an emergency motion, and the judge ordered each of the beneficiaries under Sally Fenning's will to be in the courtroom at eleven o'clock sharp.

"Good morning," the judge said. His tone was cordial, but the eyes were two smoldering black coals beneath bushy white eyebrows. A scowling judge was a bad sign in any courtroom, but especially so in the relatively courteous world of Whisper Court.

"Good morning, Your Honor." The reply was a mixed chorus of lawyers and clients. Even Gerry Colletti, supremely confident in his own abilities, had retained counsel for this hearing. Counting Jack and his client, there were ten suits altogether. Eight of them—Colletti, Sally's ex-husband, the prosecutor, the reporter, and their counsel—were crowded around a single table near the jury box, the opposite side of the courtroom from Jack and his client, as if they suddenly couldn't put enough distance between themselves and Tatum Knight. Seated behind them was Vivien Grasso, the personal representative for the estate. She seemed to be staking out a position of neutrality, sitting at neither table, choosing instead a seat at the rail that separated the lawyers from public seating.

The courtroom was otherwise empty, Jack noted, which meant that the sixth beneficiary was still a no-show.

"Mr. Anderson," said the judge, addressing Gerry Colletti's lawyer. "Would you speak to your motion, please?"

Colletti remained seated. The right side of his face was purple and swollen, and he had a large Band-Aid across his forehead. His lawyer rose, thanked the court, and stepped forward.

"Judge, it's quite obvious that Mr. Colletti is in pretty bad shape. Although this is an evidentiary hearing, we request that the court accept my client's written and sworn affidavit as a substitute for his live testimony. If counsel would like to cross-examine him, he is available."

"Seems reasonable to me. Any objections?" asked the judge.

"None here," came the chorus from the other side of the room.

"No objection," said Jack.

"Thank you," said Anderson. "Basically, the evidence before the court is that, late last night, Mr. Colletti was viciously attacked as he walked to his car in the parking lot behind John Martin's Pub in Coral Gables. He sustained a variety of injuries, mostly bruises and contusions, not to mention a concussion. Thankfully, none of them are life threatening. As set forth in Mr. Colletti's affidavit, the man who unleashed that attack upon him is his fellow beneficiary Tatum Knight."

"What a crock," said Tatum, grumbling.

"No interruptions, please," the judge said sternly. "And, Mr. Knight, watch your language."

"Did I use a bad word?"

"Borderline. When in doubt, remember, we're in Whisper Court."

"Our apologies," said Jack. "It won't happen again."

Colletti's lawyer continued, "As I was saying, the beating occurred late last night. Early this morning, Mr. Colletti found an interesting e-mail on his computer. It was delivered electronically last night at six forty-three P.M., a few hours before the attack, but he didn't get it until after. We've printed out a hard copy for the court. It's fairly short. It reads simply: 'Life is short enough. Get out of the game—now.'"

Jack glanced at his client. Tatum leaned into Jack and whispered as softly as possible, "I don't even own a computer."

"Who sent it?" the judge asked.

"We don't know. It was sent from one of those business/copy centers in Miami that leases computer terminals by the hour, so it's not traceable to anyone. Still, I believe that this message ties in quite logically with the beating Mr. Colletti suffered at the hands of Mr. Knight. As the court is well aware, we are operating under a rather unusual will. There are six beneficiaries, but only one shall inherit the estate. The only way to win this *game*, as the e-mail described it, is to outlive your fellow beneficiaries, or to persuade them to drop out and renounce their inheritance. Mr. Colletti submits that this was exactly the purpose of Mr. Knight's beating. It was an appalling attempt to strike fear into the fellow beneficiaries and to encourage all of them, and Mr. Colletti in particular, to drop out."

"That's bullshit," said Tatum, grousing into Jack's ear.

"Mr. Knight!" said the judge. "One more outburst like that, and I'll hold you in contempt."

"Outburst? My own lawyer barely heard me."

Jack shushed him, mindful that all that whispering in Whisper Court must have improved the judge's hearing. That, or his hearing aid was turned way up. "Sorry, Your Honor," said Jack.

The judge scowled, then turned his attention back to Colletti's lawyer. "What relief do you request?"

"Mr. Colletti has not yet had time to evaluate all of his legal options. At this point, we simply ask the court to enter a restraining order that would prevent Mr. Knight from communicating with the other beneficiaries, except through his legal counsel. Further, we ask that the court prohibit Mr. Knight from coming within five hundred yards of any of the other beneficiaries, except for court hearings or required meetings with the personal representative."

"All right," said the judge. "Mr. Swyteck, what does Mr. Knight have to say for himself?"

Jack started to rise, but Tatum grabbed his arm and whispered, "I want to take the stand."

"No. We agreed—"

"I don't care what we agreed. I want to testify."

The judge said, "Mr. Swyteck, if you please."

Confused, Jack looked up at the judge, then glanced back at his client's eager expression. "Your Honor, I'd like to have just a couple minutes to speak with my client."

"All right. But be aware that I've allotted one hour for this hearing. Every minute you spend jabbering with your client is one less minute you have to present your case. We'll take a five-minute recess," he said with a crack of the gavel.

"All rise," said the bailiff.

Jack and the others were on their feet, watching in silence as Judge Parsons disappeared through the side exit. Jack took his client by the arm and said, "Let's talk." They walked quickly down the aisle, through the rear entrance and into the hallway. Jack found an open waiting room by the elevators, pulled Tatum inside, and shut the door.

"I swear, I didn't lay a hand on Colletti."

"I told you this morning when Colletti served his papers on us: It doesn't matter."

"It matters to *me*," said Tatum, his voice rising.

"For purposes of this hearing, I'm telling you, it doesn't matter if you're innocent."

"Did you get a look at Colletti's face?" he said, scoffing. "Work of a fucking amateur. If it was me who done it, I can tell you this much: He wouldn't have been switchin' on his computer to check his e-mail this morning. It'd be a week before he could remember his name, let alone his password."

"Is that our defense, Tatum? Is that what you want to tell the judge?"

"I don't have to tell the judge that. I just wanna tell him I didn't do it."

"That's my whole point. If you get on the stand, you will be cross-examined. Colletti's lawyer could throw anything at you."

"Nothing I can't handle."

"Oh, really? Try this on for size." Jack stepped closer, role-playing as Gerry's lawyer on cross-examination. "Mr. Knight, the first time you ever met Mr. Colletti was at the reading of Sally Fenning's will. A week ago Tuesday, correct?"

"That's right."

"Less than two weeks after meeting you, Mr. Colletti is in the emergency room."

"I didn't put him there."

"Mr. Knight, since you're a beneficiary under Sally Fenning's will, I'm assuming you also met her at some point, right?"

"Yeah, once."

"When?"

"A couple weeks before she died."

"You mean a couple weeks before she was murdered, don't you?"

"Yeah, whatever."

"So you met her once in your life, and two weeks later she was shot in the head."

"So what?"

"Let me ask you this, sir: How many other people have ended up dead or in the hospital within two weeks of their one and only meeting with you?"

Tatum shot a cross look. "Too many to fucking count."

Jack stepped out of his role. "Good answer, Tatum."

"Shit, Jack, I just want to take the stand and tell the judge I didn't do it."

"It doesn't work that way. I'm sorry, but if you testify, Colletti's lawyer will grill you. Before you know it, everyone in that courtroom is going to know what you used to do for a living, know about the meeting you had with Sally Fenning, and know that she tried to hire you to put a bullet in her head. Now, unless you want to leap to the top of the list of suspects in Sally's shooting, I suggest you take my advice."

Tatum was seething, but Jack seemed to be getting through. "What you want me to do, exactly?"

"Keep your secrets to yourself," said Jack. "Don't take the stand. We'll stipulate to the entry of a restraining order."

"How's that gonna look?"

"I'll put the best spin on it I can. I'll tell the judge that Mr. Knight vehemently denies the allegations, but he has absolutely no need to come within five hundred yards of any of the other beneficiaries anyway. So we'll stipulate to the restraining order."

Tatum walked to the window and stared out at the parking lot below. "You know, I don't have to tell them about the meeting with Sally."

"If you take the stand and perjure yourself, you'll be looking for a new lawyer."

He let out a mirthless chuckle. "Theo warned me you were a goody-two-shoes."

"Theo warned me plenty about you, too. And here we both are. So what's it going to be?"

He turned away from the window and faced Jack. "Fine. We'll stipulate. There's just one thing you need to understand."

"What?"

"If that pussy Gerry Colletti ends up with all this money, I'm gonna beat the living hell outta both of you."

"I don't take threats, Tatum."

He gave his lawyer a big smile and a pat on the shoulder. "Just kid-din', Jack buddy."

Jack didn't return the smile. He just opened the door and started back toward the courtroom.

Twenty

Jack thought he was being watched, and he was right.

After the probate hearing he'd said good-bye to Tatum at the courthouse doors, and he continued alone to his car. Two men matched him step for step across the cracked and buckled asphalt, all the way into the fenced-in parking lot. The younger one walked with a cocky roll, chin aloft, his eyes catching his reflection in each tinted car window they passed, as if the title song to *Shaft* were on continuous playback in his head. The older man had a slight stoop and the dour expression of someone who worried too much about problems he couldn't solve, problems that kept him working late, kept him up at night, and kept his bar tab running. Even if Jack hadn't known Rick Larsen, he would have guessed he was a veteran homicide detective.

They weren't exactly friends, but Jack and he shared a certain mutual respect. Plenty of good cops had given Jack the benefit of the doubt over the years, if only because Jack's father had been a cop before embarking on a long political road that culminated with two terms in the governor's mansion. Jack's personal history with Detective Larsen ran deeper than that. As a much younger detective, Larsen had worked the file on Theo Knight, part of the team that had put the wrong man on death row. Not until the DNA tests were back could he confide in Jack—*off* the record, of course— and tell him that his rookie doubts about Theo's guilt had been squelched by his supervisors.

"Who's the new partner?" asked Jack as he turned to face them.

Larsen smiled as he pulled the unlit cigar plug from between his teeth. "You mean Calvin Klein here?"

"What's that supposed to mean?" said his partner.

"If you don't know, you got no business being a detective." He gave Jack a wink and asked, "Got a minute?"

Jack set his briefcase atop the hood of his car. "Sure. What about?"

"Sally Fenning. As I'm sure you know, I'm on her murder."

"Yeah, I was glad to hear that."

"Why?"

"You guys never caught her daughter's killer. Seemed the very least she deserved was a detective on her case who was good enough to catch hers."

"I'm working on it."

"Which leads you to me," said Jack.

"Actually, no. It leads me to Tatum Knight, which leads me to you."

"You want to interview him?"

"Love to. But he won't talk to us."

Jack hid his surprise. Tatum had neglected to tell him the police had contacted him. "Did you ask nicely?"

"Of course. I told him he could play ball or be the ball. Either way, I intend to smack a home run."

Jack chuckled. "I gotta hand it to you, Larsen. You're the only detective I know who can say that line with a straight face."

"And sometimes it even works. But all kidding aside, if your client won't talk, I am going to turn up the heat."

"What do you want to know?"

He removed his sunglasses, as if to look Jack in the eye. "Did he kill Sally Fenning?"

"The answer is no."

"Does he know who did?"

"No."

"Do you expect me to take those responses at face value?"

"Absolutely not."

"Did he beat the crap out of Gerry Colletti?"

"No."

"Then why didn't he take the stand and tell Judge Parsons that he didn't do it?"

"That was his lawyer's decision."

"What are you hiding?"

"Nothing."

"I watched the hearing. You're hiding something."

"Rank speculation on your part."

On the other side of the fence, a transit bus rumbled down the street. The air was suddenly thick with diesel fumes, but the detective didn't miss a beat. "Tell me this much: Why the hell did Sally Fenning name a thug like Tatum Knight in her will?"

"I wish we could ask her."

"I wish I could ask Tatum."

"What's in it for him?"

"He can either play ball, or—"

"Oh, please. Strike two."

Larsen smirked. "This is what bugs me. Of the five beneficiaries identified so far, four have a direct connection to Sally's prior marriage and to the death of her daughter. How does Tatum Knight fit into that group?"

Obviously Jack couldn't volunteer anything about Tatum's meeting with Sally before she was killed, but a little dialogue might not hurt. "That's interesting," said Jack. "You seem so certain that *all four* of the other known beneficiaries had some connection to Sally's prior life."

"Just a little deductive reasoning on my part."

"I think it's more than that. Sally's ex-husband, the divorce lawyer, and the prosecutor who failed to indict anyone for the murder of Sally's daughter were all obviously connected to Sally's past. But the reporter simply wrote a few fact-filled articles about a terrible crime, which hardly seems enough to put her in the same reviled category as the others."

"I'll grant you that. She's a little different animal."

"If we assume that Sally decided to leave her money to her enemies to fight over, exactly what did this reporter do to make herself into one of Sally's worst enemies?"

"You asking *me* the questions now?"

"If you can answer that one, I'll see what I can do about Tatum."

"I need a bigger commitment than that."

"I'll encourage him to meet with you. That's all I can promise."

Larsen gave him a steely look. "All right. But only because I know you're a man of your word, I'll give you this much. Deirdre Meadows did more than write a few newspaper articles about Sally Fenning."

"How much more?"

"A whole damn book. All about the murder of Sally's daughter. No publisher has bought it yet, but I understand she's still shopping it."

"And?"

"And, that's it, that's all, folks. At least until I get to sit down and talk to Tatum Knight."

Jack grabbed his briefcase. "Fair enough. Thanks for the tidbit. I'll see what I can do."

"I'll call you tomorrow," said Larsen.

Jack nodded and unlocked his car. Larsen gave a little wave as he started to walk away. Then he stopped, looked back, and said, "One other thing."

"What?"

"That's one tough client you got there, Swyteck."

"Yeah. Just like his brother."

He was suddenly stone-cold serious. "I promise you: He's nothing like Theo."

"You trying to tell me something?"

"Just be sure to do your homework."

"I already have. Tons of it."

"Do it again. For your own good."

"That's what everybody used to tell me about Theo, too. Till I proved him innocent."

Larsen turned away, as if it hadn't really registered. Jack stood and watched, nearly blinded by the sun, as the detectives crossed the parking lot and headed for the gate.

Twenty-one

Theo was too good for his own bar. That was the drunken dis he heard from his bandmates whenever they played at Sparky's. Not that they considered themselves above a raunchy rat hole like Sparky's. The comment was directed strictly at the audience. As much as Theo wished he owned a true jazz bar, he'd purchased a going concern with an established clientele. They were loyal, they kept him profitable, and they unflaggingly believed that the history of music had reached its apex with "Achy-Breaky-Heart" and had been on the decline ever since. The sax was Theo's passion, but the rednecks paid the rent.

Charlie Parker, forgive me.

He finished the set with a powerful solo worthy of the Blue Note. Two women wearing cowboy hats raced toward the jukebox, sending Theo into an *Electric Slide* panic attack. The table in front was filled with employees from the car dealership across the street. They were oblivious to the music, one of them laughing so hard that beer was pouring from his nostrils. But a few people clapped, and a woman in back even shot him two thumbs-up, which made Theo smile. Slowly, Sparky's would change its stripes, he was sure of it.

Theo carefully laid his saxophone in the stand, an old Buescher 400 that had been passed down from the man who'd taught him how to play. His great-uncle Cyrus was once a nightclub star in old Overtown, Miami's Harlem, and it would have pleased him to know that not even four years on death row could strip Theo of the passion the old man had planted in a teenage boy's blood.

"What'll it be, pal?" said Theo as he walked behind the bar and wrapped the white apron around his waist.

"Club soda."

"Hitting the hard stuff, are you?"

"Can't drink. I'm on painkillers."

Theo looked up from the well for a better look. The lighting was poor, but even in the shadows this dude was obviously hurting. "Damn, that's nasty. I seen people crawl outta here with busted-up faces. First time I ever seen anyone come in that way."

"Got a real professional ass-kicking."

"Looks that way."

"From your brother."

Theo set the glass on the bar. They'd never met, but Theo had heard plenty from Jack. "You must be Gerry the Genius."

"You and your buddy Swyteck got a real running joke there, don't you? For the last time, it's Gentleman Gerry."

"What brings you here, Gent?"

"What do you think?"

"Stupidity."

Gerry smiled, then winced with pain. "Shit, it even hurts to laugh."

"That's not my problem."

He brought the glass to his lips with care, but the left side of his mouth was badly swollen, causing a trickle to run down his chin. "You're right. It's my problem. And your brother's."

"Only because you're good at throwing around bullshit allegations."

"Are you seriously going to stand there and tell me this wasn't your brother's work?"

"You got that right."

"Who are you, his alibi?"

"No. His sparring partner. Him and me been boxing each other for years. So I can look at your face and tell you in two seconds it wasn't Tatum who done it."

"How?"

"Tatum has a mean left hook. Nobody ever sees it coming. One time my right eye was swollen shut for three days. But your right eye is perfect. It's the left side of your face that's all beat to hell. So tell me," said Theo as he delivered a mock left hook to Gerry's unscathed right eye, "how does that happen?"

"Your brother isn't a one-armed bandit. He has other punches."

"He also gots a brain. If he beats you up, he ain't gonna let you see his face."

"I saw what I saw."

"I don't believe you."

Gerry forced a crooked smile, trying hard to ignore the pain of any facial movement. "All right. Maybe I didn't get as good a look at my attacker as I led the court to believe in my affidavit. But I didn't come here to argue about the evidence."

"Then why you here?"

"Because I have something to say to your brother. Frankly, I feel safer saying it to you. I'm sure you'll deliver the message for me."

"Maybe."

"I'm offering a deal." He checked over each shoulder, as if to make sure that no one around them could overhear. "If Tatum will renounce his shot at the inheritance and get out of the game, I'll recant my testimony."

"You'll what?"

"I'll tell the judge I made a mistake. It was dark, I'd been drinking, it happened very fast. On reflection, I don't think it was Tatum Knight who beat me up after all."

"And for that, you want my brother to give up his shot at inheriting forty-six million bucks?"

A waitress pulled up to the station at the end of the bar. "Couple a' Buds, Theo." He set two open long-necks on her tray, and off she went.

"There's more," said Gerry. "If Tatum does drop out, I'll pay him a quarter million dollars, cash, right now. It's not contingent on me inheriting the money or anything else. He drops out, I give him the money. It's that clean."

"You trying to buy your way to the prize?"

Gerry pulled an ice cube from his soda and applied it to his fattened lip. "Brains, not brute force. That's what it takes to win Sally Fenning's game."

"Funny, you don't look so smart."

"I'm not the one with a restraining order entered against me, am I?"

"You must want that money pretty bad."

"There's nothing illegal about cutting deals with the other beneficiaries to induce them to drop out. It's just business. The mining business." Gerry flashed a crooked smile, calling Theo forward with a curl of his finger, as if to let him in on a big secret. "This is what I call a gold mine."

"You're using trumped-up assault charges to get my brother to settle cheap and drop out."

"I said I'd withdraw the charges. I didn't say they were trumped up."

Theo shook his head, then chuckled, "Who you think you're talking to, fool?"

"Excuse me?"

The smile drained away as Theo leaned closer and said, "This is blackmail."

"That's not the way I see it."

"Doesn't matter how *you* see it. I see it as blackmail. Tatum will see it as blackmail. And that's not a good thing for you."

"Am I supposed to be scared now?"

Theo got right in his face, pressing his huge hands into the bar top. Gerry was trying to be a tough guy, but the twitching eyelid gave him away. To his surprise, however, Theo backed down. Gerry seemed pleased to have won the staring match, until Theo walked over to the stage, grabbed the microphone from the stand, and said, "Ladies and Gentlemen, your attention, please."

The noise level dropped a notch, though it wasn't completely quiet.

Gerry shifted nervously on his bar stool, clearly apprehensive.

Theo continued, "I don't mean to rat anybody out, but I just heard that tonight we have with us Mr. Gerry Colletti, seated right over there at the end of the bar. You might be interested to know that Mr. Colletti is a former representative from the state of Massachusetts, where he was the author of the very first mandatory biker helmet law in the U.S. of A. Dude, take a bow."

A chorus of boos rolled across the room. The bikers at the pool table shot a volley of death glares that had Gerry sinking into the woodwork. Two guys with bulging biceps started toward the bar. The ugly one had identical tattoos on each forearm, the word "villain" spelled "villian," as if to brag that he was too stupid to check a dictionary. The tall guy was wearing no shirt, just tattered blue jeans and a black leather vest. His metal dog tags rattled with each tap of the fat end of a pool cue into his open palm.

Theo was feeling pretty smug as he walked back behind the bar. "Club soda's on me, Genius. Have a nice walk to your car."

Twenty-two

Jack and Kelsey were surrounded by books.

The homicide detective's tip that Deirdre Meadows had written a true-crime story about Sally Fenning was a good lead, but Jack had struggled over what to do next. Going straight to Deirdre was one option, but he wanted more facts before taking that shot. That was where Martin Kapstan came in.

Just Books was hands-down the best bookstore in Coral Gables, and Martin made it that way. The store itself was beautiful, an old Mediterranean-style building, perfectly restored, and plenty of book-filled rooms for browsing. With signings and readings virtually every night of the week, it would be difficult to name a national best-selling author in the last twenty years who hadn't made an appearance there. But it was Martin who set the store apart. He'd started out as a high school teacher, and he'd never really lost that guiding touch. Every aspiring author in south Florida sought his advice, and somehow he always found time to give it. Some of them found success. All of them found a little hope. Kelsey figured that if anyone knew anything about Deirdre's unpublished script, Martin was the guy.

"Damn, we should have come last night," said Kelsey. She was checking out the event calender posted by the door. They'd just missed Isabelle Allende.

Kelsey had worked a summer at Just Books before Nate was born, before law school, before interning for Jack, before her sphere of knowledge had begun to shrink to the point where she felt as though

she knew absolutely nothing about anything except what she happened to be working on at the moment. She seemed a little embarrassed by how long it had been since her last visit, but Martin greeted
her with his usual gentle smile and soft-spoken manner. She introduced Jack, and the three of them stepped outside for coffee in the
central courtyard. Martin and Kelsey spent a few minutes catching up,
then Martin asked, "How long you two been dating?"

They both let out a nervous chuckle. Kelsey said, "Oh, we're not—"

"No we're not . . . we're friends," said Jack. "And of course we
work together."

"Oh. I just assumed from the way Kelsey gushed on the phone
about—" Martin stopped in mid-sentence, as if someone had just flattened his big toe.

"About how crazy Nate is about Jack," said Kelsey, her smile
strained.

From the look on Martin's face, it seemed as though he had something else on the tip of his tongue. "Right. I understand you and Nate
are great buddies."

"I'm his Big Brother."

"That's terrific."

"Yeah, it's been great."

All three tasted their coffee, as if thankful for the silence. Then
Martin said, "So, how can I help you?"

Jack asked, "Have you been following the newspaper stories about
a very wealthy woman named Sally Fenning? She was shot to death
downtown about two weeks ago."

"I did read about that."

"Kelsey and I represent one of the heirs to her estate."

"Yeah, she mentioned that in our phone conversation."

"It turns out that one of the other heirs was writing a book about
Sally. She's a reporter for the *Tribune*. Her name is Deirdre Meadows."

"I've met Deirdre," said Martin.

"You don't happen to know anything about the book she wrote,
do you?"

"As a matter of fact I do."

Kelsey smiled proudly, looked at Jack, and said, "Told you."

Jack said, "I don't want to intrude on anything she might have told you in confidence, but can you tell me anything about it?"

"Not much, I'm afraid. I've never read it. I offered to read it, but Deirdre didn't feel comfortable sharing it."

"Why not?"

"The way she explained it, her lawyer told her not to let anyone read it, except for her literary agent and any publishers they sent it to."

"What was the fear? Someone stealing her ideas?"

"I think her real concern was a libel suit."

Jack did a double take. "From Sally?"

Martin nodded. "As I understand it, she started out writing the book with Sally Fenning's cooperation. About six months into it, Sally decided she didn't like the angle Deirdre was plying. Actually, to say she didn't like it is an understatement. She threatened to sue Deirdre for libel."

"So her lawyer told her not to let anyone read it?" asked Kelsey.

Jack gave the lawyer's answer. "She was probably trying to keep her legal exposure to a minimum. Obviously, if the only people who read the allegedly libelous material are a handful of potential publishers, Sally's damages would be negligible."

"That was my take on it," said Martin.

Jack asked, "Do you know what, exactly, Sally claimed was libelous?"

"I don't. It was a strange conversation we had. Deirdre wanted my opinion on whether a libel suit would help or hurt her chances of getting published. She seemed to think it was a good thing, that publishers would like the added publicity."

"What did you tell her?"

"I said, sure, the publicity department might like it. Hell, I know some publicists who would have an author set her hair on fire and run naked around the bookstore if it would move a few extra books. But publishers also have legal departments, and the lawyers weren't likely to be too keen about a libel suit."

"You didn't exactly tell her what she wanted to hear."

"I don't think it fazed her much. She said she could verify everything she wrote. Supposedly she had the full cooperation of the prosecutor on the case."

"Mason Rudsky?"

"She didn't mention his name," said Martin.

"Had to be Mason. He was the prosecutor assigned to the case."

Kelsey said, "He's also a beneficiary under Sally's will. Just like Deirdre."

Martin shrugged, as if not sure what to make of Kelsey's last remark. His pager chirped, and he checked it. "Would you two excuse me for one minute?"

"Sure," said Jack.

Martin left his coffee on the table, as if to promise a prompt return. As soon as he was gone, Kelsey looked at Jack and said, "A libel suit. I guess that's why Deirdre's on Sally's list. She was telling lies about her."

"It would be nice to know what the lies were."

"What's your guess?" asked Kelsey.

"I don't have a clue. But if Deirdre was spreading falsehoods about Sally and her daughter's murder, it could explain why Sally hated her and put her in the same category as the other named beneficiaries who had made her life no longer worth living."

"But we have to consider the other possibility," said Kelsey.

"Right," said Jack, picking up her thought. "What if the charges in Deirdre's manuscript—whatever they might be—are true?"

"Maybe Sally was ticked off not because Deirdre was spreading lies, but because she uncovered some horrible truths that Sally would have rather kept secret."

"Could be," said Jack.

"Especially if she had Mason Rudsky's full cooperation," said Kelsey.

They locked eyes, both considering it. Then Jack said, "Whether it's packed with lies or dirty little truths, one thing's for sure."

"What?"

He leaned back in his chair, his gaze drifting toward the store window and the wall of books inside. "I want to know what Deirdre Meadows wrote."

"So do I."

Then he looked at Kelsey and said, "Almost as badly as I want to know what you and Martin really talked about on the phone."

"What?"

"Whatever you said that made him think we were dating."

She blushed and lowered her eyes. "Silly boy. Didn't anyone ever tell you? Stick to mysteries you can solve."

"No mystery is unsolvable. Some are just more fun than others."

She brought her cup to her lips and peered over the rim, saying nothing.

"Don't you agree?" asked Jack.

No answer, but she didn't look away.

"You know, you can't ignore me forever," said Jack.

More silence, but Jack knew there was a grin hiding behind that coffee cup.

"Oh yeah," he said with a smile. "Now *this* is getting fun."

Twenty-three

At a court hearing on Tuesday morning, Jack was on the receiving end of a laserlike glare from Assistant State Attorney Mason Rudsky. Clearly, Rudsky wasn't happy about his seat in the witness stand, especially when it meant cross-examination from a criminal defense lawyer.

It wasn't Jack's preference to take on the State Attorney's Office, but he was being stonewalled. After he and Kelsey left Just Books early Friday evening, Jack called Deirdre Meadows and asked about her book. She didn't want to talk about it. The following Monday morning, Jack visited Rudsky and explained how Deirdre had bragged to the owner of Just Books that the prosecutor had lent his "full cooperation." Rudsky refused to confirm or deny the allegation, and he flashed the same phony smile and gave the same pat answer each time Jack asked a question: *"I'm very sorry, but the investigation into the murder of Sally Fenning's daughter is still an open file. I can't discuss it."*

Jack wasn't one to take "Up yours" for an answer. If the reporter wouldn't tell him what was in her book, and if the prosecutor couldn't talk about the investigative file, then Jack was going to see the file for himself. He filed a lawsuit under the Sunshine Act, which is Florida's very broad version of the Freedom of Information Act. The law was written to make sure that government was conducted "in the sunshine," so that private citizens had access to government records. The law applied to criminal matters, except for active investigations. One thing Jack had learned as a prosecutor was that judges took a dim view of prosecutors who tried to circumvent the law by claiming that stale files were "active."

Jack stepped toward the witness. The cavernous old courtroom was exceptionally quiet, not so much as a cough or the shuffling of feet from the gallery. The hearing was closed to the public, at least until the court could determine whether the file should be made public.

"Good morning, Mr. Rudsky."

"Good morning."

Rudsky was a career prosecutor who took his job and himself too seriously. He had an unusually large head, and when he got angry his face flushed red, as if his bow tie were tied too tightly. He was beet red already, and Jack hadn't even started.

"Mr. Rudsky, you were the assistant state attorney assigned to the murder of Sally Fenning's daughter five years ago, were you not?"

"That's correct."

"Are you handling the murder of Sally Fenning as well?"

"No. Patricia Compton is heading that team." He pointed with a nod to the lawyer seated on the other side of the courtroom. Compton was his attorney for purposes of this hearing.

"Are you part of her team?"

"No."

"Why not?"

"Objection," said Compton. "Judge, what does the composition of a completely different prosecutorial team have to do with the question of whether the investigation into the murder of Sally Fenning's daughter is active or inactive?"

"Sustained."

"Let me put it another way," said Jack. "Mr. Rudsky, does the fact that you are not assigned to the Sally Fenning murder have anything to do with the fact that you are a named beneficiary under her will?"

"Same objection."

"I'll overrule this one. The witness shall answer."

"I don't know," said Rudsky. "I don't make the assignments."

"Other than your role as prosecutor in connection with the murder of Sally Fenning's daughter, Katherine, did you have any kind of relationship with Ms. Fenning?"

"No."

"Were you surprised to learn that you were a beneficiary under Sally Fenning's will?"

"Totally."

"Can you think of any reason that she would have named you as a beneficiary, other than your role as prosecutor?"

"I couldn't even hazard a guess."

"Was Sally Fenning happy with the way you handled the case?"

Compton was back on her feet. "Objection. This is getting very far afield."

"Sustained. I've given you a little latitude, Mr. Swyteck, but please don't take advantage."

"Yes, Judge. Let me put this in more concrete terms. Mr. Rudsky, no one was ever convicted for the murder of Sally Fenning's daughter, correct?"

"That's correct."

"No one was even indicted."

"True."

"You never even asked a grand jury to return an indictment."

"I never did, no."

"You never even empaneled a grand jury, did you?"

He shifted in his seat. "You're really getting into the matter of grand jury secrecy."

"Answer the question," said the judge.

"Can I have the question again, please?"

"Sure," said Jack. "You never empaneled a grand jury, did you?"

"You mean in the Katherine Fenning murder?"

"No, I was actually talking about the Lincoln assassination."

"Objection."

The judge cracked a faint smile. "Sustained, but Mr. Swyteck does have a point. Please answer the question."

"No. We did not empanel a grand jury."

"Why not?"

Compton popped to her feet, grumbling. "Judge, this line of questioning does not go to the sole relevant issue at this hearing, which is quite simply whether or not the investigation into the murder of Katherine Fenning is active. This is a blatant attempt to invade the secrecy and sanctity of the grand jury process."

The judge looked at Jack and said, "Can you narrow your question, Mr. Swyteck?"

Jack stepped closer to the witness and asked, "Is it fair to say that you didn't empanel a grand jury because you didn't have sufficient evidence to do so?"

"I suppose that's one reason."

"Let's talk about your evidence-gathering efforts, shall we? How many subpoenas have been issued in the last three years?"

"None."

"How many depositions taken in the last three years?"

"None."

"How many witnesses have been interviewed in the last three years?"

"None."

"Are there any suspects whom you are currently pursuing?"

"Not at this time."

"Not in the last three years, isn't that right, sir?"

"That's correct."

"When will a grand jury be convened?"

"I don't know."

"And yet, you maintain that this is an *active* file, and that I have no right to see it."

"The case is still open."

"As open as it ever was?"

"Yes. As open as it ever was."

"No wonder you never caught the killer."

"Objection."

"Withdrawn. Mr. Rudsky, do you know a woman named Deirdre Meadows?"

He hesitated, as if the name alone made him nervous. "Yes. She's a reporter for the *Miami Tribune*."

"Did you ever have any discussions with Deirdre Meadows about the murder of Sally Fenning's daughter?"

"Yes. I've had general discussions with a number of reporters about the case."

"To your knowledge, how many of those reporters have written a book about the murder of Sally Fenning's daughter?"

He squirmed nervously. "Just one." ·

"That would be Ms. Meadows, correct?"

"Correct."

"Did you provide any assistance to her in the writing of her book?"

"That depends on what you mean by assistance."

"Ms. Meadows claims that she had your full cooperation. Would you call that assistance?"

"Objection."

"On what grounds?" asked the judge.

Compton was silent, stalling, as if the testimony of her own client was news to her. "Relevance," she stammered.

"Overruled."

Jack said, "Did Ms. Meadows have your full cooperation, Mr. Rudsky?"

"That depends on what you mean by full cooperation."

"Did she interview you?"

"Yes."

"Did she let you read her manuscript?"

"Yes."

"Did you share any investigative materials with her?"

He paused. Jack waited. The government's lawyer waited. Finally, Rudsky answered, "I might have."

Compton went white. She sprang to her feet and asked, "Could we have a short recess, Your Honor?"

"Not *now*," said the judge. "This is just getting interesting. Mr. Swyteck, continue."

Jack walked to the lectern and checked his notes, not because he had to, but only to make the witness stew in the uncomfortable silence. "Sir, are you aware that Sally Fenning threatened to bring a libel suit against Deirdre Meadows if her book were ever published?"

"I'd heard that, yes."

"Are you also aware that a libel suit cannot be maintained on behalf of a dead person?"

"I don't understand what you're asking."

"It's a straightforward question. Are you aware that once a person is dead, you can say whatever you want about them? There is no liability for libel."

"Yes. I learned that in law school."

"So the death of Sally Fenning leaves Deirdre Meadows free to publish her book without any fear of a libel suit. Agreed?"

"I suppose that's correct."

"And anyone who gave Ms. Meadows his full cooperation in the writing of that book would have the same protection, would he not?"

Rudsky narrowed his eyes. "What are you implying?"

Jack took a half step closer, tightening his figurative grasp. "Sir, do you have a financial interest of any kind in Ms. Meadows's book?"

Compton shot from her seat. "Judge, please."

"You'd better not be asking again for a recess."

"No," she said. "But I do have a proposal."

"There's a question pending," said Jack.

"Then I object," said Compton. "There's no foundation for any of these questions, and the inquiry is totally irrelevant. Before we waste an entire day on this fishing expedition, I would at least ask the court to entertain my suggestion."

"What is it?" asked the judge.

"In a good faith effort to streamline this process, the government agrees to provide to Mr. Swyteck all of the materials and information that Mr. Rudsky shared with this reporter, Deirdre Meadows. Perhaps that will satisfy Mr. Swyteck's needs."

"Perhaps it won't," said Jack.

Compton continued, "If it doesn't, then Mr. Swyteck is free to renew his claim under the Sunshine Act for the production of the entire investigative file."

"Why not let Mr. Swyteck finish with this witness and see if we can't resolve the entire matter here and now?" asked the judge.

"Because there is some overlap between the murder of Sally Fenning, which I'm handling, and the murder of her daughter, which Mr. Rudsky handled. I'll concede that Mr. Swyteck has the right to see anything that Mr. Rudsky shared with a reporter. But ordering us to produce the entire file would not strike the proper balance between the public's right to know and the need to preserve the integrity of criminal investigations."

The judge looked at Jack and asked, "Is that acceptable to you?"

"I'd really like Mr. Rudsky to answer my question."

"Mr. Swyteck," the judge said, "I asked if that was acceptable to you."

Jack wanted to push, but the judge seemed to be leaning in his favor, and he didn't want to lose that advantage by overreaching. "For now," said Jack. "But if I don't get everything I need, I will be back."

"Very well," said the judge. "The government has two days to produce the investigative materials to Mr. Swyteck. And I'm warning you: no game playing. I'm not going to be happy if this matter comes back to me."

With the crack of the gavel, the hearing was over. Rudsky stepped down from the witness stand, not so much as looking at Jack. As Jack packed his briefcase, Patricia Compton walked over to his table and said, "Congratulations."

"Thanks."

"It's a sad thing that no one was ever indicted for the murder of Sally's daughter."

"I couldn't agree more."

"I don't intend to have the same problem for the murder of Sally Fenning. I thought you might want to pass that along to your client."

Jack didn't blink. "Sure thing. Just as soon as I see your file. Call me when it's ready," he said, then turned and headed for the exit.

Twenty-four

I t was 2 A.M., and Deirdre Meadows was at the scene of a crime. A white van had been parked outside the grocery store for almost a week. The doors were locked, but a security guard detected the putrid odor of something like spoiled meat and rotten eggs. Deirdre heard the call on the police radio—she always kept it playing in her car, just in case something broke—and she arrived just minutes after the police had cordoned off the area. One of the officers on the scene confirmed off the record that a body was inside, which got Deirdre's heart pumping. Foul play was the rhythm that Miami crime reporters danced to, and homicide was enough to make Deirdre *bailar la bamba.*

"Man or a woman?" asked Deirdre. She was standing just on the other side of the yellow police tape, talking to a uniformed officer.

"Don't know yet," he said.

She rattled off a string of questions, gathering facts, writing the story in her head as she assimilated information. This was what she did day after day, night after night, for surprisingly little pay and even less recognition. She hoped that would change soon, with a little luck from Sally Fenning.

Her cell phone rang. She tucked her notepad into her purse and took the call.

"Hello, Deirdre," said the man on the line.

It seemed like a contradiction, but she recognized the disguised voice immediately. It was that same distorted, mechanical sound as the last call. "What are you doing awake at this hour?" she asked.

"None of your business."

She reached into her purse, pulled out her Dictaphone, and held it up to the phone.

"Put the recorder away," he said a moment before she clicked the Record button.

She froze, not sure how he knew.

"I can see you," he said.

She looked around. Two media vans had pulled into the lot and were setting up for videotaping. Three police cars and the medical examiner's van were parked on the other side of the crime scene. The large parking lot was otherwise empty, a flat acre of asphalt bathed in the yellowish cast of security lights.

"Where are you?" she asked.

He laughed, which sounded like static through the voice-altering device. "I'm everywhere you go."

She swallowed hard, trying to stay firm. "What do you want?"

"First, I want to congratulate you."

"On what?"

"For staying silent at the court hearing. You didn't mention a thing about the dog attack outside the warehouse. You showed very good judgment. The same good judgment you showed by not contacting the police."

"How do you know I haven't contacted the police?"

"Because you're an ambitious bitch."

"What does that have to do with anything?"

"I know you wouldn't just go to the police and tell them what you know. You're the kind of person who would expect something in return from them, some juicy tidbit that would have appeared in the newspaper. But I haven't seen anything of interest under any of your by-lines lately. So I can only assume you didn't go to the police."

Deirdre was silent, a little unnerved by how well he seemed to know her. "What do you want now?"

"Why do you assume I *want* something? I'm a very giving person, Deirdre."

"What are you offering?"

"A news flash. The first of Sally Fenning's six beneficiaries is going to die."

She felt chills, but she tried to stay with him. "When?"

"Two weeks from today."

"Which one?"

"That's sort of up to you."

"I don't understand."

"Here's the deal: It can be you, or it can be someone else. If it's you, it won't be quick and painless. You gotta decide. Do you want to live and share the forty-six million dollars with me, your partner? Or do you want to die?"

"Is this the choice you mentioned last time?"

"Exactly. You can choose to keep your mouth shut and make us both rich. Or you can choose to warn the others, make me mad, and make yourself dead."

"How do you expect me to make a choice like that?"

"Easy. Here's how it works. You keep quiet for a couple more weeks, and I'll take that as your acceptance. I'll assume we got a deal."

Her hand was shaking as she spoke into the phone. "Why are you doing this to me?"

"Because I know that you will make the right decision."

"Don't be so sure."

"Don't be a fool, girl. Your half of forty-six million dollars can buy a lot of grief counseling. So remember, two weeks from today, the first victim falls. If you're smart, it won't be you."

"You're sick."

"You're right. But I'm also right about one thing. If you're at all thinking that you should do something to save the others, trust me: They aren't worth saving."

She thought for a moment, wondering what he'd meant by that, but a moment was too long. There was silence on the line. The call was over. Deirdre put the phone in her purse and walked away from the crime scene, no longer interested in some story about just another body in the back of a van.

Twenty-five

J ack was eager to see what part of the five-year-old investigative
file the state attorney was ready to disclose. The judge had given
Mason Rudsky two days to turn over anything he'd shared with Deirdre Meadows about the murder of Sally's daughter, and the government waited until the fifty-ninth minute of the forty-seventh hour to
notify Jack that the materials were ready for his inspection. Jack might
have busted their chops about stringing things out, except that he'd
been busy for two days trying to convince a jury in another case that
it really wasn't robbery if his client took forty bucks and change from
the cash register but dropped his wallet on the way out with fifty-eight
dollars inside. It was sort of the criminal defense version of net-net
economic theory. Didn't work, at least not where the defendant had
left his photo ID and Social Security number at the scene of the
crime.

The government's entire production on the Katherine Fenning
murder investigation consisted of one videotape. It was in a sealed
envelope with an affidavit from Mason Rudsky in which the prosecutor swore that he'd shared nothing else with Deirdre Meadows. Jack
brought Kelsey with him. It was nice to have another point of view.

"What is this?" asked Jack.

A police officer was seated in a folding chair near the door to the
conference room. He didn't answer.

"Excuse me, Officer. I asked what's on the tape."

"I'm sorry," he said. "I'm under strict orders from Mr. Rudsky not to answer any of your questions."

"Then why are you here?"

"To make sure the tape does not leave this room."

"Seeing how this room has no windows, maybe that's a job you could do from the other side of the door. My colleague and I would like to be able to talk freely while viewing the tape."

The cop considered it. "I suppose that'd be okay."

Jack thanked him and closed the door. Kelsey was examining the videocassette. "Interview of S. Fenning," she read from the label. "It's almost five years old."

Jack said, "Sally's ex-husband told me they were both interviewed. They must have videotaped Sally's."

"Why?"

"It's a smart thing for law enforcement to do if there's a chance of getting a nice voluntary confession that will play well to a jury."

"What would Sally have to confess?"

"Let's play the tape and find out." Jack shoved the cassette into the VCR and switched on the television. A horizontal bar blipped across the bright blue screen, followed by snow and static. When it cleared, Sally Fenning was staring straight at them.

The image was the most unflattering Jack had ever seen of Sally. Her eyelids looked heavy, and her skin was pale. A punishing light shining in her face didn't help. Sally wasn't the kind of woman who needed makeup to be beautiful, but even a natural beauty had her limits, especially in a head-and-shoulders closeup like this.

"She looks so tired," said Kelsey.

"Something tells me they didn't start taping at the beginning of the interview. Looks like we're several hours into the interrogation."

"How soon was this after the murder of her daughter?"

Jack checked the date on the videocassette sleeve. "Couple of months, I think."

On screen, Sally continued to stare into the camera, waiting.

Finally, the voice emerged. *"Are you ready to continue, Ms. Fenning?"*

The focus remained on Sally's face, and the man's voice had come from somewhere off-screen. "That's Rudsky," said Jack.

"Ready," said Sally.

"I want to ask a few more questions about this stalker you said was pursuing you. First, can you tell me what he looks like?"

"Not really. I only saw him once, from behind. One night I looked out the window and saw someone running away. I'm afraid I didn't get a very good look at him."

"What does he sound like?"

"I'm not sure. Whenever he called, his voice was distorted by some kind of mechanical contraption."

"Is there anyone you suspect? Any customers at the bar who've been bothering you, hitting on you?"

"A bar waitress gets hit on by creeps all the time. Kind of an occupational hazard. Could be anyone, really."

The camera kept rolling, but there was silence. Sally took a sip of water.

"Ms. Fenning," said Rudsky, *"I have here a report on the results of your polygraph examination."*

Kelsey looked away from the screen and asked Jack, "She took a polygraph?"

"Evidently," said Jack.

On tape, Rudsky's voice continued, *"The results are interesting, to say the least. Your response to one question, in particular, showed obvious signs of deception."*

"I don't understand how that could be."

"Let's explore that, shall we? The question was this: Have you ever cheated on your husband? Your answer was no."

"That's right."

"You were lying, weren't you?"

Jack watched the tape carefully. Sally seemed to be struggling as she blinked twice and said, *"I can explain."*

"Please do," said Rudsky.

"It happened before we were married."

Rudsky's sarcastic chuckle caused a crackle in the speakers. *"How do you cheat on your husband before you're even married?"*

"Mike and I dated exclusively for two years. A few months before our wedding, we had an argument and broke up. I was devastated. I leaned on someone who I thought was a friend, and he . . . I made a mistake. It wasn't technically cheating, because Mike and I weren't married. We weren't even dating at that particular moment. But in my heart, I felt like a cheater. So I wasn't lying when I answered 'No' to the lie detector question. But I felt like I was lying, so I'm sure that's what the machine picked up."

There was silence again, as if Rudsky were trying to make her squirm. Finally, the follow-up question came, *"Do you really expect me to believe that?"*

"It's the truth."

"I'm beginning to wonder if anything you've said so far is the truth."

She tightened her mouth, seemingly defensive. *"What do you mean?"*

"You claim there was a stalker."

"There was."

"But you can't tell us what he looks like."

"No."

"You can't tell us what he sounds like."

"No."

"You can't tell us anything about him, except that he 'could be anybody.'"

"I wish I could tell you more."

"And this started how long before your daughter was murdered?"

"Several months."

"But you never told the police anything about a stalker until after your daughter was murdered."

"Calling the police would only have infuriated him."

"You didn't even tell your husband."

"I thought he would make me quit my job, which we couldn't afford. And I didn't want him to haul off and do something stupid, like buy a gun. I didn't want a gun in the house with a four-year-old child."

"Let's stop the lies, all right, Ms. Fenning?"

Jack moved closer to the screen, sensing that the prosecutor was moving in for the kill. Sally was getting emotional, the strain of Rudsky's accusatory tone having taken an obvious toll.

"*I'm not lying,*" she said, her voice quaking.

"*The real reason you didn't tell your husband about the stalker is that you were afraid he'd think you were cheating on him again.*"

"*That's crazy.*"

"*You were cheating on him again, weren't you? That's why you didn't tell the police you were being stalked.*"

"*You're so wrong.*"

"*That's why you didn't tell your husband you were being stalked.*"

"*Not true.*"

"*What happened, Sally? You wouldn't leave your husband, and your boyfriend got mad?*"

"*No.*"

"*So mad that he started stalking you?*"

"*No.*"

"*So mad that he killed your daughter?*"

"*No, no!*"

Sally was practically in tears. No one offered her a tissue. She dabbed her eye with her sleeve.

"*Come clean, Sally. The truth has already come out in your polygraph. There were signs of deception on one other answer you gave.*"

"*Which one?*"

"*You answered no to the following question: Do you know who killed your daughter?*"

Her mouth fell open. "*You think I was lying about that?*"

"*It's right here in the examiner's report. Your response shows signs of deception.*"

"*Then the machine is wrong,*" she said.

"*Or you're lying,*" said Rudsky.

Sally looked stunned, as if she could barely speak: "*Are you suggesting that I'm covering for the man who killed my own daughter?*"

"*Let me tell you exactly what I'm saying.*"

Jack watched as Rudsky's hand suddenly reached for the video camera. With the push of a button, the screen went black.

"There's no more?" said Kelsey.

"Try fast forwarding a few frames."

She hit the button on the machine, but the tape was blank. "Looks like that's the end of it," said Kelsey. "Though figuratively speaking, I'm definitely starting to get the picture."

"Me, too," said Jack in a hollow voice. "And it isn't very pretty."

Twenty-six

Kelsey had an afternoon class, so Jack drove her to the University of Miami law school. They rode in silence most of the way, listening to the radio. According to "News at the Top of the Hour," a suspected terrorist was detained at the Port of Miami and would face deportation.

"Ooooh," said Kelsey, a tinge of sarcasm in her voice. "Deportation. Now they're really getting tough."

"Yeah," said Jack, scoffing. "You'd think they'd caught a puppy peeing on the rug. 'Bad terrorist. Bad, bad, bad, bad, bad. Now go back to your training camp and don't come out until you've learned how to sneak into this country properly.'"

She offered a little nervous laughter that was symptomatic of the times, and then they continued in silence down fraternity row, past the fields of suntanned and shirtless college boys playing flag football. It was as if they both needed a little time to absorb the videotape. Not until Jack pulled into the drop-off circle in front of the law library and shifted into Park did they seem ready to talk about what was really on their minds.

"Jack, what do you think happened when Rudsky turned off that camera?"

"I'm sure he threatened her. Obstruction of justice, accessory after the fact to murder, and anything else he could think of."

"Right. He threatened to throw her in jail unless . . . unless what?"

"Unless she told him who killed her daughter."

"That's where it all falls apart in my view. Maybe it's because I'm a mother, but it's hard for me to accept that Sally would have refused to identify the man who killed her child, no matter how torrid the love affair. Assuming there even was a love affair."

"What about Susan Smith?"

"Who?"

"The married woman from South Carolina who locked her two sons in her car and sent them to the bottom of a lake so that she would be childless and more appealing to her lover."

"Do you honestly think Sally Fenning was anywhere near that extreme?"

"If Tatum Knight is to be believed, she was extreme enough to hire someone to kill her."

"That was five years after her daughter was brutally murdered. You're talking about a whole different time of her life. Before a tragedy like that, she was probably an entirely different woman."

Jack glanced out the window, thinking. "That's a valid point. But there are other reasons for Sally to have refused to identify her killer, reasons other than a sick sense of love."

"Such as?"

"She might have been *afraid* to identify him. Like you said, he'd stabbed her already, murdered her daughter. Maybe she feared he would come back to finish the job."

"Is that what Rudsky was driving at in the videotape?" asked Kelsey.

"It's not clear. Maybe even Rudsky wasn't sure if she was intentionally covering up for her lover or if she refused to identify the killer out of fear. Either way, he was clearly convinced by the polygraph results that, one, Sally was having an affair, and two, she knew the identity of her daughter's killer."

Kelsey shook her head and said, "If she was in fact covering up for her lover, then Sally was truly despicable."

"Anyone would agree on that point. But if Rudsky had it all wrong—if she wasn't covering up for anybody, and if she wasn't even having an affair—then Sally was maligned in a way no mother should ever be maligned."

"And if Deirdre Meadows was intent upon repeating those same accusations in her book, she was just as guilty as the prosecutor."

"Which might explain why they both ended up on Sally's list of beneficiaries. Her list of mortal enemies."

Silence fell between them. Kelsey checked her watch, gauging her time till class started. "So where does this lead us?" she asked.

"It all comes back to the same question. Were they her enemies because their vicious accusations were false? Or because they exposed the ugly truth?"

"How do you suppose we get an answer to that?"

"The only way I know. Keep digging."

Kelsey waved to three women walking past the car. Classmates, Jack presumed. "I'd better get going," she said. "Call me if there's anything more I can do."

"I will. Actually, I'll probably see you tomorrow night."

"Tomorrow night?"

"Yeah, when I pick up Nate. I promised to take him for pizza at the Big Cheese on Friday."

She clunked her head like a dunce. "I'm sorry. I forgot to tell you. My mother invited him over to the condo for some kind of grandkids shuffleboard marathon or something."

"Boy, is *that* going to cost you."

"Oh yes. Big time." She gave a little laugh, then cut her eyes and said, "I guess that means you're free tomorrow night, huh?"

"Evidently."

"So . . ."

"So what?"

She flashed a thin, mischievous smile. "Why don't we do dinner?"

"You mean without Nate?"

"Yes, a date."

Jack's mouth opened, but his words were on a few-second delay.

"Something wrong?" asked Kelsey. "You suddenly look as if I just asked you to be the food tester for Saddam Hussein."

"This just takes you and me to another level."

"That's sort of the idea."

"And it probably would be a great idea, under different circumstances. But I thought we had sort of an unspoken understanding that this is something we'd never do. For Nate's sake."

"I thought the same thing, until you started teasing me at Just Books. You seemed so amused by the fact that I'd somehow given Martin the impression that we were dating. It got me to thinking, maybe it's not such a crazy notion."

Jack took a breath. He recalled the conversation, and he'd regretted it. At the time it had seemed innocent enough, just a divorced guy with wounded self-esteem having a little flirtatious banter with an attractive young woman. He hadn't expected it to go anywhere, but in hindsight he could see where she might have misread it. "Kelsey, look, I'm sorry."

"Just hear me out on this, okay? With most guys I date, being a single mom is a liability. First, we have to get to like each other, and then I have to hope he likes my son. You're the opposite. Here's this great guy who totally adores my son. And I'm *not* supposed to date you because—because *why?*"

"Because if it doesn't work out . . ."

"I'm tired of living my life that way, Jack, afraid of what's not going to work out. What if it *does* work out?"

Jack considered it, allowed himself the luxury of thinking that he wasn't forever resigned to carrying around the battle scars of his divorce. "I can't deny that I've wondered about it. In the abstract, anyway."

"One date. We don't even have to tell Nate about it. If it doesn't feel right, we promise to be grown-ups about it and go back to where we were. Deal?"

He smiled tentatively, just enough to give her an opening. She took his hand and shook on behalf of both of them.

"Where do you want to go?" he asked.

"You pick. I like surprises."

"Works for me."

"Yes, I do. But we'll get past that."

"No, I meant the surprise thing works for me. I wasn't trying to pull a power play by reminding you that you work for —"

She put her finger to his lips, shushing him. "I know what you meant. Now stop being such a doofus, or I might change my mind and let you kill another Friday night with your buddy Theo." She smiled and got out of the car, then gave a little wink and closed the door.

Friday night with Theo, he thought, trying not to enjoy the view too much as he watched Kelsey walk to class.

That works for me, too.

Miguel Rios fumbled for the key to his front door. He'd enjoyed one too many margaritas with dinner and didn't realize how strong they were until it was too late. His girlfriend had offered to drive him home and spend the night, but he'd nixed that plan. She'd been coming on way too strong ever since he'd told her that he was in the running for a forty-six-million-dollar inheritance, apparently not the least bit bothered that the money would come from his ex-wife.

On the fourth try, he found the lock, turned the key, and pushed the door open. The mailbox was right beneath the porch light, and it was stuffed with at least two days' deliveries. He grabbed a handful and went inside. His legs were tired from pedaling all day, one of the drawbacks of being a bicycle cop. He plopped in the recliner, put his feet up, switched on the television with the remote, and sifted through the stack of mail. He put the junk aside and opened a letter with no return address.

Inside was a typewritten note on a single sheet of paper. It was addressed to no one in particular, just a general salutation, "To my fellow beneficiaries." The message read:

> This is not a threat. I am simply sharing information with the rest of
> you. All of the beneficiaries under Sally Fenning's will are in grave
> danger. I mean all of us, including me. I wish I could say more, but

all I can say is this: If you choose to stay in this game, be careful. Be extremely careful. *Please take this very seriously.*

The letter wasn't signed, but there was a typed name at the bottom. Miguel read it, then picked up the phone and dialed his lawyer. He was routed to voice mail, with a cheery instruction from Parker Aimes's secretary to speak clearly after the tone.

"This is Miguel Rios calling about the Sally Fenning estate. I wanted to let you know about a letter I received in the mail. It's from Alan Sirap. The sixth beneficiary."

Twenty-seven

It was time to find out more about Alan Sirap.

Jack had received a phone call from Tatum on Thursday night, and by mid-morning Friday, Jack had confirmed that all five of the other beneficiaries had received the same letter. Still, no one seemed to know who Mr. Sirap was, or at the very least they were unwilling to share what they knew. Jack set up a lunch meeting with Vivien Grasso. As the lawyer who had drafted Sally's will and as personal representative of her estate, Vivien was charged with the responsibility of locating all the heirs. In light of the latest letter, Jack wanted an update on how the search for Alan Sirap was going.

"This is one strange letter," said Vivien. Jack had shown her Tatum's copy, and she'd read it quickly.

Jack looked up from his menu, which he was only pretending to read. Old Lisbon was his favorite Portuguese restaurant in Miami, and for lunch he always ordered the house specialty, grilled squid and french fries. It wasn't for everybody, but it was definitely for anybody who was tired of the typical calamari *à la Friday's*—breaded, deep-fried, and drowning in enough marinara sauce to make a hockey puck taste good.

"Strange is one word for it," said Jack. "Scary comes to mind as well."

She smiled wryly and handed back the letter. "Come now, Jack. Something tells me that your client doesn't scare easily."

"I have a feeling yours didn't either."

"Sally had a rough life. But yes, she was pretty tough, too."

"How well did you really know her?"

"How well do we know any of our clients?"

"Some better than others."

Vivien squeezed a wedge of lemon into her iced tea. "I deal with very wealthy clients. Most of them guard their privacy rather fiercely. Sally was no different."

"So what you're saying is—"

"I knew her well enough to draft her will. That's what I'm saying."

A waiter brought them fresh baked bread and a dish of olive oil for dipping. Jack tore off a chunk but kept talking. "Vivien, you've known my father for years. You've known me almost as long. So you know I'm on the level when I tell you that anything you say here is just between you, me, and the grilled squid, right?"

"Oh boy. Here it comes."

Jack smiled a little, then turned serious. "Was it Sally Fenning's intention to construct some sick game of survival of the greediest?"

She drummed her nails on the table, as if debating how to answer— or perhaps *whether* to answer.

"I'm not trying to put you in a bad spot," said Jack. "But some weird stuff is happening."

"It's okay. To be honest, the last thing I want is for you or, worse, your father to think that I would allow myself to be part of a bloody vengeance campaign. So let me put it this way. I concede that drafting Sally's will so that everything goes to the survivor of six potential heirs is certainly unorthodox. But I never imagined that threats and bodily injury were part of Sally's plan."

"Then what was her plan?"

"This is the way I understood it. For Sally, there was no bright side to money. When she needed it, she didn't have it. When she had it, she wasn't happy."

"That much I seem to have figured out."

"As far as she was concerned, money was a curse. So she decided that when she died, she'd share the curse with people she didn't like.

The way we structured her will, each of Sally's heirs would live their whole life thinking they were just a heartbeat away from inheriting forty-six million dollars. But only one of them would ever see the money—and by the time they got it, he or she would probably be too old to enjoy it. It was vindictive, but it wasn't criminal."

"What did she tell you about her enemies—the heirs?"

"Names, addresses, Social Security numbers. Except for Alan Sirap. For him, I just got a name. Sally promised to provide an address and a Social Security number, but she never got around to it. Frankly, with a healthy twenty-nine-year-old woman as a client, I wasn't exactly hounding her every day to get it to me. The will was valid without it."

"From what you're saying, I assume that you didn't do a background check on any of the beneficiaries in Sally's will."

"No, I didn't."

"So you have no idea why my client was named as a beneficiary."

"Not really. Do you?"

Jack got out the proverbial tap shoes, unable to tell her that Tatum was a hit man. "Based on what I've learned about the others, I can only surmise that Sally considered him an enemy."

"Sally didn't explain in any great detail *why* she chose Tatum Knight or any of the others."

"That didn't strike you as odd?"

"If a client doesn't want to lay out every dirty little detail about her chosen heirs, it's frankly none of my business. It was Sally's prerogative to leave her money to whomever she wished, even her enemies. Even if it meant disinheriting her own sister."

"Rene, right?" Jack had been meaning to follow up on Sally's sister ever since her name had come up in the meeting with Sally's bodyguard, but it wasn't easy for a sole practitioner with other paying clients to jump right on top of every little lead.

"Right. She's Sally's only surviving relative."

A busboy came by and refilled their water glasses. Jack waited for him to leave, then asked, "What do you know about her?"

"I know that Sally worked side by side on a humanitarian mission with her sister for some time in Africa."

"When?"

"Before Sally remarried."

"Did they have a falling out?"

"Not that I know of. The only impression I ever gained from Sally was that she loved her sister dearly."

"But she left her nothing in her will."

"Go figure."

Jack glanced out the window. The passing cars on busy Coral Way were just a blur. "I guess vengeance can be sweet," he said in a detached voice. "But why would a woman with no other family completely disinherit a sister whom she loved?"

"I can't answer that," said Vivien.

"There's probably only one person alive who can. Does Rene still live in Africa?"

"Yes. I sent her a notice of Sally's death."

"So you have an exact address for her?"

"At the office. She's in Côte d'Ivoire."

Jack thought for a second. "I've always wanted to go to Africa."

"Now you've got an excuse to go."

The waiter returned to their table and asked, "Are you ready to order?"

"I wonder if I should update my shots," said Jack.

The waiter shot an indignant look.

"No, I'm sorry, I meant . . . Oh, never mind."

Twenty-eight

In the spirit of China Grill, Smith & Wollensky, Joe Allen's, and countless other successful New York eating establishments, Restaurant Nobu seemed to work even better with a Miami Beach suntan.

Nobu was Jack's choice for his first date with Kelsey, which seemed perfect: no-pressure Japanese dining, a lively atmosphere, and a typical South Beach crowd that made it impossible for two people to run out of things to talk about. For her part, Kelsey had also gone with a sure thing, wearing black on black with simple gold jewelry, a different look from the head-turning red dress she'd worn on their business sortie to Club Vertigo. Yet Jack found her even more captivating tonight, not because he hadn't noticed how beautiful she was before, but because he no longer felt forced to overlook the little things that would bring a smile to his face long after the evening's end. The way her hair caressed her neck. The little turn of her head whenever she smiled. Jack was still her employer, and she would always be the mother of his "Little Brother" Nate. But this was a real date, or at least a trial run, and he had to appreciate the way she was trying so hard to make it seem as though nothing else mattered.

"I have a secret to tell you," she said.

It was 10:40 P.M. and they were back where they'd started three hours earlier, standing at her front door. "What?" asked Jack.

"I have a fifteen-year-old baby-sitter."

"Why is that a secret?"

"She has to be home at eleven, which is exactly why I hired her."

"What do you mean?"

"She was my excuse, in case I had second thoughts. You might say let's go get a drink somewhere, and this made it possible for me to look you in the eye and truthfully say I had to be home by eleven."

"Oh."

"Don't look so glum. Now I wish I'd hired her older sister."

Jack smiled. "I'm glad you had a nice time. I did too."

"We still have a few minutes on the baby-sitter clock." She glanced at the porch swing and said, "You want to sit for a few minutes?"

"Sure."

Jack followed her across the porch. It was a small swing, probably built for her and Nate. They were seated side by side, looking out on the lawn, the palm trees and flower beds brightened by the moonlight. A gentle breeze stirred the oak leaves, and it sounded like the ocean.

"I can't remember the last time I was in one of these," said Jack, putting a little oomph into his kick.

"It's a porch swing, not the space shuttle, Jack."

"Sorry."

"It's okay."

She gently patted the back of his hand, and she didn't pull back. The soft pads of her fingertips and the smooth palm of her hand were lying on top of his. With the slow turn of his wrist, their fingers interlaced. It was a little thing, but it felt like much more.

"That's nice," he said.

"It is, isn't it?"

The swing continued to rock, and they enjoyed each other's company in silence. Finally, Jack said, "I don't mean to talk shop—"

"Then don't."

"This is only part work-related. I'm actually excited about it. I'm going to Africa."

"Why?"

"Sally's sister lives there. I want to talk to her. But, mainly, I just want to go. I think it'll be fun."

"Where?"

"Côte d'Ivoire. That's French for Ivory Coast."

"I know. I speak a little French."

"Great. Maybe you can teach me a few things. French is the official language there."

"Do you speak any at all?"

"Not a word. Unless you count the lyrics to 'Lady Marmalade,' You know, that old Patti LaBelle song. *Voulez-vous crochet avec moi?*"

Kelsey laughed. Jack asked, "What's so funny?"

"It's *coucher*, not *crochet*. You just changed 'Do you want to go to bed with me?' to 'Do you want to knit with me?'"

They laughed together. The silence that followed was not unpleasant, like an unspoken admission that each of them was giving serious thought to what it might be like to go "knitting" with the other. Their eyes met, and Jack felt his lips move slowly toward hers.

A noise from the house startled them. They turned simultaneously, only to catch a brief glimpse of Nate's face in the window, followed by the telling sway of vertical blinds.

"Nathan, you had better not be awake," said Kelsey.

They could hear him giggling as he ran away. Kelsey smiled at Jack and said, "So, you actually *want* to date a single mom?"

He hesitated. It felt right on one level, but he still had his reservations. "We have to think about Nate."

"You're so good with him. I really like that."

"He's a great kid."

"He is, but I'm talking about you. I've met several Big Brother volunteers. Seems to me, some do it because it makes them feel good about themselves, like they're giving back and doing their civic duty. But the best ones just really like kids."

"I'm probably in the latter group."

"That's what has me wondering. Where does that come from?"

"I'm not sure. My ex-wife and I never had kids, but it wasn't because we didn't want them."

"I'm sorry. I didn't mean for the question to become *that* personal."

"It's okay. I'm not one of those guys who goes around thinking I'd still be married if only we'd brought children into our failing marriage."

"It doesn't work. I can vouch for that."

"I do want kids someday, though."

She smiled and said, "Wondering what the world would be like with a Jack Junior in it?"

"Actually . . . aw, skip it."

"Skip what?"

"Well, this isn't exactly an even trade for the little secret you told me about hiring a fifteen-year-old baby-sitter, but there already is a Jack Junior, so to speak."

"What?"

"The woman I dated before I married Cindy gave up a baby for adoption. She says he was mine. I didn't even know about him until about a year ago."

"She told you after you and Cindy were married?"

"Long after."

"Wow. That's quite an announcement. 'Hi, I'm back, what have you been up to all these years, by the way I had your baby.'"

"It was a definite surprise."

"Have you figured out how old the boy would be now?"

"About Nate's age, actually."

"Do you think you'll ever meet him?"

"I doubt it. But if ever I do, Nate has certainly been good practice."

She withdrew her hand. "Practice?"

Jack saw the expression on her face and said, "That's probably not the right word."

"No. In fact, I'd say it's a pretty lousy word."

"I'm sorry. All I meant was that Nate's a typical mischievous boy who has prepared me for just about anything."

"Which sounds a lot like practice."

"Kelsey, come on. You know how much Nate means to me."

She got off the swing and walked to the porch rail. Jack jumped down and went to her, but she didn't turn around. "Hey," he said, speaking to the back of her head. She kept looking toward the lawn, no response.

"Nate is *not* practice," he said.

"Am I?"

"What?"

She turned and faced him. "Timing is so important in a relationship, don't you think?"

"Of course."

"Jack, be honest. How many women have you dated since your divorce?"

"I've been fixed up a few times."

"So I'm the first woman you've really pursued?"

"Pursued?" he said, his voice with a little more edge than intended. "In all fairness, Kelsey, this was really more your idea than mine."

"Well excuse me for putting a gun to your head."

"You didn't —" he stopped in mid-sentence, then brought a hand to his forehead, confused. "What just happened here? One minute we're sitting on the porch swing holding hands, the next—I don't know what."

The front door opened just wide enough for the baby-sitter to stick her head out and say, "I'm really sorry, Kelsey, but if I'm not home by eleven-fifteen, my parents won't let me sit for you anymore."

"Don't apologize. If Mr. Swyteck leaves now, you'll be home in plenty of time. You ready, Jack?"

He'd agreed earlier to drop off the sitter on his way home. "I guess so."

The girl tiptoed past them and continued down the steps. Jack looked at Kelsey and said, "Can we talk more about this, please?"

"I'll call you."

"When?"

"Soon."

They were standing just a few feet apart, but neither one moved, as if it now seemed awkward that just moments earlier they'd been headed toward a good night kiss. Kelsey gave him a tight smile and said simply, "Good night, Jack."

She went inside, and Jack waited for her to look back, catch his eye, and telegraph some sign of encouragement. It didn't come. He turned away as the door closed, then caught up with the baby-sitter in the driveway, who was peering out impishly from beneath her bangs.

"Sorry I spoiled your moment, Mr. Swyteck."

He scratched his head with the car key as he glanced back at Kesley's house. "Don't worry. About the only thing I'm sure of is that it wasn't you who spoiled it."

Twenty-nine

I'm going to Africa with you," said Theo.

Jack had taken a detour after dropping off the baby-sitter. Theo and his band were playing their Friday night gig at a jazz club on Washington Avenue. Jack caught him on his midnight break seated at the end of a long bar, though he'd almost walked right by him in the dim lighting. It was the perfect ambience for the after-midnight crowd, scores of flickering candles in a variety of shapes and sizes in one elaborate candelabra after another. Theo was picking at a blob of wax that had dripped and hardened onto the bar top.

"You are *not* coming to Africa," said Jack.

"Look, you're a hopelessly white lawyer headed for a country of sixteen million Africans whose average weekly wage wouldn't pay for the bowl of peanuts I just finished. You should be jumping up and down to have a guy like me at your side."

"All right. We'll talk about it."

"That's what you said yesterday. It's done. If you go, I go." He raised his glass in a toast, and after several long moments of consideration, Jack reciprocated with his beer bottle.

"But I'm not paying for your plane ticket," said Jack.

"Got that covered for both of us. Friend of a friend flies a company jet for oil executives twice a month. It's never more than half full. We leave this Tuesday. All you have to do is pay for our tickets to Houston."

"What kind of plane we talking about?" Jack asked with obvious skepticism.

"Jack, really. Would I treat you like anything less than the rock star you are?"

"That's what they told Buddy Holly."

Jack's cell phone rang, and he recognized the incoming number as Kelsey's. "Be right back," he told Theo, and then he hurried across the crowded bar to a relatively quiet spot near the back staircase.

"Hi." He had the phone on one ear and his finger pressed to the other to drown out the drone of nightclub noises from the next room.

"I'm sorry about the way I overreacted," she replied.

"It's okay. I'm glad you called."

"Nate loves you so much. He's never had anyone like you in his life. His father and I divorced when he was three."

"Like I said before. He's the best."

"That's why I'm just not sure about us."

Jack stopped pacing. "That's what I told you in my car when you suggested we have dinner."

"I know, and we should have listened to your instincts, not mine."

"Why the sudden reversal?"

"When you and I were sitting on the porch swing, and I looked back and saw Nate's little face in the window, my heart sank. He was so happy to see us together. But then another image flashed in my head, one of me a month or three months from now trying to explain to him why Jack doesn't come around anymore."

"But you said it yourself at the beginning. You were tired of living your life preparing for the worst-case scenario."

"Sometimes I do get tired of it."

"It's like my friend Theo always says. There's two kinds of people in this world, risk takers and—" He stopped himself. Risk takers and shit takers sounded okay when belting back beers with Theo, but it seemed a little crude here. "And not risk takers," he said, grimacing at the lack of poetry in his improvisation. "Anyway, you know what I'm saying."

"Yes. But I'm Nate's mother. I have to be careful about the risks I take."

"I can't disagree with that."

"Then you understand?"

"I do. And I don't. I guess what I'm trying to say is that I wasn't expecting to have such a great time with you tonight."

"It's complicated, I know."

"Until things went sour on your front porch, I was actually starting to think *you* had the right idea. I've been fixed up with two women since my divorce. Both had middle-schoolers who frankly scared the hell out of me. If I'm going to be dating single moms, why not date the one with the world's greatest kid?"

"There's definitely two sides to this, but—"

"But now you think my first instinct was right. Leave it to a couple of advocates," he said, scoffing. "We've persuaded each other to reverse roles."

"Look, we're not going to resolve this tonight. Maybe it's a good thing you're going to Africa. It gives us time to think."

"Right. A little time is a good thing."

"So we're agreed? We just put things on hold for a while, go back to normal."

Jack had the frustrating feeling that the right words were floating out there somewhere between them, but damned if he could find them. "Okay. Normal it is."

"Thank you. Have a safe trip, okay?"

"I will."

"Good night."

"Good night." He flipped the cell phone shut and sat on the step, alone. Already, he didn't like the feeling of "normal."

Thirty

The urinal in the men's room was busted again, and two guys were busily gratifying each other in the only stall, so Theo took the back exit into the alley behind the club. He found a dark, suitable spot between two parked cars, only to find that someone had found the very same spot minutes before he had.

"Son of a bitch," he said, stepping out of it.

He continued down the dark alley, though he was suddenly thinking more of his talk with Jack than his bursting bladder. He hadn't exactly told his friend the whole story about why he was going to Africa. Sure, it would be fun, and even more sure, Jack could use a guy like Theo to keep him out of trouble. But Theo's real agenda was much more personal. The police were zooming in on his brother as a suspect in Sally Fenning's murder, and Theo alone knew the depth of his debt to Tatum.

The alley was getting darker with each step he took, and Theo finally stopped and looked around. On either side were the unadorned backs of buildings—bars, drugstores, Laundromats. A half block ahead, the lights from Sixteenth Street were a big glowing dot in the darkness, like the light at the end of the proverbial tunnel. The walls were cinder blocks painted beige and white. Every door and window was covered with black security bars. If he narrowed his eyes, Theo could almost see one set of hands after another gripping those iron bars, hands without faces, hands he'd linked to anxious voices from within boxes during his years on death row. Those were memories he would have liked to flush. But with his own brother in trouble, and with the barred doors and windows all around him, his mind drifted back to a night on death row that he'd truly thought would be his last hours on earth.

Theo sat on one side of the prison glass; his brother, Tatum, on the other. His brother seemed taken by his baldness.

"What happened to your hair, man?"

"It's just what they do," said Theo. The prison barber had already shaved his head and ankles so that there would be a smooth connection between his flesh and the deadly voltage of the electric chair.

"Swyteck is starting to scare me," said Tatum. "What the hell is taking him so long this time? He ain't never let it go this far before."

"He's doing what he can. Sometimes you just run out of shit to throw against the wall."

"Then get a new lawyer."

"They don't give out new lawyers the night before an execution."

"But you need more time. *I* need more time."

From the day of Theo's sentencing, Tatum had vowed to track down every last member of the Grove Lords, threaten them, beat them, crack their skulls—whatever it took to find the one who had gone into that convenience store and really killed that cashier.

Theo said, "I appreciate all you done for me, but—"

"But nothin'. Don't you start with that good-bye shit now."

"We gotta face facts."

"The facts is, you didn't do it."

"You think I'm the first innocent man ever to sit on death row?"

"Sittin' here is one thing. They can't execute you, damn it."

"They can, Tatum. And they will."

Tatum checked the clock on the wall. "Where the hell is that lawyer of yours?"

"He's supposed to call in about a half hour."

"Good. I want to talk to him."

"What for?"

"I need to know if this is really it."

"We'll know soon enough."

"Don't say that. Because if he's out of ideas, I got one for him."

"What?"

With a pen, he scribbled onto the notepad in front of him. Then he leaned closer to the glass and turned the notepad so that Theo could see it. It read, "Let's just say I did it."

Theo looked his brother in the eye. "Say what?"

"I'm shit compared to you," he said, his voice shaking. "You got a brain in your head, man. You could be somebody. So let's just say it was me who done it. We look a little alike. That eyewitness was pretty shaky. Maybe she got it wrong, coulda' mixed us up, you know?"

"You would do this for me?"

"You're my little brother, man. You and me—aw, shit, don't make me say it. We're all we got, you know?"

Theo felt a knot in his stomach, wishing he could break through the glass between them. "Thanks, bro'," he said as he pressed his fist to the window. Tatum did the same from the other side, the prison handshake.

"What do you say?" asked Tatum.

"You're awesome, totally. But even if I was gonna let you try, it's just too late."

"Damn you, stop sayin' it's too late."

"It would never work anyway."

"I'll make it work," he said, his anger rising. "I can make those bastards believe."

Behind Theo a door opened, and the dull rumble of club noises rolled into the alley. He turned and saw a man step into the weak glow of a security light by the Dumpster.

"Jack?"

"I thought I saw you walk out this way. Your band's gearing up for the next set."

Theo started toward him and said, "Guess I lost track of time."

"What are you doing out here?"

He put his arm around Jack's shoulder and walked him to the door. "Just strollin' down memory lane, buddy. And you really had to be there to know what a shitty place that is."

"I *was* there, remember?"

"Absolutely. I remember everybody who was there. And I do mean everybody."

They went back inside the club, the security bars clanging as the door closed behind them.

PART THREE

Thirty-one

Côte d'Ivoire is about the size of Germany or New Mexico. Jack's problem was that getting *from* Germany *to* New Mexico is a heck of a lot easier than getting from the airport in Abidjan to the grasslands of the north.

"I don't do puddle jumpers," said Jack.

"You what?" said Theo.

"I just don't. I've had some bad experiences, and I just don't do them anymore."

"You represent a badass like my brother, and you're afraid of flying on a little plane?"

"No, I'm afraid of *crashing* on a little plane. Got no problem with flying."

And so began the ground segment of their journey, a half-day bus ride on the heels of a seventeen-hour international flight. The road system of Côte d'Ivoire is among the best in West Africa, so it might have been bearable had the nine-hour trip to Korhogo been the end of the line. Unfortunately, Sally's sister wasn't in Korhogo, which surprised Jack. Before leaving Miami, he'd managed to contact her by e-mail, and from an Internet café in town she'd confirmed the meeting. A nice retired couple who ran the Children First headquarters gave Jack the bad news.

"She's gone to Odienné," said Mr. Roberts.

"Oh, damn."

"No, Odienné," said Mrs. Roberts.

"I know, I meant . . . When is she coming back?"

"Don't know. There was a little medical emergency she volunteered for."

"How do we get to Odienné?"

It was an indisputable fact that any trip, no matter how well planned, no matter how experienced the travelers, had the potential for disaster. It was also indisputable that the trouble usually began with a question like, "How do we get to . . ."

They rented an old Land Rover in Korhogo and took turns driving, headed due west. Roads between most major towns in Côte d'Ivoire were paved, with one major exception. The road from Korhogo to Odienné was paved only as far as Boundiali, a town whose name means "drum dried in the sun," but which might have been more aptly named "dust so thick you can't even see the goat standing next to you." If all roads were like the last hundred miles from Boundiali to Odienné, the wheel might never have been invented.

They reached the outskirts of Odienné just before sunset. In two hours they'd seen only one other traveler, a skinny, naked boy riding a brown-and-white cow. On one level it seemed as though they were in the middle of nowhere, yet Jack could appreciate why leaders of another era had chosen this site as the capital of the entire Kabadou-gou Empire. To the west, the Dienguélé range rippled over to the Guinean border. To the east rose Mont Tougoukoli, an eight-hundred-meter peak that was quite impressive, if only because it rose from the midst of seemingly endless grasslands. Jack pulled off to the side of the road, giving them a moment to shake off the dust and savor the view before driving into the city.

"My back is killing me."

"Don't blame me," said Theo.

"Nobody's blaming anybody for anything."

"Which only proves what a great guy I am."

"What?"

"Next time we're hoppin' a plane from Abidjan. I don't care if I have to pistol-whip you and tie you to the fucking wing."

Jack cooled his face with a splash of water from his canteen. Theo was working on his second giant liter of Bock beer, which had been ice cold when they left Korhogo, but an afternoon temperature of thirty-four degrees Celsius had taken off the chill in short order.

"You think we'll find her?" asked Jack.

"Yup."

"How can you be so sure?"

"Cuz if we don't, you'll bitch all the way home like a teenage girl, sayin' this trip was all for nothin'. So get it through your head right now, Jacko. We ain't leavin' till we find her."

"That was truly powerful," said Jack. "Have you considered a career in motivational speaking?"

Theo sucked down the last of his beer and pretended to scratch the side of his head with just one finger, the middle one, fully extended.

They entered the city around six-thirty, minutes after the largely Muslim population of forty-seven thousand had finished the sunset prayer. It was a historic agricultural town, but the grand mosquée was all that remained of its architectural treasures. The rest of the old quarters had been hastily razed as part of a radical urbanization plan that replaced shady streets and traditional old homes with utterly unremarkable modern buildings, one more facet of the development-crazy mentality that cost Côte d'Ivoire more of its rain forest than any other country on earth.

"What's that smell?" asked Jack.

"Like charcoal," said Theo.

They drove to Hôtel les Frontières, one of the best hotels in town, which was *not* where Rene Fenning was staying. Her colleagues back at Children First headquarters in Korhogo had drawn a blank on where she was staying, and they could only tell Jack that she was at some joint right next to Hôtel les Frontières. It turned out to be Hôtel Touristel, which catered mostly to budget travelers on their way to or from Mali. The clerk behind the desk was not exactly fluent in English, but he was conversant enough.

"Was fire in market three day ago," he said.

"That explains the smell," said Theo.

"Dr. Rene come here to make help. Come. Follow."

He led Jack and Theo outside, down a dusty walkway to the back of the building, where a large cafeteria had been converted into a hospital. About a half-dozen beds lined one wall, another dozen cots lined another wall, and dozens of brightly colored woven mats covered the floor. Most of them were empty, as if the emergency had passed. Jack counted eleven patients remaining, many with bandaged hands or arms.

A woman wearing a makeshift surgical mask, the only white woman in the room, approached them and said, "You must be Jack Swyteck."

"Yes. This is my friend, Theo."

She removed the scarf from around her face, and Jack realized it wasn't a surgical mask, but rather an appropriate covering for a woman in a Muslim community, particularly a blond American trying extra hard not to offend. "I'm Rene," she said as they shook hands. "You fellas mind stepping outside with me? You're a little dusty, and we're doing our best to keep down the risk of infection."

She led them out the back door. Night had fallen, and it surprised Jack how the temperature had dropped in such a short time since sunset.

"Sorry I had to skedaddle out of Korhogo on you," she said.

"That's all right. Obviously it was an emergency."

"The worst is over now. It took some doing, but we finally evacuated the most seriously injured to Abidjan."

"Bet they wouldn't have been afraid to fly," said Theo.

"Excuse me?"

"Ignore him," said Jack, shooting his friend a look that asked, "*Is nothing sacred?*"

Rene said, "Sorry for the way I look. I've hardly slept in two days. I know you've come a long way and would like to talk about Sally."

"We can do it in the morning," said Jack.

"Lunchtime would be so much better," she said with a weary smile.

"That's fine."

She said, "There's a *maquis* next door."

"What's a *maquis*?"

"You boys haven't been here long, have you? It's like a café. Let's meet there at noon."

"Great. See you then."

She smiled and went back inside. As the door closed behind her, Jack and Theo looked at one another, as if sharing the exact same thought.

"Wow," said Theo.

"Uncanny, isn't it? She looks exactly like her sister."

"Ten minutes in the shower, and she is an absolute knockout."

"Gee, all these years I thought you were shallow, and here you are, able to look past a woman's outer layer of sweat and see all the way down to her true, naked, dripping-wet worth."

"What the hell did you just say?"

"I said she looks pretty damn good even without a shower."

"That's what I thought you said."

"Come on," said Jack, walking toward the hotel, "let's get a room."

Thirty-two

"Where's your friend?" asked Rene.

She and Jack were at the *maquis*, the open-air café next to their hotel. It was the epitome of informal dining, just a smattering of rickety wood tables and benches in the sand. They were seated across from each other in the circle of shade beneath a thatched *paillote*. The air smelled of cooked fish and some kind of steaming carbohydrate, appetizing enough, though the buzzing flies and oppressive heat would take some getting used to. Jack was sweating just sitting there, though Theo had been right about Rene: A shower and a good night's sleep had vaulted her right into another league.

"Theo's still sleeping," he said.

"Jet lag?"

"More like jet *fuel*. He and a couple of Belgians on their way to Man were up late drinking something called *pitasi*."

She flashed a knowing smile, as if she'd been there. "African gin. Deadly stuff."

A waiter brought them sodas and recited the menu in French. Jack let Rene order for both of them, trusting that he wouldn't end up with boiled eye of impala.

"You and Theo make a pretty interesting friendship."

"I hear that a lot."

"Have you known each other long?"

"Pretty long. He was convicted of murder when he was a teenager.

I picked up the case on appeal, after he was on death row. You can get pretty close to someone after counting down the hours to their death five or six different times. Especially when they're innocent."

"So you got him off?"

"Guilty people get off. Theo got screwed, and we finally made it right."

She took a long drink of cola with no ice, enjoying it before it got too warm in the midday heat. "Is that your specialty? Death penalty work?"

"Not anymore. My first four years out of law school I worked at a place called the Freedom Institute. All death penalty work."

"Sounds pretty grim."

"Not as grim as some other things. I worked for a Wall Street firm the summer before I graduated from law school. On the last day, I walk into the elevator and punch forty-two, just like every day before. Then a young lawyer walks in behind me, punches forty-one, a little older guy walks in, punches forty-three, and finally a senior partner comes and—well, I don't know what she punched. I literally ran the hell out of there. I suddenly couldn't stomach the idea that this was going to be my life, day after day, walking into the same elevator, punching the same button, going to that same little box in the sky."

"I can relate."

"Really?"

"Look around. This isn't exactly a normal career step for someone who just busted her hump through a pediatric residency."

She had a great smile, Jack noticed, and he smiled back. He hadn't thought about it before, but they did have something seriously in common, both having chosen an unconventional start for their careers. He said, "If your experience is anything like mine was, I'm sure you have a lot of friends back home making plenty of money."

"Money was never what it was all about for me."

"Me neither, but . . ."

"But what?"

His expression turned more serious. "What about Sally?"

She let out a little sigh, as if she'd known that the conversation would land here eventually. "Sally was a very complex person."

"Were you two close?"

"Yes, most of the time."

"Most of the time?"

She shrugged and said, "We were sisters. We had our differences, we got over them."

"I understand she spent some time here with you."

"Yeah. I was a bit surprised she came, but I suppose in the last few years nothing should have surprised me."

"What do you mean?"

"Charity work in Africa is not exactly for Sally. Don't get me wrong. It's not for *most* people. But after her daughter was murdered, Sally just wanted to find a way to heal. She drifted from one extreme to the other, from partying to religion, from charity work to marrying a millionaire. In the end, I guess, nothing worked."

The waiter brought their food, a lumpy, grainy dish that looked like rice mixed with a little meat. Jack tried it with caution, but it was surprisingly tasty. "Good choice," he said. "I like it."

"Really? For most people spider monkey is an acquired taste."

"Huh?"

"Just kidding."

They shared a smile, then Jack turned serious again. "I'm really sorry about what happened to your sister, so let me apologize in advance for some of the questions I have to ask."

"I understand."

"This might sound like a weird question, but do you have any reason to believe that Sally would have killed herself?"

"Suicide? She was shot in her car while waiting at an intersection."

"I know. But what I'm really asking is, do you think it's possible that she hired someone to kill her?"

She looked away, but Jack could still see the troubled expression on her face. "I don't know. I have worried about her. She had a lot of issues, many of which I'm sure you already know about. Her money problems, the stalker, the murder of her daughter, her failed marriage."

"What about the book that the reporter from the *Miami Tribune* was writing? Do you know anything about that?"

She paused, then said, "I do. If there was one thing that I think could have driven Sally toward suicide, it would have been that book. Or not the book, per se, but its premise."

"What was your understanding of it?"

"Sally felt that she was being blamed for the fact that her daughter's killer was never caught. We talked a lot about that. She was having an awful time dealing with those accusations."

"Did you ever talk to her about the polygraph exam she took? I'm not insinuating anything, but my understanding is that it showed signs of deception when Sally answered no to the question, 'Do you know who killed your daughter?'"

"You of all people—someone who has done death penalty work— should know that lie detector tests are not infallible. In my view, if that test showed signs of deception, the machine was wrong."

"There was another area that the test said she was lying about. It had to do with some question about an extramarital affair."

"If you're asking me if Sally cheated on her husband, I don't know. She never told me about a lover. I never got any awkward phone calls from Miguel asking, 'Hey, did you and Sally really have dinner together last night?'—you know, the kind of checking up you'd expect from a husband if the wife was cheating."

"Let's assume she was having an affair. Was she the kind of person who would . . . how should I put this?"

"Who would cover up her own daughter's murder to protect her lover? No way. I know that's what the prosecutor said, and I know that's what Deirdre Meadows wanted to write in her stupid book. Excuse my language, but that is total bullshit. Katherine was Sally's life. She would never have covered up the murder of her own daughter out of love for some man."

"What about out of fear?" asked Jack.

"Meaning what?"

"Again, I'm not making any accusations. Just want to consider all the possibilities. Is it possible that Sally was afraid to identify the man who killed her daughter because she was afraid he might come back and kill her, too?"

"No. Absolutely not."

"How can you be so sure?"

"Because I know—knew—my sister."

"Did you know that she was being stalked before her daughter was murdered?"

"I found that out when everybody else did, after the murder."

"If she was being stalked, how can you completely dismiss the prosecutor's theory that this stalker was her lover and that Sally was afraid to identify him as the man who killed her daughter?"

"Because I know differently. I know that after the murder, Sally was obsessed with trying to find out who her stalker was. She was hunting him down."

Jack laid his fork on the table, absorbing what she'd just said. "I wasn't aware of that."

"It's true. Unless Sally was the world's greatest actress, I'm convinced that she had never even *met* her stalker, let alone fallen in love with him."

"How do you know she tried to hunt him down?"

"Like I said, Sally came to Africa to try to get over the past. She was terribly distraught over the fact that her daughter's killer had never been caught. Finally, over two years after the murder, her stalker contacted her by e-mail while she was here in Africa. We were down at the Internet café together, checking our e-mails, when she found it."

"What happened?"

"I scrolled through my messages, then Sally scrolled through hers. All of a sudden, she went completely white. I asked her what was wrong, and she said, 'It's a message from that same guy who was stalking me before.'"

"Did you read it?"

"Yes. It was benign, really. Just, 'Hello, how have you been?' You'd never know it was from a stalker. But I guess that's the way all communications from stalkers start out."

"What did Sally do?"

"She started corresponding with him. She even had one or two on-line chats. She had a plan."

"What was it?"

"She was trying to arrange a face-to-face meeting with him."

"In Africa?"

"No. She was willing to hop on the next plane back to Miami if he would meet with her."

"Wasn't that a little risky?"

"That's finally what I said to her: 'Hey, Sally, this could be the man who murdered Katherine and stuck a knife beneath your ribs.' Finally, I talked her into a safer approach."

"Which was what?"

"Just continue the on-line communications, see if he'd divulge some tidbit of information that might help the police find this guy."

"Did it work?"

"She tried. Week after week, doing her best to coax him into say-ing something about where he lived, what kind of car he drove, any-thing. He was smart, though. Never revealed much of anything about himself. He would always turn it around and ask questions about her: What she was doing, what she was wearing, how would she like a big you-know-what in the you-know-where?"

"Did she get anything at all out of him?"

"One night, she was totally frustrated. She threatened never to talk to him on-line again if he didn't tell her his name. He gave her a name, but Sally and I both knew it wasn't real."

"What was it?"

"Gosh, I don't remember. Kind of goofy-sounding."

"Take a minute. Think about it."

Her brow furrowed as the wheels turned in her head. "I think it was . . . no. Yeah, that's it. Alan Sirap."

Jack froze. "Alan S-I-R-A-P?"

"Yes. Do you know him?"

She obviously had no idea that Sirap was the name of Sally's sixth beneficiary, the "unknown" whom they'd been unable to identify. Jack settled back in his chair and said, "No, I don't know him. But I'm starting to feel like I do."

Thirty-three

After lunch Jack took a look under the hood.

He'd offered to drive Rene back to Korhogo, and her business was finished, so she'd gladly accepted. Unfortunately, their Land Rover had developed the automotive equivalent of a smoker's hack. Jack was no mechanic, but he'd learned a thing or two from his treasured old Mustang back home, enough to know that he should at least check the filters before returning down the same dusty road that had brought them to Odienné.

Theo was reclining in the passenger seat, his feet up on the dash, fanning himself with a folded newspaper. "You know, I think this is actually going to work."

Jack was inspecting an air filter, blowing out the dirt. "How would you know? You haven't lifted a finger all day."

"I'm not talking about the Rover. I'm talking about this *chapalo*."

"Your what?"

He raised the bottle and said, "It's a millet beer my buddies from Belgium gave me. They said it would cure my hangover."

"You think drinking more alcohol is the way to recover from drinking too much alcohol?"

"It's not just alcohol. It's *pimenté*, the way the Ivorians drink it. They add hot peppers to give it extra kick. All I know is that it's kicking the crap out of my hangover."

"Brilliant," said Jack. "Next time I overeat, I'll go stuff myself with a cheeseburger *pimenté*.

"Mmm. That sounds pretty good."

Jack shut the hood, walked around to the driver's side, and leaned into the open window. They were parked in the alley beside their hotel, taking advantage of the very limited shade of the two-story building. Jack asked, "Has your head stopped throbbing long enough for you to think about Alan Sirap?"

Theo sipped his beer and made a face, as if suffering from brief *pimenté* overload. "Doesn't make no sense."

"You mean Sally naming him as the sixth beneficiary?"

"This is the guy who stabbed Sally and killed her daughter. And Rene says her sister wanted to fly back to Miami and meet him? That's what don't make no sense."

"Well, Rene talked her out of that. She realized how dangerous it could be."

"Or how pointless it could be."

"How's that?" asked Jack.

"I'm thinking maybe the reason Sally wasn't afraid to meet him is that she was convinced he *wasn't* the man who killed her daughter."

"So, you're saying she was trying to prove a negative?"

"Huh?"

"The only reason she wanted to meet with the stalker was to rule him out as a possible suspect in the murder of her daughter."

"Possible, ain't it?" said Theo.

"Yeah. It's also possible that she knew exactly how dangerous he was, but she wasn't afraid of dying. Just like she wasn't afraid to die two years later when she tried to hire your brother to shoot her."

Theo squinted. The sun had moved just enough to create an annoying glare across the top of the windshield. "Either way, I guess she hated this Mr. Sirap as much as the other heirs."

"Of course," said Jack. "It was the stalking that led to the prosecutor's accusation that Sally was trying to cover up for the man who killed her daughter."

"Okay. That means five of the six heirs are connected to Sally's past life. Which leaves a big question about my brother: What's Tatum's connection?"

Jack looked away, then back. "Maybe he's the guy who made her whole scheme possible. She rewarded him for killing her."

"No, no, doesn't fit. She didn't leave this money to reward anybody. She was trying to punish people. The only reason for her to punish Tatum is not because he made her scheme possible by killing her, but because he almost made her plan impossible. He refused to kill her."

"But think about it. Doesn't it make it more of a punishment for the other five if she makes Tatum Knight the sixth beneficiary?"

"She don't need Tatum for that. She's already got Alan Sirap, or whatever his real name is. Why would she need two—"

Jack waited for his friend to finish, and then he realized why he'd stopped. "Two killers? Is that what you were going to say?"

Theo chugged his beer, then threw the bottle out the open window. It smashed against the brick wall. "Was you who said it, not me," he said angrily.

"Theo, come on."

"Come on nothin'. I didn't come all the way over here to prove my brother was guilty. It'd be nice if you could just pretend for ten minutes that you think he's innocent."

"I'm not—"

Theo got out and walked toward the hotel. Jack followed him inside, but Theo continued straight through the lobby and into the restaurant, probably for a replacement bottle of *chapalo*. Rene was at the front desk, checking out.

"What's wrong with him?" she asked.

"Bad case of pissed-off *pimenté*." Jack grabbed her suitcase and said, "We can load up."

He led her outside and put her suitcase in back. She took shotgun, and Jack sat behind the wheel. Even with the windows open, there was no breeze to cut the mid-afternoon sun. The simple act of carrying her bag to the car had caused Jack to break a sweat.

Rene was checking her reflection in the rearview mirror, putting up her hair for the long and hot ride ahead of them. Jack averted his eyes when she caught him staring, though she didn't seem to mind the attention.

With a bobby pin in her mouth she asked, "When are you going to get around to asking me?"

"Asking you what?"

"The question that must be on your mind: Why didn't Sally leave one red cent of her forty-six million dollars to her darling sister, Rene?"

Jack removed his dusty Australian-style hat and wiped the sweat from the back of his neck with a bandanna. "That's definitely near the top of my list."

"What are you waiting for?"

"Honestly, my plan was to give it a day or two, get to know you a little, so I could tell if you were lying or not. Then I was going to ask."

She cut her eyes and said, "You think you're going to get to know me *that* well, do you?"

"No, I wasn't implying—I'm a pretty quick study, is what I'm trying to say."

She seemed amused by his embarrassment. She took his hand and said, "Put your finger right here, would you, please?"

Jack pressed his finger to the center of a long, twisted braid at the back of her head. Rene tied it all together with a colorful piece of rope, the kind he'd seen African women selling on the streets of Korhogo. In seconds, she'd completely transformed her look, and somehow it came as no surprise to Jack that she was just as striking with all that hair tucked up under her hat.

She looked at Jack and asked, "Should I tell you now?"

"Tell me what?"

"About me and Sally. And her will."

"Now's good."

"You sure? I can wait, if you think you'll be a better judge of my truth-telling after we've bounced all the way back to Korhogo together."

She was clearly poking fun at his "plan." He said, "I'll assume the risk. Go ahead."

She took a breath, adopting a more serious air. "Truth is, Sally and I had a little falling out."

"How little?"

"Actually, not so little. We were barely speaking to each other after she left Africa."

"What happened?"

"Things were great while she was here. Everybody at Children First loved her. Two sisters working side by side for a good cause, fighting against the use of children as slave labor in the cocoa fields. I was truly sad when she decided to leave, and I thought I understood. Till about two months later. That's when I found out Sally was getting married."

"To her millionaire husband."

"Not just any millionaire. Sally's mega-millionaire actually owns a cocoa plantation that hires child slaves."

"I had no idea," he said, shaking his head. "Wow. You must have felt totally betrayed."

"I was furious."

"Are you still?"

"In hindsight, I realize that Sally was so screwed up over the murder of her daughter. Like I said before, she tried everything from working for charity to marrying for money. Nothing made her happy."

"Except for maybe one thing," said Jack.

"What's that?"

"Based on her will, I'd say revenge."

Their eyes met and held. Finally she said, "You're the first person I've talked to about this. I don't even think Sally's estate lawyer knows everything."

"Thank you for telling me. I was hoping that if I came all this way I'd get to the truth."

"Maybe it's time I got to the truth, too. The whole truth."

"How do you mean?"

"I was thinking about what you said yesterday, how you wondered if Sally might have reached such a low point in her life that she hired someone to shoot her. Other than myself, I can think of only one other person who would have known her well enough to answer that question."

"I'm listening."

A sparkle came to her eye, as if she were suddenly energized. "How'd you like to meet Sally's rich ex-husband?"

"I thought he lived in France."

"He's French, but he lives here most of the year."

"You can arrange a meeting?"

"No promises, but with your friend Theo tagging along, I think we can pull off just about anything. Brains, beauty, brawn. How can we miss?"

"I know which of us is the brawn. So that must make me—"

"The *baggage*," she said with a wink, as if to confirm that she was two of the three. "Now go get your brawny friend. Time's a-wasting."

Thirty-four

The road south was paved all the way to Man, a city of about 150,000 people in a breathtaking geographical setting. It was called the "town of eighteen peaks," perhaps an overly romantic appellation for a confusing and frankly unattractive collection of urban districts that were spread across a valley and surrounded by mountains. Jack had no preconceived notion of West African cities, but Man reminded him of something else entirely, a place he just couldn't put his finger on, until Theo spoke up.

"Like a shitty Colorado town without all the white people."

They spent the night in Man, then set out in the morning for the coffee and cocoa farming region in western Côte d'Ivoire. The air had been scrubbed clean by an early shower, one last tropical blast at the tail end of a seven-month rainy season. Driving at the higher altitudes was a pleasant change from the dusty trek across the baked northern grasslands, but it wasn't as beautiful as Jack had imagined it. High, forest-strewn ridges offered some insight into how the entire region had looked years earlier, before logging and agriculture claimed the rain forests.

"Are we there yet?" asked Theo.

Jack and Rene were in front, Theo in back. Theo flashed him a big grin in the rearview mirror, revealing not his teeth but the wedge of an orange that for some childish reason made Jack laugh. It reminded Jack of something Nate would have done, which made him think of

Kelsey, which made him feel slightly guilty for having discreetly but frequently admired the shape of Rene's legs since leaving Man. It got him to thinking that maybe he wasn't interested in Kelsey after all. Maybe she'd simply managed to breathe life into a part of himself that he'd left for dead with his divorce.

Good thing we nipped it in the bud, he thought. Perhaps it was no coincidence that he'd jumped at the chance to leave the country at the first sign of anything serious between them.

"About another half hour," said Rene.

Theo grumbled and went back to sleep. Over the next few miles, the road turned into dirt tracks. All signs of forest disappeared, giving way to row after row of cultivated cacao trees. Thousands of them stretched for miles up the hills and into the valley, each one about twenty feet tall with large, glossy green leaves.

"Slow down," said Rene.

Jack cut his speed to a crawl as she pointed to a group of workers in the field. The team leaders were shirtless young men, each of them armed with a long pole that had a mitten-shaped knife at the end. It was their job to select the ripe cacao pods, slice them off the tree, and let them fall to the ground. Behind them were even younger-looking men, more likely boys, machete in hand and a cigarette clenched between their teeth as they performed the stoop-labor ritual of gathering the pods and cracking them open for a handful of cocoa beans.

"That boy over there," she said. "Probably no more than ten years old."

Again, Jack thought of Nate. "Where do these kids come from?"

"All over. Mali, Burkina Faso. The poorest countries you can imagine."

"How do they get here?"

"Sometimes they're stolen. Usually they're tricked. *Locateurs*— recruiters—will go to bus stations, city markets, wherever, and promise these kids the good life. It's all a con. That team of five over there—Sally's ex-husband probably paid some *locateur* sixty bucks for the lot of them."

"This is his plantation?"

"One of his. One of twenty thousand."

"Twenty thousand?" he said with surprise.

"Sounds like a lot, but there are over six hundred thousand coffee and cocoa farms in this country."

"That's a lot of beans."

"A lot of money," she said, her gaze drifting back toward the workers in the field. "And a lot of kids."

He glanced in her direction, catching a glimpse of the genuine concern in her eyes. He felt a strange rush of conflicting emotions, both sadness over the tragedy she was fighting and admiration for the passion with which she fought. It seemed like a strangely selfish thought, coming to him as it did while mere boys toiled in the fields around him, but Rene was definitely the kind of woman who could make a divorced man feel alive again.

"Turn down this road," she said.

The dirt tracks turned into paved highway, and Jack realized that their little detour was over. "Where to now?" he asked.

"Almost as far as Daloa. Jean Luc has a house there."

Jack had to think a moment, having almost forgotten that Jean Luc was the name of Sally's rich second ex-husband. "Have you ever met him?"

"No."

"Know anything about him?"

"He's a French citizen, but he's lived most of his life here."

"Obviously wealthy."

"Obviously. I just gave you some idea of his labor cost."

"Good money in chocolate, I guess."

"Depends on what you mean by 'good.'"

"I assume Sally wasn't unaware of his wealth when she set her sights on him."

"He was reasonably handsome in the one photograph I've seen. But he was in his mid-sixties. Draw your own conclusions."

They stopped at the gate at the end of the paved road. An armed guard emerged from the guardhouse.

Theo stirred in the backseat and said, "You want me to take care of this?"

"I'll handle it," said Rene. "This is one instance where looking like my sister should definitely be an advantage."

"Like it's ever a disadvantage," said Theo.

She gave a little smile, then got out of the truck. The guard approached and met her halfway. Jack could hear them talking, but they were speaking French.

"What's she saying?" asked Theo.

"Who do I look like, Maurice Chevalier? At this point, all we can do is trust her."

"You're cool with that?"

"I am."

"Good. Cuz if she fucking sells me to this guy, I'm coming after your ass with that machete."

Jack started humming "Thank Heaven, for Little Girls." Rene and the guard finished their conversation with an exchange of smiles and multiple expressions of *merci, merci,* all of which Jack took as a good sign. She got back in the car, and the guard opened the gate to let them pass.

"What did you tell him?" asked Jack.

"A magician never reveals her tricks," she said.

"Tricks, my ass," said Theo. "You promised him fifty bucks on the way out."

"Twenty-five. How did you know?"

"These things I know," said Theo.

"Drive on," she said. Jack followed the road past more cacao trees, small ones that grew in the shade of larger banana and coffee trees. After a half mile of ruts and dust, the road flattened into a relatively well-maintained driveway. It curved around a pond, leading to a huge house on the river at the foot of the mountain. It was the nicest house Jack had seen since landing in Africa, but it was a far cry from the mansion he had expected.

"Pretty simple digs for a multimillionaire," said Jack.

"Typical," said Rene. "You flash money here, you draw bandits. It's the inside that looks like the lap of luxury."

They parked in front beside two other SUVs. Jack brought along a dossier holding his legal papers. An African man came out and greeted them on the covered porch. The guard had apparently radioed ahead to alert him of visitors. He and Rene conversed in French, and then she turned to Jack and said, "This is Mr. Diabate, Jean Luc's personal assistant. He wants to know the purpose of our visit."

Jack opened the dossier and showed him a copy of Sally's will and death certificate. "Tell him that I'm an attorney from the U.S., and that I have some questions for Sally's ex-husband."

Rene translated, then looked at Jack and said, "What kind of questions?"

"Tell him that it has to do with the money—"

"Jack, cork it," said Theo. "Rene, do your trick again. Ask him if he wants to meet Andrew Jackson several times over."

"It couldn't hurt," the man said in English.

Jack did a double take, but it was worth a few bucks if the guy could speak English. Jack checked his wallet, then pulled back. "Is Jean Luc even here?"

"In a manner of speaking," the man said.

"What does that mean?"

Diabate tapped his foot, waiting. Jack handed over a few bills and watched him count in silence. The man stuffed the cash in his shirt pocket, seemingly satisfied, then looked at Jack and said, "Monsieur, Jean Luc is dead."

Thirty-five

Tatum knew he shouldn't do it. But with the lawyer away, the client plays. Especially when his brother goes with him.

Jack had given him a stiff warning before leaving for Africa: Under no circumstances was Tatum to have any communication with Sally's other beneficiaries. Doing so would be a direct violation of the restraining order. Tatum promised "to lay low" and "not to do anything stupid." Technically speaking, he never actually promised to heed Jack's advice. Besides, there was only one beneficiary he wanted to talk to, which meant that there were four others he wouldn't contact, which translated to 80 percent compliance with his lawyer's instructions. In Tatum's book, that was something to be pretty damn proud of.

Gerry Colletti was down the street from his house, walking his dog, when Tatum caught up with him. It was early morning, and Colletti was wearing his robe and slippers, the unwrapped morning paper tucked under one arm. Tatum approached from behind at a moment when he'd be most off guard, just as Colletti stooped down to collect fresh poodle droppings with his pooper-scooper.

"Thought you only talked shit, Colletti. Didn't know you collected it."

Colletti dropped the newspaper and looked behind him, obviously startled. He scooped the droppings into a plastic bag and said, "You're in violation of your restraining order. Get away, or I'm calling the judge."

"I'm not hurting anybody."

"You're within five hundred yards of me. It doesn't matter if you hurt me or not."

"Doesn't matter? If that's the case, I might as well beat you to a pulp. No sense doing time in jail just for talking."

Colletti took a half-step back, trying to put more space between them. His little dog growled and bared its teeth. "Easy, Muffin."

"Your dog's name is *Muffin?*" said Tatum, taunting.

"Come near me and she'll chew your leg off. What do you want to talk about?"

"I was hoping that you and me could come to an understanding."

A modicum of tension drained from his expression, as if he liked the sound of Tatum's approach. "What are you proposing?"

"First, you need to understand it wasn't me who attacked you in the parking lot."

"I don't care about that."

"What do you mean, you don't care?"

"I already made the judge believe it was you. I can make the cops believe it, I can make a jury believe it, I can probably even make your own lawyer believe it. Doesn't matter if it's true, so long as I can prove it."

"You can't prove anything. You're like that bag of dog shit in your hand."

"You're dead wrong about that, Mr. Knight. I put my best investigator on your trail. He's uncovered some pretty interesting things about you."

Tatum smiled and shook his head. "So I got an impressive résumé. Big deal. That don't change the facts. It wasn't me who pummeled you."

"You're missing my point. If you don't step aside and renounce your claim to this inheritance, a guy like me can create a ton of problems for a guy like you."

"You think it's that easy?"

"My offer still stands. In fact, I'll make it even sweeter. Three hundred thousand dollars cash is yours, no strings attached."

"That's it, huh? I'm supposed to give up my shot at forty-six million dollars just because you say so?"

"No, because you're going to land in jail if you don't."

Tatum wasn't smiling anymore. He could feel his anger rising. "You're out of your league, Colletti."

"To the contrary. You're out of yours. This is business as usual for me."

"You think you're that good, do you?"

Colletti picked up his dog, stroking its head as he cradled the ball of white, curly fur in his arms. "How do you think I ended up in this game in the first place?"

"It's pretty obvious. Sally Fenning was trying to dish out her own version of revenge to her enemies. You represented her husband in their divorce."

"You think *that's* what got me on the list?"

"Isn't that enough?"

"Oh, Tatum, you are stupider than I thought. Miguel told me to go easy on Sally, which left me with a ton of ammunition and no way to use it. It seemed like such a shame to dig up all that dirt on Sally and then let it go to waste. Then the brainstorm hit me. If Miguel didn't want to use it for his own benefit, I could use it for mine."

"What the hell are you talking about?"

"All it took was a simple warning to Sally: If she didn't give in to my demands, I'd make it a matter of public record that Sally was having an affair with the man who murdered her daughter, and that she was covering up for him."

"Where did you hear that?"

"None of your business. But again, you miss the point. I was even less sure of my accusations against her than I am about my charges against you. But I still pulled it off."

"Pulled what off?"

He flashed a thin, satisfied grin. "Ask any divorce lawyer who's ever had a wounded wife as a client and he'll tell you, getting her in the sack is like shooting fish in a barrel. But getting the wife to spread her legs when she's the client of the *opposing* lawyer . . . Well," he said smugly, "now that's a good day's work."

"You think I'm just going to spread my legs, too?"

"No," he said, his smile fading into a more serious glare. "You look more like the type to just bend over and take it."

Tatum went at him and grabbed his throat. With his other hand he tried to contain the dog, but it leaped from Colletti's arms and bit Tatum on the wrist. Tatum flung the animal across the road and recoiled in pain. He was bleeding as he backed away.

Colletti massaged his throat. Tatum hadn't held him long, but it was a hard, martial arts–style hit. He caught his breath and said, "See that, Tatum? Even Muffin gets a piece of you." He gathered up his precious dog and walked away.

Tatum just stood there, seething, watching, and holding his wrist.

Thirty-six

They traveled halfway back to Korhogo before stopping at a hotel for the night. It would have been much easier to drive around big Lake Kossou and take the main highway north, but they opted for the scenic route through Parc National de la Marahoué, as Jack wasn't about to leave Africa without seeing some form of wildlife besides Theo.

"They're throwing kids," said Theo.

"What?" said Jack.

They were having dinner at another *maquis*, eating grilled chicken and *attiéké*, a local side dish made from grated roots. A crowd had gathered in the town square across the street. A group of teenagers was moving rhythmically to the beat of a drum, but most of the audience seemed focused on a spectacle of some sort.

"I swear to God," said Theo. "There's kids flying through the air over there."

"It's the child jugglers," said Rene.

"They juggle kids?"

"It's an old tradition under the Guéré, Dan, and I think the Wobé peoples. Jugglers train for months. The girls are specially selected from the tribe. They have to be skinny, supple, and definitely not prone to crying. Five years old is a prime age."

"And they throw them through the air?" said Jack.

Theo was standing on his chair for a better view. "It's amazing. Let's go watch."

Rene said, "Africa has some wonderful traditions, but this one doesn't exactly jibe with my pediatric training."

"I think I'll pass, too," said Jack.

"Suit yourself," said Theo. He stuffed a piece of grilled chicken into his mouth and started across the street.

Jack tilted back another glass of palm wine. After half a bottle, he was beginning to acquire a taste for it. Rene refilled her glass, then raised it and said, "Well, here's to Jean Luc. May he rest in pieces."

Jack met her toast, fully understanding that she wouldn't want to wish "peace" on Sally's ex, even in death. "That was some surprise, huh?"

"Not really. Daloa can be a dangerous place, even if you're careful."

"Obviously he wasn't careful enough."

"It only takes one mistake. The Red Cross chose Daloa as this year's center of activities for World AIDS Day. What does that tell you?"

"I guess he had a weakness for the local women."

"Or some of the boys he bought."

There was bitterness in her tone, and Jack didn't even want to think about how often *that* must have happened. Jack asked, "When did he and Sally divorce?"

"A few months ago. Why?"

"I was thinking on the car ride here. The fact that he died of AIDS may shed some light on Sally's state of mind."

"I was thinking about that, too."

"Did Jean Luc give her AIDS?"

"I don't know."

"It would fit with some of the things I've been hearing about her."

"What have you been hearing?"

Jack couldn't tell her that Sally tried to hire Tatum to shoot her, since that was a privileged communication from his client. He had to keep it general, as he had in their first meeting in Korhogo. "She just didn't seem to be terribly afraid of death. And I don't say that lightly. I understand what she went through. My sense is that she had no reason to go on living after the murder of her daughter. If she had AIDS, she might have felt as though there was no point in prolonging the inevitable."

"Are you back on that theory you mentioned to me before—that Sally might have hired someone to kill her?"

"It's not much of a stretch to believe that she'd hire someone to kill her under these circumstances."

She looked away, and sadness came over her. "I'd be lying if I told you that I hadn't worried about Sally. But this idea that she would have hired someone to shoot her, I don't really understand. Why go to all that trouble? Why wouldn't she have just shot herself?"

"You could have been the reason."

"You're blaming me?"

"No, no. Quite the opposite."

"I'm not following you."

"Here's something that might help you understand. A few years ago, I saw a story on television about some Academy Award–winning actress. I forget who it was, but that's not important. The point is, before she made it big, she was so unhappy that she decided to kill herself. Problem was, she was afraid her friends and family would feel guilty that they hadn't noticed her depression in time to keep her from committing suicide. So she tried to hire a guy to shoot her, make it look like a random murder. The gunman talked her out of it."

"So you think Sally . . ."

"I think she might have found a less compassionate hit man."

"Do you have any idea who it might have been?"

Jack looked across the street. Theo was dancing with two women, laughing, waving his arms, and having a good time. It suddenly reminded him of the talk he'd had with the detective on Sally's case, who'd tried to warn him that Tatum was nothing like his brother Theo.

"That's what I need to sort out," said Jack.

Thirty-seven

K elsey was steeped in murder—all of its elements, from malice aforethought to the mortal wound.

Criminal law had been her favorite first-year course, and she'd spent probably more hours than necessary boning up on it over the last few weeks. She was devoting more and more time to the Sally Fenning case, and the media were starting to make it sound as though the police were narrowing their suspects. If an indictment was headed in the direction of Jack's client, she wanted to second chair the trial— but *only* if Jack thought she knew her stuff.

She took one last gulp of cold coffee and closed her books. The University of Miami Law Library was open till midnight, and she'd closed it down again. The vacuum cleaners were already humming across the carpet, and some frantic law-review type was cursing at a photocopy machine that had been switched off for the night.

"Good night, Felipe," she said to the ponytailed undergrad who worked behind the desk.

"Night," he said.

She passed by the sensors and exited through the double doors to the courtyard. The night was cool, so she laid her book bag on the bench to pull on her sweatshirt. It had been crowded when she'd arrived for her night class, so she'd parked at the far end of the student lot near the intramural fields. She had to cut across the campus to get there, and she didn't give it a second thought until she reached a dark stretch of sidewalk beneath a cluster of huge banyan trees. The sun had been shining when she'd arrived, and it was a very different walk at midnight. The thick canopy overhead blocked out the moonlight, streetlights, light of any sort. There were only shadows ahead, differ- ent shades of black. Banyans were strange, eerie trees with ropy roots that hung from branches and reached for the ground like long tenta- cles. Kelsey wove her way through them, dodging the hanging roots like a slow-motion slalom skier. She missed one in the darkness, bumping straight into it and giving herself a start. She took a step back and tried to collect herself, but her pulse raced. Halfway through the banyans, she suddenly felt the urge to turn and run back. She forced herself forward, only to meet another dangling root. It tangled in her hair and made her whole body quiver. She pushed it aside and hurried forward, swinging her arm like a machete through the jungle. Her pace quickened, and she was nearly at a dead run when she slammed into something that brought her to a halt and took her breath away.

One hell of a root.

She gathered herself up and started forward, but as quickly as she rose she was down again. She was about to scream when he pounced on top of her. His knees were on her belly, and she was flat on her back.

"Don't move," he said in a coarse whisper.

He talked as if he had a wad of cotton in his mouth to disguise his voice. There was barely enough light to see that he was wearing a ski mask, but the gun in her face was plainly visible.

"Don't hurt me," she said, her voice shaking.

"I hope I don't have to."

"Please, take my purse, whatever you want."

"You got forty-six million dollars in that purse, honey?"

She felt a pain in her stomach, and it wasn't just his knees. "What's this about?"

"You work for Swyteck, and he represents Tatum Knight."

"That's right."

"Tatum is one of the heirs under Sally Fenning's will."

"Uh-huh."

He pressed the barrel of his revolver into her cheekbone. "You got two weeks to change that."

"Change? I don't understand."

"I don't care how you do it. But in two weeks, I want Jack Swyteck to persuade his client to give up his shot at the inheritance and withdraw from Sally's game."

"I don't know how to do that."

"Figure it out."

"How?"

"I told you. I don't care how."

"What if I can't?"

The gun was still in her face, but she felt something sharp at her ribs, a stabbing sensation that didn't really hurt, but it definitely made his point. "You get it done, bitch. Or your little boy, Nate, goes the way of Sally Fenning's daughter."

She was suddenly breathless, barely able to get out the words. "Please, not my son."

"Please, my ass. Now, keep this between us. If you go to the police, if you make this public in any way, it's Nate who pays. Understood?"

A tear ran down her cheek, collecting at the depression from the barrel of his gun.

"*Understood?*" he said harshly.

"Yes," she said in a voice that cracked.

In one quick motion, he rose and rolled her onto her belly. "Count to a thousand before you go anywhere," he said.

She lay with her face in the dirt, afraid to make a move, too frightened to count as his fading footsteps echoed in the darkness.

Thirty-eight

The next morning Jack went for a run. It wasn't just about exercise. He wanted to check his phone messages, and it was two miles to the nearest store offering international phone service—*cabines téléphoniques*, they were called, not really phone booths but private phones for hire. He would have driven, but Theo was off in the Land Rover in search of doughnuts. Rene had warned him that it would be an utter waste of time, but Theo was having one of those bear-like cravings that could have had him scouring a rice paddy for a bag of barbecued potato chips.

Jack was soaked with sweat when he reached the general store at the end of the road. It was early in the day, and he'd run countless hours in Miami summers. That didn't matter: African Heat, 1; Jack Swyteck, 0. He put his hands on his hips and walked off the side-stitch, wondering for an instant if the sight before him was a mirage. Sure enough, their Land Rover was parked out front, and Theo was sitting on the hood, stuffing his face.

"What'd you get?" asked Jack.

"Croissants."

"No doughnuts?"

"Close enough."

Jack went inside and paid the clerk, who directed him to the private phone in back. He dialed the operator, told her to cut off the call when the outrageous cost per minute hit fifty bucks, and then connected to his voice mail.

The most recent message had come through just an hour earlier, 1:37 A.M. Miami time. It was from Kelsey. Her voice was shaking, and it sounded as though she'd been crying. "Jack, please call me when you get this message. It's very important."

That was the end of it. Some work-related messages followed, but after the call from Kelsey he wasn't exactly focused, so he hung up. He held the phone for a moment, debating. It wasn't even 3 A.M. back in Miami, but her message had sounded too serious to wait another three or four hours. He rang the operator again and returned the call.

"Hello?" she said. It didn't sound as though he'd woken her.

"It's me, Jack. Is everything okay?"

"No," she said, her voice filling with emotion. "But I'm glad you called."

"What's wrong?"

She talked fast and told him. Jack wanted to take a moment to calm her down, but he was afraid they might get cut off any minute. "Did you get a look at him?"

"No, it was too dark. I'm almost certain he was wearing a mask anyway."

"Try to remember as much as you can, and write it all down so you don't forget. His height, his smell, his weight, any accent in his voice."

"He talked like he had cotton in his mouth, so I'm not sure what his voice sounds like."

"That's okay. Just write it all down."

"I'm so scared."

"Have you called the police?"

"No."

"Kelsey, you need to call the police."

"No! He told me—" She stopped, as if there was something she didn't want to tell him.

"He told you what?" asked Jack.

"I just can't go to the police."

"Did he threaten you?"

Again she paused, and he knew she wasn't telling him something, probably to keep him from worrying about things he couldn't fix from another continent. "Kelsey, I'm coming back to Miami."

He could hear the relief in her voice as she said, "I would feel so much better if you did."

"I'm sort of in the middle of nowhere, but I'll start working on it as soon as I hang up. Somehow, I'll figure out a way to get there."

"Thank you."

"Don't worry, okay?"

"Too late."

"I can hire you a guard to stay with you, if that will make you feel safe."

"No, that's not necessary. If I get scared I'll stay with my mother."

"You sure?"

"Yes. Just get home, Jack. We'll sort everything out when you're back."

"Okay. Hopefully, I'll see you tomorrow."

"Yes," she said softly. "Hopefully."

By nightfall they were back where they'd started, in the cocoa-growing region near Daloa. Backtracking didn't seem like progress, but returning early to Miami was proving to be more difficult than anticipated. They were a full day's drive from the international airport in Abidjan, and that was the good news. Unless Jack wanted to cough up another thirteen thousand dollars to fly to Miami via Paris, they'd be stuck in Côte d' Ivoire at least another three days. That was when Theo concocted Plan B.

"You sure we can trust these guys?" asked Jack.

"They're Belgerian. You ever met a Belgerian you couldn't trust?"

"What the hell's a Belgerian?"

"They're from Brussels. You know, Belgerians."

"So that would make them what? Bulgarians who live in Belgium?"

Theo downshifted, pushing the Land Rover across some of the

darkest, roughest roads they'd traveled yet. Rene bounced so hard in the backseat that her head nearly hit the ceiling. Jack just watched the tiny raindrops that were starting to splatter against the windshield.

Belgerians?

Rene asked, "How'd you meet these fellows?"

"They were my drinking buddies back in Odienné. Swyteck here crapped out on me and went to sleep. These two guys were nice enough to introduce me to their African gin."

"Are they going to meet us here?"

"No. We're looking for a dude named Lutu."

"Doesn't sound Belgerian to me," said Jack.

Theo stopped at a crossroad for no apparent reason. They were surrounded by cocoa fields, far from city lights, shrouded in darkness by the gathering clouds overhead.

"What now?" asked Jack.

"We walk from here," said Theo.

"Walk *where?*"

Theo checked his map, which was nothing more than some indecipherable lines he'd scrawled on the back of a napkin while talking on the telephone to his Belgerian friends. "Down this road. Airstrip should be on the other side of those trees."

"The road goes in that direction. Why can't we drive there?"

"Because they told me not to."

"Why?"

"Why, why, I don't know *why.* We got drunk together. I gave them my phone number in Miami and said come get a suntan. They gave me the number of friends they were staying with in Man and said to call if I need anything. I called. They helped. Period. Isn't that enough?"

"Only for Belgerians," said Jack as he opened the door.

The three of them stepped out onto the dirt road. The rain was more like a mist, but the worst of the storm clouds were backlit by a full moon, and they were starting to look threatening. Jack put on his Australian-style hat and got his duffle bag down from the luggage rack. It wasn't all that heavy, but he wasn't thrilled about lugging it on his back for who knew how long in search of some hidden airstrip.

The steady hum of an airplane engine rippled across the farmland. Jack looked into the sky but saw nothing. The noise was coming from somewhere on the ground, presumably the airstrip beyond the tall stand of cocoa trees.

Theo checked his watch and said, "Shit, man. We gotta run."

Rene said, "I'll drop off the Land Rover as soon as I reach Korhogo."

"Thanks," said Jack. "And thanks for everything. I mean it, you were a great help."

"You're welcome. Sorry we had to meet under these circum-stances."

"Me too. But if you're ever in Miami."

She smiled and said, "Right. And if you're ever in Korhogo again . . . don't call me, because it means you are absolutely out of your mind."

Jack smiled, and then with the speed of a hummingbird she gave him a quick and tiny kiss on the cheek. "See ya around," she said.

"Yeah, see ya," he said, definitely caught off guard. He watched as she walked back to the car, got behind the wheel, and drove away.

Theo cleared his throat and said, "Yeah, yeah, yeah, and you'll always have Paris. Now come on, Bogie, the plane's leavin'."

Jack checked the night sky, which was definitely promising seri-ous rainfall. The airplane engine was whining even louder. "Let's go," said Jack.

They jogged side by side down the rutted path of dirt, taking care not to turn an ankle. Jack was huffing, Theo was grunting, and the plane was sounding awfully close. "Just—a little—further," said Theo, struggling for breath.

"Will he wait for us?"

"Hell no."

"You mean if we miss this plane—"

"It's you," he said, huffing, "me, and the antelopes."

Jack took it to a higher gear, and Theo was right with him. The road cut through the stand of cocoa trees, though it was overgrown in spots with big fanlike banana tree leaves. The mist had turned into real rain, and Jack could hear the big drops pattering against the leafy canopy. They sprinted through the foliage until they reached a clearing on the opposite side. As soon as they were out in the open, the rain became a downpour. In seconds, they were soaked.

"Shit!" said Jack.

"There's the plane," said Theo. He was pointing to a pair of headlights at the far end of a so-called airstrip that was nothing more than a field of grass and packed dirt.

"You said it was a prop-jet."

"I lied."

"What is it?"

"It's a twin engine Cessna."

"A puddle jumper? I told you, I don't do puddle jumpers."

Theo looked up into the driving rain. "Then you can spend the night here sleeping in the puddles." He turned and ran toward the plane.

Jack thought for a second, then started after him. As they reached the end of the airstrip, a man jumped out of the aircraft. He was easily as big as Theo, dressed completely in black. Jack and Theo froze. He was pointing a gun at them.

"Easy, dude," said Theo. "We're friends of Hans and Edgar."

"The Belgerians," said Jack.

"What be your names?" He spoke with an accent that Jack couldn't quite place.

"He's Jack, I'm Theo."

He smiled and put the gun in his belt. "I'm Lutu. Get in."

Theo stepped forward, but Jack didn't move. Theo said, "Come on, Jack."

The rain was falling, the engines were howling, and this friend of the mad Belgerians was packing a pistol. Jack said, "I don't think so."

Just then, another set of headlights appeared at the other end of the airstrip. It was an open Jeep filled with men. Two of them had rifles strapped to their shoulders.

"Oh, boy," said Lutu.

"Oh, boy, *what?*" said Jack.

"I knew I should never have been waitin' on you gents so long. Looks like we won't be takin' dis here plane without a fight."

"What do you mean 'taking'?" asked Theo.

"What do you mean '*a fight*'?" asked Jack.

"The owner of dis here plantation don't pay his bills, we take dis here plane back. Dat the way it is. But maybe dat don't make the owner so happy, you know what I saying?"

Jack glared at Theo and said, "We're on a repo mission?"

"How was I to know?"

Jack whacked him about the head and shoulders with his soaking wet hat.

"Hey, hey, hey," said Theo. "You want to get home or don't you?"

The crack of gunfire echoed in the darkness. The Jeep full of armed guards was speeding toward them.

"Holy shit!" said Jack.

"Get in!" said Lutu.

They scampered up the wing and climbed aboard. Lutu took the yoke, Theo strapped himself into the seat beside him, and Jack sat behind them. The plane was moving before Jack could find his seat belt, and the engines roared as Lutu asked for every bit of power they packed. They were speeding down the bumpy dirt runway, the entire plane shaking so intensely that Jack was bouncing like a pinball from one side to the other.

"Sorry," said Lutu. "Got to get dis here plane up fast!"

Jack wedged himself between the seats to keep from slamming his head against the ceiling. The rain was cascading off the windshield, the wipers working furiously. He managed to catch a glimpse of the fast-approaching Jeep. It was a game of chicken, the plane against the Jeep, Lutu against the lunatic aiming his rifle straight at them. Jack saw the sudden recoil in the man's shoulder.

They're shooting at us!

"Wooo-hoooo!" shouted Theo, loving every minute of it.

The plane hit another huge hole in the airstrip, and Jack went flying. He had to grab something, so he grabbed Theo by the throat.

"Woooo-*glupp*!"

Lutu pulled back on the yoke, and the bouncing stopped as they lifted a few precious feet off the ground.

"Pull up!" said Jack.

"Watch this," said Lutu. He held the plane steady, exactly the right altitude to decapitate everyone in the oncoming Jeep.

"Are you crazy?" shouted Jack.

The flying plane was closing fast. The men in the Jeep jumped out just before the plane passed, ditching the Jeep but saving their scalps.

"Wooo-hoooo!" shouted Theo.

"Oh shit," said Lutu.

The tall trees at the end of the airstrip were fast approaching. Lutu pulled back on the yoke, all the way back, sending the plane on a mean vertical climb. Jack fell back in his seat and banged his head, nearly knocking himself silly. He fought to keep his bearings, got on his knees, and watched, his eyes shifting back and forth between the rising altimeter and the approaching treetops.

"Come on, baby," said Lutu.

"Please, God," said Jack.

They cleared the tallest tree by a good half-meter.

"Yes!" said Theo. He and Lutu were slapping high fives. Jack was checking the knotty bruise that was taking over the back of his head.

Theo glanced back, all smiles, and said, "You owe me big time for this one, Swyteck!"

"Yeah, and I can't wait to pay you back." He slid into his seat, searching frantically for both ends of the seat belt as the plane soared into the night, climbing by the second.

Thirty-nine

The mood in Vivien Grasso's conference room was even more tense than Jack had expected. As personal representative of the estate, Vivien was seated at the head of the rectangular table. To her left were Jack and Tatum, followed by Deirdre Meadows and her lawyer. Seated on the other side of the table were Miguel Rios, Gerry Colletti, and Mason Rudsky, each with his own attorney. All eyes were upon Jack, as if to say, "This had better be good."

Immediately upon returning to Miami, Jack had called Vivien to arrange a meeting in her office first thing Monday morning. Naturally, Jack hoped that sitting down face-to-face with the other beneficiaries might lend some insight into who was threatening Kelsey. But that was a secondary objective, one that he'd have to approach subtly, as the attacker's warning had left Kelsey afraid to utter a word to the police or anyone else. Jack was far more direct when addressing the main point on his agenda.

"Rene told me that Alan Sirap was Sally's stalker."

Silence fell over the room for what seemed like a very long time. Finally, Vivien said, "So there really is an Alan Sirap?"

"No. According to Rene, it's a phony name he shared with Sally in one of their communications over the Internet. But it's the best information Sally had about him."

"I'm not sure it's good enough," said Vivien.

"Good enough for what?" asked Jack.

"To establish his entitlement to an inheritance. I'm not saying it's impossible. I'm sure that somewhere in the history of our jurisprudence a court has upheld a will where a nickname or perhaps even an alias is used to describe the beneficiary. But it would be up to that beneficiary to come forward and prove that he is in fact the person described in the will."

There was silence again, as each of them pondered the implications. Jack said, "So by naming Alan Sirap as a beneficiary, Sally was inducing her stalker to come forward and say I'm the guy, I'm Alan Sirap. In effect, she was giving him a choice: Reveal yourself as a stalker and take your shot at forty-six million dollars, or just stay silent."

"I'm not prepared to speak as to Sally's intentions in this setting," said Vivien.

"Well, I am," said Miguel. "You people seem to keep forgetting that I was married to Sally when this stalker first appeared, and if you ask me, he's the piece of shit who murdered our daughter. So let's clear up one thing right away: This Sirap character isn't going to come forward and reveal himself, not even for forty-six million dollars."

"That depends," said Jack. "Maybe he's convinced that no one can *prove* he did anything but send Sally a few e-mails."

The prosecutor piped up, as if this talk of "proof" was hitting too close to home. "With all due respect to Mr. Rios, we already know that Mr. Sirap—whoever he is—isn't going to stay silent. Each of us received a letter from him that flat-out warned us to get out of the game."

"That's right," said the others, a sudden chorus of agreement.

Rudsky continued, "So now we know several key facts. One, each of us has a warning letter from a Mr. Sirap. Two, we know that Sirap is the name used by the man who was stalking Sally Fenning. Three, at least some of us suspect that he's the same man who stabbed Sally and murdered her daughter. Basically, it boils down to this, ladies and gentlemen: It appears that each of us is now caught in a game of survival of the greediest with a cold-blooded killer."

Again there was silence, the exchange of uneasy glances—a silence that was broken by the slow, sarcastic clapping of hands. It was

Gerry Colletti offering mock applause. "Very nice ploy, Swyteck," he said dryly.

"What are you talking about?"

He glared at Jack and then glanced around the table, as if courting support from the others. "We all know there's two ways to be the one who inherits Sally's money. One is to outlive the others. The other is to persuade the others to withdraw. I think I've stated that correctly, have I not, Madam Personal Representative?"

"That's correct," said Vivien.

"So, short of killing each other off, we all have to come up with a strategy. We could cut a deal, say each of us takes one-sixth. We haven't openly explored that route yet, but we're all posturing, aren't we? Each of us trying to get in a position to take a bigger share."

"This meeting isn't about posturing," said Jack.

"*Everything* we do is about posturing," said Gerry. "Some of us are clever, some of us aren't. At least one of us is so transparent that he beat the crap out of me," he said, looking straight at Tatum, "and tried to threaten me into withdrawing. But it now appears that Mr. Knight has managed to align himself with someone who has a more workable plan: Scare the daylights out of the other beneficiaries, make everyone think this mysterious Mr. Sirap is out to kill us, so that the weakest among us drop out of the race."

"Are you suggesting that I staged this meeting purely as a scare tactic?" said Jack.

"What's your legal fee if Tatum Knight wins, Mr. Swyteck? One third of forty-six million? Not a bad piece of change."

"That's pretty cynical of you," said Jack. "All I can say is that I hope the others aren't nearly so myopic and that they'll take this seriously."

"I hope they take it seriously, too," said Gerry. "To that end, I'm prepared to make a blanket offer to everyone here, the same offer I initially conveyed to Mr. Swyteck's client. I'll pay two-hundred-fifty thousand dollars cash, right now. No strings attached. All you have to do is renounce your right to the inheritance."

A few of them exchanged glances, but no one spoke.

"Any takers?" asked Gerry.

"Is this legal?" asked Deirdre.

Vivien said, "I don't see anything wrong with it. It's quite common for beneficiaries under a will to negotiate with one another."

"There you have it," said Gerry. "Straight from the mouth of the personal representative."

Deirdre made a face and said, "Who would be crazy enough to give up a shot at forty-six million dollars?"

"I guess I would be," said Mason Rudsky.

All eyes shifted toward the prosecutor. Gerry said, "Do I have a taker?"

Rudsky's lawyer appeared to be on the verge of cardiac arrest, his voice shaking as he looked at his client and said, "Now let's not jump into anything here, Mason."

Rudsky said, "Nonsense. Somebody already beat the daylights out of Gerry Colletti. Now it looks like the sixth beneficiary is a suspected child killer. I don't see this contest ending in anything but tragedy."

"Let's talk about this in private," his lawyer said.

"No. I'm out. Ms. Grasso, as soon as Mr. Colletti's wire transfer comes through, I'll forward you whatever papers are necessary to renounce my inheritance."

"Are you sure about this?" she asked.

"I'm sure."

Gerry had a gleam in his eye. "Anyone else?"

They looked around in silence, as if checking the collective pulse.

Gerry said, "Well, that's progress. Mr. Rudsky just made himself a quarter million dollars. And the rest of us just improved our odds from one in six to one in five."

"Just remember this," said Rudsky. He scanned the room, looking each of them in the eye. "It could be a good result. It could be a disastrous result. Either way, what Mr. Colletti said is absolutely true: Your odds have just improved. For better, or for worse."

The prosecutor and his attorney rose. No one else moved, and the two men left without a single handshake. The door closed, unleashing an uncomfortable stretch of silence during which no one seemed quite sure what to say.

Jack decided to keep his thoughts to himself: *I couldn't have said it better, Mr. Rudsky.*

Forty

Kelsey couldn't breathe. At least it felt as though she couldn't. On some level of consciousness she could feel her chest swelling and lungs expanding, but her heart raced with panic as she nonetheless gasped for air. She drank it in. Cold, heavy air that singed her nostrils and burned her throat. She could inhale all she wanted, more than she wanted, but she couldn't get it out. It seemed to fill her lungs and stay there, and no matter how hard she tried, she couldn't exhale. Her eyes bulged, her arms flailed. She tried to scream, but it was no use. The air was too thick, too damp.

Water! She was sinking, fading fast, fighting the useless fight. Her legs felt dry but her head was soaked, submerged, trapped beneath something. She couldn't move, couldn't even turn her head. She could only suck harder, drink in the cold, black wetness that was suffocating her.

The room went black. Her mind was a blank. She was suddenly bone dry, her lungs completely clear. But her heart was still pounding as the images came back into focus, though it wasn't strictly a dream anymore. It was part dream, part memory—a horrible memory of Nate's worst day as a toddler, a day so frightening that her mind refused to take her back there, except when she was too tired to fight it, hovering in a semi-conscious state.

• • •

Kelsey hurried up the sidewalk and didn't bother knocking on the front door. It was her older sister's house, and she could come and go as she pleased. Walking through the living room and into the kitchen, she could hear her sister and a group of her girlfriends laughing and playing cards at the table. She said hello, then walked to the family room where the children were playing on the floor. Kelsey counted five of them, three boys and two girls, each of them dwarfed by the tower of Lego they'd constructed.

"Where's Nate?" she asked.

The children were laughing and arguing at the same time, too focused on their tower to answer. An old woman was seated on the couch, one eye on the children, one eye on the television. "He's in the kitchen," she said. "With his mother."

"No, I'm his mother."

"He said he wanted his mommy."

Kelsey's heart fluttered. She started back down the hall, poking her head into the bedrooms along the way and calling out Nate's name, but she got no reply.

"Where's Nate?" she said as she reached the kitchen.

Her sister kept her eyes on her cards. "He's in the playroom with the kids."

"No, he's not."

"What do you mean he's not?"

"He's not there. He's not anywhere!" She called his name once more, loud enough to be heard anywhere in the house. Silence.

The women threw down their cards and dispatched in different directions—one to the living room, one to the garage, one to the front yard.

"Nate!"

"Where are you, Nate?"

"Nate, honey!"

Kelsey ran to the backyard, calling his name at the top of her lungs, racing from one end of the house to the other, checking the trash bins and behind the bushes. She was at a dead run when she rounded the corner, then froze. A wood deck ran along the side of the house. On the deck was a hot tub. It was covered with a big plastic lid that kept out the leaves and critters. It was supposed to keep out children, too, when it was padlocked. But the latch had no lock. She sprinted up the stairs, then nearly fell to her knees.

On the deck beside the tub lay Nate's blankie.

"Nate!" she cried, shooting bolt upright in her bed. She was breathless, her face cold and clammy with sweat as she looked around the room. It was her bedroom, she realized, which came as a relief. She was home. It had been that nightmare again, or more precisely the memory that came back to haunt her in dreams. Nate had been just two years old at the time. He didn't know how to swim, but thankfully the tub had been only half full.

Kelsey slid out of bed and walked silently to the kitchen. The light was still on, and the photocopies were still on the table, exactly where she'd left them. Since her own attack, she'd gathered additional information about the death of Sally's daughter. She'd studied her findings before bedtime, which had proved to be a terrible mistake.

Or maybe a very timely warning.

She took a seat at the table and thumbed through the collection of old articles. She stopped at the last one, the one reporting the medical examiner's account of how Sally's daughter had died. "Suffocation caused by drowning." Kelsey skimmed the article one more time, though she couldn't bring herself to focus too intently. The very idea was too painful for any mother, for any normal human being.

This psycho—whoever he was—had rinsed his hands and knife in the bathtub, and then drowned a little girl in water made red by her own mother's blood.

Kelsey shuddered at the thought, and once again the words of her own attacker outside the law school library echoed in her mind: "Tatum Knight drops out, or your little boy, Nate, goes the way of Sally's daughter."

The dream had left her so exhausted that she practically had to prop her head up to think clearly. She was still adamant about not calling the cops. If the man had wanted to rape her or hurt Nate, he could have done that easily. He wanted Tatum out of the game—and that was all he wanted. She had to believe him when he said that Nate would pay if she involved the cops. Still, someone, somewhere, was trying to warn her that she needed to do something. Why else would she have had the dream?

Unless the message was that she was already too late.

The thought chilled her. She rose quickly and grabbed the telephone. Her mother lived in a high-rise condominium with twenty-four-hour security, the safest place Kelsey knew of. She'd decided not to go with him, however, not wanting him or her mother to see the worry in her eyes. She dialed the number and spoke at the sound of her mother's sleepy Hello.

"Mom, hi, it's me" . . . "I know it's late, I'm sorry. But I just had to check on Nate. Is he okay?" . . . "Thank God." She took a breath, her voice shaking as she added, "I really think it's best if he stays with you for a while."

Forty-one

Deirdre Meadows was staring at a blank computer screen. Not even the buzz of the busy *Tribune* newsroom could get her crime reporting juices flowing. She couldn't blame it on lack of material—there was a dead hooker on Biscayne Boulevard, a circuit court judge caught taking a bribe, and it wasn't even lunchtime—but her mind was elsewhere.

"What's cooking?" her editor asked as he breezed past her messy cubicle.

"Oh, the usual Miami spice," she said weakly.

She'd been moping around for the last twenty-four hours, ever since she'd left Vivien Grasso's office with a titanic knot in her stomach. It was all Jack Swyteck's fault. He returned from Africa and promptly warned everyone they might be in danger because of "Alan Sirap." She'd been attacked by dogs and threatened by a madman who'd vowed that he would either kill her or kill one of the other beneficiaries—and she'd told no one about it. She didn't like to think she was motivated by money. It was a matter of her own personal safety.

But was silence really the only way?

To hell with it, she thought. It wasn't her responsibility to save the others. If they stayed in Sally's game now—after the note from Alan Sirap, after Swyteck's warning that Sirap was Sally's stalker, after Tatum Knight beat up Gerry Colletti, after Gerry offered to buy them all out for a quarter million dollars apiece—then whatever happened to them was their own damn fault.

Her phone rang, and she snatched it up. "Meadows," she said.

"How's my favorite reporter this morning?"

Her grip tightened. It was that same mechanical voice—her source. "I'm not your favorite anything, pal."

"That's not true. I'm a man of my word, and your two weeks of silence makes you my partner. Hard to believe it's been almost that long since we talked last, isn't it?"

"What do you want from me?" she asked.

"Once again, I have to congratulate you. I understand you had another chance to tell the group about our partnership yesterday, and you did the right thing. You kept your big mouth shut."

"How do you know about that?"

"I have my sources. Just like you."

"Who?"

"Get real."

"How do you know they're reliable?"

"They're reliable. The kind you'd love to have."

She reached for a pen and notepad. "How much would I love it?"

"Enough to write this down."

She froze. Could he see her, or did he just know her well enough to guess that she'd gone for her pad?

He said, "I've decided to reward you. Consider it a little bone in your direction for good behavior."

"I'm listening."

"I'm sure you haven't forgotten our little understanding—be the first to die, or be the one to inherit forty-six million dollars."

Her voice tightened. "How could I forget that?"

"Good. Because I don't want you to think I've gone soft. I just want you to understand that if you do as you're told, it's in everyone's best interest."

"How do you mean?"

"Not everyone has to die."

"*No one* has to die."

"That's up to you, isn't it?"

"No," she said sharply. "Don't put this on me."

"Don't use that tone with me," he said, his voice rising. "Or I might change my mind."

She reeled in her anger, taking the edge off her voice. "Change your mind about what?"

"I have a story for you."

She fumbled again for her pad, her hand shaking as she put pen to paper. "What kind of story?"

"It's about Tatum Knight."

"That's a good start."

"Here's what I want you to write. Tatum met with Sally Fenning two weeks before she died. She drove to a bar owned by Tatum's brother, Theo, called Sparky's."

"What did they talk about?"

"She hired him to kill her."

For a moment she couldn't speak. "She *what?*"

"You hard of hearing?"

"No. That's quite a story. But I can't write something like that without corroboration."

"You can, and you will."

"But I need two sources before the *Tribune* will print—"

"Shut up and fucking listen! I didn't tell you to *run* the story. I told you to write it."

She paused, confused. "Why write it if I can't print it?"

"You take the story to Jack Swyteck and you *threaten* to publish it."

"What's the threat?"

"Tell him that the story is going to run on page one tomorrow—unless his client instructs Sally's estate lawyer to strike his name from the list of beneficiaries."

Deirdre had heard every word, but she'd written nothing on her pad. It was almost too bizarre to register. "What's this all about?"

"Like I said, not everyone has to die. If we can get some of the other beneficiaries to drop out, that's as good as dead, right?"

She thought for a second, recalling that Gerry Colletti had made the same point at yesterday's meeting. "That's right."

"So you write that story, Deirdre. Write it good. You make Tatum Knight think he's about to jump to the top of the list of suspects in the murder of Sally Fenning. Because if he doesn't drop out, then it's back to my original plan. Somebody's gonna die."

The line clicked. Her source was gone. Slowly, Deirdre placed the phone back in the cradle, then slumped in her chair, mentally exhausted. She wasn't keen on the idea of extorting anyone, but threatening Tatum Knight with a phony story was certainly preferable to standing aside and waiting for her source to bump off one of her fellow beneficiaries.

She drummed her fingers on her notepad, thinking. Sally Fenning hired Tatum Knight to kill her. Write it, but don't print it. Just the words on paper would be enough to make Tatum Knight drop out of the race for forty-six million dollars. Just the words—

No, she realized. Not just the words. The words alone had no power, or at least not power enough to intimidate two guys like Jack Swyteck and Tatum Knight.

The words had that kind of power only if they were true.

She looked across the sprawling newsroom, her gaze slowly passing over the bronze plaque on the wall in honor of the *Tribune's* past winners of the Pulitzer Prize. Finally, her focus came to rest on the office door of the editor who had slapped down her proposal for an investigative piece on Sally Fenning.

Sweet mama, she wondered. *What if it is true?*

Forty-two

South Coconut Grove is a maze of quiet residential streets that cut through a tropical forest. It's no accident that the crisscrossing courts and lanes bear names like Leafy Way, Poinciana, and Kumquat. Shade, charm, and privacy are the neighborhood selling points, each little lot surrounded by a piece of the sprawling jungle. People live there because you could be on top of the house next door and never know it.

People move away because you could be killed in your driveway and no one would see it.

Detective Rick Larsen parked his unmarked Chevy behind the line of squad cars with the swirling blue lights. He grabbed his notepad, got out, and walked around the overgrown bougainvillea and a swaying stand of bamboo that lined the street. Evenings in the Grove were like midnight in the Black Forest, even darker when skies were overcast. It had been raining since sunset, and it was hard to tell if the precipitation was still falling or if the wind was simply blowing drops off the leafy canopy overhead. Typical Grove confusion.

Larsen heard voices on the other side of the bushes. He ducked under the taut yellow police tape that was stretched across the entrance to the driveway. Pea gravel crunched beneath his feet as he entered the crime scene and asked, "What do we got?"

Cameras flashed as the investigative team photographed the area. Others were slowly canvassing the yard, searching for anything and everything. The body lay facedown in the gravel. An assistant medical examiner was kneeling over it, examining it, while speaking into her Dictaphone.

A young cop in uniform, the first to have arrived on the scene, gave Larsen the quick rundown. "White male. Fifty-something years old."

"He live here?"

"No. Owner of the house found him when she was taking out the garbage. She called the police."

"She know him?"

"No. Says she's never seen him before."

"She see anything?"

"No."

"Any witnesses?"

"Not yet."

"Any identification on him?"

"None. He was wearing a T-shirt and exercise shorts with no pockets. From his shoes and outfit, looks like he was out walking or jogging. Except that he's not in very good shape. Walking is more my guess, probably on a doctor's orders to get off his ass and lower his cholesterol."

"Anything else?"

"That's about it. Medical examiner moved in and took over."

Larsen made a few notes in his pad, then walked over to the body. The examiner was in mid-sentence, speaking into her recorder, ". . . early nonfixed lividity, torso and extremities blanch with touch."

She switched off her tape recorder, looked up at the detective, and said, "How you doing, Rick?"

"Better than him."

"That good, huh?"

He smiled just a little, about as much as he ever did. "What happened?"

"With a fractured right femur, at least six cracked ribs, a hyperextended elbow, a broken neck, and God only knows the extent of internal injuries, I'd say it was probably more than a slip and fall."

"Hit and run?"

"Pretty safe guess."

"How'd he end up in the driveway? Fly or dragged here?"

"Flew. I marked off his flight pattern. Probably became airborne somewhere south of the driveway, shot like a cruise missile right through that busted-up banana tree over there. Landed in the front yard, where we put that flag right there, then skidded into the driveway."

"Anybody checking for skid marks?"

"No one's found any yet. Street's blocked off all the way to Main Highway. You can look for yourself."

"Think I will." He started away then stopped. It was a little ritual of his, always to get a look at the victim's face before marching off to do the drawing, the measuring, the detail work. It was a sure way to remind himself that this job was about people.

He bent over and shined his penlight on the face, then did a double take. "Son of a bitch," he said softly.

"You know him?"

"Don't you? He's an assistant state attorney."

"I've only been with the Miami-Dade office a few months. Haven't worked with many of them yet."

"Well, here's one you'll never work with," he said flatly. "His name's Mason Rudsky."

Forty-three

J ack was alone on his covered patio watching the brilliant display of lightning over Biscayne Bay, when the telephone rang. He hesitated, recalling how his ex-wife had been so paranoid about picking up the phone in a thunderstorm, as if a bolt of lightning might travel down the line into the house and fry you on the spot. She always said it took a complete and utter disregard for human life to expect someone to come to the phone when there's lightning.

Maybe it's her, he thought in a sarcastic moment. He picked up the phone. "Hello."

"Good evening, Mr. Swyteck."

Jack gave his phone a quick shake. It was a mechanical-sounding voice, and he was beginning to wonder if there wasn't something to that paranoia about telephones and lightning. "Who is this?"

"Don't hang up. You'll be sorry if you do."

The voice was still distorted, but he knew there was nothing wrong with his equipment. "What's this about?"

"Mason Rudsky."

"What about him?"

"He's dead."

Jack suddenly needed to sit down. "Dead?"

"Yes, very."

"What do you know about it?"

"I know this much: The stolen car that ran him down will never be found."

"Where's his body?"

"No need to worry about that. Cops are on the scene already."

"Then why are you calling me?"

"Because you seem to be the one voice in the group of Sally Fenning's heirs that everybody listens to. And I have a message for them."

"What is it?"

"Tell them this: The man who ran down Mason Rudsky knew that Rudsky had withdrawn from Sally Fenning's contest."

Jack rose, as if pacing might help him think. "You're saying this was homicide?"

"Definitely. No one hit the brakes. They won't find any skid marks on the road."

"Killed by whom?"

"Like I said, by someone who knows that Mason Rudsky accepted Gerry Colletti's offer."

"You mean the two-hundred-fifty grand?"

"I mean Mason Rudsky was killed by someone who knew that he was no longer in the running to inherit Sally Fenning's forty-six million dollars."

"I don't understand. If he knew that, then what's the motive for killing him?"

"That's the part I need everybody to understand. Especially you, because I hear rumors that your client is feeling pressure to bow out, too."

"I'm sure everyone's feeling pressure. That's the way the game is being played."

"Well, that's not the way it's going to be played anymore," he said, his disguised voice taking on an edge.

"Sally set it up that way," said Jack. "You can win either by outliving the others, or by persuading the others to drop out."

"I don't care how she set it up. You idiots might think you can win the game that way, but let Rudsky's death send a message loud and clear. There's only one person who takes the money, and there's only one person who walks out alive."

"So, you're saying what? No more dropouts?"

"Exactly. No more dropouts."

"What is it then?" asked Jack. "A fight to the death?"

"It's personal now. New ball game. My game."

"What gives you the right to change the rules?"

"Go to your mailbox."

Jack stopped pacing. "What?"

"Just go to your damn mailbox."

Jack walked through the house with his cordless phone pressed to his ear. His mailbox was mounted on the wall outside his front door. He opened the door and stepped onto the porch, scanning the yard and checking across the street to see if someone might be watching. "I'm here," he said.

"Look in the box."

He reached slowly for the lid, wondering if a snake or rat might fly out. He stood as far away as he could, raising up the lid with the tip of his fingers. It flew open, but nothing popped out. Inside was an envelope.

"What is it?" Jack said into the phone.

"Open it."

It was unsealed. Jack opened the flap. Tucked inside was a gold locket in the shape of a heart. "It's pretty," he said. "But you don't sound like my type."

"It was Sally Fenning's, smartass."

Jack suddenly felt guilty for having joked about it. "How did you get it?"

"Look inside," he said, ignoring the question.

There was a latch on the side of the gold heart. Jack opened it like a book. Inside the locket was a photograph of a young girl. Jack had seen enough photographs to know that it was Katherine, Sally's four-year-old daughter.

Jack felt a lump in his throat, but he talked over it. "Was Sally wearing this when you shot her?"

"I never said I shot her."

"Was she wearing it the day she died?"

"No," he answered. "Not possible."

"Then how did you get it?"

There was silence on the line. Lightning flashed in the distance, and the phone line crackled. Finally, the man answered, "Sally was wearing it the night I stuck my knife inside her and drowned her little princess."

Jack heard a click on the line, followed by the dial tone. For a moment he couldn't move, but another clap of thunder gave him a start. He gently placed the locket back in the envelope, hurried back inside the house, and locked the door with both the chain and dead-bolt.

Forty-four

The following morning Jack was first in line to see Detective Larsen.

Jack had called him immediately after the phone call from the man with the disguised voice. He wished he had tape-recorded it, but the police wouldn't have been able to use a tape anyway, since in Florida it was illegal to record conversations without a warrant or consent. Jack recited the conversation as best he could from memory, and his memory was dead-on when it came to the locket. He was totally forthcoming to the police, and he asked for only one favor in return. He was back in Larsen's office at 9:30 A.M. to collect.

"We think it's for real," said Larsen.

Jack was seated in the uncomfortable oak chair on the visitor's side of Larsen's cluttered metal desk. "It was Sally's?"

"When Sally's daughter was murdered, she reported only one thing missing, a gold heart-shaped locket that she was wearing around her neck."

"Could this be a duplicate?"

"Not likely. According to the file notes, Sally said it was fourteen karats and purchased at Latham's Custom Jewelry in the Seabold Building downtown. We talked to the store's owner first thing this morning. This is fourteen karats, and he's positive this is one of his products."

"So there's pretty much only one way my caller could have gotten it."

"Pretty much."

"Okay. Thanks for the info."

"No, thank you, Jack. I really appreciate you coming in with this. When you didn't deliver on that interview of your client after I gave you that tidbit about Deirdre Meadows's book, I was beginning to think you didn't love me anymore. But I'd say we're square now. Of course, now I fully understand why you didn't want me talking to Tatum. This morning's paper and all."

"The paper?"

"Page one of the *Tribune*. You know —" His phone rang. He grumbled, apologized, and answered it.

Page one? Jack wondered. Larsen was getting deeper into some intraoffice confrontation that didn't interest Jack in the least. He caught the detective's eye, but Larsen just shrugged and continued his heated argument, managing to use the F-word as a noun, a verb, an adjective, and an adverb in a single sentence, a verbal testimonial to his veteran status on the force.

Jack needed to see a newspaper, and he wasn't inclined to wait around for Larsen to finish his stupid tiff. He gave a little wave and silently excused himself from the detective's office. Trying not to look like a fugitive, he walked to the exit as quickly as practicable, stopping at the little newsstand outside the station.

The *Miami Tribune* was staring right at him, practically screaming its message from halfway down the front page: MILLIONAIRE MURDER VICTIM MET WITH CONTRACT KILLER it read, BY DEIRDRE MEADOWS.

It wasn't the banner headline, but it was prominent enough. And the tag line in only slightly smaller font was even worse: HIT MAN IS HEIR TO $46 MILLION ESTATE. Jack purchased a copy, sat on the public bench, and devoured the story.

He could hardly believe what he was reading. It was all there, everything he and Tatum had talked about. His meeting with Sally at Sparky's. Her desire to die. Their discussion about hiring someone to shoot her. And, of course, there was a lengthy digression into the latest developments in the case, including the restraining order the judge had entered against Tatum for his alleged assault against Gerry

Colletti, followed by a strong finish that referenced a separate article about last night's hit-and-run, which had left Mason Rudsky dead.

One thing, however, was conspicuously absent from the article: Not a word was mentioned about Tatum's refusal to do the job.

Nice piece of unbiased journalism, Deirdre.

He shoved the newspaper into his briefcase, grabbed his cell phone, and dialed Deirdre at the *Tribune*. It took a minute or two for the switchboard to get the call routed properly, but finally he heard her voice.

"Meadows," she said.

"This is Jack Swyteck. I just read your story about my client."

"I'm so glad you called. Do you confirm or deny?"

He could almost feel her gloating over the phone lines. "Does it matter? You didn't even call me for a comment."

"I was on deadline. There wasn't time."

"Better to be first than right, is that it?"

"No. But it is nice to be first. Particularly when I know I'm right."

Jack rose from the bench and started walking toward the street, suddenly feeling the need to distance himself from the police station. "Who's your source?"

"Why in the world would I tell you that?"

"Can't really think of a reason. At least not from a reporter who didn't even bother to reveal her own biases to her readers."

"What biases?"

Jack stopped at the corner, almost fell off the curb. "Are you kidding me? You are one of Sally's five remaining potential heirs. If the other four withdraw or follow in Mason Rudsky's footsteps, you stand to gain forty-six million dollars. Don't you think your article should have spelled that out?"

"No. The story wasn't about me."

"This is *all* about you, and your readers should know it. Your article puts the heat on my client to withdraw from the game."

"How does it do that?"

"You know how. And don't expect me to spell it out for you so that you can twist it into some nifty quote in tomorrow's newspaper."

"I'm not being coy. I'm really at a loss. How does my truthful arti-cle about a meeting between your client and Sally Fenning put the pressure on him to renounce his inheritance?"

"Don't change the subject on me. You should have disclosed your bias."

"This story was not inspired by bias. It came from a reliable source."

"That's the whole point. The source could have had the same bias. Are you really that stupid, or are you just pretending to be?"

"Don't insult me, Swyteck."

"Then get off your J-school soapbox and play straight."

"I'm not going to tell you who my source is."

"Fine. But you should at least consider the possibility that the whole story is a plant."

"Planted by whom?"

"By one of the other potential beneficiaries. Any one of them could have simply made the whole thing up and manipulated you and the *Tribune* into printing something that would disqualify Tatum from inheriting under the will. It's like Colletti said at the meeting: It just improves everyone's odds."

"My source is not another beneficiary."

Jack stopped at the crosswalk. He hadn't expected her to tell him anything, and he certainly hadn't expected *that*. "How do you know?" he asked.

"I don't normally go to the police about my stories, but when Rud-sky turned up dead last night, I made an exception. Now that I've told them, I might as well tell you."

"Tell me what?"

"A man called me a couple weeks ago. He's my source."

"I'll ask again: How do you know he isn't one of the other heirs?"

"Because he wants to split the pot with me if I win. Another ben-eficiary wouldn't need to strike that deal. They're already in the game."

"Well, I'm not going to argue with that, but you're proving my other point. This person—your source—is clearly biased. He has a stake in your winning the jackpot, so naturally he would say anything that would hurt Tatum and force him to renounce his inheritance."

"You're absolutely right."

"I know I'm right. A newspaper like the *Tribune* shouldn't run a story based on a single source who has no credibility."

"The *Tribune* would never do that. That's why I went out and got a second source."

He paused, almost afraid to ask. "Who?"

She let out a condescending chuckle and said, "Normally I'd tell you to shove it in response to a question like that. But you and your cocky 'My Client Is Wholly Innocent' attitude have me pissed enough to tell you this much: If my source were any closer to you . . . well, let me put it this way, I don't think there is anyone closer to you."

Jack was silent, as if she'd just punched him in the chest.

Deirdre said, "Now if you'll excuse me, I have a deadline to meet."

She hung up, but Jack didn't move. He stared at his phone, still trying to comprehend what she'd just said, and the thought sickened him: *No one closer.*

A transit bus rumbled past him, leaving him in a black cloud of diesel fumes. He hardly noticed. "Holy shit," he said as he slipped his cell into his pocket.

Forty-five

The conversation with Theo did not go well.

He'd get over it, for sure, and Jack hadn't been all that accusatory anyway. The more thought Jack had given it, the more impossible it seemed. No way was Theo going to rat out his brother to *anyone*, much less an overly ambitious reporter. But Jack felt as though he had to at least touch base and completely rule him out as "the source" before confronting the person that Deirdre Meadows had assumed was closer to Jack than anyone else.

"Kelsey?" he said with surprise. "I didn't know you were coming in today."

She hadn't been on the work schedule, but she was in Jack's office seated on the couch waiting for him when he arrived. "Can I talk with you a minute?" she asked.

"Sure." Jack pulled up a chair and straddled it, facing her. He'd rehearsed his delivery during the drive into the office probably a dozen times, but he could see from the expression on her face that he was conveying some awkward vibes. "Kelsey, before we go off in some other direction, there's something I need to know."

"Please. I know what you're going to say. This morning—today's newspaper. The article about Tatum."

"Yes?" he said tentatively.

Kelsey took a breath, obviously struggling. "I don't know how to say this to you."

Jack felt a pain in his stomach, sickened by the thought, but the words came out in anger. He looked her in the eye and said, "Did you talk to Deirdre Meadows?"

She blinked twice, then averted her eyes. And he knew. He wasn't trying to be judgmental, but he couldn't help shaking his head in disbelief.

"Why?" he asked.

When she looked up, tears were welling in her eyes. "I was afraid to tell you. I knew you'd think I was an idiot. She tricked me, Jack."

"Tricked you? How?"

"She called and told me that she already knew that Tatum met with Sally before she was killed. She had all the details that Tatum gave us—the rainy night, the meeting at Theo's bar where she tried to hire him to kill her. The thing she had dead wrong was the timing. She claimed to have it from a reliable source that the meeting took place less than twenty-four hours before Sally turned up dead. I told her that her source was wrong. And then she got nasty."

"What do you mean, nasty?"

"She made it absolutely clear that unless I told her differently, she was going to print the story as written: Tatum and Sally met twenty-four hours before her death. I told her she really needed to talk to you, but she said you hadn't returned her call and she was on deadline."

"So what did you tell her?"

"I was totally firm. I said, 'I can't tell you whether there was a meeting or not. All I can tell you is that there definitely was no meeting twenty-four hours before Sally's death.'"

"Good answer."

"But she wasn't happy with it. She said, 'Tell me when it happened, or I'm sticking with twenty-four hours.' I didn't know what to do, but in the heat of the moment I couldn't imagine that the smart thing was to stand aside and let her print something I knew was false. So I told her it wasn't twenty-four hours. It was more like two weeks."

Jack groaned. "Damn it, Kesley, how could you not have known that she was fishing for confirmation that the meeting had taken place at all?"

"Because she already knew everything about the meeting."

"She made you think she knew about it. All she had was a rumor. She couldn't print that. She was bluffing. But after talking to you, she had a source."

"I'm so sorry."

"I'm sure you are. But for God's sake, you can't let a reporter manipulate you like that."

"I don't know what to say. I screwed up. You have to know that I haven't exactly been in my best frame of mind lately."

"We've all been through a lot."

"No, you don't understand." She sniffled and said, "That man threatened Nate."

"What?"

"The man who attacked me outside the law library. He said that if Tatum didn't drop out of the game . . ." Her voice cracked, as if she couldn't even say it.

"He'd do what?"

"He said—" She glanced at the framed photograph Jack kept on his desk, her boy perched on Jack's shoulders. Her lips quivered as she said, "He told me Nate would go the way of Sally's daughter."

Jack felt his anger rise. "That son of a bitch. You didn't even have to tell me, I knew that's the way that lowlife would operate."

"That's why I sent him to stay with my mother, like you said."

"I wish you'd take the rest of my advice and call the cops."

"No. I can't. He said he'd hurt Nate if I did, and I'm not taking that risk. But don't you see what I'm going through, how I could have screwed up? I'm terrified. You know how a threat like that must have made me feel. It's horrible enough what happened to that poor little girl. But Nate—I told you the whole drowning story the first time you took him on Theo's boat. I still have nightmares."

"When it comes to you and Nate, you won't find anyone more sympathetic than me. But you have to hold yourself together. You can't be putty in the hands of some reporter."

"I accept that. But I hope it at least explains it. A man threatened to drown my own son if Tatum Knight doesn't drop out of the game. I was confused, not sure what to do, what to tell anyone. Out of the blue this reporter called and started asking questions about a conversation Tatum Knight had with Sally Fenning before she died."

"You should have cut it off right there."

"I know, but I swear, Jack, she already had the whole story. I thought I was helping our client by telling her that the meeting didn't take place just twenty-four hours before Sally ended up dead."

Jack gave her a hard look. He almost couldn't believe what he was about to say, but somewhere deep inside him the lawyer had taken over. "Did you really think you were helping, Kelsey? Or did you think it was a way of giving your attacker exactly what he wanted: Get Tatum Knight out of the game?"

Her mouth fell open. "I can't believe you're accusing me of that."

"I'm just asking the question."

"The answer is no. Hell no."

Jack was starting to regret he'd asked the question so bluntly, but as Tatum's lawyer, he had to be firm.

Her voice shook. "Do you really think I'd intentionally violate the attorney-client privilege? I'm not about to put myself on the blacklist of the Florida Bar before I've even graduated from law school."

Jack took a moment, breathed away some of his suspicion. She seemed too shaken by the whole experience to be able to lie about her intentions now. "Okay," he said. "You screwed up. We'll leave it at that. But what you did is still so wrong."

"Stop it, Jack."

"Stop what?"

"I've apologized fifty times. That reporter just caught me at exactly the wrong moment. I haven't had a decent night's sleep since the attack. All I've been able to think about is Nate, that little girl, and some psycho holding them down in this tub of bloody bathwater, their little legs kicking and—"

She lost control, and the tears were flowing. She was practically slumping. On impulse, Jack went to her. She rose, and she seemed to want him to take her in his arms, but he stopped. He was suddenly feeling more like her employer than her rock. "Hey, hey," he said as he laid a somewhat reassuring hand on her shoulder. "It's going to be okay."

"I feel awful. I wish I could fix this."

"Don't worry. It's going to be all right."

He tried to step back and put some distance between their bodies, but she took his hand and said, "Are you sure?"

"The truth is we were going to have to deal with this sooner or later. Tatum really did meet with Sally. And she did try to hire him to kill her. The one item of damage control we have to address is Deirdre's failure to include Tatum's denial that he took the job."

"Can I help you with that?"

"I'll take care of it."

They were standing just a foot or so apart, a little too close for Jack's comfort. Kelsey had big, expressive eyes, and they were conveying a mix of emotions to him. Embarrassment. Remorse. She squeezed his hand and said, "It's important to me that this doesn't change the way you see me."

He didn't say anything.

She forced a weak semblance of a smile. "Do you think you can forgive a worried single mom for making a law student mistake?"

He considered it, trying to ignore the look on her face and the touch of her hand, trying to blur his memory of the one bright moment they'd shared together on her front porch and the nights he'd spent alone wondering what "might be" between them. It would take a while for him to sort out his own emotions, and it bugged him a little that she'd played the single mom/law student card in this setting. But he said what he thought she needed to hear, just words, no feeling behind them. "I can forgive you."

She smiled just enough to show her relief. "Is everything going to be okay between us?"

"Sure. But the verdict is still out on the much tougher question."

"What's that?"

"Will Tatum forgive you?"

Forty-six

The bar was packed, mostly a twenty-something crowd, young sheep who would drink battery acid so long as it was two-for-one. Deirdre Meadows was on her fourth gin and tonic, sharing a booth with her best girlfriend, Carmen Bell, a freelance journalist and self-proclaimed poet who would admit to no one but her buddy Deirdre that her true ambition in life was to write sappy greeting cards for Hallmark. They got together for drinks every Wednesday, "Ladies' Night," after Deirdre met her deadline, but tonight was more special than most.

"Page one A," said Carmen. "Nice work, girl."

Deirdre crunched an ice cube with her teeth and smiled. "Best is yet to come."

"Tell me."

Deirdre checked over her shoulder, as if to make sure no one was listening. The booth behind them was filled with the usual after-work crowd, three guys shooting tequila while their girlfriends took turns trying the old teaspoon hanging from the nose trick.

Deirdre said, "Remember how pissed I was when my editor nixed my idea for a three-part investigative piece on Sally Fenning?"

"Yeah, budget problems, blah, blah, blah."

"Well, no more budget problems. It's now a green light."

"Woo-hoo! You are on your way."

Deirdre picked a peanut from the bowl of party mix. "Looks that way, doesn't it?"

Carmen leaned into the table and spoke in the low voice she used only when trading secrets. "So tell me. Who's the source?"

"Carmen! I'm surprised at you."

She smiled knowingly and said, "You don't have any idea who he is, do you?"

"Nope," she said, and they shared a little laugh.

Then Carmen turned serious. "Are you scared of him?"

"A little."

"Just a little?"

"Well . . ." she said with a roll of her shoulders. "I'm less scared now that I've talked to the police."

"Wait a minute. Since when does a journalist tell the police about her sources?"

"This is different. This is a source who threatened to kill me."

Carmen's eyes widened. "He *what?*"

"Nothing. Forget I said that. This is a celebration. Last thing I need is for you to get me all spooked out."

Carmen gnawed her plastic stirring straw until the full two inches protruding from her cocktail were completely flattened with teeth marks.

"Will you please stop that?" Deirdre said sharply.

"Sorry. Just don't like it when my friends are getting death threats."

"I'm being very careful, okay?"

"Good. And I hope you're being smart, too."

"Oh, I am. How's this for smart? *Johnny, I'm scared, can I sleep over tonight? Johnny, can you hold me? Johnny, it would help me sleep so much better if we could wake him up just one more time and put him right—*"

"Okay, okay, I get it," she said with a smile.

"Do you *really* get it?"

"Well, technically speaking, no."

"Then that's one more way in which my life beats the hell out of yours right now, isn't it?"

"I hope you get crabs."

Deirdre laughed as she fished a ten-dollar bill from her purse. She laid it on the table, then flashed the key to her boyfriend's townhouse, and said, "Sorry to drink and run, but Johnny puts the chain on the door if I don't get there before eleven."

"Shit, Deirdre. When you gonna find a man who doesn't make you drive your own ass over to his place in order to see him naked?"

"As soon as I inherit forty-six million dollars."

"Not that the money matters to you."

"Of course not. Who needs money?"

They managed to keep a straight face for about two seconds, then burst into laughter. "I'll see you later," said Deirdre.

She zigzagged through the noisy crowd, and she could have sworn she was getting checked out more than usual. It was all in the attitude, and as of this morning she had a new one. A stranger even opened the door for her.

"Thanks," she said with a smile, then stepped outside.

The sun having long-since dipped into the Everglades, it was one of those perfect autumn evenings with just enough bite in the air to make you forget the cursed summer heat and humidity that had stuck around till Halloween. Valet was a rip-off at eighteen bucks, and as usual Deirdre had come with no coins to feed the meters on the street, so she'd wedged her little Honda into a free spot in the alley beside the drugstore. This had seemed like a good idea when the store was open, but its windows were now black and there were no more customers coming and going. Nightfall had a way of changing everything.

She dug her key from her purse as she quickly crossed the lot. A guy in a red pickup truck was sitting behind the wheel, and the look on his face gave her concern at first, until she saw the mop of blond hair bobbing up and down in his lap. Pretty safe bet he wouldn't be following her. Her car was just around the corner, and the muffled drone of the bar crowd faded with each step farther into the darkness.

Her car alarm chirped as she hit the remote button. She got in, slammed the door shut, and aimed the key for the ignition. Jittery hands made a challenge out of the simple process of starting the car, definitely more nerves than the drinks.

Damn it, settle down, girl.

The engine fired on the second try. She put it into the gear and pulled away so fast that she sent some loose gravel flying. She turned on the radio to calm herself.

She'd lied to Carmen. Her source had her more than "a little" scared. She was well aware that submitting the story about Tatum Knight to her editors was an outright defiance of his orders. She wasn't sure what he might do about it, but he would surely do *something*. She'd gone to the police, hoping they might offer protection. They gave her a pamphlet filled with canned advice for stalking victims, told her to come back when she was willing to agree to a wiretap on her home and work telephones. Maybe then they'd talk protection.

A journalist with a wiretap on her telephone. *Are they out of their minds?*

She reached Johnny's townhouse in record time. The fear, the gin, the adrenaline all had her driving faster than usual. The parking spaces in front of Johnny's unit were full, and Carmen's comment came back to her. The creep could have at least given up his prime spot and parked his own car in guest parking so that she didn't have to walk five hundred yards in the darkness. She was inclined to bag it and go home, but she did feel safer sleeping with him. She zipped her car over to guest parking, found a spot, and jumped out.

Gables Point was a quiet condominium development, lots of trees, not very well lit. She followed the sidewalk past the pool area, which wasn't the most direct path to Johnny's unit, but the lighting was better, except for the last hundred yards, where the sidewalk snaked through a forest of droopy bottlebrush trees. The ring of light that shined from the pool area seemed to follow her for a while, but she stopped when she reached the faint edge of its farthermost reach. She'd walked this way at least a dozen times over the past month, never once giving it a second thought. Tonight, her instincts told her to turn and run the other way. It was late. It was dark. There were lots of big trees for someone to hide behind.

You're making yourself crazy.

She put one foot in front of the other, and she was on her way, gathering speed, her pulse quickening. She'd entered far more danger-ous places in her career, night after night, as the *Tribune's* crime beat reporter. Interviews with killers, dead bodies galore—it was all in a day's work. This was nothing to be afraid of.

Halfway there. The sidewalk curved, but she went straight. No time for the scenic route, and there was no scenery in the black night anyway. She was cutting her own path through the grass when she heard it. She stopped and looked back, seeing nothing, hearing noth-ing. But she was certain that she'd heard something just a moment earlier. Footsteps. Behind her.

Or was she imagining it?

She turned and ran at full throttle, holding back nothing, brush-ing aside the tree branches that were lashing at her face. Her ankle turned, which made her yelp, but she ran through the pain. Twenty yards to Johnny's townhouse. She was back on the sidewalk, sprinting down the homestretch. She gobbled up the three front steps in a sin-gle leap, then searched frantically for her key in the darkness.

Jerk doesn't even leave the porch light on for me.

She got her key, used two hands to steady her aim, and shoved it home. The tumblers clicked, the deadbolt turned. She turned the knob and leaned into the door. It opened six inches, then caught on the chain.

Shit!

She shot a quick glance over her shoulder, and again she saw nothing. Or no, maybe a shadow. "Johnny, open the damn door!"

She pushed and pulled the door back and forth, shaking it vio-lently against the chain to wake him.

"Johnny!"

She heard footsteps again, and her heart skipped a beat—then relief. The footsteps were coming from inside the townhouse.

"Johnny, it's me!"

The door closed, and the chain rattled on the inside. The knob turned, and Deirdre pushed her way inside. She rushed in, eager to see him, eager to see anyone. He grabbed her, she poured herself into his arms, the door slammed, and she was firmly in his grasp before she could realize what had happened.

It wasn't Johnny.

A cold knife was at her throat. "Fucking bitch," he said in an angry whisper. "You were told to *write* the story, not print it."

She screamed, but it was heard only in her own mind, as the sharp blade slid deeply across her throat, sinking all the way to the neck bone, silencing her forever.

Forty-seven

At 4 P.M. Friday afternoon, Jack and Tatum were back in probate court.

It had been less than two days since Deirdre's murder, and everything had changed. Or at least everything had intensified, and Jack couldn't get away from it—media coverage, phone calls from lawyers for the surviving heirs, questions from investigators. It was a neighbor who'd spotted the blood seeping out from under the front door on Thanksgiving morning. The cops found her body in the foyer, and her boyfriend was tied up in his bedroom closet, unharmed but blindfolded. He hadn't seen a thing, a useless witness. Naturally, Detective Larsen turned to Jack and his client for answers, as the judge's restraining order had already labeled Tatum as the thug in the group. Mason Rudsky's hit-and-run death was still a mystery, and it didn't help matters that Deirdre Meadows had turned up dead the same day the *Tribune* ran her story that Tatum was hired to kill Sally Fenning.

"All rise!"

Judge Parsons entered the courtroom from his side chambers. The crowd rose on command, and the foot shuffling was noticeably louder than at most hearings. All fifteen rows of public seating were packed with spectators, mostly members of the media. This was the first court hearing since a state prosecutor and an ambitious reporter had met untimely deaths in a race for forty-six million dollars, and the local news geniuses had finally taken serious notice, even without a sex scandal.

"Please be seated," the judge said.

Jack and Tatum returned to their seats, the two of them once again splintered off from the others. Miguel Rios, Gerry Colletti, and their lawyers sat at the table nearest the empty jury box. Vivien Grasso, as personal representative of the estate, took a seat alongside the edge of their table, not quite on their side, but definitely not aligning herself with Jack and Tatum.

Alan Sirap was still a no-show.

The bailiff called the case, "In re the Estate of Sally W. Fenning," and the judge took over. He seemed overwhelmed at first, or perhaps he was waiting to make sure the television cameras were ready and rolling to catch his speech.

"Good afternoon," he said in a voice suitable for a funeral. "I'd be remiss if I didn't express my grave concerns over the tragedy that has befallen this matter. Especially on this day after Thanksgiving, I wish to convey my heartfelt sympathies to the friends and families of Mason Rudsky and Deirdre Meadows.

"That said, I want to assure everyone that I come to this courtroom with no preconceived notions as to who is responsible for these terrible events. I say this because we have before us today a very serious motion by Mr. Colletti, one of the potential heirs. I want Mr. Colletti and everyone else here to understand that this court will not rely on emotion or outrage to adopt any extraordinary measures. I will insist upon proof, and if the proof exists, I will grant the requested relief. But not before then. Have I made myself clear?"

"Yes, Your Honor," came the lawyers' reply.

Tatum leaned toward Jack and whispered, "I like the sound of that."

Jack gave a little nod, hiding his concern. It was eerily reminiscent of the speeches he'd heard from the bench when he was a federal prosecutor, where the judge would rail against the government for some "outrageous tactic" that "shocked the conscience of the court" and then proceed to dispatch the defendant on a millennium-long tour of the land of the walking dead.

"Mr. Colletti, proceed, please," the judge said.

His lawyer started up from his chair, but Gerry waved him off and stepped forward first, as if to say, *I'll handle this.* It was an obvious last-minute change in plans, and Jack knew exactly what was going on. The spotlight was shining far too brightly for Gerry Colletti to defer to another lawyer.

Gerry approached the lectern in the center of the courtroom, stealing one last look at the television camera before showing his back to the crowd and addressing the court. "Your Honor is exactly right. This is a very serious motion that I've filed. And I have filed it with good reason."

"I will be the judge of that," the judge said dryly.

"You will indeed. As the court knows, the State of Florida has a law on the books that is commonly referred to as the Slayer Statute. That statute prohibits a murderer from inheriting under the will of his victim."

"I'm familiar with the law. As I made clear in my opening remarks, I'm interested to know what evidence you intend to present to demonstrate the law's application to this case."

"Tatum Knight is a beneficiary under Sally Fenning's will. This motion seeks to invoke the Slayer Statute to disqualify him from inheriting under her will."

"Based on what evidence, Mr. Colletti?"

"Certainly you read the article in yesterday's newspaper. It appears that Mr. Knight is a contract killer who was hired to kill Ms. Fenning."

"Objection," said Jack, rising. "Since when did we start convicting alleged murderers based upon newspaper articles?"

"I'll sustain the objection," said the judge. "Newspaper articles are admissible in certain circumstances, but if that's all you've got, Mr. Colletti, I'd say this motion is highly premature."

"Judge, I concede that I'm not in a position at this moment to prove that Tatum killed Sally Fenning."

The judge snarled and said, "Then what are we doing here?"

"In light of the deaths of Mason Rudsky and Deirdre Meadows, I thought it was imperative to get this issue before the court now, in an abundance of caution." He glanced across the courtroom at Jack's client and said, "Just in case Mr. Knight kills me, too, before I have a chance to gather my evidence."

"Objection," said Jack. "This so-called serious motion is quickly devolving into a grandstand play without a shred of evidentiary support."

"Mr. Colletti, do you have any evidence that you, personally, are in any such danger?"

"I do. That's why I've combined this motion under the Slayer Statute with a request that Mr. Knight be held in contempt of court for violation of the restraining order. The court previously ordered that Mr. Knight should not come within five hundred yards of any of the other beneficiaries, except for court appearances and official meetings with the personal representative of Sally Fenning's estate. As detailed in the affidavit filed with my motion, Mr. Knight assaulted me once again while I was outside my house walking my dog."

The judge took a quick look at the file, peering through his reading glasses. "According to your affidavit, this happened almost a week ago. Why has it taken you so long to come forward with this evidence?"

"Frankly, this guy scares the daylights out of me. But now that two of my fellow beneficiaries have turned up dead, I decided it was incumbent upon me to bring this additional evidence to the court's attention."

The judge nodded, seemingly satisfied with the explanation. "Mr. Swyteck, we've all read Mr. Colletti's affidavit. What's your response?"

Jack rose and said, "If I may, I would like to question Mr. Colletti about the photographs he attached to his affidavit."

"Photographs?" The judge thumbed through the file, apparently having missed them.

Gerry said, "I submitted several photographs that show the severity of the blows I received from Mr. Knight in this second meeting. As I state in my affidavit, he became very agitated, grabbed me by the throat, threw me to the ground, kicked me several times."

Tatum whispered, "That's bullshit."

Jack laid a hand on his shoulder, calming his client. "Your Honor, I think I have the right to examine the witness about the authenticity of those photographs."

"Authenticity?" said Gerry in an indignant tone. "Are you suggesting—"

"Swear the witness," the judge ordered.

Gerry shook his head, as if this were all a waste of time. Then he took a seat in the witness stand, and the bailiff administered the familiar oath.

Jack approached and said, "Mr. Colletti, these photographs of your bruises—who took them?"

"I took them myself. I have a camera with a timer on it. You push a button, stand in front of it, and it takes your picture."

"Exactly when did you take these photographs?"

"Immediately after my second encounter with Mr. Knight. The one described in my affidavit."

"And the purpose of these photographs is what?"

"Well, I'm not one to brag, so I normally wouldn't put into the public record photographs of myself naked from the waist up." He smiled, clearly hoping that he'd just uttered the evening news sound byte.

The judge rolled his eyes, and the courtroom was silent. Gerry cleared his throat and said, "I filed them to show the court the severity of the beating I took once again at the hands of Mr. Knight."

Jack walked back to his table and grabbed two more stacks of photographs. He handed up one stack to the judge and said, "Your Honor, I have several zoom photographs we created from one of Mr. Colletti's originals. I apologize that I wasn't able to file these with the court earlier, but since we just received the affidavit this morning, I just a few minutes ago got these back from the photo lab."

"Apology accepted."

Jack turned to the witness, handed him the first photograph from his stack, and said, "Mr. Colletti, does this zoomed photograph appear to be a fair and accurate representation of your left arm as taken from your original photograph?"

He examined it and said, "It would appear to be my arm, yes."

Jack handed him another photograph and said, "Here's a closer zoom. Does this appear to be a fair and accurate depiction of your lower left arm as taken from the original photograph?"

"I'd say so, yes."

"One last photo." He handed it to him and said, "How about this one? It's an even tighter zoom. Does this appear to be a fair and accurate depiction of your left wrist as taken from the original photograph?"

"This is my wrist, yes."

"That's your Rolex watch, too?"

"Yes."

"It has a calendar on it, does it not?"

Gerry paused, as if sensing where this was headed. "Yes."

"Take another look at the photograph. If you would, please read the date depicted on that watch calendar."

His expression fell, and he answered softly. "It says N-O-V-Two."

"That would be November second, correct?"

Colletti shifted nervously in his seat, seeming to search for a way out of Jack's noose.

The judge took a good look at his copy of the photograph, then glared at the witness and said, "Mr. Colletti, your answer please."

"I presume that's what it means."

"And the second day of November would have been, by my count, about two weeks before your alleged second encounter with my client, correct?"

Gerry didn't answer.

Jack stepped closer. "Mr. Colletti, these photographs weren't taken after your alleged second meeting with Mr. Knight on November fifteenth. These were taken after the alleged beating you received outside John Martin's pub in the early morning hours of November second. Isn't that right, sir?"

The courtroom was silent. All eyes were upon the witness, and he kept staring at the photograph, as if willing the date to change.

Finally, Gerry shrugged impishly at the judge and said, "Gee, I don't know how I could have gotten that mixed up."

"I think I've heard enough," the judge said.

Gerry said, "Well, just a moment, Judge. If this is going to be a full-blown evidentiary hearing, I'd like a chance to question Mr. Knight."

Putting Tatum on the stand was the last thing Jack wanted. Had Gerry not overplayed his hand with the photographs, Jack might not have been able to prevent it. But now the momentum was his. "Judge, in all candor, it appears that there may have been a technical violation of the court's restraining order."

"Technical!" said Gerry. "He grabbed me by the throat."

The judge said, "Yes, Mr. Colletti. We've all seen your photographs."

A light rumble of laughter came from the galley. Jack said, "We'll stipulate to the entry of a five-hundred-dollar fine, with the express understanding that no further breaches of the order will be tolerated."

"I object," said Gerry.

"Done," said the judge, pointing with his gavel for emphasis. "And I do mean zero tolerance, Mr. Swyteck. Next time, your client's in jail."

"Understood," said Jack.

The judge looked at Gerry and said, "You may file your motion to disqualify Mr. Knight under the Slayer Statute if you wish. But let me make myself clear: Do not request a hearing and do not take this court's time unless you have evidence to present."

"Yes, Your Honor," he said, grumbling.

The judge looked out on the crowd and said, "If there is no further business before the court, then we are—"

Vivien Grasso rose and said, "Your Honor, there is one more thing."

All heads turned toward the personal representative. "What is it?" asked the judge.

She spoke with a pained expression. "I've been giving this very serious thought over the past few days, and I apologize for raising it now. But seeing what just went on in this courtroom only helped me reach my final decision."

"Final decision as to what?" the judge asked.

"I wish to resign as personal representative of Sally Fenning's estate."

The crowd came to life, as if smelling something newsworthy.

"Excuse me?" said the judge.

"One of my most important duties as personal representative is to distribute the estate to the heirs. I'm simply not comfortable distributing anything where the beneficiaries may be beating each other up and killing each other to get the inheritance."

The judge said, "Let me assure you that no one will be distributing assets or receiving any inheritance until the deaths of Mason Rudsky and Deirdre Meadows are fully explained and accounted for."

"I appreciate that, Judge. But I've made up my mind."

"I'm afraid that's not enough. By law, this court cannot allow you to resign until a replacement PR is found."

"I've taken care of that," she said. "I've been in contact with several possible replacements. One of them agreed just yesterday to step in and serve if I decided to resign."

"Who is it?"

Vivien turned toward the crowd and said, "She's in the courtroom now. Rene Fenning, Sally's sister."

Jack turned so quickly he nearly cracked his neck. A woman rose from her seat in the middle of the eighth row of public seating. She was dressed in a blue business suit, her makeup done smartly, her hair perfect, like an ad from a fashion magazine. Jack had said good-bye to a very different-looking woman, no less beautiful, on that last rainy night in Africa.

The judge said, "Ms. Fenning?"

Vivien said, "It's actually Dr. Fenning. She's an M.D."

"Dr. Fenning, has Ms. Grasso stated your intentions correctly?"

"Yes, Your Honor," she replied.

"Step forward please. We may as well make the switch official."

The courtroom was silent as Rene came forward save for the gentle scratch of pencils on notepads as reporters rewrote the lead paragraph of tomorrow's press coverage. Jack, too, watched her every move. He'd gathered glimpses of her beauty through the dirt and sweat of Africa. He'd imagined what she might look like in another place, under different conditions, but even his own vivid imagination had short-changed her. He'd hardly expected to see her again, never would have guessed it would have been this soon. It wasn't immediately clear what her involvement would mean for the administration of Sally's estate, but on an entirely different level, one that had him smiling on the inside, he was glad she'd come to Miami.

Tatum whispered, "Damn, she's even hotter than her sister was."

Jack could have told him that she had a brain to match, but he let it pass, chalking it up to some Knight brother gene that could never let the obvious go unstated.

Rene passed through the swinging mahogany gate and stood beside Vivien Grasso at the lectern. The judge greeted her with a pleasant smile, then briefly quizzed her on her background and her relationship with her sister. It wasn't anything Jack didn't already know about her, but somehow it was interesting to hear it all again in Rene's own voice.

When they finished, the judge looked across the courtroom and asked, "Do the heirs have any objection to Dr. Fenning serving as personal representative of her sister's estate?"

Silence. The judge said, "Seeing none I would ask Dr. Fenning to please stop by chambers at the conclusion of this hearing. There is some paperwork to complete, and an oath to be administered. Good luck to you, young lady. We are adjourned," he said, ending it with a bang of the gavel.

"All rise!"

On cue, the crowd was on its feet. Silence reigned for the full ten seconds it took the judge to walk to his side chambers, followed by the rumble of a hundred different conversations that commenced immediately upon his disappearance behind the heavy wood door.

Colletti glanced at Jack from across the courtroom, but he and his lawyer were in an obvious hurry to get outside and make themselves available for press interviews. They packed up quickly and merged into the crowded center aisle, followed by Miguel Rios and his lawyer. Jack started to make his way toward Vivien Grasso, just to tell her "No hard feelings," but Rene came to him and said, "Surprised?"

"In this case, nothing surprises me."

"I guess your coming to Africa started to play on my conscience. It's time I did my part to figure out what happened to my sister."

"I think that's the right decision."

She averted her eyes, then looked back at him. "I suppose that we should get together soon."

"Get together?"

"Yes. I mean, I'll be meeting with all the lawyers, of course."

"Oh, of course," he said. "Anytime."

"I'm sure you're busier than I am. I'm staying at the Hyatt till I can find an apartment. Call me, let me know what's good for you."

"I'll do that."

A reporter called out her name from the other side of the rail. Several other members of the media were waiting in the aisle, eager to speak with the new personal representative, Sally's sole living relative.

Rene looked at Jack and said, "Guess I'm about to get my first experience in the beauty of 'No comment.'"

"If you're smart."

She raised an eyebrow, and Jack said, "And they don't come any smarter."

"Nice save."

"It's what we lawyers do."

She smiled a little and said, "It's good to see you again."

"Good to see you again, too."

She turned and headed for the exit. Jack gathered his things, then glanced over his shoulder on impulse, only to catch her glancing back at him. They exchanged a little smile, as if they were having the same embarrassing thought, something along the lines of *I can't believe I looked, but it's nice to know you did, too.* Then Rene disappeared into the crowd, and Jack suddenly caught sight of Kelsey standing at the rail. He excused himself from his client, then called her to his side of the rail. She pushed through the gate, and they stepped closer to the bench where they could talk out of earshot of all but the lip readers.

"Better be careful," said Kelsey.

"Careful about what?"

"You and the new PR keep making eyes at each other like that, it'll be all over tomorrow's newspapers."

"We weren't—do we have to talk about this here?"

"Is she the reason you didn't want me at counsel's table with you for this hearing?"

Jack was starting to feel accused, and he didn't like it. "It was Tatum who didn't want you here. After the way you let your guard down and slipped attorney-client secrets to Deirdre Meadows, he doesn't trust you anymore. I'm sorry."

"And what about you?"

"Kelsey, this isn't the place."

"It's a simple question: Do you trust me?"

He paused for a breath, as if the question was far too complex to answer in this setting. "Yes. I trust you."

"More than Rene?" she asked, eyes narrowing.

"I hardly know Rene."

"Could have fooled me."

He softened his voice, not because he feared someone would overhear, but because things were getting uncomfortable. "Kelsey, before I left for Africa, I thought we agreed that it was in Nate's best interest that we put things on hold between us. So I'm not really sure how to respond."

"Just be honest with me. How am I supposed to feel when you're making eyes across the courtroom at another woman less than forty-eight hours after you told me everything is going to be okay between us?"

"I meant *professionally* everything was going to be okay between us."

"Professionally? The way you were looking at me was no more professional than the look you were shooting Rene just now."

"I wasn't—" He started to deny it, but it didn't ring true. He could see the disappointment all over Kelsey's face, as if she would have preferred some kind of denial, any kind at all, over another heartache.

Jack said, "Look, I don't know what you think you saw. But I honestly don't know what's going to happen."

She shook her head slowly and said, "Then you're blind."

"What?"

"The woman's been living in the friggin' African desert for nearly three years. Knock yourself out, Jack."

She walked away, and he didn't follow. He just watched in silence, not knowing what to think, not wanting to think anymore about it. But he couldn't stop himself from thinking, and it was making him feel guilty.

Because all he could think about was Rene.

PART FOUR

Forty-eight

It was happy hour at Sparky's, but Jack wasn't feeling very happy. He'd been brooding on a bar stool since leaving the courthouse, pouring his heart out to Theo, who was sort of tending bar but mostly keeping an eye on the cash register, making sure that his new bartender wasn't ripping him off. Sparky's attracted a rough crowd, a hangout for workingmen and -women, not the typical "suit 'n secretary" pickup joint that the professional crowd flocked to near Brickell Avenue or Alhambra Circle. There was no Ketel One vodka, no Chivas Regal scotch, and the only imported beer was El Presidente, a Dominican *cerveza* that Theo sold below cost to the tomato pickers from Homestead every Tuesday night because there sure as hell wasn't anyone else gonna cut 'em a break. But on the most basic, human level, happy hour at Sparky's was just the same old story. Bad lighting, loud music, drinks aplenty. Ribbed condoms and tongue-scorching breath mints for sale in the bathrooms. Clusters of men eyeing women, women eyeing men, people talking too loud and laughing too hard, the same scene every weekend, inhibitions dissolved and judgments impaired with each lonely misstep in the shot-and-a-beer mating dance.

"Call her," said Theo, talking over the clatter of bottles and meaningless conversations along the bar.

"Call who?" said Jack.

Theo sent a barmaid off with another tray of two-for-one cocktails. Two other orders were waiting, but he put the tabs aside and reached under the bar, which could only mean trouble—his personal stash. It was just then that Jack noticed his friend was wearing his infamous "I'm not as Think as You Drunk" T-shirt.

"Please, not that," said Jack.

Theo flashed an evil grin as he pulled up two glasses and his special bottle of Herradura Tequila Añejo. "You pick up that phone and dial Rene's number. Or we're doing shots."

"Would that be with or without training wheels?"

Theo pushed the salt shaker and little bowl of lemon wedges aside. "Without."

"You're brutal, man."

"We don't stop till one of us hits the floor. And let's face it, Jacko: We both know it won't be me starin' at the ceiling."

"What makes you think I want to call her?"

"Because you been talking about her for half an hour. So you call her now, or you spend all day tomorrow with an ice bag on your head."

"Herradura never gives me a hangover."

"Forget the tequila. I'm talking about slapping you so hard upside the head that you'll have to walk into the next room to hear your own ears ringing. So don't ask me one more fucking time if I think you should call her. *Call* her."

Theo slid the phone across the bar top, but Jack was still debating. Strictly from the standpoint of case strategy, he should have been all over her without delay. Last thing he and his client needed was for Rene to get an earful about Tatum from Gerry Colletti or Homicide Detective Larsen before Jack could speak to her. But something was troubling him, holding him back. He looked at Theo and said, "I'm not gonna say she was flirting, but it was damn close."

"You trying to make me jealous?" he said, then puckered up and shot a squeaky, exaggerated air kiss in Jack's direction.

Jack ignored it. "Why would she even be nice to me, let alone flirt? If you believe yesterday's newspaper, Sally Fenning—Rene's *sister*—hired my client to pump a bullet into her brain."

"You just said the magic words, Jacko: *If you believe* yesterday's paper. Obviously, Rene don't believe it. Which is all the more reason for you to get on the phone and get into her—"

"Theo," he said, groaning.

"Camp. I was gonna say *camp*."

"Yeah right."

Theo handed him the phone. "Call."

Jack took it and got the hotel number from directory assistance. Theo stood over him, watching in silence, as if to make sure that he actually dialed it. The hotel operator connected him to Rene's room, and she answered on the third ring.

"Rene, hey, it's Jack." Then he added, "Swyteck," like an idiot, which had Theo rolling his eyes.

"Hi," she said. "I was just on my way out the door."

"I won't hold you up. I just wanted to follow up on what we talked about earlier. You know, about setting up an appointment."

Theo screwed up his face and said, "An *appointment?*"

Jack waved him off, waiting for her reply. The delay felt longer than it actually was, but Jack got the definite impression that she was mulling something over.

Finally, she said, "Can you pick me up in half an hour?"

"Tonight?"

"Well, if tonight's not good—"

"No, tonight's fine."

"You sure? I was just going to catch a cab. But now that you've called, and the more I think about it, I'd really rather not go alone."

"Forget the cab. I can take you. Where you going?"

She answered in a flat, serious tone. "Sally's old house."

"The mansion over on Venetian Isles?"

"No." Again she paused, then said, "Her real old house. The one Katherine was murdered in."

Jack gripped the phone, but he didn't speak.

Rene said, "You don't have to come if you don't want to."

The music, the laughter, the endless bar chatter all around him—it all suddenly merged into an annoying buzz in the back of his brain. "I want to," he said. "I'll pick you up in twenty minutes."

Forty-nine

They caught the tail end of rush hour out of downtown Miami and didn't reach the Ninety-fifth Street exit until almost seven, well after dark.

The business district for Miami Shores was built around a little hitch in the road that connected I-95 to U.S. 1, and most of the community had the same small-town feel—quiet residential streets, drugstore on the corner next to the local diner, white church steeples protruding through the broad green canopy of palm trees and sprawling live oaks. It was a neighborhood in transition, much of it updated with the influx of younger families, especially in areas away from the interstate. But Sally's old place wasn't just built in the sixties; it was trapped there, just two blocks away from I-95, a two-bedroom, ranch-style house, still sporting the original jalousie windows, aluminum awnings, and terrazzo front porch that screamed "rental property." Jack almost expected a pink plastic flamingo on the front lawn.

Jack parked his Mustang in the driveway. A potbellied man wearing blue jeans and a V-neck undershirt was waiting on the front steps, visible in the yellow glow from the porch light.

"Who's that?" asked Jack, peering through the windshield.

"Property manager," said Rene. "Just follow my lead, okay?"

"Your lead?"

"I didn't tell him that my sister used to live here and that I just wanted to look around. I said I needed a place in a hurry and that I'd give him ten percent more than the going rate if I like it. That's why he agreed to meet me on a Friday night."

"Anybody live here now?"

"An old guy, lives alone. Ever since the murder, I'm told it rents month to month, if it rents at all."

"With that kind of history, I guess you have to be pretty down on your luck to live here."

"Yeah," she said, and then her voice trailed off as she added, "Even more down than Sally was."

They headed up the walkway, and the property manager greeted them at the steps. Rene said, "You must be Jimmy."

"That's right." A toothpick wagged from his lips as he spoke, his thumbs hooked on his belt loops.

"I'm Rene, this is Jack," she said, handshakes all around. "We're here to see the house."

He closed one eye, a nervous habit, and said, "Y'all know 'bout the li'l girl got kilt here, right?"

"Yes, we know."

"Good. I want that out in the open. Cuz people comes here all the time, ya know. They look around, likes the place, then find out 'bout dat girl, and it changes their minds right quick. Jis wastes my time."

"We're okay with it."

"No children, huh?"

"No," she said. "No children."

He pulled a big ring of keys from his pocket, found the right one, and turned the lock. He pushed the door open, then immediately took a step back. The pungent odor of old kitty litter hit Jack in the face like an ammonia-soaked rag.

"Cats," said Jimmy. "Screwball who lives here now gots eleven of them."

"Eleven?" said Jack.

"Yeah. Can't stand them smelly bastards. Y'all go ahead. Look around. I'll wait right here."

Rene went first and switched on the light. Jack followed, and Jimmy stayed behind. The door closed just as soon as they were inside. Jimmy was apparently determined to contain the cat odor.

The living room was small and cluttered, with threadbare green carpet stretching wall to wall. A dingy white sheet was draped over the camelback sofa, and Jack counted five cats sleeping on it. Two armchairs, an ottoman, and even the coffee table were likewise covered with old sheets, and Jack accounted for three more cats.

"Man, it stinks in here."

Rene simply shot him a look that said, *Try living in Africa for three years, bucko.*

Jack took a step forward, then jumped at the sound of a cat toy squeaking beneath his shoe. He let out a nervous chuckle, but Rene didn't even flinch. She suddenly seemed oblivious to the sounds, the smells, the sights—to anything but the past she'd come here to uncover. Jack, too, could feel the mood shifting. No more little jokes, no more playful smiles, no more contrived distractions to keep them from breathing in and absorbing the tragedy that had occurred right here in this house, the horrible crime that had ended a child's life and changed a young mother forever.

"She was twenty-four when it happened," said Rene, her voice quaking.

Jack just stood there, as if he could feel his own blood coursing through his veins. Twenty-four. Could he remember what it was like to be twenty-four? Could he even fathom what it felt like to be a twenty-four-year-old woman with a four-year-old child, flat broke, working nights at Hooters, her husband working two jobs just to keep them out of bankruptcy? Was that the life of the princess Sally had dreamed about as a little girl, coming home at midnight six nights a week smelling of cigarettes and spilled beer, too much makeup on her pretty face, her nipples protruding from her too-tight tank top and her nylon shorts riding up her ass like a thong bikini, because looking like a slut would fetch her a few more bucks in tips? He wondered if there was a time in her entire adult life when Sally was ever truly happy. He wondered, too, if Sally could possibly have realized that her shitty little life wasn't all that bad, that it could have been so much worse, that the real nightmare was only about to begin.

"I don't think I can go back there by myself," said Rene.

Instinctively, Jack went to her, took her arm, and together they started down the dark hallway. They walked slowly, their heels clicking on the cracked terrazzo floor, *click-clock, click-clock, click-clock,* as if to mark the reversal of time, their descent into an unspeakably dark past. Jack didn't make her go any faster than she wanted, but they were barely moving, and finally she brought them to a stop at the open bathroom door.

Jack was right with her, so he switched on the hall light, which gave them enough illumination to see inside. A cat was perched on the lid of the toilet seat, as if waiting for a drink, then scurried away. The sink was stained with a broad streak of rust, and mildew had darkened the white ceramic tile. A deep crack arced across the medicine chest mirror. Directly opposite them was a cabana door that presumably led to the patio.

"That's where he got in," said Rene.

"The jalousie windows?"

She nodded once and said, "He slid his arm through, reached inside, and unlocked the deadbolt."

Jack stared at the lock, imagined the knob turning, wondered what Sally and little Katherine were doing when the stranger had joined them, wondered what was going through that monster's mind when he closed the door behind him, stepped inside, and started toward the bedroom. Was he all tingly and excited, sexually aroused, fearful of nothing? Or maybe he did have fear, a sociopath's only fear, the sick fear that reality couldn't possibly measure up to his endless hours of twisted fantasies, fear that all the planning and anticipation would be for naught because it simply wouldn't be enough that the girl was all his, the hot mom too, and that he could do with them as he wished.

Rene stepped inside, past the sink, then stopped and gasped. Jack immediately understood why. The bathtub. It was gone. It had been ripped out and replaced with a stand-alone shower, but its footprint remained like a giant scar, a crude confirmation of what had happened there. Jack had seen many crime scenes and crime scene photos, but he never got used to it. Looking at it made you realize that it really had happened, that it could never be undone, that the awful bitterness would rise up in your throat until you could taste the pain, the screams, the utter horror of the victims. Right there, that very spot, was where he'd knelt on the tile floor, filled the tub with water, and rinsed Sally's blood from his knife. Right there, that same spot, he'd wrung the blood from Sally's blouse, dipping and squeezing until the water turned bright red. Then he carried Sally's daughter—still alive, her feet and hands bound—and placed her in the tub, undoubtedly drawing one last moment of pleasure from the horror in her eyes. And then he slowly rolled her over, facedown in the water, and he watched, watched with delight. Jack knew he watched, because he'd spent four years of his life defending monsters like this on death row, he'd seen the gleam in their eyes as they recounted their conquests, killers who didn't see the point in killing unless they could watch every fucking last minute of it. That son of a bitch just watched her body writhing, her head bobbing, her bound legs flopping like some vulgar abomination of the Little Mermaid, his own curiosity unsatisfied until he saw with his own two eyes how much of the bloody mixture her tiny lungs could hold.

"We should go," said Jack.

"No. I want to see the bedroom."

They retreated from the bathroom and continued down the hall. The door was open about a foot, just enough for a cat to come and go. Rene pushed it all the way open, and flipped the light switch. The fixture on the ceiling had four bulbs, but only one was burning, which left the room dim and full of shadows—cat shadows, dozens of them. Cats on the bed, on the dresser, on the floor, in clothes baskets scattered about the room. Cats everywhere, and Jack felt his eyes starting to water.

"Looks like his eleven cats have had a few kittens," he said.

"I want to check the closet."

From what he'd read about the crime, Jack knew that the attacker had been hiding in the closet. Rene stepped around a sleeping ball of orange fur, and Jack followed her across the room. She stopped before the closet door.

"You want me to open it?" asked Jack.

She stared a moment longer, then simply nodded.

He'd offered to open it without a moment's hesitation, but as he reached for the handle, he felt something pulling inside him. It had been five years since the crime, dozens of different people had lived in this house since then, and he knew in his mind that there was nothing to fear on the other side of that door. But in his gut, where it mattered, he felt a slight reservation.

"Please," said Rene. "Open it."

The metal door handle felt cold in his hand, cold as the ice water that must have run through that killer's veins. He turned it. The latch clicked. He pulled the door open and saw a sudden black flash, which sent his heart into his throat.

A cat raced across his shoe tops.

He and Rene exchanged glances, as if to calm each other's nerves. Jack opened the door all the way and looked inside.

"You say he got in through the bathroom door, huh?"

"That's what Sally told me. The police report said there were signs of break-in at the bathroom door."

"So, he comes in the bathroom, walks down the hall to Katherine's bedroom, and hides inside the closet."

"That's the theory."

Jack pointed to the access door in the ceiling inside the closet and said, "Where do you suppose that leads to?"

Rene looked up and said, "The attic?"

A wall of built-in shelves inside the closet led upward like a ladder. Jack climbed up to the third shelf, pushed on the plywood, and opened the ceiling door. "It's an attic, all right. Wonder if he could have come in this way?"

"I suppose it's possible. I don't even think Sally knew every theory the police considered or rejected. The prosecutor was extremely tight-lipped about his investigation."

"Tell me about it. I had a little run-in myself a few weeks ago. So

long as they consider the investigation active, they aren't going to tell
you much."

"You mind taking a look?"

"In the attic?"

"The police have had five years to solve this crime. Why not have
a look for ourselves?"

Jack shrugged and said, "Okay, sure. Why not?"

Jack climbed up the shelves, pushed the ceiling door aside, and
poked his head into the attic. The air was stuffy, and he was sweating
almost instantly, as the temperature in the attic was at least ten
degrees hotter than the main house. Jack let his eyes adjust and found
a naked bulb hanging from a wire. He pulled the cord, and the attic
brightened.

"Got light," he said.

"Good," she replied, her muted voice wafting upward through the
ceiling.

Jack climbed the rest of the way and pulled himself up. The attic
had no floor, just exposed joists and insulation, so he distributed his
weight across three joists—feet, seat, hands. The lighting wasn't
great, but it was good enough to see that the attic ran the length of the
house, from one end of the gabled roof to the other. He was at the
highest point, dead center, and even there the head clearance was
only about three feet. He saw no windows.

"Don't see how he could have gotten in here from the outside," he
said. "Don't see any outside access at all."

"How about access from another room?"

He was afraid she was going to say that. "I'll check."

He crab-walked across the joists, careful not to slip and stick a foot
or hand through the ceiling. The farther he traveled from the opening, the hotter it got. He could feel his shirt starting to stick to his
back with sweat. His foot dragged across the exposed insulation, and a
cloud of musty fibers was suddenly airborne. Jack coughed the thirty-
year-old particles out of his lungs. He didn't see another ceiling access
door anywhere.

"I think the closet's the only way up," he shouted.

"Why don't I just check the closet in the other bedroom," she shouted back.

Jack considered his position, his head banging against the roof, his body spread out across the joists as if he were training for the county fair wheelbarrow race. *Now she thinks of it.* "Good idea," he said.

He could hear her footfalls below him as she traversed the hallway that connected the bedrooms. He heard a door open, presumably the master bedroom, then another one, presumably the closet.

"Nothing," he heard her shout.

The lightbulb flickered, and the attic went dark.

"Oh, shit," Jack muttered. He stayed in his crab-walk position, hoping the light would flick back on. Some light was shining through the opening to the attic from the closet below, so it wasn't completely black. He knew the joists were the standard sixteen inches apart, so he could find his way back even with the bad lighting. He waited for his eyes to adjust, and then he noticed something.

Down at the other end of the attic, over the master bedroom, a ray of light was shooting up into the attic. *What the hell?*

"Rene, where are you?"

"In the master."

"Do you see a hole in the ceiling?"

He waited for her reply, which was simply, "No."

The beam of light was still shining up like a laser from the master bedroom. He hadn't noticed it earlier, but that was because the attic light had been burning. In the dark attic, and with the light glowing in the bedroom below, it was plainly visible. Jack crawled toward the beacon until it was within an arm's length.

He stared at the light for a moment, noticing that insulation had been cut away next to the joist. The hole itself was smaller than a dime, but there was definitely a hole, and with the insulation trimmed back it appeared as though someone had deliberately put it there. He squatted down and peered through the opening.

"Rene? You sure you don't see a hole?"

There was a brief pause, as if she were searching. "No," she said. "Just the ceiling fan."

Ceiling fan. Jack pulled away a little more insulation. He found an electrical box and a mounting bracket for a ceiling fan. Beside the fan bracket was another bracket. It was attached to the joist but not to the fan, and it didn't seem to be serving any purpose at all. He took a closer look, and there was just enough light emanating upward through the hole to let him read the manufacturer's name printed on the side of the bracket: Velbon.

It probably wouldn't have meant anything to him, had his ex-wife not been a photographer. Velbon was one of the best-known manufacturers of tripods and mounting brackets for video cameras. At that moment, Jack realized exactly what he'd found.

He took one more look down through the hole—a hole that from the bedroom probably looked like nothing more than a vent in the ceiling fan—and he had a perfect view of the bed.

Five years earlier, it would have been Sally's bed. He could have watched Sally climbing into bed. Sally sleeping in her bed. Sally doing whatever it was she liked to do in bed.

"Rene?" he said in a voice loud enough to carry into the room below.

"Yes?"

"Your sister was definitely being stalked."

Fifty

At six o'clock Monday morning, Gerry Colletti was in his kitchen, dressed and ready to leave for work. He checked his reflection in the glass display cabinet and, as always, liked what he saw. A lot of lawyers had fallen into the casual dress mode, but not Gerry. The suit was Armani. The shoes, Ferragamo. His silk tie and socks—you could measure a man's true net worth by the quality of his socks—both by Hermès. The shirt was custom made in Hong Kong, as were all his shirts, because there wasn't a designer in the world that made shirts to fit a freak of nature with a nineteen-inch neck and a thirty-inch sleeve length. Gerry hadn't worked out since he quit the wrestling team in college, unless you called banging your female clients a workout, so it was truly the clothes that made the man— clothes and a good tailor.

"Gabby, order more Hawaiian Gold," he said into his Dictaphone. He kept a running list on audiotape of all the personal things his secretary needed to do for him, but he suddenly realized that with Gabby a general order for "Hawaiian Gold" might fetch him anything from a box of pineapples to a bag of premium pot. "That's Hawaiian Gold *coffee*," he said, then slipped the Dictaphone into his inside pocket.

He poured himself a cup for the road, tucked the *Wall Street Journal* under his arm, and headed for the door that connected the kitchen to the garage.

It had been a quiet weekend, and Gerry had wanted it that way.

He was still smarting from the way Swyteck had embarrassed him at the court hearing on Friday afternoon. It wasn't like him to make a stupid mistake like that with the photographs and the date on his wristwatch. That kind of slipup told him one thing: He wasn't being patient enough. Brains and patience were all it took to win this contest, two things Tatum Knight and Miguel Rios didn't have. That would be their downfall. They alone stood between him and forty-six million dollars. Well, them and Alan Sirap.

Whoever the hell that is.

Gerry entered the garage and hit the button on the wall that switched on the light and opened the garage door. His emerald-black BMW was ready for a ride, washed and polished, glistening beneath the hanging fluorescent tube. He paused to admire it as the garage door noisily lumbered upward. He'd always been a car guy. His father had been a car guy—a greasy coveralls, dirt-under-the-fingernails, minimum-wage auto mechanic who'd never in his life owned a new car. His father never had anything new. *They* never had anything new. His mother had left them when he was ten, came back for Gerry, filed for divorce, cleaned out the old man, waited for the divorce to become final—and then married her divorce lawyer. A *smart* divorce lawyer. She married that son of a bitch, and then sent Gerry back to live with the old man, flat broke, not a pot to piss in.

What goes around, comes around.

With the press of a button on his remote, the car alarm chirped and the doors unlocked. Gerry got inside, slid behind the wheel, and closed the door. He got himself situated—coffee cup in the holder, newspaper open on the seat beside him for easy reading in stopped traffic, loose change for the tolls in the dispenser. He checked himself one last time in the rearview mirror, then turned the key.

Nothing.

He turned it again, but there was just a click, and then nothing, a pathetic sound that was even more pathetic when you were used to hearing the glorious rumble of eight perfectly tuned cylinders.

The battery was his first thought, but then he thought again. The electronic keyless entry had responded to his remote, and the dome light had come on when he'd opened the door. The clock was working, too. Something was screwy with the starter.

Or somebody had screwed with it.

Another man might have been frightened, but Gerry only smiled. He prided himself on being fearless. In his line of work, many an ex-husband had threatened him, and a few had even come after him. You couldn't do this work without balls as big as globes, and his were made of brass.

Somebody messing with his car—how beautiful was that? It was exactly the kind of additional evidence of intimidation he needed to box Tatum Knight into disqualification under the Slayer Statute. That idiot just couldn't control himself, and Gerry was suddenly cocksure that Tatum Knight had yanked the wires from his alternator in retaliation for his clever courtroom maneuvering. Swyteck may have scored a few points for style at Friday's hearing, but Gerry had the long-term winning strategy. And if Knight kept doing stupid things like this, he'd reap the rewards sooner than expected.

He pulled the hood release, got out of the car, and walked around the front to check things out. If this was what he thought it was, he'd definitely file a police report. But he didn't want to be crying wolf, either. He wanted to see those wires ripped from the starter, maybe even take a few more pictures.

The hood had risen up about four inches before it caught on the safety latch. He reached underneath to find the trip switch that would completely release it. He couldn't remember the last time he'd opened the hood, and wasn't exactly sure where the release was. Both hands were under the hood, fiddling for the switch, when a black blur fell from above him, swooping down like Spider-Man from atop the opened garage door that lay directly overhead suspended from the ceiling. It was a huge blur that took the shape of a man who pounced on the hood of the car, his sheer weight slamming it shut on Gerry's fingers. He felt the back-spray of blood against his belly, heard the sickening crush of bones that just a split second earlier had been his precious hands.

A cord closed tightly around his neck, silencing his screams, as the man reached up and manually pulled the garage door closed. Gerry's head rolled back, and that's when he saw it, right above him: The access panel to the attic had been pushed aside—a passageway that had been hidden by the opened garage door in its rolled-back position, an opening that hadn't been there when he'd entered the garage with the door closed.

Gerry stood face-to-face with his attacker, unable to run away or raise his mangled hands in defense, unable to pry his fingers loose from beneath the crushing car hood that had trapped him like an animal. The pain was so intense that his entire body tightened with spasms. He tried to scream, but the wire noose around his neck drew tighter. He could barely see, his vision blurred by the trauma, but he could see well enough to know that his attacker was looking right at him, his face hidden behind a ski mask.

The tension on the cord eased. Gerry could breathe again, hear again. The man was saying something.

"Poor Gerry Colletti," he said taunting him. "Tried to hard-nose negotiate his way to the prize."

"Huh?" he tried to say, but it was only a grunt.

"If only he'd known all the deals had already been cut."

"What are—" he started to say, but the cord tightened around his neck, and again he was fighting for air. His knees buckled, and he would have fallen to the ground if his attacker hadn't held the cord high like a rope from a tree limb. He could feel his life slipping away as he heard the man say, "See you in hell, Gerry. I hear it's one big gold mine."

Fifty-one

Homicide Detective Rick Larsen arrived at the home of Gerry Colletti just after dinnertime. It had been a comfortably cool autumn day, but temperatures were dropping with the setting sun. White short-sleeve shirts with a loosened necktie were the trademark Larsen attire, but tonight he broke down and pulled on a windbreaker, which was perfectly fine. His old buddies up in Buffalo were already trudging through eighteen inches of Thanksgiving snow.

Two squad cars were parked at the end of the driveway, blocking off traffic. The medical examiner's van was parked just inside the squad cars, and yellow police tape marked off the entire yard as a crime scene.

Larsen was technically off duty, but he'd left word to be called immediately if anything happened to any of the remaining heirs under Sally Fenning's will. With Mason Rudsky and Deirdre Meadows already in the morgue, it didn't take a genius to see a pattern developing. He'd considered putting a tail on Rios, Colletti, and Knight so that the police would be right there if anything happened to one of them. But stakeouts were expensive, and there just wasn't room in the budget for one of them, let alone three, especially when his instincts told him that the killer would probably lie low for a while until the media hoopla settled down, wait a few weeks or possibly even a few months before striking again.

In one of the few lapses in his long career, his instincts had steered him wrong.

Larsen got out of his car and walked over to the uniformed officer in charge of controlling access to the scene.

"Is it who we think it is?" said Larsen.

"No official ID yet. But it's his house, his car, and as best I can tell the face matches the mug shot on his driver's license. If it ain't Geraldo Colletti, it's his twin brother."

"Who found him? Someone driving by?"

"No. Garage door was closed."

"Doesn't look closed." There was reproval in his tone, as if to convey his sincere hope that someone on the team wasn't in line for a severe ass kicking for having altered the crime scene.

"His secretary opened it. She saw him through the window, thought he might still be alive, so she opened the door."

"His secretary?"

"He missed eleven scheduled appointments for the day, didn't answer his beeper or his cell phone. By late afternoon she was getting pretty worried, drove over. Found him there in the garage."

Larsen looked up the long driveway of Chicago brick. The forensic team was at work in the area around the garage opening, and the assistant medical examiner was tending to the body.

"His secretary still here?"

"In the squad car. I took her statement, but she's too shook up to drive home."

"Ask her to stick around, okay? I may want to talk to her." He gave him a wink and a slap on the shoulder, then started up the driveway toward the garage.

A gust of wind stirred up some fallen mango leaves, sent them swirling past the opening. It was a northeast wind, the kind of wind that ushered in those awful cold fronts that could send late November temperatures plummeting all the way down into the fifties or even forties. Larsen actually liked a little nip in the air, though he sympathized with the poor slobs who were spending two months' salary to walk around Miami Beach dressed in winter coats. He was a sympathetic guy, or so people told him. Took every homicide personally, showed real compassion to the families and the victims. Even when the victim was an asshole lawyer.

"Gerry Colletti," he said to no one in particular as he stopped at the entrance to the garage.

The cord was still around the victim's neck. His bloody hands were still trapped beneath the hood, his limp body draped over the front of the car like a hapless deer that someone had nailed while barreling down the highway at sixty miles per hour. Larsen focused on the hands and said, "Ouch."

"No kidding," said the examiner. He was on his knees, taking measurements. "Man, I remember when I was twelve, my sister slammed the piano key cover on my fingers."

"Has to hurt bad."

"Shit yeah. Of course, ligature strangulation with a fifty-pound picture-hanging wire has a way of taking your mind off your fingers."

"That our cause of death?"

"Take a look for yourself. Cord's still around his neck, and I don't think it was planted there to throw us off. We got bleeding sites in the mucosa of the lips, inside the mouth and eyelids. Face and neck congested and dark red. All consistent with strangulation."

"I guess we can rule out suicide."

"I'd say so. The bruising pattern on the neck is a horizontal straight line," he said, indicating. "With a suicidal hanging you find the more vertical, inverted V-shaped bruise. Suicide by straight strangulation is pretty rare."

"Especially with your hands trapped beneath a car hood."

"Good point, Columbo."

A guy inside the garage climbed down from a ladder. It was Larsen's young partner. "Rick, have a look at this."

The ladder was right beside the car by the passenger door. Larsen climbed up to the fourth step, high enough to get his head between the ceiling and the suspended garage door in its rolled-back position. The access panel had been pushed aside, and Larsen shined his penlight through the opening to the attic. "Point of entry," he said.

"Looks that way," his partner said.

Larsen spoke as he climbed down the ladder, the scene unfolding in his mind. "Perp hides in the attic. Hears the garage door opening. Slides the access panel away while the garage door opener is clanging away. Colletti never hears a thing. Can't see a thing either, because the opened garage door hides the hole. Perp climbs out, waits for Colletti to come around to the front of the car, pounces on him."

"Why are his hands beneath the hood?"

"Perp took care of that. Car doesn't start. I'll bet the keys are still in the ignition." Larsen peered through the passenger side window and answered his own question. "Yup."

The medical examiner rose from the garage floor and said, "Hey, Columbo, look at this."

Larsen grumbled as he walked to the front of the car, wishing he'd stop calling him Columbo. "What?"

The examiner held a magnifying glass over the victim's left shoulder blade. "Looks like we got a dried stain here."

"Blood?"

"Nah. Dried blood on a tan suit would be your basic brown. All we have here that's visible to the naked eye is the outer ring of the stain."

"What does that tell you?"

"It's a silk-blend suit. You ever dropped water on silk, like a tie or something?"

Larsen screwed up his face and said, "A silk tie? I don't think so. But I did accidentally piss on a pair of polyester pants once."

"Be glad it wasn't silk. Water will stain silk. Leaves a ring just like this."

"You're saying this is water?"

"Something with a high water content that dries relatively clear, but not water." He raised an eyebrow to give added weight to his words and said, "Semen, maybe."

Larsen's partner chuckled. "What? You think he strangled this guy and then whacked off over his work?"

Larsen and the examiner were deadpan, as if they'd seen stranger things. Then Larsen took another look at the body, the mangled hands trapped beneath the hood, the bruises around the neck—bruises that reflected the use of far more force than was necessary to choke the life out of the victim. "Got a lot of rage here, contempt for the victim."

"Which is consistent with a guy who does this to get his rocks off. Literally."

Larsen shook his head and said, "I don't think it's semen."

"Lab will tell for sure."

"I'll bet dollars to doughnuts it's saliva."

"Saliva?"

Larsen nodded slowly, absorbing the scene, watching more of the crime unfold in his mind's eye. "Like I said, we got real contempt here. Something personal. Killing him wasn't enough. He took one last look at this pathetic heap hanging from the front end of his eighty-thousand-dollar BMW, dredged up every ounce of hatred in the back of his throat, and then let it fly."

"He spat on him?"

"Yeah," he said as a dreamy smile tugged at the corners of his mouth. "Thank our lucky stars. He spat on him."

Fifty-two

"They want you to submit a DNA specimen for testing," said Jack.

Tatum wiped the beer-foam mustache from his lip, silent, as if his lawyer needed to say more before a response was merited.

A restaurant wasn't Jack's first choice of venue, but Tatum lived in north Miami Beach, and he'd groaned like a sick water buffalo about driving "all the way to Coral Gables" for a meeting with his lawyer. So Jack had suggested they meet for lunch at Gusto, a Cuban restaurant near the Lincoln Road area. The service was friendly and the food was good, perfect for a first date or a leisurely dinner with friends. But the colorful stories that came with the meal seemed downright goofy when the basic objective was to get your client to give up bodily fluids.

The waiter placed Jack's medium-rare palomilla steak before him, then slid the house specialty in front of Tatum and said, "*El balsero* for you, señor."

"What the hell's this?" he asked. "I thought I ordered regular old shrimp."

Jack said, "The special has shrimp in it. *El balsero*, they call it. It means 'the rafter,' I think."

"*Sí, sí.* The rafter." The waiter smiled proudly, and Jack smiled back, though somewhat bewildered. Jack had clients, friends, and even relatives who had actually come to Miami by raft, so he wasn't quite sure what the politically correct reaction was to a dish called "the rafter." But this *was* a Cuban restaurant, the waiter was more Cuban than he was, and a nostalgic mural of Havana Harbor was painted on the wall, so he just kept smiling.

Tatum was staring at his plate.

El balsero, the waiter explained, was the personal creation of a talented chef with a quirky sense of humor and, arguably, too much time on his hands. The banana-shaped raft was made from the hollowed-out shell of a plantain so lengthy that Freud would have had a psychological feast. The rafters inside were six stuffed shrimp tail-up and held fast by a tomato enchilada sauce. Thin french fries on either side of the raft were, naturally, the paddles.

"Looks more like a gondola than a raft," said Tatum.

"I was thinking a canoe," said Jack. "Say, Lewis and Clark paddling down a river of mojo sauce."

"Ah," the waiter said with a wide smile of recognition. "Sooper Mahn."

"No, no, not Superman. That's *Lois* and Clark. I'm talking about the nineteenth-century explorers—you know, Lewis, Clark, Sacajawea?"

The waiter just shrugged, lost. Jack considered trying to explain it in his stilted Spanish, then decided against it, figuring that although he wasn't exactly ahead, he might as well quit while he wasn't quite so far behind. "Never mind. *Gracias por la comida*," he said, thanking him for the food.

"*De nada*," he replied. You're welcome.

Jack sprinkled chopped onions and parsley on his palomilla steak, poured the black beans over his white rice and added a little hot sauce, just the way he liked it. When he looked up, Tatum's shrimp were gone.

"Pretty damn good," Tatum said. "Lois was especially tasty."

"*Lewis*," he said, dismissing it with a wave of his hand.

Tatum sat back, seeming to have had his fill of shrimp passengers and small talk. He looked at Jack and said, "Tell me why I should give Larsen my DNA."

"To get a swarming pack of homicide detectives off your back."

"They think I killed Colletti," he said, more a statement than a question.

"Of course they do."

"I didn't."

"I know. Theo told me you two were out on his boat fishing last night. Didn't get home till this morning."

Tatum took another long drink from his tall glass of beer. "Did you tell the cops that?"

"Yes."

"And they still want my DNA?"

"Larsen doesn't put much stock in an alibi that can be corroborated only by your brother. Frankly, I don't blame him."

Tatum leaned into the table and said, "Is it that you don't blame him? Or do you think Theo's lying for me, too?"

Jack looked away, not sure how to answer. "Where are the fish, Tatum?"

"They weren't biting," he said flatly.

"Not a single one all night long, huh?"

"Fishermen come home empty-handed all the time. Theo even made a joke on the boat ride home, how it's like Jack always says, this is why they call it fishin' and not—"

"Catchin', I know, I know. Look, the bottom line is, your alibi isn't going to fly all by its lonesome. I talked face-to-face with Larsen this morning. I'm not saying they're going to come out and arrest you tonight, tomorrow, or the next day. But the heat is on. I'm fielding calls from the cops, Miguel's lawyer, lawyers for the dead heirs, the press. I'm starting to feel more like a juggler than a lawyer. Larsen's offering us a scientific way to exonerate yourself before we drop all the balls and he comes to slap the cuffs on your wrists."

"Explain this to me."

"There's a stain on Colletti's suit. Turned out to be saliva, and there's enough of it to allow for DNA testing. Since it was on his back, doesn't seem likely it was from the victim, himself, so they think that whoever killed him also spat on him."

"Pretty stupid thing to do."

"Homicides can get personal, emotions take over. Anyway, the cops want a DNA sample from you. The lab compares the two, and if they don't get a match—bingo, someone else jumps to the top of the list of suspects."

"What if I say no?"

"If they have enough other evidence to link you to the crime, they could go for a court order, force you to give a hair sample, a cheek swab, something nonsurgical."

Tatum picked at the empty shell of the plantain in his plate, saying nothing. Jack gave him a moment, then asked, "So, what do you say?"

Tatum looked up, his expression dead serious. "Let 'em arrest me."

"What?"

He drained his beer, and said, "Sorry, Jack. I can't give the cops my DNA."

Fifty-three

Theo understood, but he knew he could never explain it to Jack. It was Jack who'd told him about the meeting at the restaurant, and Jack was cool in Theo's book, but a Yale-educated lawyer whose daddy was once a governor couldn't even begin to understand why Tatum wouldn't give a DNA sample. Didn't matter how cool Jack was. Only Theo could understand, but that didn't mean he agreed with the decision. He'd even called Tatum himself, which got him exactly nowhere.

"This could prove you innocent. Don't you see that, man?"

"I'm not givin' no DNA."

"But this shit works. A DNA test is what got me off death row."

"You didn't have no choice, Theo. You was already on death row."

"And that's where they wants to put you, too. Take the test."

"No."

"*Shee-it*, Tatum, why the hell not? We was out fishing all night. You're innocent. I *knows* you're innocent."

"Then stop askin' me to take the fucking test."

The conversation could have lasted another thirty years, and Theo would have been no closer to convincing him. When Tatum had made up his mind, there was no changing it. He'd been that way all his life. But maybe this time he was right. If Jack Swyteck couldn't understand it, well, that's the way it breaks, buddy. If Theo didn't want to accept it, hey, that's your choice, bro'. People didn't think of

Tatum Knight as a man of principle, but nobody knew him the way Theo did. And Theo knew exactly what was going on in his head. Two black guys, brothers—not soul brothers or gang brothers or You-Can-Share-My-Needle-for-a-Taste-of-Crystal-Meth brothers—but real brothers, brothers from the same womb, born of the same crackhead mother who'd gone out one night and gotten her throat slit by some asshole who didn't think her blow job was worth the ten dollars. Maybe they did and maybe they didn't have the same father (and they probably did, because they looked so much alike), but either way they'd never know who the hell he was. An alibi from these dead-end kids from Liberty City wasn't good enough for Detective Rick Larsen and his lynch mob. They needed DNA—ironclad, scientific proof-positive of innocence, or his alibi didn't mean shit. Well, fuck *them*, was all Tatum was saying. All of them.

Theo could understand that. At least he wanted to understand. It wasn't easy to stand by and watch his brother pass up a golden opportunity to prove himself innocent, clear his name, get the blood-hounds on somebody else's trail. Not after losing four years on death row for someone else's crime. It took balls to stand up to a homicide detective that way, to look the demon in the eye and say, "You want me? Come get me." Theo admired that in his brother. Actually, they were a lot alike in that respect. The Knight brothers were never the ones to back down from anyone or anything, never afraid to butt heads with their worst nightmares. With one exception. There was one demon Theo had never confronted. He'd never gone back to that all-night convenience store where he'd found that clerk in a puddle of blood.

'Bout damn time you did.

Theo remembered the way. He drove the exact route they'd taken that night, last night it seemed, or was it a million years ago?

It was nine o'clock in the evening, much earlier than his disastrous visit at 4 A.M., just as dark but much more traffic. The street was freshly paved, and there was a new median down the middle. Public works had planted a few palm trees to pretty-up the neighborhood, not the towering and beautiful royal palms or the Canary Island date palms you saw on wide boulevards cutting through tony Coral Gables, just the straggly, brown variety that got planted for no other reason than to shut people up whenever they bitched and moaned about the lack of green space in *their* neighborhood. So after all these years, they finally got the weed palms, sickly looking trees plucked from somewhere in the Everglades, one or two puny fronds reaching aimlessly for the sky like Alfalfa's haircut, their trunks propped up by two-by-fours and covered top to bottom with gang graffiti, clearly some bureaucrat's idea of landscaping.

Theo turned at the traffic light. The pool hall was gone, the whole building boarded up and scorched around the edges, the fire probably caused by a careless cigarette or more likely the owner's dumb-ass refusal to make good on a gambling debt. The gas station was still on the corner, but the new self-serve pumps looked like something out of *The Jetsons* compared to the old equipment Theo remembered. And Theo did remember. He'd forgotten nothing, having gone over that night many times in his mind while lying alone on a prison bunk. But just the thought of actually retracing his steps had his heart pounding.

He parked the car and switched off the radio. The music had been playing loudly that night, as he recalled, until they parked behind the convenience store, where Lionel, the gang leader, gave him his instructions and started the initiation.

"*You want to be a Grove Lord or don't you?*"

"*Shit, yeah.*"

"*You got five minutes to prove it. Then I'm gone, wit or wit'out you.*"

Theo got out of the car and shut the door, his head clear of alcohol this time yet clouded with so many memories, so many doubts.

Loose gravel on the pavement crunched beneath his feet as he started down the alley. He was approaching the store from the back, just as he had before. It was a solitary journey, the passageway narrow and dark, brightened only by the streetlight at the front entrance. He'd sprinted up this alley the last time, but tonight he walked, absorbing the details. The dirty bricks on the walls on either side of him, the cracks in the pavement beneath his feet, the sound of the traffic somewhere ahead of him. He reached the sidewalk and turned left, toward the entrance to Shelby's, except that it wasn't called Shelby's anymore. The sign on the door said MORTON'S MARKET. Theo had heard that old man Shelby had sold it. He couldn't take it anymore, his business off badly from all the talk on the street about that poor nineteen-year-old kid who got beat to death by that black piece of shit from Liberty City and his pocket-size crowbar.

"Got a buck, bro'?" asked the homeless guy sitting on the sidewalk outside the entrance.

"Get you on the way out," said Theo, and then he stopped at the glass doors. He remembered the butterflies in his stomach the last time he'd come here, how relieved he was to see no one inside the store, the cash register unattended. It was a little different at this hour, two customers inside that he could count, the clerk seated at the counter and watching ESPN on the little television. But everything else looked virtually identical, the aisles configured the same way, the same beige tile floors, the beer and snack foods stacked the same way near the entrance. It may have been called Morton's Market, but he was going back to Shelby's.

He pushed the door open and walked inside.

The clerk glanced over his shoulder, checked him out, then turned his attention back to the television. Theo walked around the stack of newspapers and the barrel of iced-down singles. The clerk didn't give him a second look. Theo Knight, former death row inmate, had just walked into the store, and the kid didn't seem to care. Did he know what had happened here? Had anyone told him?

Have you been in that stockroom?

Theo stopped and looked down the hall, his gaze carrying him all the way back to that first sight of blood, the bright crimson trail that he'd followed like a fool, followed all the way to Florida State Prison and four years of near misses with the electric chair.

The front door opened. Theo turned, the clerk's head jerked. Two teenage boys walked in. Both were black. Both wore baggy pants, Miami Hurricane football jerseys, thick gold chains, and black knit caps, which seemed to have replaced the backward baseball caps of Theo's era, even in the tropical climates. They walked with the typical gang swagger, something that never seemed to change from one generation to the next. This time, the clerk looked nervous. The boys separated. One went down the far aisle, the other took the near aisle. Up and down they walked, as if casing the place, biding their time until the customers had the good sense to leave them alone with the clerk and the cash drawer.

Theo watched them. This time he wasn't going to run. *I'm here for you, pal.*

Finally, the nearest one burst into laughter. The other laughed even harder, no apparent reason, some kind of private joke that was at the expense of Theo or the scared clerk. Either way, Theo didn't like it, and they were starting to piss him off.

Their laughter faded; the joke was over. The one who'd laughed first grabbed a couple of Gatorades from the cooler, walked up to the counter, and laid down his money. The clerk still looked nervous, but it was no longer a fear of the unknown but rather the fear of a danger that was all too familiar. He handed over the change and said, "Thanks, Lenny."

"I'm Leroy, dumbshit. Lenny's the ugly one."

Theo watched as the two boys walked out the front door, laughing and hassling each other. "Who you calling ugly, motha' fucka'?"

Then they were gone, on to the next joint, no place in particular. Lenny and Leroy, like Theo and Tatum. Teenage brothers. Couple of neighborhood badasses who got their kicks just skulking around and watching people scare. Looked alike. Dressed alike. Acted alike. People always getting them mixed up, confusing one for the other.

Theo suddenly went cold. It was a sickening thought, but he was beginning to understand his brother's refusal to take the DNA test on a whole different level, one that had nothing to do with courage or principle or standing up to Detective Larsen. It boiled down to just one thing, the very thing the test was about: genetics.

Theo shook his head, not wanting to believe it but believing it nonetheless.

Tatum, you chickenshit son of a bitch.

Fifty-four

J ack had time enough to smell but not taste the coffee before Theo came barging into his office on Wednesday morning. He had Tatum in tow, so Jack knew it was serious.

"What's wrong?" asked Jack, rising from behind his desk.

His secretary suddenly appeared behind the double-barreled hulk of humanity that was blocking Jack's doorway, standing on her tiptoes and waving from the hallway to get Jack's attention. "Knight brothers are here," she said.

"Thanks, Maria."

Theo closed the door and said, "Siddown, Tatum."

Tatum took a seat, and so did Jack. No one told him to sit, but with Theo speaking to his own brother in that tone of voice, it seemed wise to anticipate.

Tatum glared at his younger brother and said, "You think now you could maybe tell me what the hell this—"

"Shut your mouth," said Theo.

It had been a long time since Jack had seen his friend so worked up. "Theo, calm down, all right?"

"Calm down?" he said with an angry smile. "I been calming myself down all night long, and it just gets me more pissed. So don't tell me to calm down."

"What happened last night?" asked Jack.

"I went back to Shelby's."

Jack and Tatum exchanged glances, as if neither one knew where to go from there.

Theo kept talking, pacing. "I was trying to understand, why would Tatum refuse to take a DNA test to get found not guilty when his own brother got hisself off death row that way? And then it hits me: That *is* the reason he won't take the DNA test."

Tatum said, "What you talking about?"

"You *know* what I'm talking about."

"Ain't got a clue."

"Four years I wasted on death row. No more lies, Tatum."

"You're pissing me off now. Don't be calling me no liar."

"Then stop the lying," said Theo, his voice rising. "Ain't no more excuse for it. That's why I dragged your ass all the way over here, held off talking about it till you and me both was sitting down in front of our lawyer. Tell him, Jack. Everything we say here is protected by the attorney-client privilege, right?"

"You're both clients. But it's two different cases. I'm a little confused as to what's going on here."

"Jack, let's just agree that nothing leaves this room. Can you fucking do that for me?"

Theo's eyes were bulging. "Sure," Jack said in a calming voice. "This is all privileged."

"Nothing that we say here can ever be repeated in a courtroom. No one can run out of here and tell the cops what the other one said, right?"

"That's right," said Jack.

Theo glared at Tatum and said, "Talk to me, brother."

"Talk what?"

"I want the truth."

"The truth about *what?*"

"Was you the one who killed that clerk at Shelby's?" Theo wasn't shouting, but his voice was firm and harsh, and the question hit like ice water. Jack looked at Theo, then at Tatum, then back at Theo, wondering what in the world had happened in the last twenty-four hours. He expected Tatum to jump any second and grab his brother by the throat for talking such shit.

Tatum simply chuckled and said, "Wha-at?"

It was a nervous chuckle. Jack could hear the little break in his voice, and he knew Theo was on to a horrible truth that was about to change things forever. Jack looked at Tatum and said, "He wants to know if you're the member of the Grove Lords who let him take the fall."

Tatum gave his lawyer a look that said, *Stay the hell out of this, Swyteck*.

Theo was pacing again, speaking in what sounded like pure stream of consciousness. "This is what I realized last night. You refused to take the DNA test for Gerry Colletti's murder because you was worried about a match."

"I didn't kill Colletti."

"I know you didn't. But I'm not talking about a match between your DNA and the DNA found in the dried spit they took from the back of Colletti's suit coat. You were afraid of a match with the human hair and skin the cops scraped from under the fingernails of that convenience store clerk at Shelby's. That kid fought like a tiger, right, Jack?"

"That's what the crime scene suggested."

"The forensic guys who testified at my trial said the kid fought back and put a nice scratch into the top of his attacker's head. Got some skin and hair under his nails. My first lawyer tried to use that at trial. He asked the jury, Why no scratch on top of my client's head if the victim had skin and hair under his nails? Too bad for me that I wasn't arrested and examined by a doctor until seven months after the crime. Scratch could have healed in all that time. At least that's what the prosecutor made the jury believe. But it all worked out in the end. The scrapings of skin and hair gave us a nice DNA sample. DNA wasn't used that much at the time of my trial. Four years later, it was. When Jack came in to handle my habeas corpus petitions, he got the test, got me off death row."

"And the only one happier than you was me," said Tatum.

"Yeah, now I know why. I don't understand all the details, but,

Jack, help me out here. Once there's a DNA test, the cops keep that shit around, don't they?"

"You're talking about CODIS," said Jack.

"Tell him, Jack. Tell Tatum what he already knows, and what I just figured out."

It was strange, the way this was coming off as if Jack and Theo had rehearsed it. But Jack had wondered about the real killer for almost as many years as Theo had, and now that Theo was on a roll, Jack was right with him, step for step. "CODIS is the FBI's Combined DNA Index System," said Jack. "If a DNA test is performed on a specimen sample taken from a crime scene, that DNA profile is entered into the forensic files of CODIS. Once I was finally able to get the test done to compare Theo's DNA to the hair and skin sample taken from the victim, the DNA profile of the unknown killer would, as a matter of course, have been entered into the CODIS forensic database."

"Which is exactly the reason my brother didn't want to give his DNA profile. Even though his DNA would have proved that he didn't kill Gerry Colletti, a simple run through the FBI's database would have proved that he *did* kill the store clerk."

A tense silence filled the room as the two brothers stared each other down.

"That wasn't the way it was supposed to go down," Tatum said quietly.

"Oh, man," said Jack, his response involuntary.

Tatum continued, "It was my next step up in the Grove Lords. I had to take someone out, you know, if I ever wanted to have my own turf. So Lionel, he picks out this clerk at Shelby's. No real reason, just picked him. So, I did him."

Theo looked ready to explode. Jack knew he had to say something before he had another homicide on his hands. "Why'd you pin it on Theo?"

"Wasn't supposed to be no one else in the store. But when I came out, I ran past some guy on the sidewalk. I was afraid he could ID me. I had to think fast, man. I was scared, you know? So when I get back to the car, that's when me and Lionel come up with the plan."

"What plan?" asked Jack.

"We had to get someone else, you know. Someone else to go in that store."

Theo's voice shook with anger. "Someone who looked like you."

He shook his head, his voice filled with regret. "I didn't want it to be you, Theo. That's what I told Lionel. All the Grove Lords dressed alike. Black pants, Miami Heat jerseys, gold chains, backward baseball caps. We could have picked almost anyone. But Lionel picked Theo."

"And you didn't fight him?"

"At first, yeah. I said no way. But it made sense for it to be you."

"Bullshit, Tatum. It was dark, we all dressed alike. There were ten other Grove Lords that could have looked like you."

"We didn't pick you just because we looked alike. It was smarter than that."

"Smart?" he said, almost screeching.

"You was fifteen, man. Lionel said no way you'd be charged as an adult. I was almost eighteen. No question I was looking at adult charges. So that's how we picked you."

Jack could hear Theo breathing in and out, the anger scorching his lungs and throat, taking his words away. Jack spoke for him. "So you served up your little brother thinking he'd get off on a juvenile charge, serving time in detention until his record was expunged at age eighteen."

"That was the plan."

Jack kept probing. "That guy on the sidewalk who you nearly ran over on your way out of the store—he was the eyewitness who mistakenly picked Theo out of the lineup."

"That's right."

"And with a solid eyewitness, the state attorney started feeling pretty good about the case. They charged Theo as an adult, not a juvenile. And the jury nailed him for murder one."

"Next thing I know he's on death row," said Tatum. "It was like a nightmare for me."

"For *you!*" Theo shouted. "Fuck you, Tatum!"

"Don't you think it was killing me, too?"

"No! You would have let me die."

"No way was I gonna let that happen."

"I always knew I was set up by the Grove Lords. How many conversations did you and me have between the prison glass, Tatum? The two of us wracking our brains trying to figure out who the scumbag was. We never was able to narrow it down to less than about fifty. Not once did you even hint it was you who was the killer. The whole time, you was just *pretending* to stand by me when I was on death row. But you would have just stood silent right to the end, let me die for something you did."

"You know that ain't true. What about that night I offered to confess, remember? I said I would confess if that's what it took to get you off death row."

"That wasn't real, man. That was guilt talking."

"It *was* real."

Theo glared at him, then looked to his lawyer. "Tell me something, Jacko. Last time you got me a stay of execution, how close was I to getting fried?"

"Seventeen minutes."

"You get any last-minute phone call from my brother saying, 'Hold everything, they got the wrong man, I'm guilty, it's me, Tatum—I'm the killer!'"

They all knew the answer, but Jack said it anyway. "No."

Theo stepped closer, his eyes filled with hatred. "Just how fucking close were you going to cut it, brother?"

Tatum wouldn't look at him, his gaze cast downward to his shoes. "You're my brother," he said, "I can make good, man."

"Too late," said Theo.

"No, listen to me," he said, his voice quickening. "I'm gonna get this money, this forty-six million from Sally Fenning."

"What, you want to buy me back, now?"

"Just give me a chance to do right by you."

"Give me back my four years."

"I would if I could, but I can't."

"That's your problem, isn't it?"

"I'm doing all I can. It's a lot of money, Theo."

"Don't want your money."

"A shitload of money, even split three ways."

"Leave me out of this," said Jack.

"I wasn't talking about you, fool!" said Tatum.

At that moment, it was as if everything came to a halt. Jack had heard it. Theo had heard it, too. And from the look on Tatum's face, he clearly wished he hadn't said it.

"*Three* ways?" said Jack.

"Did I say three?" said Tatum. "I meant to say two."

"No," said Jack. "You said three, and you meant three. If I'm not the third, who is?"

Tatum's eyes darted from Theo to Jack several times. He looked as if he wanted to say something but knew there was nothing he could say. It was out there, the words had fallen from his own lips, and now it was a known fact: Tatum already had a deal to split the money with someone. He had a partner.

"I'm outta here," he said as he popped from his chair.

"Tatum!" said Jack, but his client was already out the door and barreling down the hallway. Jack followed. "Tatum, if you expect me to be your lawyer, we need to talk."

Tatum stopped halfway down the corridor, wheeled on the balls of his feet, and said, "You're fired, okay? We don't need to talk about any-thing."

"Which ones did you do?" asked Jack.

Tatum's eyes widened. "Watch yourself, Swyteck."

"We know you didn't kill Colletti, because you and Theo were out fishing. So that must have been your partner's work. Did you do the reporter or the prosecutor?"

He took a step closer, pointing a menacing finger as he spoke, but Jack didn't back away. "You listen to me," said Tatum. "It's like Theo said in there. Everything we talked about is attorney-client privilege. You keep your mouth shut."

"The privilege has exceptions."

He gave Jack a sideways glance. "Are you threatening me?"

"I'm just telling it like it is. A lawyer can't reveal what his client did in the past. But if a lawyer thinks his client is about to commit a future crime, the privilege doesn't necessarily apply. From what I heard, it would seem that Sally's ex-husband is next on your list."

He flashed a thin smile, as if he thought it cute the way his lawyer was standing up to him. "What are you gonna do? Call the cops?"

Jack said nothing.

Tatum's smile widened. "Didn't think so," he said as he turned and walked to the exit.

Jack followed past his secretary, who looked terrified by what she'd obviously overheard. When they reached the empty lobby area, Jack called to Tatum and said, "Maybe I'll tell Miguel Rios first. Then I'll tell the cops."

Tatum stopped at the door. The smile was gone.

Just then, the door opened, and Kelsey walked in, arriving for work. Tatum grabbed her and pulled her into his grasp.

"Stop!" said Jack.

"Don't move!" said Tatum.

Tatum was holding her in front of his body like a human shield, Kelsey's eyes as wide as silver dollars. Tatum formed his hand into the shape of a gun, the index finger pointed to her temple, the thumb cocked like the hammer.

"Don't threaten me, Swyteck." He pulled the mock trigger, jerked her head forward as if a 9 mm slug had just shattered her skull, and then pushed her to the floor.

Kelsey rolled across the carpet and let out a blip of a scream that sounded like fear and relief combined as she went to Jack.

Tatum shot one last angry look at them. Jack glared right back as he watched his former client slam the door and then disappear behind a pane of translucent glass and the painted block letters that spelled JACK SWYTECK, ATTORNEY AT LAW.

Fifty-five

"I could kill him," said Theo.

Jack and Theo were back in Jack's office, alone. Jack had taken a minute to calm Kelsey's nerves and asked her to wait in the conference room while he and Theo sorted things out.

"Killing him isn't the answer," said Jack.

"I know that. But I at least gotta get him back in the ring, no gloves this time."

"I understand you're pissed," said Jack. "I am, too. But for the time being, we have to put that aside and think clearly."

"Think about what?"

Jack took a seat behind his desk, straightening a paper clip as he spoke. "Tatum just threatened Kelsey right before my eyes. If we don't stop him, Sally's ex-husband is likely to be next on the hit list. Tatum thinks that either I can't do anything to stop him, because I was his lawyer, or that I won't do anything, because I'm afraid. Tatum needs to think again, but that doesn't mean the answer is to run outside and tackle him."

"You gonna call the cops?"

"Let's think this through first, okay?"

"Okay. Shoot."

Jack pulled a notepad from his desk drawer, feeling as though he should be jotting things down, but he was thinking and talking too fast to write. "Let's start at the beginning. Vivien Grasso laid it out on the table in the first meeting she had with the beneficiaries as personal representative of Sally's estate. She flat out told us: 'If any of the beneficiaries is thinking about bumping off the others in order to be the sole survivor, forget about it. Your motive would be obvious, and you'll never get away with it.'"

"Tatum figured out a way around that."

"He thinks he has. My guess is he teamed up with a partner—someone who could do the killing while he was out building alibis."

"Like, 'I was out fishing with my brother,'" said Theo.

"Exactly. So long as he has a workable defense, like an alibi or whatever it might be, the fact that he's the last man standing at the end of the day won't be enough to send him away on murder charges. He may be right about that. He may be wrong. But a forty-six-million-dollar inheritance can buy one heck of a good criminal defense lawyer."

"One thing's for sure," said Theo. "I know my brother. If he's come this far, he won't stop."

"Which means we need to figure out who his partner is."

"Any guesses?"

Jack leaned back in his chair, considering it. "I've been giving this a lot of thought. It seems possible that there are two killers at work—or, at the very least, someone has gone to the trouble of trying to make it appear as though there are two killers at work."

"How do you count two?"

"The first is the guy who called me after the prosecutor was murdered and said that no one can opt out of the game, 'Everyone must die.' If this guy is taken at his word, money is not his primary objective."

"A psycho like that doesn't sound like Tatum's partner."

"No. But the other killer—or, at least, the other personality—is the guy who attacked Kelsey and said he wanted Tatum to withdraw from the game."

"Wait a sec," said Theo. "If you're saying that this guy is Tatum's partner, why would he want Tatum out of the game? Seems like the opposite would be true."

"It has to be a ruse," said Jack. "It makes a nice cover for Tatum and his partner, doesn't it? It would appear that Tatum is being threatened into withdrawing, but in reality Tatum and his partner are killing off the other beneficiaries so that Tatum can stand firm and inherit the jackpot."

"You sound pretty convinced that this partner is not himself a beneficiary."

"It only makes sense if his partner is *not* already a beneficiary. He wouldn't need Tatum if he was already in the game."

Theo rose, pacing as he thought aloud. "So, we're looking for a friend of Tatum's who is not a beneficiary and who is not squeamish about blood."

Jack and Theo looked at one another, as if the name came to them simultaneously. "You thinking who I'm thinking?" asked Jack.

"Seems pretty obvious, doesn't it?"

"The guy who got Tatum into the game in the first place. The dirtbag who linked up Sally with Tatum."

"Sally's old bodyguard?" said Theo.

"Yup."

They locked eyes, mulling it over in the silence between them. It seemed to fit. Theo asked, "Now what? You go to the cops?"

Jack shook his head. "Your brother isn't one of my favorite people on earth, but the fact remains that everything I learned about his possible wrongdoing arose from the attorney-client relationship."

"But I heard you say it yourself as he was walking down the hall: The privilege doesn't apply if the client is about to commit a future crime."

"I'm a criminal defense lawyer, Theo. I'd better be damn sure about my facts before I breach the attorney-client privilege for any reason."

"You're not sure?"

"Not sure enough. I can't just run to the police and tell them, hey, my client had a slip of the tongue and said let's split the pot three ways instead of two ways, and based upon that I *think* he may have conspired with Sally's old bodyguard to kill off the other beneficiaries."

"So what do we do?"

"Basically, I do whatever I can to let you even the score with your worthless brother. I help you to help yourself."

"I'm listening."

"I think you should pay a visit to Sally's old bodyguard."

He smiled wryly, curling his right hand into a fist, massaging it with his left. "It would be my pleasure."

"No rough stuff," said Jack.

"Then what is it you want me to do?"

"Just follow my plan."

"Your plan?" he said with a chuckle. "Last time you had a plan, I ended up kidnapped by some Russian-speaking Latina babe, locked in a seedy hotel room, and chained to a bedpost for three days."

"And your complaint would be . . . ?"

Theo's smile widened as he reconsidered. "You the man, Jack. What's the plan?"

Fifty-six

They settled on a short frame Smith & Wesson revolver with a polished nickel barrel.

It had taken only a few minutes for Jack and Theo to formulate their strategy. Kelsey wanted to help, and since she was the one whom Tatum had threatened most directly, Jack figured that she deserved a shot at redemption. She agreed to take a ride with Theo over to a gun shop on Biscayne Boulevard and point out the gun that most closely resembled the one her attacker had shoved into her face outside the law school library.

"That's the one," said Kelsey. She was pointing through the locked glass door on the display cabinet.

"You sure?" asked Theo.

"It was dark outside, and the guy was wearing a mask. But that gun was right in my face, and there was enough light from the library to see at least that much. It may not have been that exact model, but it was one just like it."

"Thanks," said Theo. "That's just what I needed. You want me to drive you home?"

"No, my car's still on the street by Jack's office. Could you drop me off there?"

"No problem."

• • •

Jack was at the watercooler when Kelsey returned to his office. She said she'd forgotten something in her desk, but Jack walked her to her car, sensing that more important things were on her mind. They were standing at the curb between her parked car and a black olive tree that had sprouted from a square landscaping hole in the sidewalk.

"Would it surprise you to hear that I was coming into the office this morning to clean out my desk?"

"No one asked you to quit."

"No one asked me to stay."

Though it hadn't been a conscious decision on his part, he couldn't deny the inference she'd drawn.

Kelsey said, "I'm sorry for the way I acted in court the other day, corralling you at the end of the hearing. It wasn't very professional."

"I understand."

"Do you, really? Or are you just saying that?"

"I guess it is getting pretty crazy."

"Crazy? Jack, I got attacked at gunpoint walking home from the law library by some creep who threatened to drown my son. Today, your client grabbed me and pretended to blow my brains out. I don't blame you for any of that, but here's the part that's really nuts: I still walk around feeling as though I have something I need to make up to you."

"I'm not trying to make you feel that way."

Her tone softened, but her expression was pained. "I want us to get past this—this awkwardness that's come between us ever since that reporter called me about Tatum."

"I wish it hadn't happened, but I can't pretend it didn't."

"She tricked me. I slipped up."

"It was the kind of slipup that could have landed our client in jail."

"Which is apparently where he belongs."

"Which is not at all the point."

"I know. I made a mistake. I said I was sorry."

Jack lowered his eyes and looked away. Kelsey stepped closer, cocking her head a little to catch his gaze. "Hey," she said with a weak smile. "If you're about to say 'Love means never having to say you're sorry,' I think I might strangle you."

The way she was looking at him, he knew that honesty was the only option. "Kelsey, I—"

"Don't," she said.

"It's important. All I'm trying to say is that for five years I was married to a woman who heard my every secret. Personal, professional—it didn't matter. I trusted her completely, and we *still* fell apart. What chance does a relationship have when that trust is destroyed before we even get started?"

A woman passed on the sidewalk while walking her cocker spaniel. She nodded hello, tugged her dog away from Jack's shoe, and kept walking.

Kelsey looked at Jack and said, "You really like her, don't you?"

"Never saw her before."

"I didn't mean her. I meant Sally's sister. Rene."

Jack shrugged, not sure what to say.

Kelsey drew a deep breath, then let out what sounded like a sigh of resignation. "You're a good guy, Jack. Frankly, I think this trust issue you've latched on to is an intellectual game you're playing because you're afraid to follow anything that doesn't make intellectual sense. But you deserve to have what you want, even if you aren't very good at figuring out why you really want it."

"Thanks. I think."

"I hope it works out for you."

"Not sure there's anything to it yet."

"There will be."

He gave her a quizzical look, wondering how it was that women saw things in other women that men couldn't find with a microscope.

"I'll still do my part to make your plan work. Whatever you and Theo need." She reached out as if she were about to brush his cheek, then pulled back. "See you around, Jack."

"Yeah. See you."

He watched as she got into her car and started the engine. He offered a little wave as she drove off. Maybe she'd seen it, maybe she hadn't. But the hole in his gut and the emptiness he felt wasn't really about her. It wasn't about Rene, either.

Damn, he said to himself. *I'm really sorry, Nate.*

Fifty-seven

Theo was in the mood for acting. This was not to be confused with his frequent cravings for *action*, which usually involved an ample supply of massage oil, edible panties, and glow-in-the-dark, double-extra-large condoms (when it came to Theo getting lucky, luck had nothing to do with it). Rather, he was preparing himself to act in the "I'd like to thank the Academy" sense of the word, as in displaying his skills as an actor.

You talkin' to *me*?

Even without the cameras rolling, there was no truer form of art than turning a fraud like Tatum's friend Javier into an honest glob of Jell-O.

"Can I come in?" asked Theo. He was standing on the front step. Javier was on the other side of the screen door, wearing only exercise shorts, no shirt. He looked like he'd just rolled out of bed, and sleeping past noon was probably pretty normal for a bouncer at a South Beach club. It was obvious that he'd done some serious weight lifting in his teens and early twenties, probably some steroids, too, but he was starting to turn that proverbial corner on the fast track to fatville. A thick gold chain hung around his neck, and Theo noticed that the skin on his pecs was red and irritated, like the guys at the gym who had their chest waxed for the girls who didn't like hair.

Javier gave him a hard look, as if trying to figure out if he knew him. "You look an awful lot like my buddy Tatum. You must be his pain-in-the-ass little brother."

"Theo's the name. It's time you and me talked."

"What about?"

"Business."

"What kind of business?"

"The kind you can't do standing on the front porch."

He gave a little smile, then let Theo in and led him back to the kitchen. Theo pulled up a bar stool as Javier cleared the counter of four big plastic jugs filled with powered protein and body-building supplements.

"Beer?" asked Javier.

"No, thanks. Already had breakfast."

Theo did a quick scan of the apartment as Javier fetched himself a brew from the refrigerator. A new big-screen television dominated the room just off the kitchen. The rest of the furniture looked as though it had come with the dumpy apartment. If Javier was into anything illegal, he was either a small-time player or a high roller who hid success extremely well.

Javier popped open a beer for himself, then took a seat on the opposite side of the counter. "So, what's up?"

"I've reconsidered Tatum's offer."

He drank from the can, then wiped his mouth with the back of his hand. "What offer?"

"Sally Fenning's forty-six million."

"What about it?"

He narrowed his eyes, ready to assess Javier's reaction to his next line. "I've decided that I'm okay with a one-third cut."

"Yeah," he said, scoffing. "Who wouldn't be?"

"So, you're okay with it?"

He took another drink, then belched. "Okay with what, dude?"

"A three-way split instead of two-way?"

He smiled quizzically. "You know something I don't know?"

Theo had come here feeling pretty confident about his bluff, but he was beginning to wonder if Javier really was his brother's partner. "You playing dumb on me, Javier?"

He chugged the rest of his beer and crushed the aluminum can in his fist. "Do I look like I'm playing dumb?"

No, thought Theo, and that was the problem. He looked just plain dumb, and it was throwing a crimp into Jack's plan. The whole idea had been for Theo to come here bluffing, trying to find out if Sally's bodyguard was indeed Tatum's partner. But if their theory was correct, Theo should have been making more headway with this blockhead.

Unless he's really playing it cool.

The telephone rang. "Hold your thought," said Javier. He pitched his empty can into the trash and started across the kitchen.

Theo watched him reach for the phone, and he was suddenly uneasy about the way this plan of Jack's was unfolding. What if Javier was just playing it cool? What if that was Tatum on the line, calling to tell him that Theo can't be trusted—that Theo has to go?

He took another quick and dirty look around the room, his pulse quickening as his gaze settled on the assortment of kitchen knives in the butcher block beside the stove.

"Hello," he heard Javier say into the telephone, and Theo wondered if the caller on the other end of the line was who he hoped it was, or who he feared it was.

Fifty-eight

The big question was what to do about Miguel Rios.

Jack hadn't been bluffing entirely in that final exchange in his office, when he'd warned Tatum that Sally's ex-husband would be the first to know about Tatum's apparent "two-way split" with a partner who was likely as dangerous as he was mysterious. Implicit in the threat, however, was the assumption that Jack would first have to come around to the view that breaching the attorney-client privilege was the ethical and proper thing to do. That, of course, was a huge assumption. The issue wasn't whether his client (or former client, it didn't make any difference) had killed in the past. Jack could never reveal that information, not even if he had a sworn confession, not without being disbarred. The question was whether Tatum was going to kill again in the future. Unless Theo hit a home run in his meeting with Javier, Jack wasn't anywhere near close enough to establishing that his client was about to commit another murder and that the life of an innocent person was in imminent danger. Certainly he didn't have the level of proof required for a criminal defense lawyer to take the extraordinary step of betraying his own client's confidences.

Still, morality played a role here. He at least wanted to meet with Miguel, if for no other reason than to make sure that one of Sally's few remaining heirs had a healthy appreciation of just how much danger he was in.

"You think I'm not shittin' bricks already?" said Miguel.

Jack was seated on the edge of the couch, watching Miguel pace across the rug. Miguel hadn't been able to sit down since inviting Jack into his living room. He spoke fast and with an edge to his voice, and Jack could understand the nervousness.

"I guess it doesn't take a genius to know what's going on," said Jack.

"Well, what is your client doing?"

Jack wasn't sure what to say. There wasn't much he could say, but he did his best. "I no longer represent Tatum."

"Why not?"

"That's all I can tell you."

Miguel finally stopped pacing. He looked Jack in the eye, seeming to sense that Jack was trying to convey more. And Jack was indeed sending a message. It was like at trial, when a criminal defense lawyer knew that his client was committing perjury. Some lawyers believed that the only ethical response of the lawyer was to stand aside and let the client tell his own story, no involvement by the lawyer. No lawyer could stand up and say, "My client is lying," but the moment he clammed up and did nothing to elicit any further testimony from his own client, anyone who knew the rules knew exactly what was going on.

Miguel was a cop, and Jack hoped he was savvy enough to pick up the similar drift he was casting across his living room.

"Are you saying . . ."

"I told you, that's all I can say."

Miguel lowered himself against the arm of the couch, then bounced back up and started pacing again. "This is just great. First Rudsky. Then Meadows. Then Colletti. That leaves me in the running with Tatum Knight, who scared me from the first time I saw him. And this Alan Sirap, which is apparently an alias for Sally's stalker. And need I remind you that I still think Sally's stalker is the man who killed our daughter?"

"You seem to have a pretty firm grasp of the picture."

"Better than you think. Have a listen to this."

He walked across the room to his stereo on the wall unit, then pulled a cassette tape from its plastic case. "I gave this to the police this morning. It's a recording of a message I received on my answering machine."

"This morning?"

"Yeah. It came around eight-thirty—eight thirty-two A.M. according to my machine."

Jack didn't say anything, but he made a mental note that Tatum had been in the car with Theo en route to his office at that time. He wondered where Javier had been.

Miguel kept talking as he adjusted the controls on the tape recorder. "I was in the shower when the call came, so the machine picked up. Scared the crap out of me when I listened to it. Called the cops right away. That's why I took the day off. Detective Larsen wants me home to take the call in case he calls again."

"Was the voice at all familiar?"

"Nah. It's disguised. Here, have a listen." He pushed the Play button, then stepped back from the stereo. The speakers hissed with silence, followed by a crackle or two, and then Miguel's voice on tape.

"Hi, this is Miguel. Leave a message at the tone."

There was a beep, then nothing. Jack glanced at Miguel, who seemed to signal with his eyes that it was coming. It took several moments, then finally the silence was broken.

"You're next, Miguel. But you knew that, right?"

It chilled Jack to hear it, and he could only imagine how it had made Miguel feel. That Jack had heard the voice before made it all the more scary. It was the same mechanical, hollow-sounding voice from his own phone call, the lunatic on the line who'd told him that "Everyone must die." But there was one big difference. He sounded much more agitated in Miguel's message.

"Don't even think about dropping out of the game, asshole. It won't help. Didn't help Mason Rudsky, did it? It's like I told Swyteck—every last one of you will die. And you know why? Because that's what Sally wanted. She didn't have the guts to say it, much less do it. But I know what she really wanted. She wanted to punish you. And now it's up to me to give you bastards the punishment you deserve. Chew on that, Mikey. The surviving heir

gets forty-six million dollars. Too fucking bad there won't be any. None. No survivors."

The speakers hissed again, marking the end of the recording. Miguel switched off the cassette player. He seemed to be waiting for Jack to say something, but it hardly seemed necessary. It was just as Jack had suspected. The killer saw himself as Sally's protector and avenger. Money was not his motivation. He wanted justice for Sally, the sick kind of justice that was born only of a sick kind of love. The message was perfectly clear.

Sally's stalker was back—with a vengeance.

Fifty-nine

Theo was able to overhear enough of the bodyguard's telephone conversation in the kitchen to know that it wasn't Tatum on the line. It was Kelsey, exactly according to plan.

It wasn't part of Jack's overall strategy, however. This was something Theo had cooked up for Kelsey's benefit on the way over to the Biscayne Guns & Ammo Shop. If there was one thing Theo hated more than anything, it was a thug who threatened children. Theo promised Kelsey that, with her help, he'd tried to find out if the bodyguard was the bastard who'd stuck the gun in her face and threatened her son. All she had to do was to call Javier while Theo was over there visiting and tell him she's been thinking about him ever since they met that night at Club Vertigo. She'd have to tie him up for a good ten or fifteen minutes, lay it on pretty thick—how she thought it was really sweet and respectful the way he was trying not to look at her mouth throughout their conversation because of his addiction to porn, how it's really tough to find a guy that thoughtful in Miami, especially one who's even cuter than the Rock.

"You really think so?" Javier said into the phone with a boyish grin.

Theo had to get out of the room, not simply to keep himself from laughing out loud, but because it was part of the plan. He tapped Javier on the shoulder and said, "Bathroom?"

Javier just waved, as if afraid that even a curt "Thatta-way" might break his rapport with Kelsey.

Theo started down the hall, confident that Kelsey could keep this loser tied up forever in the futile hope of voice sex.

Theo walked right past the bathroom and into lover boy's bedroom. Kelsey had promised to beep him on his vibrating pager before she hung up with the bodyguard, which would give Theo time to get back to the kitchen before Javier could catch him snooping.

He was looking for the gun. Kelsey wasn't able to get a look at her attacker's face, nor could she ID his voice, since he spoke with what sounded like a wad of cotton in his mouth. But that gun was right before her eyes—the gun that looked like the one she'd selected at the gun shop with Theo that morning, a short frame Smith & Wesson revolver with a polished nickel barrel.

There was no way to know for certain where a gun owner might keep his weapon, but with a thug like Javier, a single guy with no kids in the house, it seemed reasonable to guess that he'd keep it someplace like a nightstand, well within reach if he were surprised in the middle of the night. It was a longshot, to be sure, but if Theo found any kind of weapon that remotely resembled a short frame Smith & Wesson, there would be hell to pay.

The bedroom door was open, and Theo entered quietly. There were no draperies on the lone window, only mini-blinds, and the bands of morning sunlight streaming through the slats created a zebra-stripe effect across the floor, the dresser, and the unmade bed. It was a disorienting pattern, but Theo forced his eyes to adjust rather than switch on the lamp. With the door open, he could still hear Javier talking on the phone to Kelsey, which gave him extra comfort. He crossed the room, his footfalls muffled by the thick wall-to-wall carpet. He stepped around the empty pizza delivery box on the floor beside the bed, moved quickly to the nightstand, and opened the top drawer.

He started at the sight of a cockroach staring back at him, but it scurried away in an instant. Inside the drawer was just a half-empty bag of potato chips, some loose coins, and the crumbled remnants of countless other snack foods that Javier didn't seem to mind sharing with his six-legged friends. Theo closed the top drawer and opened the bottom one. It was cluttered with junk—a disposable camera and film, old magazines, videocassettes. But no gun.

Theo went to the dresser. The top drawer was underwear and socks, as good a place as any to store a gun. But it wasn't there. Not in the middle or bottom drawers, either.

What the hell kind of a bodyguard has no gun?

He turned and looked at the bed. It was unmade, so he could see the slightest separation between the mattress and the box spring. It would make sense, he realized—easily accessible to a man caught unawares while sleeping. He shoved his hand into the void, then stopped as his fingers touched the cold metal. Pay dirt.

He grasped the handle and pulled out the gun, his heart thumping at the expected sight of a Smith & Wesson revolver with a polished nickel barrel. But it wasn't the gun Kelsey had described. It was totally black, not even a revolver. Theo had seen enough guns to recognize it as a Glock 9mm pistol. Even Kelsey, someone completely unfamiliar with handguns, could easily distinguish between a nickel-plated revolver and a black pistol.

Of course, no one said that this was the only gun in the house.

Theo could still hear Javier talking in the kitchen. Kelsey was doing a nice job of keeping him occupied. He swept the room with his gaze and then decided to check the closet. He slid the mirrored door open, then stopped cold. He'd expected to see clothes hanging inside, but the entire closet was lined with shelves, floor to ceiling, and on each shelf was a row of videocassette cases arranged with the spine facing out. They looked identical, black plastic cases with a white label on the spine. Each label had only one word on it, and they were arranged in alphabetical order. Alicia. Amanda. Brittany. Two tapes for Caitlin. Four for Pauline. Hundreds of tapes, each with a woman's name on it.

Theo wasn't sure what to make of it at first, but it soon dawned on him. Jack had told him about the camera bracket that he'd found in the attic at Sally's old apartment. He scanned the rows of videocassettes, searching for a case with the name Sally on it. But the bottom shelf ended at "P." The second half of the alphabet must have been stored somewhere else.

The silent pager on his belt vibrated. It was the previously agreed-upon signal from Kelsey that she was running out of things to say to Javier and that their conversation would soon come to an end. He stuffed Javier's pistol into his waistline, thinking he might need it. Then he grabbed one of the tapes at random and shoved it inside his jacket, just so that he could later test his theory. He quickly but quietly left the bedroom, hurried down the hall to the bathroom, and shut the door. He dialed Jack's cell phone, eager to test his thinking.

"It's me," said Theo.

"What's up?"

He hesitated, as if giving himself a moment to absorb his own discovery. He wasn't a hundred percent sure of it, but why else would a guy like Javier have a closet full of videocassette tapes with the name of a different woman on each one?

"You want to give me odds?" asked Theo.

"Odds on what?" said Jack.

"I'll take your five to my one that Sally Fenning's stalker was able to get himself hired as her bodyguard."

Sixty

Jack kept the telephone conversation short. Theo had laid out his findings quickly, and Jack was eager to put the question to Sally's ex-husband: Could Javier—the man who became her bodyguard—have been her stalker, the man who murdered their daughter?

Miguel sat on the edge of the couch, staring pensively into the steeple he'd formed at the bridge of his nose with his index fingers. Jack watched his expression tighten, his face grow redder.

"Are you okay?" asked Jack.

"I can't believe it," he said in a low, angry voice.

"It's still just a theory for now. But we know Sally was being stalked. We know that someone was probably videotaping her from the attic over her bedroom. And now we find a stash of videotapes in her bodyguard's closet."

Miguel didn't answer. He seemed to be taking it all in.

Jack continued, "It fits with the message you got on your answering machine this morning, too."

"How do you mean?"

"He was her bodyguard. Her protector in life. The guy who left that message seems to be playing the same role. Protecting her, avenging her death."

"Should we call the cops?"

"Not yet. Theo wants to probe a little more, see if he can get Javier to cough up the tape with Sally's name on it. We haven't found it yet, but—"

"And you never will," he said.

"Why do you say that?"

"What idiot would be stupid enough to keep that tape around this long, after all that's happened?"

"You'd be surprised. It's like collecting trophies for some of these guys. They keep jewelry from their victims, snippets of hair, clothing, all sorts of things that a rational person would burn at the first opportunity. But that's why I say we should let Theo press him a little more. You call the cops, I guarantee that tape will disappear."

He shook his head slowly and said, "How could she hire that creep as her bodyguard?"

"She was fooled. She never saw her stalker. So when he came applying for a job as her bodyguard years later, she didn't have any reason to make the connection."

He looked down, gnawing his lower lip. "I don't believe that for a minute. No way Sally was fooled."

"Well, if she wasn't fooled, then that would mean she knowingly hired the man who . . ."

Miguel's eyes were smoldering. "Now you get it, don't you? Can you imagine being so cock crazy that you cover up for the guy who murdered your own daughter?"

Jack took a half-step back. "That's a pretty big leap you're making. You're saying she had a thing for her stalker?"

"I didn't say he started out as her stalker. He became her stalker. It's like I thought all along. The guy started stalking her after she dumped him or cooled off the relationship or something like that. I knew that bitch was seeing someone. I always knew it."

Jack paused, perplexed by his response. "Wait a minute. The first time you and I talked, you told me the same thing you told the police in their investigation into your daughter's murder. You said that Sally never told you or anyone else that she was being stalked until after the murder."

"Yeah, so?"

"That seems inconsistent with what you just said—that you knew Sally was seeing someone. That you *always* knew it."

Miguel narrowed his eyes, seeming to resent the way Jack was picking apart his words. "You fucking lawyers, always trying to twist things."

"I'm just trying to reconcile your own statements, that's all."

"All I meant was, you know—when I said that I knew she was having an affair, I didn't realize she was a cheater until after our daughter was murdered, after Sally claimed that she was being stalked."

"No, that's what you said the last time we talked. What you just said was different. You said you always knew it."

"What do you want from me, Swyteck? You like playing these little word games? Yeah, I said always. Ever since our daughter was found dead and Sally came up with this stalker story, I always had my doubts. That's always. I didn't mean from the beginning of the fucking world."

Jack thought for a second, figured maybe he had pressed too hard. "Okay, gotcha."

"I had my doubts, all right? I always had my doubts as to whether she was speaking the truth when she said she didn't know who her stalker was. The prosecutor had the same doubts after she failed the polygraph."

"Okay, I got it."

"Maybe I should remind you that I was the one who passed the polygraph when the cops asked me three different ways if I murdered my daughter, stabbed my daughter, or hurt my daughter in any way."

Jack let his gaze linger. Miguel was starting to sound like the many clients he'd visited in prison, the ones who proclaimed their innocence a little too forcefully.

Miguel said, "I'd love to sit and talk all day, but I got some things I gotta do."

"Sure," said Jack. "Thanks for your time."

"You bet."

Miguel walked him through the living room, through the

enclosed front porch that Miguel had converted into an office area. Jack didn't stare, but he quietly took it all in as they headed for the door. He wasn't looking for anything in particular, but his gut was suddenly telling him to learn as much about Miguel as he possibly could, right down to the paint color on the walls and the type of computer he owned.

Miguel opened the door, and Jack stepped out. "Call me if there's anything I can do for you."

"I will," said Miguel.

The door closed, and as Jack started down the sidewalk, he had the distinct impression that he wouldn't be hearing from Miguel. Not anytime soon.

Sixty-one

Javier was sitting in the TV room when Theo returned to the kitchen. Theo walked around the bar stools, pulled up a chair, and straddled it, his arms resting atop the backrest. Javier was no small man, but Theo still dwarfed him, not with size but attitude.

"So, how's our friend Kelsey?" asked Theo.

The goofy grin slid off Javier's face. "You know her?"

"Know her? I'm the one who told her to give you a call."

"You? Well, hey—thanks."

"Don't thank me, moron. You didn't think that was real, did you?"

"Were you listening to us?"

"Hell no. I scripted it. It was Kelsey's job to drag you off to fantasy land, so I'd have time to look around your bedroom."

His mouth fell open, but the words were a few seconds behind. "You went in my room?"

Theo shot him a look that would have sent most men running. "If there's one thing I hate more than a guy who threatens a single mother, it's a guy who threatens her kid. So, where is it, lover boy? Where'd you hide the revolver with the polished nickel finish? The one you shoved in Kelsey's face."

Javier looked as if he were about to explode. He started to rise, then stopped.

"Sit the fuck down," said Theo as he took aim with the borrowed pistol.

"Hey, that's mine."

"Didn't anyone ever tell you? Guns make really shitty pets. Turn on you in a minute."

"Be careful, all right? That thing's loaded."

"I know. I can tell from the weight." It was a nice way to let Javier know he was no stranger to guns with a magazine full of ammunition.

Javier settled back into the couch, his eyes darting nervously from the stern expression on Theo's face to the black hole at the end of the barrel.

Theo said, "I think I will have that drink you offered earlier. Not beer, though."

Javier pointed with a nod toward the liquor cabinet. "Help yourself."

Theo rose and walked to the cabinet, keeping one eye and the gun trained on Javier at all times. "Let's see what you got here," he said as he sorted through the variety of bottles. "Scotch. Rum. Bourbon—if you can call this bourbon. My grandma used better liquor than this to make bourbon balls at Christmas."

"Beggars can't be choosers."

He nodded, smiling on one side of his mouth only. "Sit tight, friend. I'll teach you a thing or two about begging."

Javier sank a few inches into the couch.

Theo checked the labels on a few more bottles, then selected one. "Here we go. One-fifty-proof vodka. Now that's what I call a drink. One for you, lover boy?"

"No, thanks."

Theo walked toward him, unscrewed the cap, and shoved the gun into Javier's cheek. "I'd really like you to have a drink."

"Whatever you say."

Theo poured the vodka onto Javier's head, emptying almost the entire two-liter bottle until Javier and the couch were soaked.

"Say when," said Theo.

Javier was silent. Theo stopped the shower with about an ounce remaining in the bottle. Then he went back to his chair and poured the remaining vodka into a little puddle on the cocktail table in front of him. He pulled a cigarette lighter from his pocket and said, "You can always tell the good stuff. True one-fifty vodka should burn with a nice blue flame."

Javier went rigid. Theo put the lighter to the spilled vodka, then gave it a flick. It burst into a blue flame that danced atop the cocktail table. Javier jerked back against the sofa, getting as far away as he could. Theo let it burn for about a minute, watching Javier sweat through his vodka-soaked pores. Then he slapped the table with the palm of his hand and extinguished the flame with a loud crack that nearly made Javier jump from his seat.

He aimed the gun at Javier's left eye and asked, "You a smart guy, Javier?"

"What?"

"You got a brain in your head? I just want to know."

"People say I'm pretty smart, yeah."

"Good. Because there's something I want you to figure out for me. You think you can do that?"

He shrugged, saying nothing.

"I asked you a question," said Theo, his voice gaining force. "Can you do that for me?"

"Sure," said Javier, his voice quaking. "Whatever you want."

"Let's say I start your house on fire."

"Man, please—"

"Shut up!" his voice boomed. "You let me finish, and don't interrupt. Got it?"

Javier nodded.

Theo softened his tone, but it only seemed to put Javier even more on edge. "Let's say I start your house on fire. And let's also say you're in it."

Javier was struggling to show no reaction, his left eye twitching. Theo said, "This is just hypothetical, okay, lover boy? Now, once the fire's out, people are gonna say things like, 'Hey, you hear Javier's house burned down?' And then some guy will say back, 'Yeah, I hear he burned up with it.'" Theo scratched his head and said, "I just don't get that, do you?"

Javier looked confused. "Get what?"

"Listen to what I'm saying, numb nuts. Your house burns *down*, but you burn *up*. What the hell's with that? Do the fires burn in different directions? Do the flames somehow magically meet in the middle? And if they do, at what point do you start burning down and the house start burning up?"

Theo flicked his lighter, let the flame spike into the air. The look of fear on Javier's face was instantaneous, as if he was suddenly aware of how flammable he was, soaked with one-hundred-fifty-proof vodka.

"Watch that lighter, okay?" said Javier. "Please, don't burn me."

"Don't worry. I won't let you burn long. Maybe thirty seconds, tops, before I have to put a bullet in your head. Neighbors and whatnot. Can't have you running around the living room screaming like a wild banshee. Flaming, no less." His lips curled into a sinister smile. "Flaming wild banshee. I like that. Great name for a drink. One-fifty vodka and maybe a sliced jalapeño pepper. I'm a fucking genius, don't you think?"

"Sure, man. Whatever you say. Just put the lighter away, okay?"

Theo sat back, his smile fading. Theo had a disarming smile, and it came naturally. But he could look as bad as Tatum if he put his mind to it, and at that moment he was doing his very best to be exactly like his older brother. "Tell me how you picked the name Alan Sirap, jerk-off."

"Who?"

"The phony name you passed along to Sally Fenning over the Internet."

"I swear to God, I don't know what you're talking about."

"Really? Then why'd you videotape her?"

"What videotape?"

"I saw your little library, all those tapes in your closet. Didn't see one for Sally, but I'm sure we'll find it here some—"

"That's not—"

"Shut up!" Theo shouted. "What did I say about interrupting me?"

"I'm sorry, okay? But—"

"Don't give me no lip, asshole. I'll bet you weren't even her body-guard. You probably didn't even work for her, did you? What were you, her *self-appointed* bodyguard? Bodyguard is a nice way of saying you were her stalker?"

Javier was turning ash white.

Theo flicked his cigarette lighter, then adjusted the flame upward until it was shooting a six-inch tongue of fire. "Show me your tape of Sally."

"There is no—"

"I'll turn you to toast, man."

"I'm telling you, there is no tape."

"Don't lie to me!"

"I'm not lying! Please, don't burn me, man. Just don't burn me!"

Theo extinguished the lighter, then ripped the "Pauline" tape from inside his coat and threw it at him. "Play it. Let's see your work."

"This isn't my work."

"Play it!" he shouted.

"Okay, okay." Javier took the tape, rose slowly, and walked to the television. Theo kept his gun trained on his head with every step. He inserted the tape into the VCR and adjusted the television. The screen flickered, then turned blue. Theo waited anxiously, expecting to see a crude surveillance tape of an unsuspecting woman sleeping in her bed or sitting on her toilet—a woman named Pauline whom this pervert had stalked with a hidden camera, just as he'd stalked Sally.

But it was something else entirely. Theo heard a woman moaning, then a man grunting as the image on screen came into focus. A gor-geous blonde was lying on her back, floating naked atop a waterbed, her legs pointing up to the ceiling in the shape of a V with stiletto heels. Some guy with incredibly strong hips was directly underneath her, doing the absolute best he could in one of those painful front-to-back positions that made sense only if sex was intended to be fun strictly for viewers and not participants.

"That's Pauline Preston," said Theo.

"You know her?"

"She's one of my favorites."

"I got four of hers. Buddy of mine copies the tapes for me over at the video store. I keep them alphabetical by actress. Titles never mean anything to me."

"Are you telling me that every tape on those shelves in your bedroom closet is bootleg porn?"

"It's kind of a hobby of mine."

"A hobby? There must be a hundred tapes in there."

"Okay, it gets a little out of control sometimes. I admit it. I even told your buddy Jack when we met over at Club Vertigo. I think I'm —"

Theo waited for him to finish, but Javier was suddenly glued to the set. It seemed that Pauline needed a shower, but somehow she'd lost her way and managed to wander straight into the locker room of a men's rugby team.

"You think you're what?" asked Theo.

"I'm addicted," he said in a weak voice, unable to tear his gaze away from the screen. "I'm totally addicted to this shit."

Theo gave a little shrug and said, "Isn't everybody?"

Sixty-two

You threatened to burn him alive?" said Jack. He was stopped in his car at a traffic light, one hand on his cellular, the other pressed between his eyes as if to stave off a migraine.

Theo said, "It's not like I doused him with gasoline or anything. I used vodka. It's like that game you play as a kid where you squirt lighter fluid on your hand and then start it on fire."

"I think I missed that game," said Jack.

"The fuel burns, but your arm doesn't. Anyway, worst that would have happened to lover boy was like a bad sunburn. But he was too stupid to know that, so he told me everything."

Jack wasn't so sure that the stunt was as harmless as Theo thought it was. "Theo, no more tricks like that, okay?"

"No need for it now. Turns out that the videotapes weren't surveillance tapes after all. They're all just bootleg porn."

"What?"

"Lover boy is quite the pervert, but he's no stalker. At least he wasn't Sally's stalker. I'm telling you, there's nothing like the threat of fire to drag the truth out of someone. He's definitely not Alan Sirap."

A misty rain was starting to fall, hard enough for little beads to gather on Jack's windshield and then zigzag their way down to the wipers. Crazy Miami weather, sunny one minute, raining the next. "He could still be Tatum's partner," said Jack.

"No way. Tatum wouldn't have a partner this stupid."

"You may be right. To tell you the truth, I'm starting to get a gut feeling about Miguel."

"How do you mean?"

The light changed, and he was about to pull into the intersection, but an ambulance was cruising toward him from the opposite direction. Jack stayed put, catching sight of the backward painted letters on the front hood of the emergency vehicle as it flew past him.

And that was when it suddenly came clear in his mind.

"Holy shit," he said.

"What?" asked Theo.

"I'm going back to Miguel's house."

"Jack, what's going on?"

"There's something I want to check out."

"You want me to help?"

"That's okay. If I need a fire, I'll rub two sticks together."

"That was harsh."

"I'll call you." Jack ended the call and pulled a U-turn. In less than five minutes he was back on Miguel's front step. He had to knock three times before Miguel answered.

"Back so soon?" he said as he opened the door.

"I think I left my sunglasses here."

"I didn't see them, but I'll take a look."

"Mind if I wait inside? It's starting to rain out here."

He hesitated, as if more than a little suspicious, then acquiesced. "Sure. Wait right here."

Jack stepped inside and closed the door. Like many Florida houses built in the sixties, Miguel's house had no true foyer. The front door opened to what was originally a screened-in porch, but Miguel had enclosed it and converted it into a small home office space.

Out of the corner of his eye Jack could see Miguel in the living room as he checked for sunglasses behind the couch cushions, on the table, in the general area where Jack was seated. Jack had only a few seconds, which was more than sufficient. The computer was nearby, and all he needed was to get a look at the screen from the right angle. He took two steps forward, stole a quick glance, and froze.

The computer was turned off, and Jack had approached it in the same way Miguel had undoubtedly approached it day after day, before switching it on. The screen was black, but there was a reflection on the glass. Directly behind the computer was a typical work of framed commercial art that was sold at places like Z-Gallery, a huge replica of an Art Nouveau poster for the 1900 World's Fair—*Exposition Universelle*. Across the top in big arching letters was the name of the host city, which reflected backward on the screen: S-I-R-A-P. Paris.

In a flash, Jack envisioned Miguel at his computer late one night, posing as the stalker and communicating in an Internet chat room with his ex-wife Sally in Africa. She suddenly asked for his name. Of course he couldn't give his real name. He conjured up a bogus name, any old name that popped into his head. Without even realizing it, he typed in the name he'd seen in the reflection of his computer screen day after day, week after week, month after month, every time he approached that black screen and switched on the power. The name had been planted in his unconscious mind, just as it had been planted in Jack's mind a few minutes earlier, the first time Jack had passed through Miguel's Florida room on his way out the door, though it hadn't really registered until he spotted that passing emergency vehicle with the backward letters—Y-C-N-E-G-R-E-M-E—painted across the hood.

"Sirap," he said, the word coming like a reflex.

Jack heard the cocking of a pistol. Before he could move, the barrel of a gun was pressed to the back of his head.

"Don't move." It was Miguel's voice, but it was from the opposite side of the room. Miguel had entered from the stairwell that led to the upstairs bedroom. Jack couldn't see the gunman behind him, but it was obvious that someone other than Miguel was pressing the gun against the back of his head.

"Turn this way," said Miguel. "Slowly."

Jack turned, the gunman still behind him, the gun still at his head.

Jack was staring straight at Miguel. He, too, was pointing a gun at Jack.

"I knew it was you," said Jack. "Sally cheated on you once, right before you were married. She admitted that much on the videotaped interview with the prosecutor. Was she cheating on you again, Miguel, is that what you were afraid of?"

"I'm not afraid of anything right now, Swyteck."

He felt the gun press more firmly against the base of his skull. He needed to buy time, so he kept talking. "Interesting thing about that surveillance camera over the bed in your old house. There were no windows in the attic. It had to be installed by someone with access to the house—regular access, someone who could get up and down to change tapes. Got any ideas on who that might be, Miguel?"

"Just like I told the police. I got no idea."

"I think it was someone who lived there," Jack said, his glare tightening. "You were stalking your own wife, weren't you. What was the plan, Miguel? Scare her so badly that she stops cheating on you?"

Miguel met his stare, but his expression tightened with anger. "Is that too much to ask for? A wife who doesn't cheat on you?"

"That's no excuse for killing your own daughter."

"Yeah," he said, scoffing. "That."

The cold reaction confirmed Jack's suspicions. "Call me nosy, but I checked this out when I was here earlier, and this second visit only confirms it. All the framed photographs around your desk, on the coffee table, hanging on the walls. I didn't see a single one of your daughter."

Miguel didn't answer, but he was still aiming his gun at Jack's chest.

Jack narrowed his eyes, giving him the look that had worked countless times on cross-examination in the courtroom. "She wasn't yours, was she, Miguel?"

It was almost imperceptible, but the gun was starting to shake. Miguel was furious.

Jack said, "That's how you passed the polygraph exam. The cops asked you, Did you kill your daughter? You said no. It was the truth. She wasn't your daughter. How did it happen, Miguel? Was it the lover Sally took right before you got married?"

The look on Miguel's face only confirmed that it was true. "You think you're smart, don't you, Swyteck? The only one to figure it out."

"No," said Jack. "I think Sally had it figured out, too. That's why she flunked the lie detector test when the cops asked if she knew the man who murdered her daughter. She didn't know in her mind. But somewhere, deep down in her heart, she knew. She knew in her heart that the killer was her husband. She was just too afraid of him to say it."

Miguel glared at Jack, then lowered his gun. For a brief instant, Jack thought that maybe he'd miraculously gotten through to him. But he seemed to look past Jack, focusing instead on the gunman standing behind him.

"Shoot him, Tatum."

Jack flinched. It wasn't really a surprise, but hearing Tatum's name gave him a jolt anyway.

Tatum said, "Actually, I think it's your turn, boss."

"Turns?" said Jack. "You idiots are taking turns?"

"Didn't start out that way," said Tatum. "But after I told Miguel that Colletti fucked his wife, literally, in the divorce, he couldn't wait to smoke that dude. Which was okay by me. So long as we could make them all look like the work of this made-up psycho stalker, Alan Sirap, we were home free."

"Whose turn was it when it came time to shove a gun in Kelsey's face?"

"That would have been mine," said Miguel, and at that moment Jack noticed that he was holding a revolver with a polished nickel finish. "No one ever wanted to hurt her," said Miguel. "That was all about making people think that the killer wanted Tatum out of the game."

"Sounds like you were in charge of the threats, eh, Miguel? The phone calls to Deirdre Meadows, the call to me after the prosecutor was murdered, the phony message on your answering machine this morning. Those were all you, weren't they?"

"Does it matter? Could have been me, could have been Tatum. Go buy yourself a forty-dollar voice-altering gadget from a spy shop and it could be anybody."

"Do you really think you can get away with this?"

"Maybe," said Miguel. "Maybe not. But for forty-six million dollars, I say it's worth the risk."

"But you're both named as heirs. One of you has to pull out of the game, and then the two of you split the pot, right? Or one of you has to kill the other and take it all."

"First things first, Swyteck. Shoot him, Tatum."

"No. I said it's your turn."

"What the hell does it matter whose turn it is? Shoot him."

"It matters to me," said Tatum.

"Why?"

"Because I know you can kill when your Latino machismo is on the line, like with Gerry Colletti. And I know you can dish out the threats, like with Kelsey. But I want to see you kill for money. Nothing but money. Like I did with Deirdre and Mason Rudsky."

"All right, you pain in the ass. I'll shoot him myself."

Jack looked straight at him, hoping that direct eye contact might unnerve his would-be shooter. It seemed to work for a moment, as Miguel kept the gun at his side. But then he simply lowered his gaze, as if shifting the target from Jack's head to his torso. His arm went up, and suddenly Jack was staring down the barrel of a gun.

Before Miguel could pull the trigger, the window exploded in a barrage of gunfire. Four quick shots, all slamming into Miguel's chest. He stammered backward, pelted by each projectile, and then fell to the ground in a pool of blood.

Tatum dived for cover, pulling Jack down with him. He pressed the gun firmly against Jack's head, keeping him as a hostage, his ticket out.

Jack was nearly crushed beneath Tatum's weight. He couldn't move, and he didn't dare move anyway with the gun nuzzling up to his skull. With his cheek to the floor, Jack could see the bottoms of Miguel's shoes at the other end of the room. A rivulet of blood drained slowly down the grout line in the ceramic tile.

Finally, there was a voice at the door. "Let him go," said Theo.

"Get your ass in here," shouted Tatum. "Or I'll blow his brains out."

Jack lay perfectly still. He wanted to scream out at the top of his lungs, tell Theo to get lost, go away, run for it. But he knew it would have been pointless. He knew that Theo wouldn't leave him.

Jack heard the door open, then the sound of Theo's heavy footfalls on the tile. "Prize patrol," said Theo.

It was classic Theo, a line that they might laugh about someday, if they lived to tell the story.

Tatum pulled Jack up from behind the couch, using him as a human shield, his gun to Jack's head. Jack's eyes met Theo's, but only for an instant. Theo was staring down his brother.

Tatum asked, "Did you call the cops?"

"No. This is something I want to settle myself."

Jack's eyes widened, as if to say "You *better* have called the cops." But he could see the determination in Theo's expression, see that this *was* something he wanted to settle himself.

"Pick up Miguel's gun," said Tatum.

The gun was lying on the floor beside Miguel's body. Theo started across the room, and Tatum swiveled Jack's body—the shield—as Theo passed by them on his way to the corpse. Theo stepped around the puddle of blood, then stooped down to reach for the gun.

Tatum said, "Not with your bare hands, moron. Use your jacket."

Theo pulled off his windbreaker and wrapped it around his hand like a glove. He picked up the gun, then looked back toward his brother, as if to say, *Now what?*

Tatum said, "We gotta kill him."

"We don't gotta do anything."

"You're right. You gotta do it. Do it with Miguel's gun."

Theo didn't respond.

"Do it, Theo. Shoot Jack right now. If you don't, I will."

"You think I'm taking orders from you?"

"I'm talking a deal, man. Forty-six million dollars. We split it. Don't you get it? They're all dead but me. It's mine. Mine and yours. All you gotta do is pull the trigger, and we're partners. It's clean."

"Say what?"

"Listen to me. Here's the story. Jack, you, and me came over to confront Miguel the pussy here. He confessed to the killings and shot Jack. Then you shot Miguel. We're home free, brother. All we gotta do is get rid of Jack."

Theo didn't answer.

"You thinking about it, ain't you?" Tatum said through his teeth. "Half of forty-six million dollars. Come on, do right by your brother. Shoot Jack with Miguel's gun."

Theo was stone silent.

"Do it now, damn it!"

Theo knelt down beside Miguel's body. He pressed the gun into Miguel's hand and raised it slowly.

"Even better," said Tatum, his voice racing. "Let Miguel's own finger pull the trigger."

It was as if the gun were in Miguel's grasp. Theo held Miguel's lifeless hand between his own huge hands, taking aim at Jack's head.

"That's right, Theo. One little squeeze."

Jack's heart skipped a beat. Theo was a friend. He'd never shoot his buddy, the lawyer who'd saved his ass on death row. Not in a million years. Not for anything.

Except maybe twenty-three million dollars.

"Theo," said Jack. "This is crazy, pal. Tatum screwed you before, he'll screw you again."

"Do it!" shouted Tatum.

In a flash, the gun jerked, a shot whistled across the room. Tatum's gun was airborne, and his head snapped back violently. Jack dived forward to the floor. Theo rushed to his wounded brother.

Tatum was flat on his back, gasping and holding his throat. The bullet had passed through his neck. Blood was pouring from the severed carotid artery, pumping in surges with each beat of his fading heart until he was surrounded by a growing circle of red. His eyes glazed over with a helpless expression, a look that Jack hadn't seen since his days of defending death row inmates, that unmistakable, almost incongruous look of fear and bewilderment in the eyes of a murderer who was suddenly forced to come to grips with his own mortality.

Tatum looked up at Theo. He could barely speak, his throat filled with blood, but the bullet had passed through his neck off-center and had spared his voice. "You piece of shit," he said in a thick, distant tone, choking on his own blood. "You shot your own brother."

Theo looked at Jack, then back at Tatum, his expression deadpan. "Wrong again, Tatum. I saved him."

Tatum's head hit the floor, and his body was suddenly still.

Sixty-three

Jack watched from the helm as Theo walked alone to the bow of the fishing boat and scattered the ashes. It was early Sunday morning. The horizon was still orange from the rising sun, and a warm wind carried the ocean's whispers from the east—from Nassau maybe, which seemed fitting, since Tatum used to love to go there and gamble. Seagulls trailed their boat across the deep blue swells, ready to steal a fisherman's bait. One of them splashed into the waves, snatched up a floating fragment of bone in its beak, and then dropped it from mid-air.

"Not even the scavengers want him," said Theo, his voice falling off in the breeze.

The burial at sea had been Theo's idea. Fishing out on the boat was the one place he'd felt connected to his brother, miles of blue water between them and a world that hadn't exactly welcomed the Knight brothers with open arms, a world that seemed to have known all along that it would be better off without Tatum. He was a badass, to be sure, but his death was no cause for celebration. Theo needed time, not so much to grieve but simply to come to terms with his brother's betrayal. Jack was determined to give Theo the space he needed.

The two of them had told all to the police at the crime scene. Jack took the media calls in the ensuing frenzy, not because he enjoyed the publicity but because Theo hated it even more. Within hours, it was all over the evening news that Tatum Knight had shot Sally Fenning to death in a strange murder for hire in which the victim was her own target, and that Miguel Rios had murdered Sally's daughter in a crime of jealous rage that had gone unsolved for five years. The details played out differently depending on which newscast you watched, but the newspaper got it mostly right, thanks largely to the background work of the late Deirdre Meadows. The *Tribune's* final, lengthy feature ran in the Sunday edition. It relied heavily on excerpts from Deirdre's unpublished manuscript, which was preceded by a glowing tribute to Deirdre from her editor, and included dubious assertions that the editors were behind her pursuit of Sally Fenning's story "one hundred percent from the very beginning"—all of which seemed just a wee bit calculated to set her up *posthumously* for the Pulitzer nomination she'd so desperately wanted in life.

"I'm ready," said Theo, wiping the salty sea spray from his brow. "Let's go in."

"This is a good thing you're doing," said Jack.

"Yeah. At least this way I won't be tempted to come piss on his grave."

Jack started the engine and steered for home. The ride back took almost an hour, completely in silence. Jack thought it would do Theo some good to get out of the house, and Theo was always up for eating, so they went for a leisurely breakfast at Greenstreet, a sidewalk café in Coconut Grove. Before the Sally Fenning matter, Greenstreet had been a favorite Saturday lunch spot for him and his Little Brother, Nate, after rollerblading along the bicycle paths on Main Highway, a shady and windy way that emptied into the little shops and restaurants in a part of the Grove that still bore some resemblance to the tree-lined hippie village it had once been. Thoughts of Nate still saddened him, though he was optimistic. Kelsey no longer worked for Jack, and the budding romance between them was dead, but after the way Kelsey had helped out Theo in the end, everyone seemed cool with each other. Jack and Nate might be as good as new once Nate got used to the idea that Jack and his mother apparently weren't meant for each other.

All that was complicated, too complicated for a simple Sunday breakfast. Winter was just a couple of weeks away. The sun was shining warmly, joggers and cyclists everywhere; people wearing shorts and T-shirts were out window shopping and walking their dogs—all the telltale signs that life went on and that December in south Florida definitely didn't suck. Jack was too wrapped up in the newspaper to notice that Theo had already finished his pancakes and was halfway through Jack's. He skimmed through the rehashed material on page one A, then picked up the second half of the feature story on Sally Fenning with a mix of emotions, but mostly a sense of relief that it was all finally over:

> "Sally was dying of AIDS," says her sister Rene Fenning, a pediatrician working for a charitable organization in Africa, who also served as the final personal representative of the estate. "She never really wanted to go on living after her daughter was murdered, and although I personally never found out for certain that she had the disease until I saw her autopsy report, I would imagine that she became even more despondent after her second husband infected her with the deadly HIV virus." Rene denies claims that her sister's second marriage was strictly "for money," but the *Tribune* has confirmed that her ex-husband was one of the twenty-five richest men in France at the time of his death. A large portion of that money, eighteen million dollars that grew into stock worth some forty-six million, went to Sally upon their divorce after less than two years of marriage. "The money never made her happy," says Rene.
>
> Eventually, that unhappiness led her to a murder-for-hire that was effectively a suicide. According to sources close to the investigation, Sally could apparently think of no better way to check out of this world than to let the people who had ruined her life fight for her millions—a deadly game of survival of the greediest in which a hired killer and a stalker known only as "Alan Sirap" were sure to make things interesting.

Jack skipped the lengthy description of Sally's will, the game, the murders—things he already knew. He went straight to the end, picking up with a quote from Homicide Detective Rick Larsen.

"She [Sally] probably hadn't scripted it this way, but she had to have known that alliances would form, that some players might even go to the extreme measures that Tatum Knight and Miguel Rios had gone to—effectively a tag team approach to eliminating the other heirs, all done in a way to make it look like the work of a psychopathic stalker, the missing Alan Sirap." Larsen shrugs, almost philosophical in tone as he unscrews the cigar plug from his mouth and adds, "The consensus view among Monday-morning quarterbacks is that Sally probably figured it would come down to a final battle between Tatum Knight and Alan Sirap, never knowing for certain that Sirap was actually her husband."

In the end, that gap in Sally's knowledge had tragic consequences for Miami attorney Gerry Colletti, Assistant State Attorney Mason Rudsky, and *Tribune* reporter Deirdre Meadows. "Clearly this got out of hand," says Rene Fenning. "I'm sure Sally expected some bickering and maybe even some lawsuits among the heirs. But I think she also expected people to drop out of the game before it came to physical violence. Never would my sister have put this thing in motion if she thought people were actually going to die over their own greed."

Editor's Note: Tribune *reporter Deirdre Meadows contributed to this report through articles previously published in the* Tribune *and materials from a book she was writing before her death.*

Jack pitched the newspaper aside. Theo was seated across from him at the little round table, chewing roundly, as if he were trying to swallow an entire pancake in the fewest number of bites ever recorded.

"Something wrong?" he said in a muffled voice, his mouth completely full.

"Pretty lame article."

Theo's whole body jerked as he swallowed too much food. Jack half-expected to see the bulge in his neck, like a python having a bunny for lunch.

"Lame in what way?"

"It doesn't even come close to answering the really big question."

"Which is?"

Jack reached for his wallet to pay the bill, knowing without even asking that Theo had "forgotten" his again. He looked at Theo and said, "The question five people just died trying to answer: Who gets the money?"

Sixty-four

I'm going back to Africa," said Rene.

She was standing on Jack's front step, dressed in a sleeveless shell and a pair of jeans that fit loosely but still couldn't deny her figure. Jack stood in the open doorway to his house, not sure what to say. "So soon?"

"I'm afraid so. I was on my way to the airport. Just thought I'd stop by, say thanks."

"I'm glad you did. Come on in, please. If you've got a minute."

"Thanks."

Jack stepped aside and let her pass. Theo came from the kitchen to greet them. He'd been out fishing in the boat he kept behind Jack's house, and he smelled of it.

"Sorry for the odor," he said.

"No problem. My tolerance is quite high."

He had to think a moment, then Jack said, "Rene's on her way back to Africa."

"Ah," said Theo. "Back to fight the slave traders, are you?"

"My work isn't finished there."

"Good for you. You're one amazing babe, you know that?"

"Thank you. Sort of."

"Hey, I was wondering about something," said Theo. "A while ago on TV I saw something about how the same rush you get from eating chocolate also comes from having sex."

"Theo, come on," said Jack.

"It has to do with the part of the brain that's stimulated," said Rene.

"Exactly. Which means that people who don't have enough sex are the ones who crave chocolate, right?"

"I suppose that follows."

He raised an eyebrow and asked, "Does that mean that people who don't have chocolate crave sex?"

She just smiled.

"Theo," said Jack, groaning.

"Well, shit, Swyteck. She's gonna be three thousand miles away sleeping by herself in some hovel by the time you ever get around to asking her."

"Theo, would you mind getting us something to drink?"

He considered it, then said, "Got just the thing. Be right back."

Jack waited until his friend disappeared into the kitchen, then he offered Rene a seat in the living room. They sat in armchairs on opposite sides of the cocktail table, facing each other.

"He's nonstop entertainment, isn't he?" said Rene.

"He's nonstop. I'll give him that much."

They shared a smile, then Jack said, "You mind if I ask you something a little personal?"

"I might not. Depends on what it is."

"It's about Sally."

"That seems like fair territory, after all you've been through."

"It puzzles me that she put the whole forty-six million dollars into this game she created for six—or as it turned out, five—people she considered enemies. Seems to me that she could have accomplished the same objective with forty-six million or twenty-six million or even six million."

"She went with everything she had."

"That's exactly what confuses me. A guy like Tatum would have fought just as hard for a lot less money. I guess what I'm saying is this: She didn't *have* to completely disinherit her sister. She could have left you twenty million dollars and let the others fight over the remaining twenty-six."

"She could have. But she didn't."

Jack waited for her to say more, then simply asked, "Why not?"

She lowered her eyes, as if searching for the fortitude to say what she was about to say. "That's one of the things I came here to tell you."

Jack didn't even realize it, but he had scooted forward to the edge of his seat. "Yes?"

"Turns out she didn't disinherit me."

Jack blinked, as if he wasn't sure he'd heard correctly. "Say that again?"

"One of my jobs as personal representative of Sally's estate is to find all wills and codicils. Well, turns out there was another will."

"Another will?"

"Yes. It was in French. She kept it in a safe deposit box in Paris. It postdates the one she made in Florida."

"Which means that it supersedes the one she made in Florida."

"That's my understanding."

"And it leaves her fortune to . . . ?"

Her expression turned very serious. "To me."

"Everything?"

"Yes. Everything."

Jack couldn't help but smile. "That's beautiful. So that means these jokers here in Florida were fighting, clawing, and literally killing each other over a will that was . . ."

"Not worth the paper it was written on," she said flatly.

"What do you know?" said Jack.

"Yeah. What do you know?"

"Or maybe the more important question is, What *did* you know?"

"Meaning what?"

"Were you surprised when you found that will? Or did you know that Sally had AIDS? Know that she was planning some kind of scheme to destroy her enemies, to get even with the people who had ruined her life? Know that she'd guaranteed herself the last postmortem laugh with a second will that left everything to her sister?"

"I was hoping that you and I could agree that I was totally surprised."

"Do I have reason to think otherwise?"

"Not unless you want to believe that I stood by and watched this bloodbath play out, knowing full well that I alone had the power to reveal the existence of this second will and put a stop to it."

"I hate to think you'd do that."

"I would never do that. Mind you, I'm not overwhelmed with grief over the passing of any of them. The divorce lawyer, the prosecutor, the reporter who wanted to get rich and famous writing that damn book. Every last one of them made life unlivable for Sally. But I'm a healer, not a killer."

Jack considered it. She was looking him straight in the eye, and he could feel it all the way to his bones. He wanted to believe her, and he felt convinced. He'd been fooled before, big time, by his ex, and he was pretty sure he knew the difference.

Theo emerged from the kitchen with six glasses on a tray, three of them cocktail glasses and the others filled with water. "Drinks?" he said.

Rene said, "I'd like to, but with all this added security at the airport, I really have to be going. I'm sorry. Rain check?"

"Sure." Jack rose to see her out. She said good-bye to Theo, who obviously couldn't help himself and had to give her a hug, fish stench and all. Jack walked her to the door.

"So, what are you going to do with all that money?"

"Hmmm . . . I know this really good charity in Africa."

"I was hoping you'd say that."

"Of course, I'm not an idiot. I was thinking I might squirrel away one or two million for my early retirement."

"I was hoping you'd say that, too."

"Anyway, you might be surprised to see how much forty-something million can do for my little operation. Come visit sometime." She took a half-step forward and kissed him at the corner of the mouth. "Anytime, actually."

He watched from the front porch as she walked to her rental car. Theo joined him and offered a drink.

"Gonna let her go, huh?"

"She'll be back."

"No, she won't."

He took a breath, then let it out. "You are right again, my friend."

Theo forced the glass into Jack's hand. "Have one of these. You'll feel better."

Jack downed the drink, then cringed and immediately chased it with one of the tall glasses of water. "Whoa! I think my mouth's on fire."

"That's because the vodka's so cold it almost burns going down. Or it could be I overshot on the jalapeño juice."

"Jalapeño? What the hell is this thing?"

"Flaming Wild Banshee."

"Never heard of it."

"Lover boy and me just invented it a few days ago."

Jack did a double take, recalling how Theo had threatened Javier into spilling his guts. "I don't think it's going to catch on."

"Damn. I was hoping it would make us rich."

Rene's car door slammed, and as he heard the engine start, he couldn't help but imagine Rene stepping off the airplane in Abidjan, taking that long and dusty road outside Korhogo, and finally trading in that fly-infested shack with dirt walls and a rotting roof for a decent place to live and treat her patients. He thought also of Gerry Colletti and the others, the ones who'd literally died trying to snag Sally's fortune. And then he caught Rene's eye as she was backing out of the driveway, and he saw the contentment all over her face, the same kind of contentment that made Theo so much fun to be around.

He gave Theo a little smile and said, "Now, why would anybody want to be rich?"

"You want me to list the reasons alphabetically by subject matter, or numerically from one to forty-six million?"

Jack chuckled, his eyes clouding over as Rene beeped the horn and drove away. "Theo?"

"Yeah?"

"I could really use a vacation. You think I'd be crazy if I took it in Africa?"

Theo belted back a Flaming Wild Banshee without so much as a grimace. "I think you'd be crazy if you didn't."